RAQUEL RILEY

"I'M ALWAYS GOING TO SHOW UP FOR YOU, REAPER. ALWAYS."

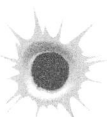

I reached down into the darkest pit of hell and snatched your ass out of there. Now you're stuck with me.

"Someone is always going to have to bleed in order to keep the stripes red on the flag. It's the price of freedom. That's just the way it is."

"THERE'S NEVER GONNA BE A DAY THAT I DON'T LOVE YOU, OR THAT I DON'T WANT YOU, WES. THIS RING MEANS I'M NEVER GOING TO LET YOU FALL."

I never took myself for a jealous guy until West
I also never had anything worth losing Until West

"I'M NOT ASKING YOU TO MARRY ME. I'M TELLING YOU HOW IT'S GONNA BE FOR THE REST OF OUR LIVES. IT'S GONNA BE ME AND YOU. FOREVER. FROM HERE ON OUT. ON THE GOOD DAYS AND BAD DAYS AND ALL OF THE DAYS IN BETWEEN."

"I LOVE YOU," I BREATHE AGAINST HIS LIPS.
"LOVE YOU MORE."

"I've got you, Reaper. Three legs. You can't fall with three legs."

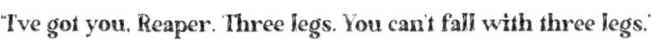

We're two souls that were always destined to be mates, beautifully broken and carefully mended. We belong to each other. I am the keeper of his body and his heart, and he is the protector of mine. To him, my imperfections are perfect. To me, he has no imperfections, he was always perfect.

THE LUCKIEST DAY OF MY LIFE WAS THE DAY I SAT DOWN BESIDE YOU IN THE MESS HALL AND STOLE YOUR BISCUIT.

Gran, Brandt isn't just my best friend anymore. He's the man I love with all my heart.

"YOU CAN BE MY WINGMAN ANYTIME."
CHOKING ON A LAUGH THAT'S PART SOB, I SAY, "BULLSHIT. YOU CAN BE MINE."

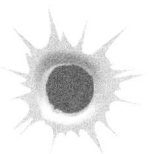

"WEST WAS LIKE A LIVE GRENADE. YOU COULDN'T PUT THE PIN BACK IN ONCE YOU PULLED IT OUT. HE WAS DRAWN IN BOLD LINES AND BRIGHT COLORS."

"I CAN'T WATCH YOU TAKE YOUR LIFE. NOT WHEN IT MEANS SO FUCKING MUCH TO ME. WEST, YOU MEAN SO MUCH TO ME." HIS VOICE CHOKES UP. "I DON'T WANT TO BE LEFT ALONE IN THE DARKNESS EITHER."

"You can snap at me, bite my head off, or you can hit me, but I'm not leaving you alone in the darkness that's trying to swallow you."

"I'M ONLY ALIVE BECAUSE OF YOU. IF YOU GO, I'M COMING WITH YOU."

ALL I WANT TO DO IS GIVE UP. JUST CLOSE MY EYES AND FLOAT AWAY AND NOT RETURN. FOR THE FIRST TIME IN MY LIFE, I DON'T WANT TO BE ME ANYMORE.

I don't usually watch men. Being surrounded by them day in and day out, I've become immune to them. But with West, I'm aware that I stare a little too long. Longer than what is acceptable.

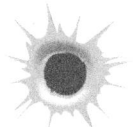

All of my senses exist in the space between my legs, in the parts that are covered by his mouth. I can't think of anything else of this being awkward, of this being wrong—only how good it feels and how right.

A feeling of ease settles over me. No matter where in the world we're stationed, if Brandt is there, I'm good. I'm home.

"DON'T FORGET, JUST BECAUSE I'M NOT WITH YOU DOESN'T MEAN YOU DON'T HAVE MY LEGS." "AND I CAN'T FALL WITH THREE LEGS. I WON'T FORGET, REAPER."

Goddamn, I will never deserve this man, not as my friend, and not as my lover. In no capacity, in no lifetime, will I ever be worthy of him.

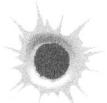

"I WANT YOU TO WRECK ME. I WANT YOU TO MAKE ME FORGET EVERYTHING BUT YOU."

West is the most touchy-feely guy I know. I think touch is probably his love language or something.

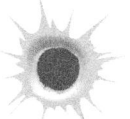

"You know what? Home isn't a place, it's a feeling. Doesn't matter if I'm standing on American soil, or my boots are covered in a sandbox in the middle of hell halfway across the world. As long as you're by my side, I'm home."

It's been sixteen years since my first bj, and I can't recall a single one. I can't even spare a moment to grieve the loss of those memories because Brandt eviscerated them with his wicked mouth.

"I'LL SEE YOU ON THE OTHER SIDE 'CAUSE I'LL BE THERE WITH YOU. IN THIS LIFE AND THE NEXT. TOGETHER FOREVER."

Copyright © 2024 by Raquel Riley

www.raquelriley.com

All rights reserved.

No part of this book may be used, reproduced, or transmitted in any form or by any electronic or mechanical means, including information storage and retrieval systems, without written permission from the author, except for the use of brief quotations in a book review.

This is a work of fiction. Names, characters, places, and incidents either are the product of the author's imagination or are used fictitiously. Any resemblance to actual persons, living or dead, businesses, companies, events, or locales is entirely coincidental. The use of any real company and/or product names is for literary effect only. All products and brand names are registered trademarks of their respective holders/companies.

This book contains sexually explicit material which is only suitable for mature audiences.

Cover design by Raquel Riley

Photography by Tom Cullis Photos

Model Alex Minsky

Editing by Jenn ReadsBooks

Proofreading by Laurie Cappolino

For West,
*You jumped into my head and
screamed at me to tell your story.
I'm so glad I listened, and that you chose me.
There will be good days and bad days,
but you are NEVER alone.
You can't fall with three legs.*

For Brandt,
*There are no words to describe the kind of man you are, I just
hope I was able to tell your story with truth and describe your
heart and soul accurately.
Take care of yourself and our boy.*

CONTENT WARNING

This book deals with heavy sensitive topics like mental health and depression, low self-esteem, survivor's guilt, PTSD, and healing after loss.

On-page death of side characters, On-page suicide attempts, Disfigurement and amputation, anger, and self-hatred.

Alcohol and marijuana use.

FOREWORD

I spent hours researching for this book, but I'm no expert on military life and law. There may be inconsistencies mentioned.

Careful research and sensitivity screening was done for amputees and survivors of trauma. Any derogatory words mentioned by the main character are his own feelings about himself, not others, due to his grief process.

Some parts of this book may be hard to read, but it only makes the hard-earned HEA that much sweeter.

Please read with an open heart and heed the trigger warnings. I hope West and Brandt hold a special place in your heart like they do mine.

With Love,

Raquel Riley

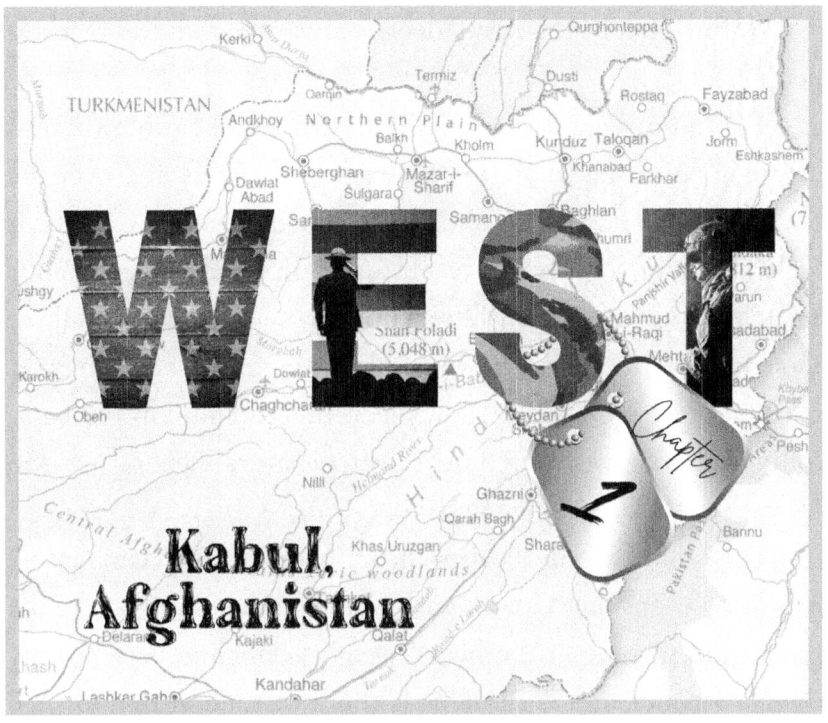

MY SKIN FEELS as dry and rough as sandpaper as it scrapes across my sac.

You would think with as much as I sweat, it would feel softer, but the arid desert has a way of sucking the moisture from your body until you're as wrinkled and parched as a prune.

Reaching under my pillow, I grab the bottle of lotion I keep stashed there. The supply chain doesn't carry lube, and it's not a common item in care packages. Soldiers existing in this wasteland have to make do with whatever they can find. I've seen some creative solutions with this being my second tour. Sunblock, cooking grease, shampoo, petroleum jelly—hell, one guy used shoe polish. His dick was tinted black for a week.

Unfortunately, the Army doesn't always recruit the smartest people.

Two pumps are enough to fill my palm and I rub my hands together, smearing the lotion between my fingers and over the backs of my hands before sliding them back inside my briefs. It feels cool and slightly sticky but eases the glide considerably. Snatches of conversation filter through the thin metal walls of the containerized barracks, but I block them out. *Feels so good.* Closing my eyes, I take a slow, deep breath and cup my balls, rolling them between my fingers as the natural heat of my skin warms the slick covering my hand.

The sound of my beating heart booms in my ears as my breathing evens out. Coarse curls tickle my hand as I stroke the thick skin, tugging at the heavy weights dangling between my thighs. I'm not in a rush. This is the best time of day to steal thirty minutes of privacy. Thirteen-hundred is chow time. Soldiers rush to get in line while the food is still lukewarm, not that it improves the flavor much.

I can wait. The pleasure of rubbing one out in peace and relative quiet is well worth the cost of eating reheated food.

Taking hold of my shaft, I squeeze as I draw upward, milking the first drop of precum from my slit. Rubbing it around the dry head of my cock, feeling the stickiness of it moistening my skin, always gives me a small thrill of satisfaction.

Did Brandt have a jack-off ritual? Was that a thing? I'd have to ask.

The muscles in my stomach clench as I draw my hand back down the rigid length. *Fuck, that feels good.* Up and down, the easy rhythm stokes a fire in the pit of my belly. Bucking my hips into my fist makes the fire burn hotter. I drift my left hand down under my balls, passing over my taint. Maybe just the tip of my finger in my ass would get me–

The door to my barracks slams open and bangs against the wall with an echo. "Wardell!"

Fuck! I snatch my hands out of my pants too late. His left brow arches. *Fucking busted.* My spine stiffens as I scramble to sit up and offer him a sticky-handed salute.

"Yes, Sir!" John Bannon is a real prick on a personal level, but he makes a decent Squad Leader.

"Go wash your fucking hands and report to Command. New orders."

He disappears before I can reply.

The Street Sweepers are the best Fire Team on this base, in my completely unbiased opinion. That's why we always get called up first. Up ahead, I see Brandt heading to the mess tent. Sneaking up behind him, I grab him around the waist and knock him off balance, laughing. He clings to my shoulders before he realizes it's me and shoves me away. The dust we kick up burns my eyes.

"Fucking dick."

"Always be prepared," I warn, wiping away the grit from my tear ducts.

"That's the Boy Scout motto, not the Army," he scoffs, rolling his eyes.

My laugh dies as I straighten his shirt, catching a whiff of sourness over the smell of detergent. It's the damn washing machines here; they're never cleaned properly. Everything comes out smelling musty. Clearing my throat from the dust, I snap, "Round up the team. We have new orders and we're heading out in two hours."

Brandt looks less than thrilled, his broad shoulders slumping. "Fuck. I was looking forward to playing cards tonight and getting drunk."

Slapping him hard on the shoulder, I tease, "Night's not over, sweetheart. There's still plenty of time for that."

We both know that's bullshit. We would never drink in excess on base knowing we could be called up at any moment, like now. But out on the road? On a mission? There would be no alcohol, not even the smallest drop. We're already gambling with our lives. Not one of us is interested in lessening the odds.

Brandt's dark blue eyes travel up and down the length of my body before settling on my face. "I'll get the guys together and meet you inside. Save me a biscuit."

The base doesn't offer much in the way of convenience and luxury, but it beats sleeping rough on the side of the road. We have a gym, a commissary, an Internet café, if you can call it a café because they sure as hell don't serve refreshments, and a laundromat—we even have a coffee stand, run by privately contracted Russians. Everything is constructed of plywood or pallets with armored roofing, or made of repurposed metal shipping containers.

No matter what time of day we receive new orders, Brandt and I have a routine we follow to the letter. A hot meal and a lukewarm shower because neither is something we will ever find roadside, and we never know how long it will be before we get to experience such luxuries again.

Making my way into the chow hall, I'm waylaid by several people I recognize that stop to slap my shoulder or give me a high five or just a head-nod. With over a thousand soldiers stationed here, it blows my mind how many of their faces are familiar to me. Grabbing two trays, I make my way down the galley line, cherry-picking two of anything that looks semi-edible. It looks like they're serving meatloaf today. This shit isn't even brown, more like a faded gray, and the consistency of dog food. It contains so much water that it doesn't even hold its shape. They are basically serving us reconstituted MREs. No, I take that back. The chili mac MRE beats this meatloaf any day.

Fucking delicious. There goes my hot meal.

Wisely skipping the meatloaf, knowing we wouldn't have access to a toilet tonight, I go for the apples, granola bars, garlic bread, then add a little dessert—a handful of oatmeal raisin cookies, and two cups of yogurt. The drink dispenser looks like something you would see in a fast-food restaurant, but with different choices. They offer apple, grape, and orange juices, although none of them tastes good. Reconstituted from powdered mix by people who can't get the consistency right, it was more like drinking flavored water, or sometimes fruit-flavored sludge. I skip it and fill two cups with water.

After making a circuit of the room, I choose a seat at an empty table so that we can discuss our plans without being overheard. Minutes later, Brandt joins me. Stretching his long legs over the bench, he folds his six-foot frame into a seated position and grabs his tray.

A feeling of ease settles over me. No matter where in the world we're stationed, if Brandt is there, I'm good. I'm home.

We've been stuck together since boot camp back in Ft. Moore, Georgia, over twelve years ago. He grabs for my garlic bread, and the memory comes flooding back as if it happened just yesterday.

Taking a seat at the only empty table in the relatively crowded DFAC, I scratched my head, my scalp already itchy from the two-day-old shave, as I passed a discerning eye over my tray. The food was a far cry from my Gran's southern cooking, but I was starving. Hunger made everything taste a tad bit better. A tall guy with a shaved head just like mine sat down across from me. Dressed in standard issue fatigues also like mine, the only thing that set us apart, that set any of us apart, was the name badge sewn on his jacket's breast pocket, and his eyes. He had the darkest blue eyes, like sapphires. The same color as the stone in my class ring.

Aguilar. That was the name sewn on the badge.

He picked up his biscuit and inspected it closely, as if he were debating putting it back. Mine weighed as much as a hockey puck and was just as hard. I wouldn't blame him if he passed on it. Then, his face scrunched in revulsion, and he plucked a hair from the biscuit. I watched in fascination as a kaleidoscope of expressions danced across his face as he tried valiantly to get a handle on his roiling stomach. Taking pity on him, I handed him my biscuit. I hadn't planned on eating it, anyway.

Aguilar accepted the biscuit warily, eyeing me with his piercing blue gaze.

"Thanks?" I remained silent, and he began picking the biscuit apart, popping pieces in his mouth only after he inspected each one carefully. "My name's Brandt."

"Weston," I replied.

And then, as if I'd known him all my life, he began to ramble about his family and his friends back home in Charlotte, North Carolina. I listened as I ate, not contributing very much to the conversation, until finally I blurted, "My friends call me West."

Brandt's next word hung in the air, unspoken. His eyes softened, and a smile touched his full peach lips. "Then I guess I gotta call you West."

He kept right on talking as we ate, filling any silences that might have been awkward between two strangers meeting for the first time, and twelve years later, he's still stealing my bread and talking my ear off.

All at once, we're joined by the rest of our team. Corporal Micah Jennings, also known as Sharp Shot or just Sharp, is our rifleman. He's an expert marksman and a damn fine cook. Corporal Tommy Estevez, aka Boom, is our grenadier. The guy is scary smart when it comes to explosives. Like *MacGyver* smart. He also knows his way around the engine of a Humvee. Specialist Annemarie Legaro is our linguist who speaks fluent Pashto. She hates it, but we call her Rosie, as in the Rosetta Stone. She's a new addition to our team, but I welcome her skills. They crowd around the table like ants swarming a grain of sugar.

"Talk to me, Goose," Brandt quips, his expression eager and bright.

I swallow my smile and roll my eyes. His *Top Gun* references are just one of his many annoying traits. Stealing a cookie from his tray so we're even, I explain, "There's a small village down highway A75 along our supply route from Quetta in Pakistan." Breaking the cookie in half, I shove one piece in my mouth, chewing as I speak. "They recently finished construction on a new school and they want us to clear the building and surrounding area before they allow students in."

Some of the interest dims from Brandt's eyes and he focuses his attention on his cup of yogurt. No doubt he was hoping for something more exciting.

"We're not just playing hall monitor here, Reaper." As our automatic rifleman, Brandt can be a ruthless killer, akin to *Rambo* when he unleashes the furious vengeance of his weapon, hence his nickname, the Grim Reaper. "Intel said the village has transient residents that come and go often. There are reports that insurgents have already moved in and have taken over the school and are using it as a bomb factory. Where in the fuck are they traveling to? And why would they keep coming back?"

Tommy's face pinches. "I don't math well, but one and one doesn't seem to be adding up to two here."

Shoving the other half of the cookie in my mouth, I lick my fingers clean, and Brandt's gaze falls to my lips. Did I have crumbs stuck to my mouth? Swiping them clean with the back of my hand, I still feel a bit self-conscious as I chew, and I wait until I swallow before speaking again.

"It's possible they are Taliban spies or insurgents. We'll leave just before sundown and make camp tonight along the highway. Tomorrow, we'll check out the school, talk to the locals, and make sure we sweep the village clean before we leave."

Rosie gives me a half-assed salute. "I'll be ready to report for duty at seventeen hundred, Sergeant." She was the first to leave the table.

"Count me in, Professor," Tommy adds. They insist on calling me Professor because of my love for military history, a subject Brandt teases me endlessly about. In fact, he was the one who came up with the nickname. Tommy follows Rosie out of the Mess.

"See you in the parking lot," Micah assures us.

"And then there were two," Brandt quotes, finishing off the last spoonful of his yogurt before licking his lips clean.

I study him while his attention is diverted by his meal. The hard angles of his squared jaw, covered with dark stubble. The tiny mole next to his full lips that resemble a beauty mark. His thick fringe of dark lashes that hood his ocean-blue eyes. After all these years, I know his face better than my own. My heart squeezes, full of gratitude for him, for his unwavering loyalty and his unconditional friendship.

It will always be just the two of us. No matter what.

I HAVEN'T BEEN able to take a deep breath since I arrived here six months ago.

The air is layered with fine particles of powdery dust—moon dust—that make your teeth grit together. I can feel that shit coating my lungs by now, slowly suffocating me from the inside out. When I'm indoors, the recirculated air is rife with germs and the stench of unwashed sweaty bodies. In the showers, the thick blanket of steam that doesn't vent well fogs the bathroom, amplifying the smell of mildew. Even as I walk through the base outdoors, the putrid aroma from the retaining pond where our waste is dumped is intensified by the relentless heat and smacks me in the face like a ten-pound brick, robbing me of what little breath I dare take into my lungs.

I would give almost anything for a fresh breath of air, to smell something sweet and clean and new.

Every night, I lay my head down and close my eyes and pray for a dream where I'm back home again, walking through the woods that surround Charlotte, or the mountains of the Blue Ridge. Hell, even the semi-stale city air of Fort Bragg would be a welcome salvation.

I miss the smell of food cooking on the stove, the musky spice of my designer cologne, and even the cheap *Glade* air freshener and scented candles that littered my apartment. I miss a lot of things that I used to take for granted. And considering the high price I'm willing to pay to appreciate them at this moment, I know from past experience that it won't take me long to begin taking them for granted again as soon as I return home.

When I step into the mobile showers, a converted eighteen-wheeler, I see West is already there, along with one other guy at the end of the row, trying to find a modicum of privacy. There are no shower curtains, in fact, there never are. They disappear as soon as they're replaced. The best you can hope for is to turn your back to the room and accept that showing your ass is considered modest.

I choose the stall across from West and place my soap on the shelf. Turning on the water, I cringe and tense all my muscles from the deluge of icy cold that hits my skin. Every one of my nerve endings are screaming out as I wait for the temperature to turn a mild and bearable cool. It will never be hot. It will never be lukewarm. Cool is the new warm in Afghanistan.

As I stand under the weak spray to wet my hair and begin soaping my body, I turn and face the room. The guy occupying the last stall turns off his water, wraps his hips in a towel, and grabs his clothes from the bench. I turn back to the wall as he passes by, but turn again to face West when I hear the suspicious but unmistakable repeated smacking that can only be the sound of his balls slapping against his thighs as he jacks his cock. He only does it when no one else is around. I suppose I should feel honored that he's comfortable enough around me not to care that I witness it. He grunts as his arm works furiously to bring him to the edge. The sound of his shallow breaths becomes loud in the confined space.

Forbidden heat winds its way through my body, warming me against the chilly water, and I can't help but reach for my balls, cupping them in my hand as I roll them between my fingers. The soapy glide feels so good, and I sigh a deep breath of satisfaction, loud enough that West turns.

A roguish grin stretches across his rugged face, and his dark eyes bore into mine as he slows his strokes, prolonging the show while drawing out his pleasure. I stroke my hand up my shaft, feeling it harden more with every second that ticks by in the steamy silence.

I don't usually watch men. Being surrounded by them day in and day out, I've become immune to them. I much prefer the soft curves of women. The long silken hair and coy looks that tease and tempt. But with West, I'm aware that I stare a little too long. Longer than what is acceptable.

I've spent so many years showering with him, sharing barracks and beds, and at times, even a sleeping bag. I've become so familiar with his body that I feel almost possessive of it.

Which is ridiculous. But I can recall every mole and scar that mars his skin. I know his body as well as I know my own. And he's so free with his affection. West is the most touchy-feely guy I know. I think touch is probably his love language or something.

It all just makes me feel… I don't know, open to him, in all ways. For whatever reason, I have not one defense erected against him, in my heart or my mind. I can't deny how beautiful he is. Maybe it's because I know he's just as beautiful on the inside. Maybe it's because his body is cut perfectly, every muscle is toned and defined, every inch of his tanned skin broadcasts his attractiveness like a billboard in Times Square.

And then there's his blatant sex appeal. Like right now, the way he's looking at me, the way he's touching himself, daring me to watch. West isn't gay, and he's not attracted to me. Not in the least. He just likes the attention. He loves to have his ego stroked. He chases the thrill of the dare, pushing the boundaries of decent behavior. And with me, he knows he can push it as far as he wants, because I'm safe and no matter what he does, nothing will ever change between us.

"Bannon interrupted me earlier. I never got to finish." He looks down to where his hand is wrapped around his shaft and hisses a sound of pure pleasure from between his teeth. "Agh."

Biting his bottom lip, West drops his head back under the spray of water, eyes closed, and brings himself off with a final grunt. The muscles in his stomach contract, rippling beneath his inked skin in a wave, and I swear I can feel it in my own body, the heat, the crescendo. I stroke a little faster, getting more into it, because Christ, it feels good to touch myself, and even better to do it while he watches. I'm not supposed to feel that way. It's so taboo, considering our friendship, and only recently have I become aware of it. But I still don't know how I feel about it.

West shampoos his hair, looking back at me several times to watch my progress. "You gonna finish?"

My stomach flips. Does he want to watch? Or is this just another dare because he knows how private I am? My gaze bores into his, locking his eyes with mine as I stroke, thrusting into my fist, bucking my hips, tightening my abs. Suddenly, I imagine it's his hand stroking me, the heat from his calloused palm encircling my shaft, and that's all it takes to lose control. I come over the top of my fist in thick spurts while he watches. Turning back to the wall, I finish my shower in solitude.

We turn off the water and towel dry in silence, and I can hear my heart beating inside my body. This is the farthest we've ever pushed the boundary. I imagine he did it for the rush, or the attention. To him, it was probably nothing more than an immature game between friends. Showing off how thick and long his cock is, proud of his hard-earned, perfect body. But it's becoming harder and harder to deny *my* reasons. The truth is, it gives me a sick thrill to imagine he had participated, that he craved me, like I did him.

Slipping my legs into fatigues, I'm overcome with guilt, filled with shame from my thoughts. It settles over my chest and shoulders like a heavy weight. West doesn't deserve that. He's good to me. His friendship and his motives are pure. He doesn't deserve for me to perv on him.

Exiting the trailer, he holds the door for me, and I vow to

apologize to him without words. I will find a way to make it up to him and be the friend he deserves.

The Kabul-Kandahar Highway, also known as Highway One, connects the two largest cities in Afghanistan. It's the only paved road for hundreds of miles. Although our Humvee is equipped with automatic weapons, my stomach clenches in knots every time we pass a convoy of vehicles passing us in the opposite direction. There's no way to tell who's behind the wheel. You only have a split second to react in order to save your life and the lives of your team.

As the automatic rifleman, it's my job to man the guns, with backup from Micah. Instead, I'm driving. West is riding shotgun, navigating our direction, while Micah has his head sticking out the top, manning the saw. There aren't many signs along the highway pointing us in the right direction, and the sandstorm kicking up dust decreases visibility considerably.

Just another beautiful day in the desert.

The sounds coming from my stomach draw West's attention. My anxiety from driving the highway, coupled with memories of our earlier shower, and the guilt that followed, are stirring my gut into a toxic brew. And I do feel guilty, plenty guilty, but there is a side helping of heat that accompanies that guilt. No matter how ashamed I feel of my attraction to him and the fantasy of him touching me that pushed me over the edge, I'm still incredibly turned on thinking about it.

Fucking hell, like I need this distraction right now, with a mission looming on the horizon. I need to get my head in the game and push this ridiculous desire from my mind.

"I'm telling you, the best gun of World War II was the Johnson rifle," Micah insists heatedly, ducking his head back down inside to add his two cents.

West's face bears his signature *are you fucking kidding me* look. "You can suck *my* Johnson. Everyone knows it was the M1 Garand."

But Micah isn't ready to give in. "Yeah, but they had to wait until they ran out of bullets to reload. What if you're in the middle of a firefight? Wouldn't you have preferred to reload and top off your clip beforehand?"

"It only held eight fucking rounds, dipshit. If it was good enough for Patton, it's good enough for me." West smirks and slaps my thigh, like he delivered the ultimate argument-ending theory.

It was always like this when the team got together, debating over the best tank, the best gun, the best artillery. And I have to hand it to West; he knew his shit better than anyone.

Hence why I named him Professor.

We drove for hours, fueling our bodies on protein bars and beef jerky. In the Afghan desert, everything looks the same. Bleached, brown landscapes and ramshackle tenement housing. There is no skyline, no buildings that rise above the city squalor. But when the sun rises and sets, it's the prettiest damn sight I've ever seen. A giant, blazing ball of fire, painted the boldest shades of orange, fuchsia, gold, and crimson you can imagine. I only get to see it when I leave the base. The FOB is surrounded by concrete walls for our safety, and it becomes tedious to feel so closed-in day after day. So, although the province isn't much to look at, I appreciate just being able to look.

"Do you want some jerky?" West's tone is full of concern, emphasized by his hand on my thigh.

He's trying to distract me from my anxiety, knowing how my stomach twists whenever we're on the road. As if he doesn't have enough responsibility on his shoulders, leading an entire team through a hot zone on his way to report for a mission he also has to coordinate, apparently, he's going to add my shit to his long list as well. But that's why he's such a dynamic team leader.

It's also why he's my best friend.

"Nah, I'll wait until after we make camp." I couldn't eat right now if I tried. It would probably just come right back up.

After four more hours of driving, another debate about artillery, and a bathroom break on the side of the road, I pull off the highway and about half a mile down, West instructs me to park the Humvee behind a concrete blockade about eight feet wide. I can't begin to guess where it came from, but it will serve well as a barrier from the road for the night.

We make camp in short time, pitching tents to block the sand thrown by the windstorm, and remove supply crates from the back of the Humvee to use as seating. There are no campfires or folding chairs, or s'mores. This isn't an overnight Scouts' campout. We have to be ready to bail at a moment's notice. And just like the Scouts, our motto is *'leave no trace'*. That sentiment not only applies to our gear and trash, but also the light of a campfire will only draw attention to our position. We have to act as if we were never here—and as if we aren't here even now.

I only have three things in my tent—my rucksack, which also serves as a pillow, my rifle, and a bottle of water, which is less for staying hydrated, and more for just rinsing the dust from my mouth.

"Think fast, Reaper," Tommy shouts, tossing a rolled up pair of his socks at me. "Found them in my ruck. We can play *Hacky-sack* or keep away."

When you're stuck in the middle of absolutely fucking nowhere, you find creative ways to stay busy.

"I'm going to pass, but thanks." The last thing I need with my twisted stomach is to jump around.

Planting my ass on a plastic crate, I pull my balaclava up over my mouth and ears and try to tune them out. If I can just retreat inside my head for a few minutes and find something to focus on, I can calm my nerves enough to settle my stomach for dinner.

I jump when strong hands land on my shoulders and begin to knead the tense muscles. I don't have to turn and look to know it's West. His capable fingers dig into the tight muscles of my neck, digging out my worries with his thumbs and grinding them to dust. I relax into him, leaning against his hard stomach.

The heat from his body warms me to my core, melting away my troubles. My body begins to loosen under his touch, and the memory of our shower earlier comes back to me again, the moment where he came in his fist, his milky-white seed flowing over the top of his knuckles, his golden-brown eyes burning me alive. He's touching me with the same hands he used to touch himself.

Goddamn, I really need to stop thinking about that.

And the more I think about it, the more I *want* to think about it. Maybe even want it to happen again.

His deep voice, filtered through the knit layers of his balaclava, caresses my ear as he bends low over my shoulder. "Now that I've got you nice and loose, stay that way while I make you something to eat."

Everything inside of me melts and softens. "With the wind kicking up, we're going to have to eat inside our tents."

"Come on, then. Come, keep me company." Then he addresses the team. "Not much risk with the storm making such poor visibility. We're almost camouflaged by the sand, but I still need you on watch. Tommy, you take first shift. I will relieve you at twenty-three hundred," he shouts over the rising wind before tugging me inside his tent.

We sit facing each other, with our knees touching. The tent is barely big enough for one person, and together, we're a tight fit. Digging into his ruck, he pulls out two brown packages and two plastic spoons.

"I've got chili mac and beef stew."

We both know I'll lose a hand if I reach for the chili mac. It's his favorite. I feel touched that he even offered. Grabbing the beef stew and a spoon from him, I tear open the pouch and stuff my mouth with food. I haven't eaten since lunch, and my stomach is growling now that I've settled down some.

"You don't even want me to heat it first?"

"I'm good," I reply around a mouthful.

Shrugging his shoulders, he follows suit. We eat in silence, inhaling the bland food as if we're on the verge of starvation. Outside the tent, the wind howls like a wild beast, with grains of sand pelting the thin nylon like tiny bullets. When we finish, West wraps up the garbage in a plastic bag and tucks it back inside his ruck.

With only the dim light from his LED lantern, the atmosphere feels subdued and relaxed.

"Are you feeling better?"

"Much," I mumble.

"Tomorrow, we only have four hours on the road. Highway A75 is a lot less traveled than A1. Should be quieter."

"I don't know whether that's good or bad."

"I guess it could be both." West smirks, an expression of his that is as familiar to me as the sound of his deep voice. "Don't worry, I promise you we'll get there in one piece. No Afghani with a lick of sense would fuck with our Humvee. Not with my automatic rifleman behind the wheel. He's fucking terrifying. They don't call him the Reaper for nothing."

I half-smile, half snort at the ridiculousness of his compliment. I'd been inspecting the dirt under my fingernails while he spewed his teasing banter, but I raise my eyes to his, a warm feeling spreading through my gut. Sometimes, when I look at him, all I see is my friend, my buddy for the last twelve years, my brother to the soul. Someone I know better than I sometimes know myself. But sometimes, I look at him with his cock in his hand, with his confident, cocky grin, and I can't help but think, *fuck he's hot.*

Right now, he's both. "How's that blister on your foot?"

"What blister?"

"The one you were complaining about like a baby yesterday."

"I was not," he defends with a laugh.

"Were, too. It's probably bleeding into your sock right now. Give me your foot."

I grab for his boot, and he kicks my thigh. "I can take off my own boot."

A heavy sigh accompanies the rolling of my eyes, and I shove him in the chest. "Lie down and give me your foot."

"Fine," he huffs, "if you wanna rub my feet so bad, you can take it off yourself."

West lies down on his bedroll and shoves his foot in my gut.

"I'm not going to rub your damn foot, princess. I just don't want it getting infected when your blister pops." He huffs again and I have to bite back my grin. Such a tough guy. Such a faker. "You still have that ointment I gave you?"

"Side pocket," he grunts.

I dig the tube from his ruck. "It's almost empty. When we get back to base, I'll get you another one."

"I can get my own tube, thanks." He sounds so petulant as I unlace his boot.

"I know you can, but I also know you won't. Not until the damn blister is infected." He glares, and I glare right back, peeling his sock from his foot. "Go ahead, tell me I'm wrong."

"Shut up and rub my foot."

I have to fight the urge to dig my thumb into the blister, to prove a point, and to shut him up. Then I regret it when I apply the ointment, and he sighs with relief and pleasure. So, I end up rubbing his fucking foot. It isn't completely terrible.

As I continue to rub small circles over his heel, he becomes more relaxed, quieter, until I swear he's fallen asleep. But then his eyes pop open, and a grin spreads across his face.

"You hear that?"

Instantly, I'm on guard, my body tensing for a threat. I still, listening but hearing nothing. He realizes I don't get it and his grin stretches wider.

"The storm, it stopped."

He's right. All I hear is silence. No howling wind. No grains of sand pelting against the walls of the tent. Touching his skin had drugged me into such a deep, hypnotic state I hadn't even noticed the storm had ceased. West sits up and grabs his boot, and when it's laced up again, he crawls out of the tent.

"Come on, Nurse Aguilar."

The plastic crates we sat on earlier are half buried in sand. Tommy, Micah, and Rosie emerge from their tents like turtles poking their heads out of their shells. They kick the sand off the crates and resume their seats.

West heads away from the group. "Let's check out the Humvee. I want to wipe the sand off the windows, in case we have to clear out in a hurry."

The concrete blockade had shielded most of the sand from smothering the armored vehicle and our tents. I'm grateful for West's foresight in choosing our spot. He's a kick-ass team leader. He grabs a towel from beneath his seat and begins to wipe down the windows, while I dig drifts of sand away from the tires with a small entrenching tool. Then he climbs up on the hood and clears away the debris. West smacks his hand down on the metal top.

"Climb up here." When I'm seated beside him, with my

long legs stretched out like his, he points to the sky. "Look up. There must be a million stars out tonight."

We lie back against the windshield so we don't have to crane our necks. The stars glow like neon lights. It's a beautiful sight. Every once in a while, the desert wasteland gives you something to appreciate, like a gift for having endured its misery.

I breathe out a deep sigh of appreciation, beginning to truly relax for the first time today. "You know what this means, right?" The words aren't even out of my mouth before we feel the first fat drops of rain.

"There it is," he agrees, laughing. It always rains after a storm.

"Like Mother Nature washing away the dirt and beginning anew."

"Fuck, a flood wouldn't clean this place up. There's dirt everywhere. It's the fucking desert." West sits up and wriggles out of his khaki t-shirt. "I only brought one other shirt, so I better keep this one dry."

He balls it up and sticks it behind his head, like a pillow. I decide to do the same, and pull mine over my head before balling it up. The rain feels blessedly cool against my heated skin, and I welcome the refresher by sticking out my tongue to catch a few drops to drink. The temperature will drop fast now that the sun has set, but for these few minutes, it feels like the closest thing to heaven I'm going to find out here.

West rubs his hand across his stomach, smearing the water over his skin. I look down the length of his body, appreciating the ripples and valleys of his abs, the tight definition, his skin bronzed from the relentless sun. Black and colored ink covers his broad chest and obliques. His thick arms are heavily tattooed, as are his thighs and calves. I'd been there by his side for every one of them. Every time he added another one to his body, he dragged me along with him. Yet I only have half as many as he does.

It's a sort of addiction for him, a way to process his stress and anxiety.

He lets his hand drift down by his side between us, and when his fingers brush against mine, I don't pull away. Nor do I pull away when his pinky deliberately rubs against mine. In fact, I let him hook our little fingers together. Muted fragments of the team's conversation hover in the darkness. It sounds like they're playing *'name that show'* by singing theme songs from nineties sitcoms. We lie here in silence for several minutes, staring up at the sky, processing our own thoughts. God only knows what's running through his head.

"Do you remember the last time we did this?"

A snicker that holds no amusement trickles from my lips. "Yeah. You got pulled for guard duty overnight and dragged me along with you. Then you fell asleep on my shoulder and I had to stay awake and do your job."

"You're a real friend. Someone I can count on in a pinch." He laughs and rests his head on my shoulder, staring at me with a blinding smile.

"And you're an asshole," I return, shrugging him off. "Two days later, I got called up, and you were nowhere to be found. I was still exhausted, and I ended up falling asleep. My ass got written up."

He rolls onto his side, facing me, laughing so hard his body curls around mine. "They made you wash every vehicle in the parking lot," he wheezes.

Fucking dick. "You're a real friend. Someone I can count on in a pinch," I parrot.

His laughter dies off, and he sits up, leaning on his elbow as he stares into my eyes. "You can always count on me, Reaper. Nobody loves you like I do." A moment of silence passes between us, and I swallow hard, the intensity of the moment making me feel vulnerable. He lies back down, but this time, his hand doesn't find mine in the space between us. "You gonna stay with me again tonight?"

"Of course. But if I get called up for duty when we get back to base, I don't care where you are or what you're doing; I will find you, and I will drag your ass to the parking lot with me."

West sighs long and loud, folding his hands across his bare wet chest. "Deal."

WEST

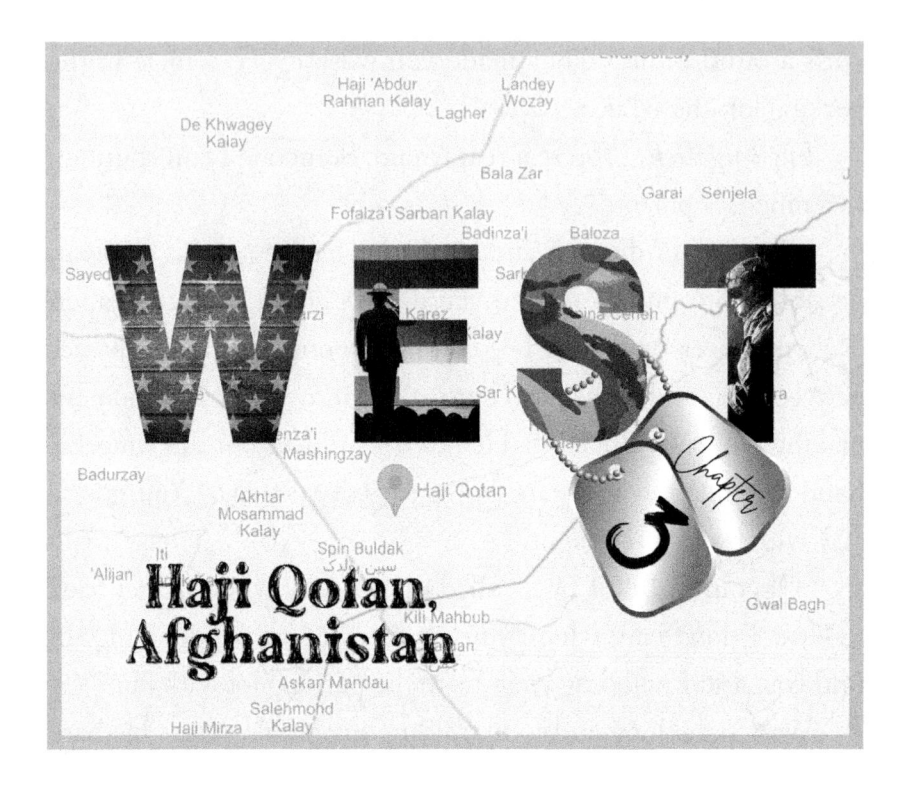

Chapter 3

Haji Qotan, Afghanistan

"PACK UP! We head out in five."

I watch my team scramble to pack up their tents and rucks as ordered. The curve of the morning sun teases the horizon, threatening to set the world on fire with its blazing orange-and-red hues. My gaze falls on Brandt, already behind the wheel and ready to go. We slept there last night, inside the Humvee to avoid the rain, and early this morning, before any hint of the sun breaching the horizon, I woke him and we broke camp quietly. Last night we took turns sleeping as the other kept watch so that we would both be rested enough for our mission today.

That's the best part about having a partner. You're never at your weakest because there are two of you. Two of you to share the burden, the struggles, and the victories. How can I fail with him beside me? Brandt is like my emergency battery pack. When I'm running on empty, he recharges me.

Last night's rain made a mess of things, turning the landscape into a swamp of thick sludge. The sand that had piled up from the windstorm is now wet quicksand, sucking at our tires as we make our way back to the paved road. It's slow going as we crawl through the spongy terrain. At one point, Rosie jumps out to check the depth of a puddle too wide to go around before we carefully make our way through it. We all breathe a sigh of relief when we're back on the A75, except Brandt. I think he actually prefers the mud.

"It's my little girl's birthday today," Micah muses, ducking his head back inside.

Rosie turns in her seat and looks up at him. "Were you able to call her before we left base?"

"Nah, communications were down because that storm started kicking up, but my girl got her something from me and put my name on it. I'll call her when we get back to base."

I feel both regret and relief that I don't have a family stateside sitting around missing me, lighting candles for my safe return and shit. After I lost my grandma, there was no one left for me to count as family, aside from Brandt. His parents live in Charlotte, not far from Fort Bragg, but he doesn't make it a priority to go home and see them often, nor do they make it a priority to visit the base.

We have each other, and that's enough for us.

"I talked to my wife the day before yesterday," Tommy recalls with a grin. "It was our anniversary. Been married for four years now. She said she wants to start a family when I make it back home."

"You ready for that?" Rosie asks excitedly.

"Been ready. I don't think I have another tour in me. I'm ready to go home and get fat, kick around the house on the weekends and grill shit, watch the game, and argue with my wife."

"Sounds like heaven," Micah seconds, "but I think I'll stay in the service in some way, maybe reserves or something. What about you, Rosie girl?"

"I've been talking to someone," she admits shyly. Catcalls and whistles ensue, elevating the noise level in the vehicle to a roar.

"Hey, settle down back there," I bark. "This isn't a Taylor Swift concert. Reaper's trying to concentrate." They catch my grin in the rearview mirror and realize I'm kidding.

Tommy taps me on the shoulder. "What about you, Professor?"

"What about me? I've got my wife right here." I slap Brandt's thigh. "He's going to have to improve his foot rub game though, if he wants me to give him kids."

His straight white teeth glisten as he smiles back, shaking his head.

He always takes my ribbing good-naturedly. It's just one of many perks of a decade-long friendship. You can tease the other person, insult them, even say hurtful things at times, and all will be forgiven.

"As long as they all look like me and not you, I'll rub anything you want me to," he teases.

Predictably, the peanut gallery goes wild with comments and jokes. I let it slide because not only does it pass the time on the road, but hopefully we're distracting Brandt from his anxiety. Until finally, we pull off the highway onto an unpaved road only wide enough for a single vehicle.

As we drive through the city of Spin Boldak, children run alongside the road, keeping pace with our vehicle, shouting at us, waving, and some even throw small rocks. It's hard to tell if these people are friends or foes. Most are just indifferent. As long as we keep the terrorists from attacking their village and recruiting their children and raping their women, they're happy to leave us alone. But the children are desperate, always asking for handouts, whether it be food, clothing, or supplies. They would take anything we were willing to part with.

If we were riding with more security in a convoy, with plenty of backup and firepower, I would stop and share what I could, but this isn't a humanitarian effort, and we're woefully under-manned and under-armed. Additionally, and more importantly, it would only heighten Brandt's anxiety, which makes it a solid no for me.

We leave Spin Boldak in our rearview in a cloud of dust and continue through villages that become smaller and less populated until we reach Haji Qotar, our final destination.

After making two rounds through the small village, cruising at a snail's pace as we check for signs of anything and anyone out of place, Brandt kills the engine in front of the newly constructed school.

"This place is like a ghost town," Rosie remarks.

Frowning at her, I add, "Just another thing that doesn't

make sense about this town. Intel says their population isn't more than a hundred people."

Tommy's brows pull together. "What the fuck do they need a school for?"

"Your guess is as good as mine. Let's check it out. Tommy, how many grenades have you got on you?"

"Two, Sergeant."

"Micah, are you fully stocked on clips?"

"Yes, Sir."

I don't have to ask Brandt if he's ready. I know he is. He's anal about his preparedness. Annmarie specializes in linguistics, and her main job is to provide communication between us and the locals, but when her services aren't needed, she's expected to carry a gun and cover her ass, as well as ours. A soldier is first and foremost always a soldier, before any specialty or rank.

"Rosie, are you fired up?"

"I've got eight clips, Sarge."

"Let's roll out. Vee formation until we make our way inside the building. I don't have the layout yet, so I'll call it when we get in there."

I survey my team on the dirt path that leads up to the building. They look sharp as fuck, eager and ready, and I wait for that feeling of rightness to click within me. That feeling that tells me we're ready to move. A huge weight settles over me. The weight of responsibility. It's a weight no one wants to carry. I'm responsible for their safety. One bad call, one wrong move, and I would shoulder the regret of those decisions for the rest of my life, however long that is.

From the outside, the building doesn't look like much. It's as plain as every other building in this village. Most are constructed from dried mud and sand, adobe style, all blending together in a sea of beiges and browns. But from the inside? It's even worse. There is no way you can convince me this is a school. Even in a village this poor, the villagers take pride in teaching their children. The walls are made of bare plywood, no paint or spackle coating them. Some rooms are only divided by hanging sheets. The floor is made of packed gravel.

As team leader, I'm trained to assess a location or situation in the blink of an eye. It only takes seconds for me to discern whether we're under threat or not. As we move through the front door in a single file line, we pause at the base of the stairs while I survey our surroundings. I note there are no overhead lights, no safety measures. Hell, there aren't even doors on the classrooms. The building is stripped bare down to the basics. Our Intel said the construction was complete. It looks like another bomb factory or training facility for insurgents. They were popping up faster than we could shut them down.

The good news? The place doesn't seem inhabited currently, which considerably lessens the risk for my team. We'll scope it out, seize any supplies we find, and then either burn the building down or detonate it. I vote for detonation. It's always more exciting than a fire.

"Sharp, Boom, Rosie, upstairs," I motion with my head, as both my hands are on my gun, "Reaper, with me." My voice carries through the microphone attached to my helmet that keeps us all connected.

We stay on the first floor, circling around the staircase. I come upon what should be a janitor's closet, except that it's missing a door and is empty.

"This is a total front operation," Brandt mutters in his comms.

"Nothing but crickets up here, Sarge. Just an empty shell," Tommy comes back over my headset. "I see stripped wiring and lots of plastic packaging discarded on the floor. Other than that, nada. We'll take the secondary stairs down and sweep as we make our way back to you."

"Roger that," I call back.

The walls are so thin, I can hear the echo of their boots overhead and wonder what the flooring is made of. Probably another sheet of plywood. Tense moments pass in silence. The beating of my heart is the loudest noise in the room. We duck into another classroom, only to find it empty, just like all the others.

"Looks like a dry hole," I report into my headset.

It grows so quiet you can hear a pin drop, and I figure they must have hit the back stairs. Brandt and I move through the narrow halls, with me clearing rooms on the left and him on the right, working in tandem to sweep the first floor. I see nothing, not even debris. Perhaps they haven't moved in yet. Before we leave, we'll make sure there is nothing left of this building for them to move into.

A click echoes through the headset, and every muscle in my body tenses as I recognize the sound. Moving on autopilot, we duck into the janitor's closet. The force of Brandt's solid body crashing into me from behind knocks the breath from me as I hit the gravel floor face first.

"Frag out," someone screams into the mic, their voice so

loud in my ear it bounces around inside my head, and I brace for the inevitable explosion.

I scramble to cover Brandt's body with mine, rolling over him to protect him from falling debris. Time stops, even though it continues to move. The sound of wood splintering like sheets of paper fills my headset. The force of the blast reverberates through my body, shaking my bones and teeth until they rattle. I can taste the dust and debris in my mouth. Brandt shouts in my ear and through my headset, so that I hear and feel him everywhere. Nothing exists but my fear and his body and voice. The smell of burning wood and chemicals fills the air like a toxic cologne. It's the scent of death and destruction.

"Sharp! Boom!" My call goes unanswered as my fear mounts. "Rosie!"

Two more explosions in rapid succession shake the entire building, and I can hear the creaking and cracking of it breaking apart, preparing to bury us in its rubble. The floor beneath us becomes a weapon as gravel tears through my fatigues, imbedding into my skin. The impact of the blast forces us apart, throwing my body several feet away from his, and I land in a broken heap. Chunks of the ceiling come crashing down on our bodies, the walls cave in.

The pain is blinding, and almost too much to bear, and then I–

WEST

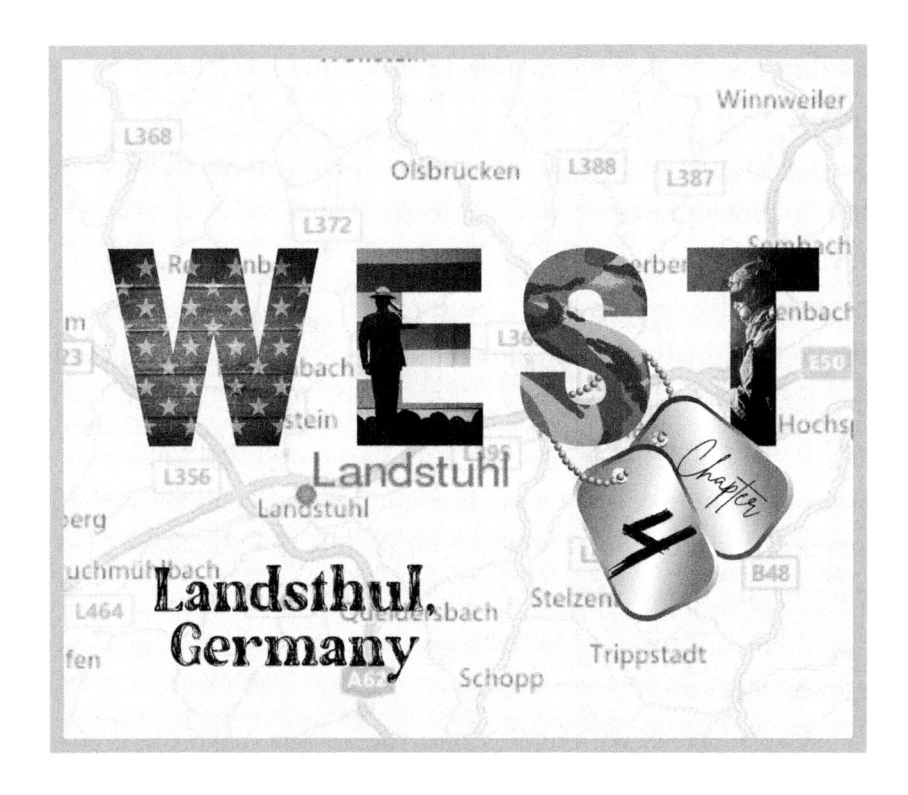

Landsthul, Germany

Chapter 4

IT'S DARK..

And cold.

So dark, I can't see.

But I can feel the chill seeping deep into my bones.

The icy cold makes my body feel numb.

My limbs feel heavy and sluggish, as if I'm underwater.

Am I swimming?

I must be under the water, deep in the ocean, where the sunlight doesn't reach, where it's cold and dark.

The pressure is closing in on me.

That's why my head hurts.

The throbbing beats against my skull, a slow, steady rhythm in sync with my heartbeat.

But... There's no water in the desert.
We're stationed miles from the ocean.
Why would I be swimming?
If I could just get my–

I'm burning alive.

Cell by cell, every molecule and atom in my body is evaporating under the relentless, scorching inferno that consumes me.

The heat from the core of my body is spreading through my veins like wildfire, making my limbs tingle.

Why did he leave me for dead in the middle of the desert?

The sun is going to bleach my bones as white as the rocks.

Reminds me of that time Brandt and I took four days' leave in Cancun.

I burned my skin so red I couldn't even get laid because I was in so much pain and discomfort.

Are we back in Cancun? I fucking hope so.

It sure beats dying alone in the desert.

Goddamn, can't he snag us an umbrella before I fucking waste away?

Brandt!

I know that motherfucker can hear me because I can hear him.

He's talking to someone while I lay here dying.

Completely fucking inconsiderate!

Bra–

My tongue isn't cooperating, probably because my mouth is so dry, it feels glued shut.

If he would just stop flirting with the ladies long enough to grab us a couple of drinks, maybe I could speak clearly.

Tequila Sunrise, Brandt.

I reach for him, but I'm not even sure if my hand is actually moving. It feels like dead weight.

I'm dead weight.

Brandt, get us—

I'm—thirsty. So fucking thirsty.

My saliva has become a thick paste, being churned by my tongue into a sticky froth that coats the inside of my mouth.

I need Bran—no, he's here with me. Touching me. I think he's holding my hand, if I could just see his face.

"–bringing him out of it today. His head looks good."

Good? My head looks fan-fucking-tastic. Cut, smooth, and fat.

Why is Brandt's girl talking about my cock? Why is Brandt?

"He'll be waking up soon," she says.

Can't open my eyes. They're so heavy.

Did she fucking roofie me?

I'd have shown her my cock without putting up a fuss if she would have just asked.

I squeeze his hand, so he'll help me open my damn eyes.

"He's squeezing me! West...it's me, Brandt. Wake up."

Of course it's fucking you. Who else would be holding my hand and shouting at me?

"Help...Me..." Even to my own ears, my voice sounds raspy and faint, barely recognizable.

"I'm here, West. Talk to me, Goose."

If he's going to start with the Top Gun shit, I'll punch him if I ever get my eyes open.

"So...Fucking...Loud..." It's exhausting just trying to spit those three simple words out.

"Sorry," he chuckles. Then his voice is in my ear, just a soft whisper of his breath and sound. "Is this better?"

"You have...big...mouth."

"Yeah," he laughs again, but softer this time. "You can call me whatever you want. Just open your eyes for me first."

Slowly, I peel my eyes open millimeters at a time. It's so bright, the light blinds me through the narrow slits of my lids.

"There you are," he beams, his white smile more blinding than the lighting.

When I finally manage to crack them open all the way, I immediately have to squint when the too-bright fluorescents cause my head to throb.

"Too bright," I croak.

"Turn the lights off," Brandt hisses at his girl.

I give it another shot, this time managing to locate him in the darkness. His face hovers above mine, blurry and smiling, but full of concern.

"Hi," he breathes, glowing at me like I'm someone fucking special.

His girl hovers over his shoulder. "Welcome back,

Sergeant."

I don't like the look of her. I don't trust her. Returning my gaze to Brandt, I squeeze his fingers again. "She roofied me."

He laughs out loud and then seems to remember he's supposed to be quiet and whispers, "No man, we had to put you out. But you're back now. You're back," he beams, and kisses my knuckles.

I try to untangle my hand from his, but even that slight movement is fucking exhausting.

"Where...the fuck did I go?"

"I'm going to get the doctor. I'll be back," she says before disappearing.

Brandt doesn't even spare her a glance. "You're in the hospital. You've been asleep for quite a while."

"Did I...OD? How much...did she give me?" I'm struggling to speak each word around a mouth full of bitter-tasting glue.

"Nobody gave you anything, West. We had to put you to sleep."

"Sleep–" I repeat, thinking how good that sounds right now.

When I wake again, we're alone. He's still holding onto me, like a lifeline. His touch grounds me, making the pain in my head recede slightly.

"Water," I rasp.

My voice sounds like it belongs to someone else. Someone who crawled on their hands and knees through the desert for days in search of water.

"Oh shit, yeah. I'll be right back." He drops my hand and scrambles out the door, returning minutes later holding a paper cup with a straw. "Tiny sips. Take it slow," he advises, bringing the straw to my chapped lips.

But, of course, I'm greedy for anything liquid, and I take too much. A fit of coughing ensues, and I spit most of the water back out, cringing as I feel it dribble down my chin.

Fuck, my throat isn't working right.

In fact, nothing is working right. My body feels like a lead weight. My limbs tingle with numbness, like my skin is being pierced by a thousand pinpricks, as if they've fallen asleep.

The pain in my head is so bad that I can feel it behind my eyes. Every time I look left or right, my vision blurs, and my eyeballs are fucking sore, if that's even possible. I try to sit up to take another sip, but it's futile. I'm too weak.

How long have I been asleep?

I didn't realize I'd asked the question out loud until he answers.

"It's been a while."

Brandt won't look me in the eye when he talks to me. Instead, he busies himself with my comfort—grabbing for the remote on my bed to raise my head, adjusting my pillow, and holding the paper cup in front of me, as if I'm too weak to do it myself.

Though I am.

Now that I'm sitting up slightly, I can feel how stiff my neck is. Rolling my head from side to side, I try to loosen it, but it takes too much energy. Again with the cup in my face, and I manage a small sip without drooling on myself.

Even in the dim light, I can make out my surroundings, however blurred they still are, and realize I'm in a hospital, though I can't recall what the fuck I did to land my ass here.

"Brandt, talk to me. I need some answers."

My voice still sounds as if I swallowed broken shards of glass.

"The doctor should be here any minute."

That's a non-answer if I've ever heard one. I don't want to talk to the doctor. I don't know the doctor. I know Brandt. I trust Brandt. And I want him to look in my eyes and tell me why I'm here.

"Just tel–"

"There you are. It's good to finally meet you, Sergeant Wardell. I'm Doctor Müller."

The doctor is tall and stocky, with shaggy brown hair, and a mustache that covers most of his top lip. Reaching into his pocket, he pulls a penlight from his white lab coat and clicks it on before warning me, "This is going to be bright, and I understand your eyes are sensitive right now, but please try not to blink."

Once, early in my military career, I made the regrettable mistake of mouthing off to my drill sergeant. He made me stand outside in the pouring rain and mop the parking lot of my barracks. It was forty-two degrees outside that day with a stiff wind. That was easier than trying not to blink right now.

"Better. Much improved," he declares, and I realize his speech is heavily accented with German. Where in the fuck am I?

I find Brandt with my useless fucking eyes and I feel a little bit like Dorothy from *The Wizard of Oz* when I ask him, "We're not in the desert anymore, are we?"

Of course we're not.

There's no hospital there besides the field hospital, which is really just a converted shipping container stocked with first aid supplies. As I look around, I finally take note of the state-of-the-art machines beeping and glowing with my vital statistics. Everything looks... newer, modern.

No, we're not in the desert anymore.

Why is my mind so sluggish? It hasn't even occurred to me until now to piece things together. I'm a fucking Sergeant First Class, a team leader, and yet I'm relying on others to inform me when I can damn well figure shit out for myself.

And still, Brandt won't look me in the eye.

That tells me everything I need to know.

Out in the hall, the sound of someone dropping something, some sort of medical equipment or perhaps a food tray, explodes in the silence. The sound is a shock to my senses, and I jump as my body tenses, which makes everything fucking hurt.

And the sound I heard is echoed again, but this time inside my head. Much louder and in high definition. White light so bright that it's blinding explodes behind my eyes, and I can see it and hear it inside my head. I can smell it. The chemical burn, the metallic iron of blood, the acrid smoke. They scream out at the top of their lungs and the sound ricochets inside my ears through my headset.

The sound of a building coming down around me, burying my body under its charred rubble.

The sound and smell of death.

I choke on a gasp of air so deep and sharp that it seizes my lungs momentarily, and in those few vital seconds, it all comes rushing back to me.

Feeling as if I've been shot through the heart with adrenaline, my heartbeat spikes, making the machines I'm hooked up to go crazy, and the increase in blood flow makes my head throb even harder. This time, when I look at Brandt, he reluctantly meets my eyes.

My answers are right there in front of me, written all over his face. It's in his guilty expression, his down-turned mouth. It's the regret in his eyes.

Even in the darkness, I can see him plain as day. He can't hide the truth from me any longer.

"Where are they, Reaper?" The tone of my voice is a warning he can't ignore.

"Doc, can we have a minute?" Brandt asks.

The doctor hesitates, looking back-and-forth between us. I can't tell if he's more worried about my health or Brandt's safety.

"I'll return shortly," he warns before leaving us alone.

He drags a plastic chair to my bedside and drops down in it with resignation, sighing deeply as he rests his head in his hand. "What's the last thing you remember?"

I can see it clearly now, memories of that day playing through my head like a reel on repeat. It won't stop—the screaming, the static in my headset, the blinding flash of light, and the blast of heat and force as the explosion pushed into my body.

My gaze settles on the small gold cross he wears around his neck. "There was an explosion. I heard three of them. You pushed me into that closet, and then...nothing." Brandt lifts his head and finally looks at me. "I've got nothing after that."

He swallows three times before he can speak. "They tripped an IED on the stairs. That was the first blast."

"And the other two?"

The intensity of his gaze burns a hole right through me. No doubt he's hoping his silence will lead to me filling in the blanks so he won't have to.

"Reaper."

His throat works, sliding up and down the long column of his neck, and he licks his dry lips. "Those were Boom's grenades."

The Grenadier isn't considered fully armed if he doesn't have at least two grenades on him at all times in combat. If those were his explosives I heard, then that meant...

I find his eyes again, and I can see the regret swimming in those blue depths. He shakes his head slowly back-and-forth, and I know, I know what he's trying to say without words, but I have to ask.

"Are any of them alive?"

His head stops moving, and he swallows again before dropping his eyes to my lap, to the blue blanket that covers my body. A hot flash of anger rushes to the surface, burning a fiery path in my chest.

How dare fate try to fuck with me? How dare she take my team from me?

It was my job to lead the mission, to plan for their safety, and I feel blinding rage at my incompetence, at my inability to save them, and at preventing their deaths.

Hot tears bubble up and burn my eyes before spilling down my cheeks. So many tears they blind my vision until Brandt's face becomes a wavering blur in the darkness.

"No," I whisper.

Maybe if I refuse to accept it, it can't be true. Maybe there's a way to go back in time and do something different. His head is in his hands again, and when he raises his tear-stained face to mine, we both know there's nothing we can do differently to change the outcome. We lost our team, the Street Sweepers, and we're the only two survivors.

I can't even begin to process the anger and grief consuming me, so I put a pin in it and move on to the next issue. "Where are we?"

"Landstuhl, Germany." He sounds utterly defeated and broken, just like how I feel.

"How long have we been here?"

"Three weeks."

Somehow, the tubes and wires connecting me to the machines that surround my bed haven't registered yet through my grief and confusion and shock, but now I wonder.

"What happened? Why am I in this bed?" And then another thought occurs to me. A more pressing one. "Are you a patient here, or just visiting? How bad were you hurt?"

The questions come rapidfire now, and I can't seem to stop as the logical part of my brain comes back online.

"I'm...both. Technically, I'm still a patient here. We both are, until they transfer us back stateside."

"Stateside? We're being sent home? What the fuck for?" My voice is rising with my panic as my anger and confusion swells.

I have a fucking job to do right here in this godforsaken desert. I have lives to avenge by finishing this goddamn war, and I'll be damned if they're gonna send me home before I complete my mission.

Because otherwise, it was all for nothing. I refuse to believe I lost three members of my team for nothing.

But right now, my concern for him outweighs everything else. "How bad were you hurt?"

"It's nothing, it's—I'm fine."

Bullshit. Does he think after twelve years I can't tell when he's lying? "Take off your shirt."

The bewildered look in his eyes is almost comical, *almost*, except nothing is funny right now.

"What? No. Why?"

"So I can see for myself that you're fine." I challenge him by staring him down, waiting for him to fold. "If you have nothing to hide, prove it. Show me."

He reaches for the hem of his T-shirt, and then stops. "I took a lot of shrapnel. And gravel. Wood splinters, too."

"Define a lot."

"Over most of my body. My torso and back, my arms and legs. I've lost hearing in my left ear. It looks like it's permanent. Blew out my eardrum. And these broken fingers," he says, holding up his left hand. His middle, ring, and pinky fingers are bandaged in a splint.

A sick feeling clinches my gut. The hearing loss sucks, but he still has one good ear. It's an accident that happens frequently, even stateside on bases all across the country. But imagining that his body will bear the permanent scars of the tragedy for the rest of his life sickens me. He'll remember every time he looks in the mirror, every time he showers and dresses. His skin was so beautiful. Perfectly unblemished. But now...

I take note of the cuts and bruises that mar his face and arms. His right eye is tainted red with broken capillaries. He looks like he's been through hell and back, and it dawns on me that if he's up and walking around after sustaining those injuries, and I'm still stuck in bed hooked up to the machines after three weeks of recovery, I must be in worse shape than he is.

"And me? Why am I still in this bed?" Besides the fact that my head hurts like a bitch.

Brandt reaches for my hand again, but I'm able to pull away, and he shoots from his chair like his ass is on fire and begins to pace the room. His apparent anxiety is only increasing mine.

"TBI. You suffered a traumatic brain injury. Fractured ribs, broken toes, and some internal bleeding, but it's resolved itself now. You had a terrible fever, but you're over the worst of it. They had to keep you asleep until the swelling around your brain lessened."

TBI? Fuck. I just thought it was a concussion at best. The fever must be why I thought I was dying or in Cancun. I'd much rather be in Cancun right now than here.

"Now that you're awake, they'll probably send us back home in a matter of days to begin your therapy."

"Therapy? Fuck that, I'm going back to the FOB to do my fucking job. They can take their therapy and shove it up their–" I grab the handrail of my bed to pull myself up, intending to get the fuck out of here, but reality sets in quickly, and I realize that's a joke. I'm not going anywhere like this. I'm so weak I can barely sit up. Sharp, blinding pain shoots through my right leg like I'm being burned with a hot poker, and I gasp as my muscles give and flop back down against the pillow.

Brandt rushes to my side. "What are you doing? Sit the fuck down."

"No! If you wanna go home, fucking go, Goddammit, but I'm not coming with you. As soon as I'm strong enough, I'm gonna walk the fuck out of here and go back to–"

His broken sob rips from his throat as tears fall from his eyes, and he collapses in the plastic chair and drops his head on my lap. His dark hair is such a contrast from the blue blanket, and I stroke my fingers through the strands, wondering why he's falling apart. The grief? Returning home solo?

"West," he cries, and I realize he's grieving for me, not them. But why? Why me? I'm right here. I'm whole. Brandt raises his head, and when he looks at me, I've never seen him look so wrecked. He looks absolutely lost.

"What is it?" Whatever it is, I'll fix it. I'll fight any battle for him, slay any dragon, anything, just to wipe that hopeless look off his face.

He grabs the edge of my blanket, and slowly, with his eyes on my face, he pulls it back, revealing my bare thighs, my knees, and then...

Panic has me frozen, and my heart stops beating. "Brandt," I say a little desperately. "Where the fuck is my leg?"

His throat works over and over, like it's convulsing. "They couldn't save it." His voice is so full of anguish it sounds almost foreign.

My heart starts beating again, too quickly now, and the sound echoes inside my throbbing head. My breathing quickens, and I feel a panic attack coming on. Though I've never had one before, it can't be anything else.

He slips his hand behind my back to rub down my spine. "Just breathe."

"Get. The fuck. Off. Me." The words are stilted between the short, harsh puffs of air that I'm trying to drag into my lungs.

"West, you have to believe me. There was nothing–"

"Fuck you!" I don't have the ability to scream, not with my throat still raw, and the shortness of breath. It comes out as more of a growl. "There's always something…Else…They can do. It's not your…Fucking leg…" He just stands there, hovering, staring, breathing, waiting for me to absolve his guilt. It's not going to happen. Not today. "Just get out," I breathe. My voice is nothing but a heavy whisper because I have no fight left in me.

"Fine. But I'll be back."

Don't fucking bother.

The rational part of my brain understands that losing my leg is nothing compared to the lives that have been lost. I'm sure the rest of my team would gladly give their leg to save their life, but I'm not feeling rational. The oppressive weight of everything I've lost is too much to bear right now. My friends, my leg, my career—it's too much to process all at once.

All I want to do is give up. Just close my eyes and float away and not return.

For the first time in my life, I don't want to be me anymore.

WEST

Ft. Bragg Fayetteville, NC

Chapter 5

THE METAL FORK chases the nurse out of the room as I hurl it after her, hitting the linoleum floor with a clatter which is drowned out by her curse.

"Shut the fuckin' door while you're at it."

Brandt's large body fills the doorway. He picks up the fork and smirks like he finds something funny. "Making friends already, I see. You really know how to charm the ladies."

"Fuck them. And fuck you."

"What is it now, a sponge bath? You used to like the idea of those."

"Yeah, well, the reality is less sexy than the fantasy. She

wants me to get in that thing," I accuse, pointing at the wheelchair beside my bed.

"And?" he asks, taking a seat in it. "It's pretty comfortable."

"I don't want to be seen in a wheelchair. I'm not a fucking invalid. What's the difference between sitting in that thing and sitting in this bed?"

"If you don't want to be an invalid, then get the fuck out of that bed and stop acting like one."

Of course, he doesn't pull any punches.

I traded one prison for another. After a brief stint at Walter Reed Hospital for evaluation, I was transferred back home to Ft. Bragg. Womack Army Medical Center wasn't much of an upgrade from Germany. Same shitty food. Same fucking staff that want to treat me like a helpless child. Same four fucking walls, day in and day out.

The view from my window is of the parking lot. I can see people come and go about their daily lives and all the while, mine is on hold indefinitely. Like time stopped when that bomb went off, and I am existing in a stasis that never evolves. Every day I wake up with the same stump that prevents me from living my life, at least the way I used to. And every day I wake up and wish I hadn't.

And every day Brandt shows up with a smile on his face and encourages me to keep going, keep fighting. For what? What the fuck am I fighting for? I have nothing. Zero motivation to recover. What kind of life am I returning to when I'm discharged?

My head hits the pillow and rolls toward the window, and I stare. And stare. Because what else do I have to do?

"Doc says you're starting therapy tomorrow."

His words have no effect on me. I couldn't care less about physical therapy. That's for people who want to recover, who have a life to return to.

Anger has annihilated my grief, and it consumes me completely. Anger is easier than grief. Grief is exhausting, it's draining emotionally and physically. Grief hurts.

Anger doesn't cost me anything.

In fact, it's the only thing keeping me alive right now.

Liza pops her head back in the room, eyeing me warily before turning her attention on Brandt.

"Staff Sergeant Aguilar, the doctor is ready to see you now."

"Thanks, Liza. And Sergeant Wardell has something he would like to say to you," he prompts, looking at me like I'm supposed to know what he's talking about.

The longer I stare back in silence, the wider his eyes get, like he's imploring me.

"Fuck," I curse softly. "I apologize for throwing a fork at you. It's not my best day." Just like yesterday, and the day before that, and the day before that, and the…

With her hands on her hips, she declares, "You're forgiven. And don't do it again. I don't get paid enough to dodge utensils."

The soft soles of her shoes whisper along the linoleum as she exits the room, and I grab onto Brandt's arm and tug him back down.

"Why are you seeing the doctor?"

"It's nothing, just a routine check-up," he lies straight to my face. And I know he's lying because he's looking right into my eyes, trying to sell it to me. The longer I hold his gaze, the more he starts to fall apart; his nostrils flare, and then he bites his bottom lip.

Without invitation, I reach for the bottom of his khaki T-shirt and pull it from his cargo pants, revealing his scarred torso. It's the first time I've seen it, and I don't know what I was expecting, but Jesus fucking Christ, he's covered in half-healed wounds. His beautiful skin will never be the same again. But there's one that stands out among the rest, a large white bandage under his right pec. The gauze is damp with leaking yellow fluids.

"Christ, West!" He tries in vain to tug his shirt back down.

"What's that?"

"Nothing, just another shrapnel scar."

I raise my eyes from his ribs to his face. "Lie to me again and see what happens."

His throat works, and he tugs his shirt back down. "It's nothing. It got infected, but I'm sure the doc will give me something for it."

If I was angry before, it's nothing compared to the rage building inside of me now. Heat suffuses my face. "If you weren't so busy babysitting my fucking ass all day, you might have more time to take care of yourself!" His eyes roll at my outburst, just one of many lately, and the thin thread of my self-control snaps. Next to my bedside is some sort of breathing apparatus from respiratory therapy used to strengthen my lungs that I chuck at him. "Don't come back until you're loaded up on antibiotics!"

"Settle the fuck down, West, jeez."

The dam of anger holding back my grief cracks wide open,

and hot tears spill over my cheeks. "I can't...Brandt, I can't lose you, too. It's too much. Please," I beg, and I'm not even sure what I'm begging for. I just need one less person to feel responsible for. One less burden to carry. It's so fucking heavy, and I'm so fucking exhausted.

"Hey," he coos soothingly, rubbing my shoulder, "I'm right here. I'm not going anywhere. Let me get this taken care of and I'll be right back."

All I can do is nod through my humiliating tears and snot. The gentleness in his voice makes me feel so vulnerable, and I just want to crawl into his embrace and let him erase the myriad of emotions that are eating through my gut like a corrosive acid. But he pulls away too soon, and I'm left alone again with my thoughts and my feelings. I hit the button again on my morphine drip, and in minutes, I'm drifting through the clouds, feeling weightless, feeling free. There's no burden to carry up here in the morphine haze.

Everything is just... Easier...when I'm flying high.

Sometime later, the warmth of a solid body comforts me from behind as I lay turned on my side, on my good leg. His hand on my hip tugs me from a dreamless sleep, courtesy of the morphine. Brandt's deep voice is a soothing lullaby in my ear.

"I'm back. Doc said everything's gonna be alright."

The intimate connection of his hand covering my hip is a soothing comfort I crave, and yet, it makes me want to cringe. I'm the last person on earth who deserves the comfort of another's arms, but the relief I feel knowing he'll be okay is like breathing a deep breath of fresh air after being suffocated.

Brandt shifts, bringing his body closer to mine, until his chest is flush against my back, and he sighs deeply, a sound of relief and contentment. How long has it been since he had a good night's sleep? I don't want to rob him of it—of the peace he finds being so close to me. In truth, I miss him just as much, if not more. If he can just remain silent and enjoy this unguarded moment without calling attention to the fact we were stealing comfort from each other when I'm so undeserving, I can let it pass. We can enjoy a few hours of rest and wake up recharged and ready to fight another day. *Just please*, I beg silently, *don't say how much you miss this. Don't say it out loud.*

His breathing evens out to a soft snore, and I can feel his warm breath puff against my shoulder through the thin cotton of the hospital gown. I choke down on my inner demons that want to crawl to the surface and push him away, and I just let myself feel—for a few precious moments, I just allow myself to feel the proof of his life, his breath against my skin, the heat from his body, and the solid weight of his hand on my hip. Just for a moment, I can allow myself to feel connected to another person.

It's at this moment I realize that if I do wake up tomorrow, and I will, unfortunately, it's only because of him. With the loss of my team and my career, and my family, I really only have Brandt. Sure, he can do without me; he's a big boy. Completely self-sufficient. But I know how I would feel if I lost him. It would bury me six feet under the ground where I belong. I can't do it to him. I've taken enough lives, I can't take his. I can struggle through the wasted existence of my life, if only to save his.

As I drift off to sleep, I carry that thought with me. As if I've been given new orders, it was now my mission. To live—for Brandt.

God only knows how long we sleep before we're woken by Liza. She pushes into the room carrying my dinner tray. Brandt stirs behind me and sits up, wiping the sleep from his eyes.

"You know, you almost look human when you're sleeping, especially when you let him near you. It's like you're hiding a streak of kindness deep inside of you," Liza taunts.

"Don't believe it. I'm still an asshole."

"I believe that," she agrees, arching her brow. She holds up a plastic package containing utensils.

"Plastic forks?" I almost have to admire her foresight. It doesn't hurt when I throw plastic.

"I don't get paid enough to take your shit, Sergeant, which means I'm not going to from here on out. I've read your chart. It clearly states you're thirty-two years old, but if you want to act like a child, I am going to put you last on my med rotation. After my twelve other patients. After my dinner break. And after my fifteen minute coffee break. Oh, did I mention my charting?" she asks smartly, tapping her bottom lip. "It will be a long, painful night before I make my way back to you again."

"Duly noted, Nurse Ratched."

She glares, unamused, and then, in a sweeter voice dipped in sugar, she asks, "Staff Sergeant, may I get you a dinner tray? I'm sure you're hungry by now."

"Thank you, Liza, I would appreciate that."

She leaves, and he sits up. "Don't go," I half-joke, "your presence makes me more likable, apparently."

"I'm not sure much of anything can make you more likable. And I'm not leaving, just going to sit up in a chair so I can eat."

I take his measure as he settles into the plastic chair beside my bed, checking his phone for messages. He looks more rested than before, and in less pain, which brings me a small amount of satisfaction.

"You know," he muses, without looking up from his phone, "there was a time when your vanity wouldn't allow you to treat her like that." Now he looks at me and smirks. "You had to be the most popular guy in the room, the most liked."

I scoff and roll my eyes. "Those days are long gone. I'm at my worst. What the fuck do I care if she likes me? Getting laid is a thing of the past. I have bigger problems."

Brandt sobers. "You're right, you do have bigger problems. Tomorrow you begin physical therapy, and I won't stand for you not taking it seriously. You better eat up and get some rest tonight because tomorrow begins a new chapter. The first day of the rest of your life."

———

If I thought my life sucked lately, it's nothing compared to how bad it's going to get now that I've met my physical therapist, Navarro Riggs. The man is a fucking sadist. In fact, I'm convinced his calling in life is to make me suffer.

His six-one frame is packed with tightly defined muscle, and his dark eyes and hair highlight a harsh, sinister face. And if all that isn't enough of a caution flag, his don't-fuck-with-me attitude sure is.

"Sergeant Wardell, it's an honor to meet you. I'm Navarro Riggs, but you can just call me Riggs. We've got a lot of progress to make in a short time. Are you ready to get to work?"

Is he fucking kidding me with his clipboard and his Boy Scout pep talk? He's even got a pen tucked behind his ear, like a real go-getter. He can fucking get gone for all I care, because I'm not here to work.

Apparently, my lackluster response really burns his ass because he leans down low to get right up in my face, gripping the armrests of my wheelchair, and lowers his voice at least four octaves.

"I hear you hate being in that chair. Which is great because when you're in here with me, you won't be using that chair whatsoever."

Taking the bait, I reply, "Where in the fuck am I supposed to sit, then?"

"You're not going to be sitting at all."

"Well, in case you haven't noticed, I sure as fuck can't stand."

An unholy light illuminates his dark eyes, putting me on guard. "I promise you, not only can you stand, but you're going to walk, run, swim, ski, and do any other fucking thing you wish to do when I'm done with you."

I snort right in his face, but it lacks humor. "You're fucking dreaming. You can sell that bullshit to your other patients if they're dumb enough to believe it, but I know better."

Riggs smirks, looking completely self-satisfied. "I'm going to make you eat those words, Sergeant. The only thing standing in your way of getting out of this hospital is me. If you want to go home, you better fucking cooperate and prove to me you're ready."

His attitude is only igniting my temper further, and at this point, I just want to challenge every word that comes out of his mouth. Then again, I'm dying to get the fuck out of this hospital, and I'll do just about anything he wants if it means getting him to sign off on my discharge.

"So what do I have to do to be a good little patient?" I sneer.

"You can start by losing the attitude. It's not doing you any favors. And you're wrong, you *are* going to get out of that chair. And you'll be able to do all the things I promised you."

Fuck this guy, with his two good legs and his you-can-do-it attitude. Who the fuck does he think he is, talking to me like that? "In case you haven't noticed, *Riggs*," I stress his name with all the attitude I can muster, "I only have one fucking leg."

"That's pretty fucking obvious," he says, standing up and gripping his clipboard again, arms crossed over his wide chest.

"Exactly, so I won't be swimming, running, hiking, skiing, or fucking—" He stops me there, smiling like an asshole.

"Why not? Did your dick get blown off in the blast, too?"

"What? No! I've still got my dick."

"That's good to know. Does it work?"

What the fuck was it with this guy? "The fuck do I know? I haven't exactly tried to use it yet, being stuck in the hospital night and day with nurse Liza barging in on me unexpectedly every fifteen minutes."

He laughs now, and I'd give anything to get out of this chair and take a swing at him.

"Well, there's your homework for tonight. Find out if your dick works."

"What the fuck do you want to know about my dick so bad for? Do you want it or something?" I know I'm pushing the bounds of decency, but really, why is he so fucking interested in my cock?

"Trust me, a working dick is a great motivator for recovery. Find out if it works."

I give him my signature *'what-the-fuck-ever'* expression that Brandt loves and shake my head, letting my eyes scan the room. Soldiers of every size and shape, color, and gender are grunting and sweating in pain as they push their broken bodies to the limits. I'm not the only one in here missing a leg, or worse. A small measure of shame fills me because they're working hard to regain use of their bodies and I'm sitting on my ass, complaining and crying like a little bitch. God himself can't get me to believe that I'll be cross-country skiing someday, but if I could just get up and walk to the bathroom to take a piss by myself, I'll count it as a win.

Navarro Riggs seems like a real asshole, but if he can help me get my ass out of this wheelchair, maybe I should listen to what he has to say.

Chapter 6 — Brandt

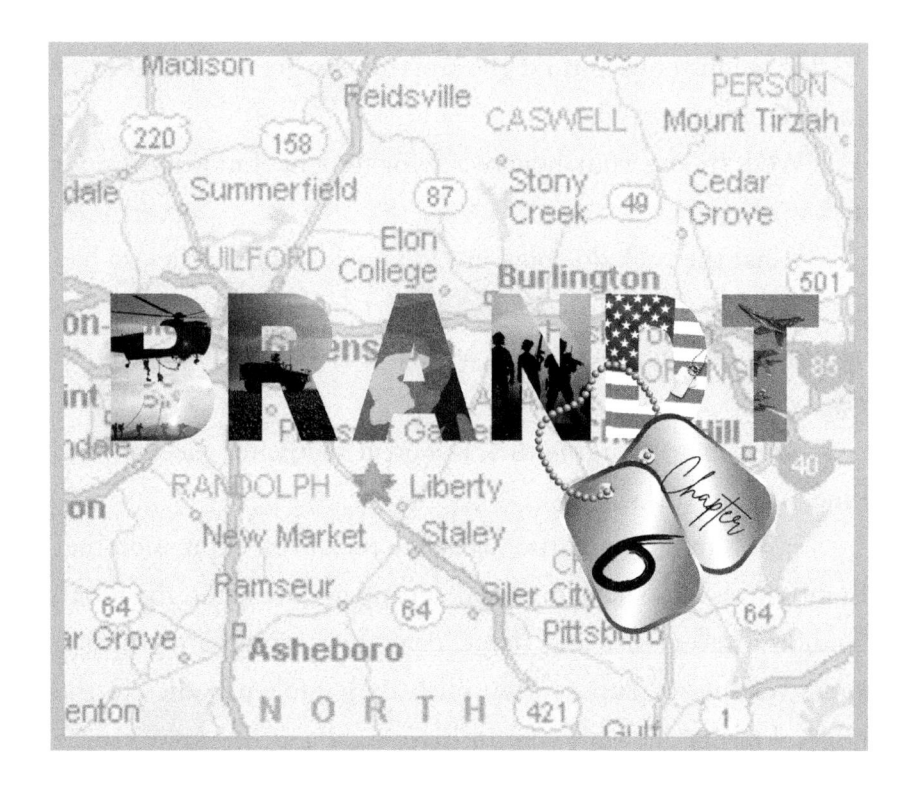

"WHAT'S A SIX-LETTER WORD FOR DIMWITTED?"

If I'm going to spend hours with my ass glued to a plastic chair, I'm going to need a new hobby. Playing word games on my phone is getting old fast.

"Brandt."

"What?" I look up from my phone to see him staring into a cup of *Jell-O* as he mutilates the chunks with a plastic fork.

West slides his gaze to me. "Six-letter word for dimwitted. Brandt."

"You're a fucking comedian." Dismissing him, I return to my phone, racking my brain for the answer.

"Christ," he curses, making a disgusted face. "I can smell myself."

It's hard not to laugh. "I can smell you from over here." Which is true, I can. He's really let himself go lately. His beard is growing in, his hair is greasy and unwashed, and I'm not sure when the last time he brushed his teeth was. Liza tries to bathe him in the bed, but West usually refuses. I don't know if it's because he's depressed and content to waste away, or if he's too self-conscious to show her his body now that it's so altered. Probably both.

I pocket my phone and just study him for a moment. He's staring out the window, which he does for hours on end every day. I'd give anything to know what he's thinking, but I'm pretty sure it's all very dark.

West was like a live grenade. You couldn't put the pin back in once you pulled it out. He was drawn in bold lines and bright colors. He had a loud, filthy mouth and no filter, and was usually willing to take stupid risks, as long as no one else's life was in jeopardy but his own.

That was the old West, the guy I used to know. The SFC. The Team Leader. My best friend.

He was larger than life.

The guy lying in his bed right now is someone else, someone I don't recognize any longer. A washed-out, pale version of himself.

I'd give anything to have him back.

"It's bad enough being the one-legged cripple in the wheelchair. I don't want to be the smelly, greasy one-legged cripple in the wheelchair." He pushes his tray table away, and looks directly into my eyes. "Will you help me?"

I hate to hear him talk about himself like that. It turns my fucking stomach, but I can't chastise him every time he does it or I would sound like his mother.

"Sure, help you with what?" I stand, ready to do any favor he asks of me.

"Help me take a shower."

I'm a little startled, because until now, he hasn't shown the slightest interest in hygiene. "Yeah. Let me call Liza–"

"Fuck Liza. I want *you* to help me."

I guess I shouldn't be that surprised. Of course, he'd rather have my help than hers. He trusts me, is less self-conscious with his body around me.

"Okay, but is it safe to take a shower? Isn't it like, a fall risk or something?" I'm already lowering the bed rails, knowing damn well the risks.

"Not if you don't let me fall." There's a hint of a smile teasing his lips, and it's a quick glimpse of the old West I miss so much.

"Easier said than done, smart ass. You're gonna have to help me." I grab the handle of his chair and wheel it over to the bed, lining it up like Liza showed me.

"I'll do the best I can. But I have faith in you, Reaper. You would never let me fall." I'm touched by his words. Of course, I would never let him fall. Not in battle, not in the shower, either. "'Cause if I hurt myself, it means we've got to stay in this shithole even longer."

Despite turning it into a joke, I feel like he's half-serious. He knows I would never fail him if I could help it.

"What about your bandage? Should we get it wet?" Liza is going to kick my fucking ass for doing this undercover.

"Just take it off. The stitches are closing nicely. It won't hurt to get it wet. She can put a new bandage on when we finish."

Together, we scoot him into his chair, and I wheel him toward the bathroom. It's a lot easier than it used to be just days ago, before they removed his IV drips and heart monitor.

Reaching into the shower, I turn on the water and adjust it to scalding hot like he prefers. The tiny bathroom fills with thick steam. I grab towels, washcloths, and a bar of soap and stock it in the shower stall.

"Grab onto the bar and I'll help you stand."

He reaches for the metal safety bar screwed into the wall, and I hoist under his arms to help him balance on his leg, making sure he's steady before I scoot the chair away. Then I untie his gown and slip it from his shoulders.

"Put your arm around my shoulders and lean on me, and we'll walk into the shower together."

"You're gonna leave your clothes on?" He sounds surprised.

"I don't need to shower. Do you really want to get in that tiny stall with me naked?"

"This is fucking stupid," he gripes, looking for his chair.

I'm making him feel self-conscious by remaining dressed. The spotlight is all on him, and it's too much for him to bear. I get it. I might feel the same way if it were me.

"Okay, Okay. Just give me a second to get undressed while you hold on to the bar. Don't let go," I warn in a dire voice as I strip quickly. For a moment, I debate whether I should leave my briefs on or not, but it will just feel more awkward for both of us if I leave them on.

"All right, come on, put your arm around me. Step slowly."

We shuffle into the tiny tiled stall, and I guide him to the safety rail. "Your job is to hold on to this and don't let go. I'll do the washing."

Soaping up the cloth, I begin with his back because it's the easiest place to start. He still has cuts and bruises that are in various stages of healing, and I rub over them gently. We're quiet, nothing but the sound of the water, and the tension is growing thicker than the cloud of steam.

I laugh nervously. "Why is this suddenly awkward as fuck? It's not the first time we've showered together."

"Yeah, but it's the first time you're washing me." He leans his head down under the spray, shifting his spine and the muscles in his back in stark relief. No matter what he's been through, he's still beautiful. He'll always be beautiful.

"I think it's awkward because you feel vulnerable."

"I fucking hate this," he whispers harshly.

"I know, I hate it too," and I do hate it. I hate that he has no confidence anymore. I hate that he hates himself. Sliding the washcloth over his shoulders, I leave a trail of suds in my wake as I wash down his arms. "You have such nice skin."

West laughs and shrugs me off. "Fuck off, Hannibal Lecter. What, are you gonna make a skin suit out of me?"

I can't help but laugh with him. "No, that was stupid. I just–"

West leans back against my body, fusing his wet skin with

mine. With my right hand on his hip to steady him, I trail my left hand holding the rag down his rib cage.

"Reaper?"

My lips hover over his ear. "What?" The word is just a caress, and he shivers in my arms.

"Just...Don't ever feel sorry for me. If I thought you pitied me, I would kill myself in a hot second."

It's hard to swallow, almost impossible, as everything inside of me tightens painfully. "Don't say shit like that."

"I mean it."

"I don't feel sorry for you. I'm just–" my voice sounds broken, like it's been dragged across gravel, and hot tears burn my eyes. "–heartbroken. Watching you in so much pain breaks my fucking heart. Seeing you struggle..." I try twice more to swallow before I can speak again. "It breaks my heart, but it's not pity. You're the strongest motherfucker I know." Fuck, my voice is cracking like a pubescent teen. "Weston Wardell is larger than life. You have a face and body that puts mine to shame, *and* you outrank me. I don't fucking pity you."

"Good. 'Cause I couldn't take it if you did."

I move the cloth across his chest, holding him to me in a bear hug, and then wash down his stomach, stopping just above his pubes. He grabs the rag from me, chuckling.

"It's okay. I can do that part myself."

With only one hand on the rail, he soaps up his junk while I hold him steady, and then he's handing back the rag to me so I can finish. Slowly, I wash the perfect white globes of his ass, scraping his skin with my fingernail.

West flinches. "What the fuck are you doing?"

Laughing, I explain, "Stay still. You have a clump of surgical glue stuck to your ass cheek. It's probably been there for weeks, but it's coming off today." He relaxes again as I scratch the glue off, and I take advantage of the moment to lighten the mood. "Obviously you don't wash your ass."

"Fuck you. My ass is clean enough to lick."

Shut up, Brandt. Shut. The fuck. Up. Do not take the bait.

I'm so paranoid that he can read my mind that it takes me a moment to realize what he's doing.

"*Ungh*," he moans, the sound echoing off the tiled walls.

A peek over his shoulder reveals he's only got one hand on the rail, and it doesn't take a genius to figure out what he's doing with the other one.

"Seriously? You think this seems like a good time for that?" *While my bare cock is just inches from your ass crack? While I'm struggling to suppress thoughts of licking your ass? Fuck me.*

"It's homework..." he pants, increasing the pace of his strokes. "Riggs wants...*mmmhhn*...to know if it...still works."

Wtf?! "Why? Why is that something he needs or wants to know?"

"He has...a theory...that it's motivating for my...*ungh*...recovery. Fuck, that feels good. It's definitely still in working order." The slapping of his balls against his thighs resonates deafeningly in the silence as I'm processing his words, and then he adds, "Who knows, maybe he's just deeply closeted, and he gets off on this shit."

"I doubt it." At least he can't see me peeking over his shoulder, my eyes traveling down the length of his body to where his fist beats against his groin. I'm going to hell for watching, but I was probably already headed there anyway, so fuck it. "You about done?" I wouldn't care if he wasn't. I'm enjoying the show, but the longer he stretches this out, the more awkward it's becoming.

"Jesus, Reaper, cut me a break. The last time I came was… fuck, it was in the shower with you," he laughs.

My stomach flips remembering that day, and I realize it's the first time I've heard his laughter since the accident. Maybe Riggs is right, maybe this is what he needs to get motivated about his recovery. I'm all for anything that helps him find his smile again, his sense of purpose.

"Have at it. Beat it till it falls off."

His chuckle morphs into a pleasured-filled groan, and I peek over his shoulder again to watch as he shoots ropes of thick, white cum down the drain. My cock twitches, and I have to will it to stay soft.

Enough of this torture. Reaching around him, I shut the water off and grab him a towel. Droplets of water fall from his dark hair to drip down his back and I start there, toweling his skin dry. I work my way down his butt, and then his good leg, before turning him slightly to step in front of him. After his arms and chest are dry, I keep going down his stomach, following the trail of dark hair that leads to—

"Go ahead, you're the last person who's ever gonna touch it."

"Don't be ridiculous," I return as I pat him dry.

"You're ridiculous! Who the hell is going to want me now?"

"Who wouldn't?!" I get that he's feeling down on himself, but why can't he see what I see?

"Pull up some girl's number from your phone. We'll send her a picture of our bodies. Guess which one she's going to respond to?"

"Whatever, don't be a jackass. In fact, those girls don't know how good they have it. You're doing them a favor." While I continue gently drying his partial leg, I look down at his foot and laugh. "The only thing missing is your damn foot. I swear, I love you like a brother, but you have the nastiest fucking feet." I straighten up to my full height and wrap the damp towel around his hips. "Always with the foot powder and the blisters. Hell, you're better off now," I tease.

It works like a charm. West smirks, but there's also sadness in his smile. "I'm serious, Reaper. No one is ever going to want me like this."

My heart breaks for him all over again. What if he's right? And what does that mean for me? I could never be happy with someone if he's lonely and miserable. If he's not dating, neither am I.

"Someday you're gonna meet–"

"Don't! Don't fucking say it. Someday I'm just going to meet a nice girl who loves me for who I am and not how I look? Is that what you were gonna say?" I'm speechless, because that's exactly what I was going to say, and he sighs deeply. "You don't get it. I don't want someone to *settle* for me. I want to be *enough*."

I'm sick of it. Fucking fed up with his *I'm-not-good-enough* spiel. I slip my finger under the gold chain that hangs around his neck and pull him close. "Don't you get it? You're *not* enough. You were *never* just enough, Wes. You've always been *more* than anyone deserves. And if they can't see that, in spite of your missing leg, they're fucking trash."

Apparently, when my heart is broken beyond measure, or when I'm incredibly turned on, I drop the t from his name. I wonder if he even noticed.

"Wes?" he smirks. "Is this something new you're trying out?"

Of course, he's going to focus on that instead of what I said. Ignoring him, I insist, "Someday you're going to meet some miserable soul who doesn't deserve you, and because you never make good decisions, you're going to fall head over boot for them."

"And you're gonna be right there to pull me back," he assures me, pointing his finger into the center of my chest.

Chapter 7 — WEST

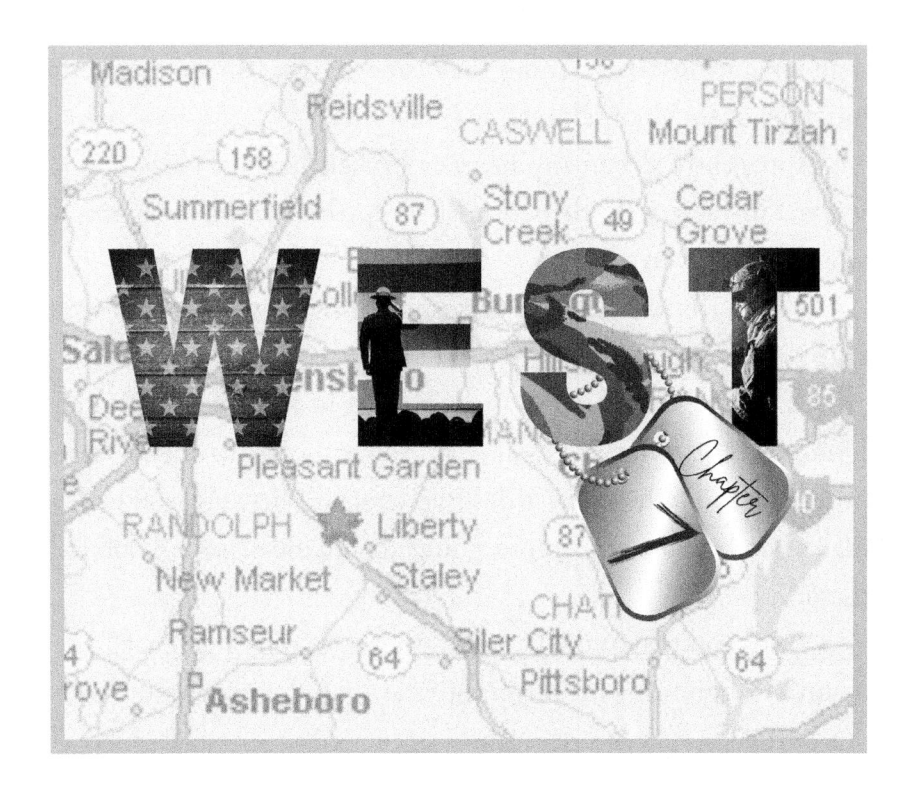

"WHAT IN THE fresh hell is going on in here?" Liza shrieks, pushing her way into the room. Of course, she has to walk in right when we're hobbling from the bathroom with a cloud of steam billowing out behind us.

"What's it look like? We're getting cleaned up."

"Do you realize you're at high risk for falls?" She must mean business with her hands on her hips.

"Can't fall," I grunt, as Brandt deposits me on my bed. "I've got three legs. Can't fall with three legs." I'm referring to both of Brandt's legs plus my one, but from the way she's glaring, she doesn't find it funny.

"The least you could have done was shave your face while

you were in there," she huffs. "Lay down so I can wrap your leg."

"You mean my stump?"

As she's gathering her supplies, I can see her eyes roll. Liza doesn't appreciate my dark sense of humor. She spreads everything out on the rolling table beside my bed.

"You look almost human again. I guess you're not too bad when you clean up." It's a backhanded compliment, but it's the best I'm going to get from her.

"You hear that, Brandt? She's starting to come around. She might even like me by the time I'm discharged."

Brandt notes the look on her face and laughs. "That might be stretching it." He's dressed in a clean pair of BDUs and he catches me looking. "Tomorrow, before you head to therapy, I'll bring you a fresh pair to change into. We can't have you rolling down the hall with your ass hanging out."

After smearing some sort of ointment over my stitches, Liza tears open a new roll of gauze and begins to wrap my limb. I sit up a little straighter and check out what she's doing down there.

"Do you want to watch? It wouldn't kill you to learn how to do this yourself. I have a feeling you won't be here much longer, and you'll need to know this when you get home."

The pleasure I feel at breaking free of this sterile prison is overshadowed by a rush of anxiety. Going home alone is filled with so many unknown factors that it's overwhelming to even consider.

"I've never looked at it," I confess. But I'm mildly curious.

"You haven't seen your leg yet?" She sounds shocked, her

eyes growing wider when I shake my head. "I'll get you a handheld mirror so you can see it better." Liza disappears into the hall and comes back minutes later, carrying a plastic purple mirror. Then she removes the gauze she already applied, uncovering the stitched and puckered skin on the tip of my thigh. My limb now ends just above the knee. Or where my knee used to be.

Brandt slides his hand over mine and squeezes, and I pull away, feeling childish. I don't need him to hold my fucking hand to help me accept the reality of my lost leg.

Liza tilts the mirror left and right until she finds the perfect angle. It doesn't hurt to look. In fact, I feel almost numb, strangely detached, as if I'm looking at someone else's leg. But the longer I stare, the heavier the pressure feels in my chest, and I can feel my heart begin to squeeze. It's not the sight of the stitches or the scarring. It's the implications that come with it—the memories, the what-now. My future looks a lot different from my past. I have to relearn the most basic things that I learned as a toddler. And it galls me to admit that I'm afraid.

Quietly, I lace my fingers with Brandt's, noting his small smile from the corner of my sight. I'm a fool to think I don't need him.

It's been a grueling week of rehab, and there's not one muscle in my body that isn't screaming out for mercy. I thought I was fit, more or less, but now I'm rethinking my definition of fit. Riggs has me doing impossible shit, like push-ups on the armrests of my wheelchair, while I'm sitting in it. Strapping thirty pounds of weight to my ankle and making me do leg lifts. And today is my favorite, the parallel bars. Or as I call them, the bitch bars, 'cause I sure feel like one now that I'm failing spectacularly at it.

How hard is it to brace my weight on the rails and hop ten feet in a straight line? Apparently, harder than I imagined. And with my heart rate up, blood is rushing through my veins, and I can feel it throbbing in my stump like a pulse.

I want to sit back down.

I want easy.

I don't want to be reminded that I'm crippled.

That I'm half the man I used to be.

I'm tired, and my arms are beginning to feel like limp noodles.

Weak—like me.

Riggs stands off to the side with his fucking clipboard, and his fucking stopwatch, and stares as I struggle. My breathing comes faster and shorter, and I'm sweating profusely. My attention is on him, hoping for an intervention instead of focusing on my path, and my leg gives out at the knee. I stumble and fall face first on the padded mat.

"Fuck!" I raise my head to see him still staring, looking almost amused. "You just gonna stand there and laugh, or are you gonna help me up?"

He looks like he has all the time in the world. "You'll get up when you're ready."

"Fuck you, this isn't a game." I'm snarling the words and spittle flies from my mouth and pools on the mat in front of my face. I'm so angry, I could shred the padding with my bare hands. "Help me up." Riggs widens his stance and braces his thick arms across his chest as he watches in silence. "Fucking help me!" I hate myself for even having to ask, let alone beg.

His face hardens in the blink of an eye. He's not playing anymore, but neither am I. "Get up," he snaps.

"I can't." I'm too winded to even yell at this point. The words sound as defeated as I feel.

"Get. Up." He enunciates each word clearly, and each one sounds like a command I can't disobey.

"I can't!" Twisting my head, I check to see if we've drawn an audience, but thankfully, they're ignoring us. I'm sure it's nothing they haven't seen before.

"You can and you will." Riggs shakes his head in disgust and scoffs. "And you call yourself a Sergeant First Class. Look how easy you give up. You must've made one damn fine leader."

My face heats with shame and anger. "Fuck you. When I get up, I'm gonna kick your fucking ass."

"Sounds like a plan. But you have to get your ass off the floor first." He's not glaring at me, but he's not grinning either. Riggs just stands there, calmly waiting for me to get my shit together. It's fucking infuriating. "Get up. I'm not gonna tell you again."

"How?" I shout in frustration. I have no more gas in the tank. My will and my energy are completely depleted.

"Roll onto your knee." Following his orders, I grunt and huff as I roll my body. "Good, now brace your arms and push yourself up with your good leg." When I'm on all fours, or threes, he says, "Reach for the bar. Pull yourself up." I just might stroke out before I'm on my feet again. "Just like that, soldier. Was that so hard?"

I'm struggling to catch my breath, and I swipe sweat from

my brow and wipe it on my T-shirt. "I'm still gonna kick your ass."

"Now that, I'd like to see," he says, looking at my missing leg. "When you finish the parallel bars, you can have a seat."

I absolutely refuse to go through that again. I'll finish these fucking bitch bars if it kills me, and it just might. It's a struggle, but I eventually make it to the end. Riggs is waiting with my wheelchair ready, and I plop into it with all the grace of an elephant.

"You've got to stop relying on your good leg to do all the work. It will grow stronger, but eventually, it will give out on you. You can do real damage to your knee. If you lose both legs, you'll be shit out of luck." He has a point, but I don't see the solution. "You're going to start training with your new prosthetic, learning to put your weight on it, and trusting it to hold you." Riggs catches my unsure look and smiles. "It's made of titanium. It's a lot stronger than your damn leg."

Then he looks to the waiting area, where Brandt is loitering in the doorway, looking murderous, but also scared shitless.

"Who's your sergeant at arms?"

The nickname makes me smirk. "My best buddy, Staff Sergeant Aguilar."

"He looks…intense, and wholly focused on your recovery."

In a nutshell. "Yeah, that's understating it."

"Good. That's good. You need someone like that in your corner. Will he help you at home?"

"Yeah, he's going to move in with me. I don't know where I would be without him. He's become my right hand."

"Your right leg, you mean."

"Yeah." How perfectly apt.

"Was he in the blast with you?"

"He was there. Right beside me." A flash of heat moves through my body, remembering the blast. "I think he saved my life."

Riggs eyes Brandt once more before returning his gaze to me, and he swallows, like he's remembering something significant. "I don't doubt it. That's what brothers do."

―――

The grueling hours of strenuous work I put in at rehab paid off, and with Riggs's recommendation, the doctor signed off on my discharge papers, and I was sent home. I was still expected to report to rehab four days a week, and in addition to that, I had to start occupational therapy, as well as see an actual therapist, to shrink my head.

"That doesn't mean you're only working out four days a week," Riggs insisted. "You have a full range of exercises I expect you to do at home every day, several times a day. And I'll know if you don't. I'll be able to see your piss-poor performance in my gym."

I had a feeling he *would* know, and he'd work me twice as hard.

When we left for the desert, Brandt had a shitty one bedroom apartment on base, and he gave it up gladly, hoping he would return with a promotion and a raise and be able to get something nicer. Now that we're being med-boarded, or discharged painstakingly slowly, he's moving in with me until we're finished with Fort Bragg. It makes sense really, considering my injuries. I need his help around the clock, not to mention I also have a nice-enough two bedroom townhome.

And now that I'm back after being gone for nearly a year, I can't say it feels like home anymore. Like I lived here in a different life. To be fair, the man that used to live here was a different man than the one that came back home.

A silver-framed picture of me and Brandt sits on the entry table in the hallway, taken years ago when we were first transferred to this base. It's the only thing I feel any attachment to in this house. The knickknacks and pictures that used to define me or bring me comfort just feel insignificant now. None of it holds any sentimental value or connection to who I've become.

Maybe it's because I don't know who I am anymore. I'm a stranger in my own skin.

"Let's get you upstairs, so you can settle in and rest," Brandt suggests, coming up behind me. He kicks the front door shut with his boot and drops his ruck.

Staring up at the flight of stairs seems daunting, nearly impossible. It used to be something I took for granted. Now, it would be my greatest challenge.

"Where's all your stuff? You can't just have one bag."

"Don't you remember?"

The TBI makes it difficult to remember a lot of things. So much knowledge, so many memories, lost and forgotten.

"I stored a few boxes in your garage before we were deployed. I'll grab them later. There's not much in there, just some pictures and medals, civvies, and a bunch of junk." With his hands on the handles of my chair, Brandt sighs deeply. "How should we do this?"

"Fuck it, just leave me here. I'll live on the couch."

"Cut your shit. I came by earlier and put fresh sheets on your bed. Now we've just got to figure out how to get you up there in it. We can try using your crutches, and just sort of hop up each step. Or you can climb on my back."

I give him *the look*, the *are-you-fucking-kidding-me* West Wardell special. "Just fucking shoot me and be done with it."

Brandt smacks me on the back and laughs, and then he crouches in front of me, presenting me with his back. "Come on, hop up."

My stomach turns. *I hate you. I hate myself, hate what I've become. Nothing more than a parasite. A fucking leech.*

If there's an ounce of pride left inside me, it dies a quick death as I wrap my arms around his neck and let him haul me up from my chair. Our ascent up the stairs is slow going, and Brandt struggles under my weight, grunting as his breathing becomes heavier. He pauses at the top of the stairs to catch his breath with his hands on his knees before shuffling into my bedroom, where he dumps me unceremoniously on the mattress. Huffing and puffing and laughing, he collapses next to me in a breathless heap.

"Welcome home, Professor."

I remain quiet until he nudges me. "I don't even know where home is anymore."

He looks at me like I've lost my mind. "Do you feel this?" His big solid body bounces on the mattress. "A real bed. Not a cot, or a sleeping bag, or even that paper-thin wafer the hospital calls a mattress. A real fucking bed. How long have we dreamed of a good night's sleep on a soft mattress?"

With a shrug of my shoulders, I brush off his excitement. "Doesn't feel like home."

"Are you fucking kidding me?"

"I've lived in so many countries—so many places I've laid my head—and said 'I'm home', but I never really felt it."

He folds his arms under his head. "You know what? Home isn't a place, it's a feeling. Doesn't matter if I'm standing on American soil, or my boots are covered in a sandbox in the middle of hell halfway across the world. As long as you're by my side, I'm home." His words bring up all these feelings that I'm trying to keep buried so I can make it through the day without falling apart, and I can feel tears burn the backs of my eyes, but I refuse to let them fall. Brandt rolls into my side and grins at me. "You are my compass. A strong and steady presence at my back holding a rifle." The hand that squeezed mine for weeks in the hospital finds mine and squeezes again. "You're my home. Always. No matter where we are, I'm home with you."

This time, I squeeze back and the tears fall unbidden. "Same."

Chapter 8 — BRANT

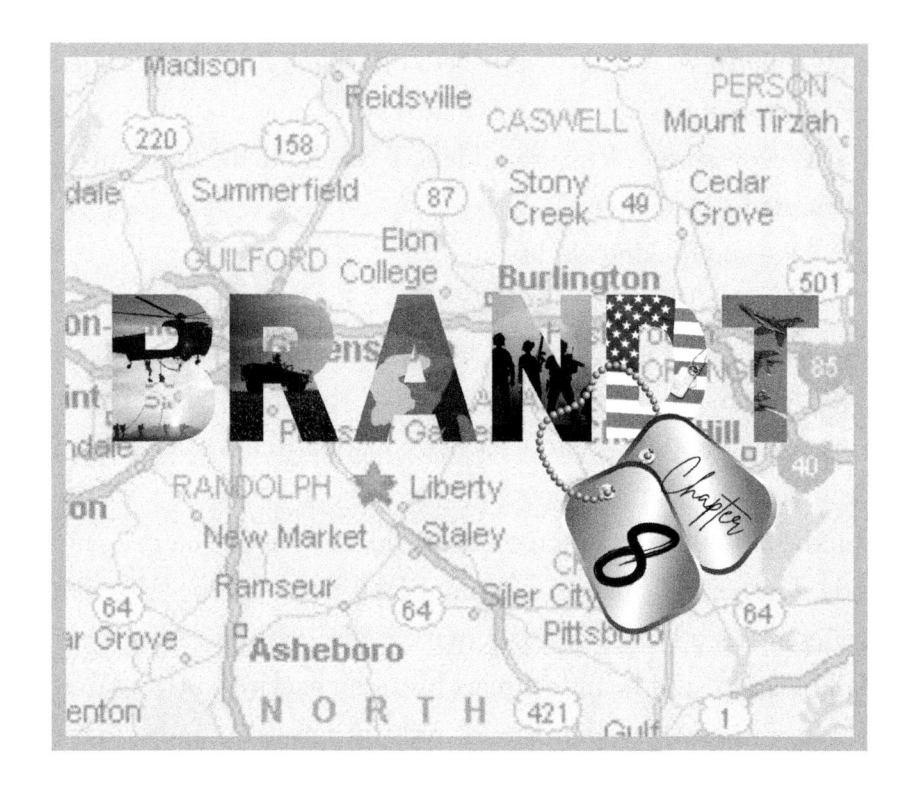

COMING HOME ISN'T much of a homecoming.

I was never under the impression that being home would be a magic cure for either of us, and even knowing that, the melancholy and depression hits harder than I was prepared for.

I'm lost in the day-to-day routines, distracted by laundry, dishes, and doctor appointments. The silent minutes of my day are filled with echoes of their voices, the sound of their laughter, past conversations we had. Their faces haunt me. I'm drowning in the past, and I'm losing myself. Or maybe I just don't want to find out who I am now.

I'm buried under the weight of their memory, and I can't forget.

It's draining me dry. I have nothing left to give, nothing left to feel. I'm just numb. Numb, and so fucking done. But I don't have the luxury of giving up, like West. He needs me; he needs my strength, he needs my legs, and as much as I would love to give up, to crawl into bed and never wake up, I have to be strong —for him.

I won't let him fall, and I won't let him fail. I'm going to make sure he heals and lives the best life he can, even if it kills me.

I'm running myself ragged, burning both ends of the candle, just trying to stay afloat. Every morning I have to wake up and report to my CO. Then I hit the track and run five miles before rushing back home to start the laundry and make breakfast. I'm trying to keep West on a routine, so I wake him up, help him get washed up, dole out his meds, and deflect his rotten attitude. I'm already exhausted by this point, but there's no rest for the weary. The rest of our day is filled with PT, doctors' appointments, and enough paperwork to give me carpal tunnel.

But in the evenings, when the sun sets and the chaotic day grows dark, the minutes slow down to a crawl. West chooses to be solitary, and he remains in bed, usually passed out on painkillers... or maybe he's just pretending to be asleep to avoid me. Television only holds my attention for so long, and I feel like I'm climbing the walls looking for something to keep busy. I just want someone to talk to, some place to be, anything—any distraction from my head.

Fresh from the shower, I step into clean sweatpants and head across the hall. Ducking my head into West's room, I make sure he's settled before I head downstairs. His bed is empty.

Where in the fuck is he?

His chair, which is always parked next to his bed, is also gone. "West? Yo, West!"

He doesn't answer, and I duck into his bathroom only to find it empty. Standing there, I wonder what the fuck is going on, wonder how a guy who can barely sit up on his own can disappear without a trace. A flash of light catches my eye and I whip my head around to the sliding glass door that leads to his balcony. The sun reflects off the metal of his chair—that's what caught my eye. With a smile, I shake my head, amused that he got one over on me. I'm just thrilled he had the motivation to get his ass out of bed. He hasn't sat outside in the sun since… Well, not since before his accident. And as I stand here and watch, he grabs the railing and pulls himself up out of his chair, and I'm almost too late before I realize what he's doing.

Motherfucker!

In a panic, I take off at a dead run, vaulting over his bed, and I throw the door open. "West! Stop!"

Half his body is already dangling over the ledge, and if he had two good legs, he'd be on the ground already, a floor below. Then again, if he had two good legs, he might not be on this balcony in the first place. Desperately, I grab onto his leg, pulling him back with all my strength. I'm yelling and sobbing, a complete fucking wreck, but West doesn't say a word. We land in a heap on the balcony floor.

"What are you doing?" He still doesn't answer. My tears are falling so hard and fast they're blinding me, and I'm choking on snot and the lump in my throat. "Why? Why would you do that?" But I don't need him to answer. I already know why.

At this height, he wouldn't even have killed himself, most

likely, unless he hit his head. His fall would only have caused further injury to his body. My arms are around his waist and I squeeze him tighter, in anger and relief, and because I just need to reassure myself with the solid weight of his body that he's still here. Still alive.

As much as he doesn't want to be. And I can't will him to live. How many more times am I going to have to save him? He clearly doesn't want to be saved. But I'm not giving him a choice.

"Try that again, and I'll kill you myself."

"I wish you would," he says, and I have to physically restrain myself from clawing his face with my bare hands. That's how angry I am. I want to hurt him like he's hurting me. I want to shake him hard enough to knock sense into him. I want to make him want to live, and I don't know how.

Even though I'm with him practically every minute of every day, I've never felt more alone.

While West meets with his occupational therapist, I have an appointment with my doctor. After waiting forty-five minutes past my scheduled time, a nurse finally comes in.

"I'm sorry Staff Sergeant, the doctor is running behind and won't be seeing you today. I'm just going to check your wounds myself."

Welcome to TRICARE. Army medicine, Army strong.

"Looks like your infection cleared up. And I see a note here in your chart about your hearing loss. Did you want me to order you a hearing aid?"

I realize how petty it is for me to balk at using a hearing aid, but it stings my pride. And I want to kick myself for being angry with West. What I feel isn't even a fifth of what he feels.

"Nah, but thanks anyway. I've still got one good ear."

"Well, let me know if you change your mind. I'm going to have the doctor schedule you for a follow-up X-ray on your ribs. But other than that, you're good to go."

I'm pulling my shirt back on just as West wheels himself into the room. "What'd the doc say?"

I chuff a harsh breath. "What doc? The one who's too busy to see me?"

"For real?"

"Nurse says my infection cleared up, and I need a hearing aid."

"What's that? I didn't hear you?"

"I said, the nurse said my–" I catch his smile growing wider by the second and realize he's fucking with me. "You're an ass. You need me to repeat that louder?" God, his smile is beautiful. Feels like forever since I've seen it.

"I'm gonna start calling you old man Aguilar."

"The hell you are. I don't need a damn hearing aid. I've still got one good ear."

"Hey, what do you know? I've still got one good leg!" I can't help but laugh at his sarcasm.

"Are you ready for PT?"

"About that. I ran into Riggs in the hall. He said to meet him at the pool today."

"At Tolson?"

"Yeah, they've got that full ramp that leads into the pool. He said I can wheel my chair right in."

"Well, hell, I'll grab my speedo and we'll head over there," I tease.

Instead of calling me an idiot, or brushing me off, West plays along. "You might have to show me that. I'm imagining it's red, no, purple. Is it purple?"

"Yeah West, it's purple," I deadpan. His grin is bigger than mine, and it warms my gut. "You want me to get you one?"

"Fuck, yeah." He cups his junk and his face lights up. "My shit would look great in a speedo."

It would. And then I immediately kick myself mentally for thinking that.

I haven't thought about him like that in weeks, with all his negativity and pain. But when he smiles like this, when he laughs, it's easy to see how attractive he is.

His black sweatpants are a far cry from a purple speedo. West still isn't comfortable showing his leg, and he keeps it covered 24/7. I throw on a pair of navy blue basketball shorts from my ruck and wheel his chair down the long ramp that leads into the shallow end of the pool. Riggs is already in the water. He's holding a blue noodle float, and he's got a bucket of workout equipment sitting on the side of the pool.

"Park his chair on that ramp and float him over here, Aguilar."

It took some convincing for him to drop our ranks and just use our names. Just like with the stairs, West holds onto my neck, and I carry him on my back. West floats the noodle under his arms, reclining with his leg out in front of him, and I spot him from behind.

"Now, I want you to do some leg lifts and bicycle kicks. The reclining position will help strengthen your core at the same time."

I watch helplessly as West struggles through his workout, and I grow more anxious by the second. Sometimes it feels as if I'm walking on eggshells, constantly overcompensating to placate him and avoid setting off his temper. When he struggles and fails at new challenges, he becomes frustrated easily. That frustration feeds his self-hatred, and I worry about another suicide attempt.

I'll never forget that day in the hospital in Germany. I went down to the cafeteria to grab lunch, and when I came back up to his floor, I knew right away something was wrong. The nurses were tense, giving me sideways glances, anticipating my reaction. When I walked into his room, three nurses were working frantically to pump his stomach. He'd OD'd on his morphine drip and had fallen unresponsive during the nurses' rounds.

Terror and fear like I've only known one other time in my life, weeks before in the blast, gripped my heart so tightly I couldn't breathe. Not until he did. And when he opened his eyes, he looked at me and said, "You're still here?" The disappointment in his voice made me want to choke him out. There I was trying not to fall apart because the only thing in my life that mattered was trying to leave me, and he was disappointed he was still stuck with me.

I felt so alone, like I'd been orphaned, although my parents still lived. I was losing him, slowly, or maybe he was already gone. His soul had died despite the fact he was still alive. West was slipping away from me, and without him, I had nothing left.

The other day on the balcony, I felt that same paralyzing fear. The only thing scarier was the realization it probably wouldn't be the last time I'd have to save him.

"Aguilar, hold his hips. Wardell, I want you to do the same leg exercises, but now use the natural resistance of the water to build your muscles."

West has lost weight since the accident. Spending the last few weeks laid up in bed with no appetite will do that to you. My hands easily span his hips, and I can feel the sharp edges of his hip bones beneath my fingers. It feels so good to touch him again, if for no other reason than to just feel his warm, solid body beneath my hands and reassure myself he's still alive and well.

Drops of water trickle down his inked skin as he splashes, and his already dark hair becomes jet-black when wet.

"Good. Let's try something more advanced. I want you to swim to me. Use your upper body and kick with your leg."

He splashes water in my face as he kicks off, grunting as he heads toward Riggs. I breathe a sigh of relief when he makes it with a triumphant smile. On the return trip back to me, I hold my breath in anticipation until he reaches the safety of my arms.

"That's good, Wardell. The more time you spend in the pool practicing, the stronger you'll become. We tend to use muscles in the water that we don't normally use outside the pool."

West looks up at me with his spiky wet lashes, his breath still coming hard and fast, and asks, "Will you help me?"

Until my dying breath. "Of course, I'll help you."

"All right gentlemen, I've got another patient to meet back in the gym. Feel free to use the pool a little longer until you're ready to get out. Keep practicing, Wardell. You're doing great."

I have him all to myself. A feeling of peace and serenity cradles me. The lights aren't as bright here, and the sound of the water gently lapping at the sides of the pool is a calm, soothing lullaby. Apparently, West thinks so too.

"Can we be done exercising and just relax?"

"Sounds perfect."

We tuck pool noodles under our arms and just float on our bellies. I can feel the tight muscles in my body begin to relax for the first time in… Fuck, I've lost count.

"We should go for massages," I blurt, impressed with my own bright idea.

West barely grunts in response. He probably doesn't want anyone to touch him. I see him get tense when the nurse examines him. Even if one of the staff casually touches his shoulder when they're talking to him, he gets all stiff and scowly.

"I could massage you," I offer.

"Yeah? Maybe."

Well, that wasn't a no. He could really use it though. I'll bet he's so tense he's ready to snap. Reacting without thinking, I drift over to him and ditch my pool noodle, taking his hips in my hands again.

"What are you doing?"

"Just relax and lean back against me." My voice sounds as mellow as the water. West doesn't resist, just sort of melts against my chest with a sigh. My hands move over his hips, down his thighs, and back up again to his waist. I slide them up under his lower back, kneading his flesh with light but firm strokes, and I feel the last of his resistance bleed away.

"I didn't know you have magic hands."

"Just ask around, the girls will tell you."

He chuckles. "Speaking of, I think my occupational therapist has a thing for you. She spends most of our session asking questions about you."

"How frustrating for you," I tease.

"She said I get my leg tomorrow. My prosthetic. I have to come in an hour earlier than my normal time to get squared away with it. She's going to show me how to put it on and take it off, and how to care for it and my skin."

"West, that's fucking awesome. It's gonna be great, you'll see."

He *would* see. I would make him see.

"Yeah, maybe. You want me to give her your number?"

"Fuck no." Here I am excited about his leg, about his future, and he's worried about me? *Christ*.

"Why not? She's kind of cute."

"So are you. Since we're already living together, and we shower together, I'll just stick with you."

"You're a funny guy, you know that? A real fucking comedian."

To fuck with him, I slide my hands down his back to cup the perfect cheeks of his ass, giving them a gentle squeeze. I'm prepared for him to headbutt me, or say something cutting, but instead, he just sighs with pleasure.

"Oh my God that feels so good. Been a long time since I've had a butt massage."

"When did you have a butt massage?"

"You've never been to one of those places? They're all over Fayetteville."

"What places? Massage parlors?"

"Fuck yeah. I mean, I didn't get a happy ending, but she massaged my ass real good. It was life-changing."

"Where in the fuck was I?"

"Beats me. Probably on rotation."

"Thanks a lot, buddy. Thanks for thinking of me."

He laughs at my sullenness. "All I'm saying is, anytime you want to massage my butt, I'm not gonna say no. I'm not gonna let toxic masculinity ruin a life-changing experience." He tilts his head back and looks up at me. "And neither should you."

He wants to touch my ass? Fucking have at it.

"I can arrange that. I think it would do us both a world of good to relax some. The stress is going to kill us." I wanted to bite my tongue as soon as I said it. How could I be so fucking callous?

West turns his head to drag his scruffy cheek across my chest. "Don't threaten me with a good time, Reaper."

The following week is a nonstop reel of agonizing failures where West struggles with his new prosthesis. Every time he falls, every time his big body hits the floor, my gut churns with anxiety. I pop antacids like they're candy, but nothing helps.

West is miserable and angry, and obviously in a lot of pain.

And there isn't a fucking thing I can do to help.

"Stop leaning on your leg and trust the prosthetic," Riggs insists for the hundredth time.

And for the hundredth and one time, he falls.

My self-control snaps like a dry twig. I can't take another second of watching him fail. He's frustrated with himself and his therapist, and with every failed attempt to walk, he's losing more of his confidence. At this rate, he's never going to have the hope he needs to succeed.

"I can't! I'm weak. Just let me lie here."

I step forward from the background, no longer an invisible bystander, and I crouch down in front of his face.

"What's weak? Your body? Your mind? Or your will? The only thing I see weak about you is your fucking attitude. You're acting like a damn pussy." I'm so angry I can feel my face grow hot.

West stops sputtering and whining, and stares up at me in wide-eyed awe. "Excuse me?"

"You heard me. I don't need to be excused. I'm sick and tired of listening to you bitch and moan. I realize what you've lost. You're not the only one. But I can't take one more second of listening to you fucking cry about it." Wisely, Riggs stays quiet. "I'll tell you what, if Jennings and Estevez had gone through this shit and said the things you do, you know what you would tell them? You would punch them in the fucking mouth and tell them to man up and stop acting like bitches. Not even Rosie would pull this shit." I pause to swallow past the lump forming in my throat. "That's exactly what you would do. Your body is strong. Your mind is strong. Your heart is strong. We just need to work on your piss-poor attitude."

West is speechless. He just stares, but he's seething with anger because he knows I'm right.

Apparently, so does Riggs. He clears his throat and orders, "Get up, Wardell. We've got work to do and we're a long way from finished."

———

At home, I refuse to carry him up the stairs any longer. He has a leg, and he needs to use it to get his ass where he needs to go. If I continue to baby him, he will never improve, never get stronger. My enabling is going to put him six feet under the ground, and that would kill me too.

He falls plenty of times, just about every fourth step, but at least they're carpeted. I try to help him stand, grabbing hold of his hips to help him back up on his legs, but West is done with me. His arm strikes out to punch me in the chest.

"Don't fucking touch me!" Of course, I ignore him. "I mean it. Get your hands off me."

Christ, I'm done with his shit. "I'm about to put my fucking hands all over you in a way you're not gonna like." My words hiss in his ear as I get my hands around his waist. "What is your goddamn problem? Why are you so angry?"

"Because I feel like a fucking cripple!" He's so frustrated and angry he's on the verge of tears, and he struggles to hold them back.

No more kid gloves. They will only hurt him worse in the

end. West needs a heaping dose of tough love. "You are a fucking cripple, now get up."

"Fuck you, fucker! I'm not a fucking cripple!"

It's a good thing I'm standing behind him and he can't see my smirk, 'cause I'm sure he'd wipe it off my face with his fist. "Exactly! You've got an extension on your leg that makes it work perfectly fine, so get your ass up those stairs. Now."

He begins his struggle to ascend again, but I halt him, slamming his back against the wall with my hand on his chest.

"What the fuck?" he cries.

Getting right up in his face, I warn, "The next time you call yourself weak, I'm gonna show you just how much stronger I am than you. Maybe the cripple likes to be dominated?"

West pushes back, cursing me, his face scrunched with anger.

But I just laugh, making him angrier. "You're so much fun when you're pissed off."

He pushes me aside and grabs the handrail to continue pulling himself up, step-by-step, but he falters when I smack his ass, turning back to glare at me so hard I'm surprised it doesn't burn me alive.

In the end, he gets to the top of the landing. It might have taken forty-five minutes, but he did it—on his own. Tough love is exactly what he needs.

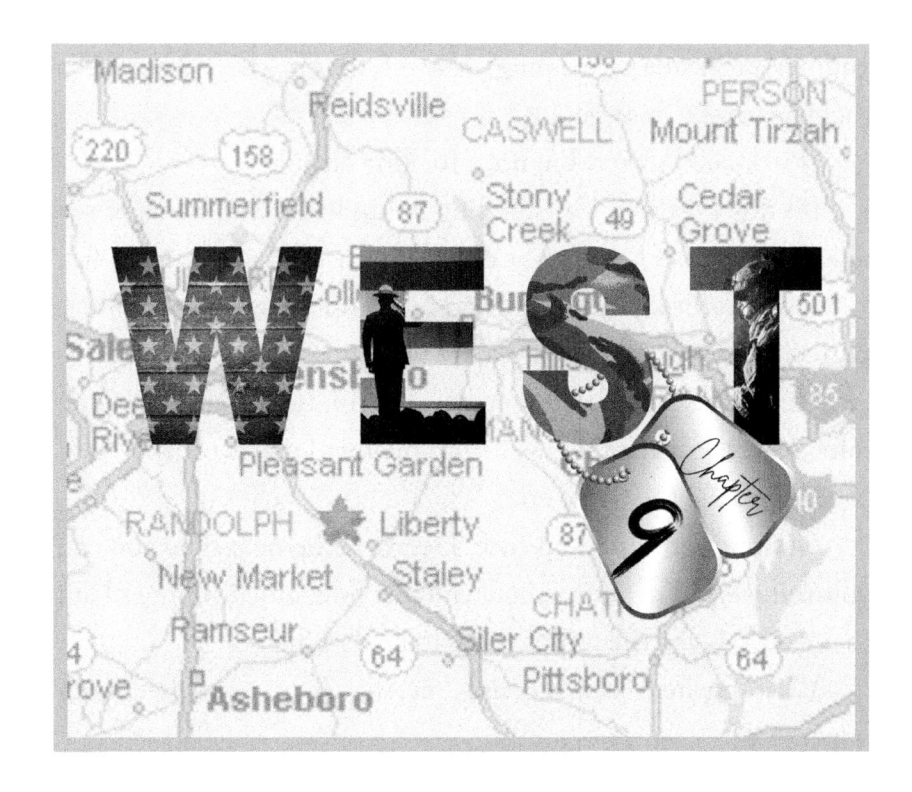

EVERYBODY LOVES A HERO.

The truth is, most heroes can't stand themselves. Most heroes are chased by demons, haunted by memories of the good deed they did until it turns into a nightmare.

You can't appreciate Heaven until you've crawled through Hell on your hands and knees.

I've been to Hell, I've crawled on my hands and knees, but that doesn't make me a hero. I'm just a soldier, or at least, I was... Now, I don't know what I am.

And this certainly isn't Heaven.

I'm not scheduled to meet with Riggs for another twenty minutes. Brandt is meeting with his therapist, mandated by his CO. I wheel my chair to the edge of the pool and look down into the clear blue water. There's no one here but me. The smell of the chlorine has become a familiar comfort to me, something I associate with floating—feeling free—being held by safe, strong arms. Brandt's arms. Sunlight filters through the dirty windows, reflecting off the water like glitter. The ripples create moving shadows that dance along the concrete walls. It's almost pretty.

It's now or never.

I take a deep breath and check the Velcro straps on the weight bags tied to my chair. On the exhale, I tug at my seatbelt to make sure it's fastened tight. I've got one shot at this, and I can't blow it. I'm not sure how many more chances Brandt will give me. He watches me like a hawk. For the past week, he's cut my pain meds in half. He insists on shaving me himself, because he can't trust me with a razor. The sliding glass door to my balcony is now padlocked.

By the time Riggs or anyone else finds me, I'll be long gone.

Maybe I'll be at peace. Maybe I'll burn in hell. But I'll be gone.

Releasing the brake, I push my chair forward and plunge into the deep end of the pool. The weight of my chair and the weights tied to it take me straight to the bottom. The water is a cooling caress around my ruined body, and I look up toward the surface, toward life, and release the air from my lungs. A rush of tiny bubbles bathe my face as they escape, but I'm content to stay where I am. In a few minutes, I too will escape.

My chest tightens, and I fight the natural urge to take a deep breath. Maybe I should. Lungfuls of water will only kill me faster. But my brain resists. That primal part of me that wants to live, that's screaming out for me to save myself. Fight or flight.

My blood thickens with adrenaline and my mind races in a panic.

I'm sorry, Brandt. So fucking sorry.

I made him a promise that I'm breaking right now.

But in a minute, I won't even care anymore. I'll never have to care about anything again. No more carrying the weight of other people's burdens. No more suffering. No more pain.

I can't hold out any longer, and I breathe in a mouthful of water, silently choking as I embrace the death I deserve.

My head throbs and my throat burns. Black shadows creep around the edges of my vision, and my eyeballs feel as if they're going to burst.

And then there's nothing but silence. *Peace.*

.

.

.

I can feel the pain in my head before I can see, and I choke on bitter vomit as I struggle to take a breath. My chest burns like fire. My head throbs like I have a migraine. And some piece of shit is pressing on my stomach like he's trying to squeeze the life out of me all over again.

"Mother...Fucker..." he pants as he squishes my intestines. "I'll fucking...kill you...myself."

Must be Brandt, 'cause I've heard that threat before.

And then he's gone, replaced by medical staff that whisks me away on a stretcher. Again, with the wires and the tubes. Again, with the bright lights shining in my sensitive eyes. They swarm around me like ants, shouting orders, rattling off my stats and vitals. They save my life. *Again.*

I'll never forgive him for this.

When the hustle and bustle dies down and my vitals are steady, the staff empties out one-by-one, leaving me alone with my savior.

I'm afraid to be alone with him, because of what I might say, afraid of what *he* might say. I never expected to have to face the consequences of my actions. The anger on his face doesn't scare me, it's the hurt in his eyes. The stark, naked fear that he can't hide.

I'll add it to the list of things I can't forgive myself for.

He's holding up the wall across the room, and I'm sure there's a reason he won't come near me. Maybe it's for the best. If he gets his hands on me, he'll probably put them around my throat.

"Brandt–"

"Three times," he hisses, his nostrils flaring as he seethes. "Three times now you've tried to leave. Tried to leave *me!*" His voice becomes increasingly louder.

"Get the fuck out of here. I wasn't trying to leave you, asshole. I was trying to leave this world." I roll my head away from him toward the ceiling so I don't have to see the anger on his face any longer. "My head is fucked. It's not about you. Why do you have to see it that way? This isn't personal."

Brandt comes closer, and he crouches down beside my bed so we're eye to eye, so I have to look at him.

"Do you think you're the only one? The only one of us with

thoughts like that? I don't know how many times I've thought about it."

He sounds so intense, like he needs me to believe every word. And I do. He may not wear his pain and misery on his sleeve like I do, but I know he's torn up inside.

"But you've never attempted it." I could almost hate him for being so much stronger than me.

"Nope."

"Why not?" My throat is raw and my voice sounds like a frog croaking.

"I couldn't save them. But I can save you." The resolve in his eyes is stronger than his will, stronger than steel.

And I'm angry again in a flash, my face heating with the intensity of it. "Can't you understand? I don't want you to save me! I'm not your fucking mission!"

"I know that," he states calmly. "You're my reason for living. I can't help but think tomorrow might be a little bit better than today." Brandt clasps my hand, ignoring the IV running through my vein. "Even if it's not. But if it is? There's nobody else I'd rather face the day with than you."

There's so much he isn't saying, so much he's holding back, but I don't need to hear it because I can feel it; in the way he squeezes my hand so tightly and in the way his tourmaline eyes bore into mine.

"You're hurting. You're in pain. You're scared." His warm lips brush across the back of my hand and he squeezes his eyes shut. Most likely to stop the flood of tears I know are threatening to spill. "And you feel all alone, even though I'm right here." He blinks his eyes open and focuses on my face. "It's grief, and it's to be expected after what we went through. There's no right or wrong way to grieve, and there's no time limit on it." It hurts to swallow, but I manage to do it twice.

"It comes and goes in waves and stages. And you have every right to feel all of it, whether you want to or not. But I promise you two things," he whispers fiercely. "One, this is temporary; it's not going to last forever. And two, I promise you, Wes, you are not alone. I'm not going anywhere." His voice is husky and warbled with emotion. "You can snap at me, bite my head off, or you can hit me, but I'm not leaving you alone in the darkness that's trying to swallow you."

He loses his battle with his tears, and they run down his cheeks and soak into his already soaked shirt. *Because he jumped in to save me.*

"I won't let it have you," he cries brokenly, and I want to die all over again for the pain I've caused him. "Lean on me. Take from me. My strength, my conviction, my hope, and my love." He clutches my hand to his stubbled cheek and squeezes. "Take all my love and let it fill up all your broken, empty places."

"Brandt–" I don't even know what I want to say, I just need him to know I hear him. The beeping machines are a somber reminder of the severity of the situation. He brings his forehead to mine, and I close my eyes with relief, needing the warmth of his touch. I need him to pour all that love he has for me into my empty chest so it can heal me.

"I know you feel lost. But I swear I've got you, and I'm going to hold on to you so tight." He clutches the back of my head, his fingers almost pulling on my hair. "So fucking tight," he whispers. "I'm not gonna let go until you're strong enough to stand on your own again. However long that takes." Brandt pulls back so he can look into my eyes. He's ravaged by his grief; grief that I caused him. Why do we hurt the ones we love most? "I will hold you up and be your pillar," he vows.

All I want is to take away his pain and make him stop hurting. "Three legs. You can't fall with three legs."

"No, you fucking can't." He presses a kiss on the back of my hand.

Up until now, I've let my anger numb my pain. But his love and his hurt have thawed the wall of ice protecting my heart. The tears that have been pooling behind my eyes for weeks finally fall in a hot rush down my face.

"Take me home."

"I can't, not until the doctor says—"

"No, home, to the cabin. Take me back home." Away from the base. Away from the Army. Away from soldiers dressed in uniform, who look just like the members of our team we lost. I want to go home to the forest and the mountains. It's the only chance I have of healing myself.

The front of the house isn't much to look at, but the back more than makes up for it. The massive deck stretches across the entire back of the cabin. A seating area and a hot tub take up most of the space. Towering pine trees and giant oaks shade the deck and most of the windows. The built-in stone fireplace generates enough heat to warm the seating area on chilly nights.

With my head in his lap, I gaze up at the setting sun,

grateful that I lived to see another glorious sunset. The pinks and purples and fiery oranges blend together like watercolors on a canvas. I would have missed this if I wasn't here. Brandt would have missed this, too. It isn't as pretty as watching the sunset in the desert, but it's the next best thing.

His fingers card through my hair. "Where you at?"

"Right here. Just remembering the last time we had all the guys here for a barbecue."

Brandt's laugh is a balm for my soul. "Hell, which time? They practically lived here. We had to start lying about where we were going on the weekends because if they saw us throw a duffel bag in the back of the Jeep, they knew we were headed up here."

It wasn't just our team, either. It was guys in our company and anyone left behind at the barracks with no plans for the weekend. They would show up here with hunting rifles, fishing poles, cases of beer, and packages of meat for grilling.

The peace I felt earlier vanishes and a heavy weight settles over me. Moisture gathers in my eyes as my feelings rush to the surface.

"Fuck, man. We didn't even get to say goodbye." My voice cracks wide open, along with the floodgates holding back my tears. "Those motherfuckers robbed us of the chance to say goodbye."

Tears glisten in Brandt's eyes like sapphires. "We could always get in the car and make the rounds, go visit each one of them—their families, their graves." His blinding white smile shines through his grief. "Are you down for a road trip?"

I laugh and swipe at my tears, sniffling like a snotty mess.

"Shit, I can barely walk to the bathroom. I don't think I can handle that. It's too much pain and suffering and—fuck no. That's not how I want to remember them. And what the fuck for? Closure or some shit? Fuck that. I'll never get over what happened to them. Visiting their families isn't going to help."

My gaze drops to my leg—half leg. Losing them isn't the only thing I can't get over.

"You're right, it was a terrible idea," he agrees.

I struggle to sit up, feeling inspired as a smile stretches across my lips. "You know what we need? We're gonna light that fire, power up the hot tub, put some fucking music on," I spread my arms wide to encompass the entire deck, "and we're gonna light the grill and put the beer on ice, and we're gonna play some fucking cornhole."

His smile starts small and grows wider the longer he stares at me. Then he stands and claps his hands together. "Hell, yeah!" Brandt starts toward the house and then stops and turns back. "Is this supposed to be some half-assed memorial?"

"It's whatever the fuck you want it to be, but it doesn't change what we're about to do."

"Micah loved cornhole," he recalls wistfully.

"Fuck yeah he did. Didn't you lose to him and have to wash his car or something?"

The memory dawns in his eyes, and his chuckle starts out slow, and builds momentum. "If only. He made me wash it in a jockstrap."

I laughed out loud, a sharp crack. "Was it purple, like your Speedo?"

"You fucking ass," he laughs.

"Well, come on. Let's get in our jockstraps and do this right."

"I don't have a fucking jockstrap, you dick."

"What did you wear that day?"

"I borrowed his!"

I threw a pillow at him, which he easily sidestepped. "That's disgusting. Didn't he have some kind of crabs or some shit from that girl he met at the laundromat?"

Brandt doubles over at the waist and grabs his knees, laughing so hard I'm positive he's crying. "That was before he met his wife. Thank God for Marissa." He straightens and swipes his eyes. "For the record and the honor of his memory, he cleared that shit up with meds."

"How do you know?" He picks the pillow up off the ground and throws it back at me, and I catch it. "Did you look?"

"No! That's just what he said."

"Yeah," I say with a laugh, shaking my head, "he said a lot of shit. You're not itchy are you?" I ask, checking out his groin.

Brandt rushes me, grabs the pillow from my grasp, and smothers my face with it. "Quit scoping out my junk and go get the damn beer while I grab the meat."

"Wash your hands first," I call out as he heads inside.

BRANDT

Chapter 10

Black Mountain, NC

"I WANT you to slide your ass in that hot tub and relax."

West grabs my hand when I start to walk away. "Wait, aren't you getting in?"

"Yup, just got to grab something from inside. Get started without me."

In the top drawer of my nightstand, I've been saving something for West to help improve his pain and his mood. He's been having a hard time since I cut back his narcotics. I grab the joint and the lighter and head back outside. West is already waist deep in the water. He tips his head back to rest against the edge of the tub and looks up at me with a loose smile on his face, courtesy of his beer buzz.

"You coming in with all that on?"

I can't see what he's wearing clearly through the bubbling surface, but I'll bet it isn't much, so I strip down to my briefs and climb in. Reclining in the built-in lounger, I tug on his hand.

"Come over here."

"Over where? What're you doing?" He laughs, unsure of what I'm asking.

"Come sit over here, on me."

"Sit on you?" He laughs again, but floats over to me, and I pull him down on my lap and situate him so he's laid out over me, reclining with his back against my stomach and chest. I hook my leg over his to keep him locked in.

We don't usually do this kind of thing. I mean, we used to cuddle together sometimes, but it's been a long time since he's felt like letting his guard down around me—around anyone. Barring our nightly showers, where he continues to jack off as I stand behind him, holding his hips steady, we haven't had any moments that come close to crossing a boundary. I'm guessing with West's confidence and self-esteem at an all-time low, he doesn't care to seek attention like he used to. He doesn't want eyes and hands on his body—not even mine, the safest person in the world for him.

But tonight, with both of us feeling loose from the alcohol, a beautiful sky above us filled with stars, classic rock playing softly in the background—our moods are relaxed. The most relaxed I've seen him in weeks. I just want to keep it going as long as I can, whether it's just for tonight, or I can milk a few days out of it.

West needs this, and so do I.

Because he's lying on top of me, his body is closer to the

surface, and his chest rises from the water. His dark brown nipples are hard and tight, and the longer I stare at them, the harder and tighter I become. To distract myself, I grab the blunt from the edge of the tub, slide it between my lips, and light it before offering it to him.

"Open up."

"Where'd you get that from?"

"A guy I know on base. I thought maybe it would help you relax."

"As long as you don't get busted." He takes it from me and hits it.

"What are they going to do, kick us out?"

West chuckles and hits it again. "I guess you have a point," he says, blowing out a stream of thick white smoke. "When we're done with Bragg, you want to live here?"

"Long-term or short-term?"

"Either. I have no fucking clue what we're supposed to do with ourselves now. I just feel like if we're making a fresh start, we could do it here."

He passes the joint back to me. "I don't care what we do, West. As long as we do it together."

"Damn right," he says with a sigh, easing his head back against my chest.

I slide my hands over his shoulders and knead his tense muscles, digging my thumbs into his stiff neck. He reaches back and grabs the blunt from between my lips and sighs with pleasure. In fact, the more I rub, the more he continues to sigh, making little groans and moans that only make my dick harder. It might be the first time he's had such an effect on me, and maybe it's because his body is in contact with mine, maybe it's the sounds he's making that remind me of sex, or maybe it's the fact that I haven't had any in so long, but I'm rock-fucking-hard for West Wardell, my best friend.

"Are we gonna talk about what we're gonna do for money?"

"I don't fucking know, West. Can't we talk about something else right now?"

"We can talk about the fact that your dick is hard." He settles his ass back-and-forth over my cock to make his point.

"Fuck, West, really?" He chuckles and lays the blunt on the rim of the tub. "Get off me."

"No, I'm comfortable. Rub my shoulders." He blows out a long stream of smoke he was holding in his lungs. "Is it hard for me?"

I can hear the laughter in his voice. He's laughing at me. "Come on, get off me for real." I slide my hands to his hips, to urge him to move, but he locks his leg around mine again.

"I'm not moving. Rub my shoulders." One hand remains on his hip, while my left hand returns to his shoulder. "Mmm, feels good. Keep going."

I dig my fingers deeper into his bare hip as I fight my baser instincts. Am I really trying to convince myself not to hump my best friend? This is fucking nuts.

West slides his hands down his stomach and moans again as he rolls his hips. I watch as the toned muscles in his abs ripple beneath the inked canvas of his skin. He doesn't stop his descent, and I can't look away as he skates his hand down his shaft to cup his balls. When he rolls his hips again, he breaches the water, and I can see the outline of his hard dick through the thin, wet cotton of his briefs. He tugs them down his hips and continues to rub his length, and I can feel myself growing harder.

"Oh, come on. Are we really doing this here? The shower is one thing, but I don't want jizz in the hot tub." It doesn't surprise me that he ignores me and continues, really getting into the moment, the mood, and I have to wonder where he is in his head. Is he here with me, or is he imagining someone else?

"Touch me," he hisses, as his fist moves up and down.

I press my fingers harder into his neck. "I am touching you."

"No, touch me," West insists.

I slide my hand from his shoulder down to his pec and skim my fingers over his tight nipple. He purrs like a kitten. My gut swirls with adrenaline.

"More. Touch me more."

This is fucking nuts. I want to, but I know better. West is lonely and desperate for human contact and validation, but I'm the wrong man for the job. Partly because I'm a man, and partly because I'm his best friend and nothing more. This can only end badly.

Against my better judgment, I creep my hand from his hip, ever so slowly, toward his hand, the one that covers his cock. My lips brush over his wet hair and I breathe in the scent of his shampoo—citrus and sandalwood.

"Wes, what ar–"

"Shhh. It's okay."

My heart beats painfully hard, loud enough that he has to hear it, and I feel like this is the ballsiest thing I've ever done—and the stupidest. "It's not like you can't do this yourself."

He rubs his head back-and-forth across my mouth. "I know I can. I just want to feel someone else's hands." I close my fingers around his shaft. His skin is warm, even underwater, and the breath I've been holding in rushes from my lips.

Someone else's hands. Jesus Christ, I could be anybody. Anybody but *me*. Anybody but his best friend. But does it stop me? Fuck no, it doesn't stop me for a second. I've never admitted to myself I wanted this, wanted to touch him like this, but now that I am, I'm not going to deny that it was always there, in the back of my head. His dick kicks in my hand. *I definitely want this.*

My lips move to his ear, and I try once more. "Wes."

"Don't stop, Reaper. I need this."

He wraps his hand around mine, keeping me in place so I don't pull away, and guides my hand up and down his shaft.

I need this, too.

With my left hand, I tweak his nipple, still in awe of my daring, and continue to stroke him with my right. West bucks into my fist to urge me to go faster, to squeeze him harder.

We're really doing this.

"I've got you. Just relax. Close your eyes." With my last ounce of nerve, I nip the shell of his ear with my lips and he shivers and reaches for his balls.

The background music accompanies the sounds of his pleasure and I want to slow my strokes, I want to draw this out as long as I can, 'cause fuck knows when or if I'll ever get to do this again, but more than that, I just want to make him feel good.

Pumping faster, I work his cock like I would my own, stoking the flame in his blood, until he grasps my wrist, almost halting me as he urges me on. He's just making sure I don't stop —not until he comes. And when he does, he gasps my name like a plea and spills over my fist. I can feel the warmth of his seed and can't help but imagine what it tastes like.

It's the first time I've ever had that thought about any man, and it's sobering.

How long can I leave my hand on his cock before he asks me to move it?

I'll never know because he goes soft in my grip, and I realize he's fallen asleep.

I check my watch again for the thousandth time. "Two hours. Two fucking hours we've been sitting here."

"Welcome to the Army. Hurry up and wait." West taps his pen against the booklet of Mad Libs. "Give me a noun and an adjective."

"Cannon and hairy."

He grins, and it's sexy as fuck. I can't stop noticing these things about him lately. The way his smile lifts higher on the right corner, how he arches his left eyebrow but not his right.

"Reminds me of that guy in Kabul. You remember him?" he asks, cracking up. "He was in charge of the mortars, and he was hairy as fuck."

I chuff and shake my head, trying not to smile, but it's difficult the longer I stare at him. The shit he remembers... but he can't recall what we ate for dinner yesterday.

"All right, give me a number."

"Fifty-two. You know, we could be out of here today."

"It don't work like that. You know that. They might say we're done, but even then, it can take weeks. The papers come in the mail."

"Yeah, but if the med-boarding process is over, we can fucking leave. Fuck the papers. They'll get there when they get there."

West fills in the blanks in his notepad, and when he looks back up at me, he grins. "I'm ready to get the fuck out of here right now."

"You can thank me anytime for making sure they believed it was accidental that you went for a swim with weights tied to your chair. Otherwise, I'd be going home today, and your ass would still be under observation."

"Thank you, master of the bullshit. I know you hated lying about it, but being strapped to a bed in Womack wasn't going to help me."

He's got his prosthetic on today, and though he's still getting used to walking in it, I look at him and think for a second how easy it is to forget that he's not complete, like he used to be. With his long legs dressed in BDUs, his boots on, he reminds me of the team leader he used to be.

"Okay, here's what we've got. The clown and the cashier had the cannon ready to shoot out fifty-two hairy guinea pigs into a kiddie pool full of Jell-O." He reads from the notepad, and when he glances up at me, smiling, he's confused by my blank expression. "What?"

"You need a fucking psych eval."

"It's not supposed to make sense," he insists, tucking the pad away. "Riggs! Hey man, what's up?" West flags Riggs as he passes by.

"Gentlemen, how are you?"

"Just waiting for our final decision from the PEB. Fingers crossed today is the day."

"You've got nothing to worry about. The Physical Evaluation Board is going to medically retire both of you. I've seen your files. When you're finished here, come see me. I've got something I want to talk to you both about."

Two and a half hours later, we step into Riggs's office.

"Well, gentlemen, how'd it go?"

"You're looking at two retired old men," West teases.

"Hundred percent disability," I add.

West pushes me playfully. "Man, you got eighty percent. Don't try to one-up me."

"Wardell, you need to apply with the VA right away. You're far from done with your rehab. You have a long way to go. I'm talking years. And I'm not gonna let you give up and get lazy." He tosses a brochure across his desk.

"What's this," West asks, grabbing it up. He thumbs through the brochure as a myriad of expressions dance across his face.

"Beyond the Army Legion of Love Soldiers is an organization that helps guys like you. They help soldiers who've been discharged get back on the road to recovery."

"Isn't that what the VA does?"

"Sure, that's what they say they do," he smirks. "But the

Legion of Love doesn't clinch their asshole when they have to reach into their pockets to help the vets."

"I don't know, Riggs. Don't I have everything I need? I've got the chair and the leg, and I guess I've got to continue with therapy. What can they do for me that the VA can't?"

"Well, for starters, they can get you a decent chair."

"What's wrong with my chair?"

"It's a piece of shit. Standard medical equipment. Have you ever tried to wheel your chair off the sidewalk or any paved surface? Try it and tell me what happens."

"Okay, so a better quality chair. What else?"

"How about a new leg?"

"What's wrong with my leg?" He asks, tapping his prosthetic knee. "That leg is a piece of shit, to tell you the truth, and you and I both know it. You can't stand on that leg for more than three hours at a time without being in pain. The Legion of Love can get you a custom fitted prosthetic. They can get you a running blade. They can put you in clinical trials for your vertigo and your migraines."

I grab the brochure from West and flip through the glossy pages. It was your typical propaganda, guys in wheelchairs with big smiles on their faces, women holding babies in their one good arm.

"But most importantly," Riggs continues, "the Legion will give you a support group of men and women in the same boat."

"Oh, yay, more therapy."

"It's not like that, West, I promise you. Look, I'm heading over there tomorrow. I volunteer there. Why don't you meet me over there and I'll give you a tour and show you around. Then you can decide for yourself if it's something that feels like a good fit."

West snatches the brochure back from my grasp and flips through it before settling on the cover. "BALLS? What kind of place names their organization BALLS?"

Riggs drops his head in his hand, and I can hear him trying to smother his laughter. "I agree, they could have done better. Just say you'll meet me."

"All right, I'll check out your balls."

"Jesus Christ," Riggs mutters, "get out of my office, gentleman. I've got work to do."

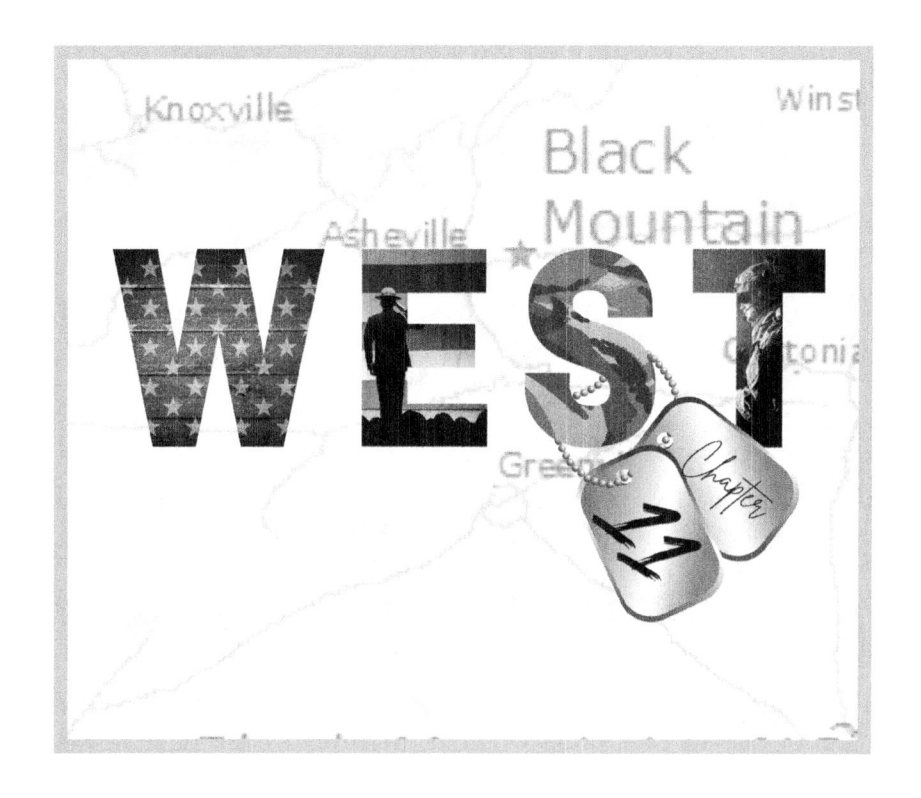

TODAY IS A *BAD* DAY.

Some are better than others, but not today.

I'm struggling. It's two o'clock in the afternoon and I still haven't gotten out of bed. I can hear Brandt in the kitchen, banging pots and pans and muttering to himself. No doubt he's pissed at me. Or maybe he's just disappointed. I've done well the past few days, and he probably fooled himself into thinking it would stay that way.

His mistake. He should know better.

He has good and bad days too, he just hides it better than I do. Brandt is steady like a rock, whereas I'm a buoy bobbing in the ocean, dipping high and low in the turbulent waves.

The sound of his boots echoes down the hallway as he approaches my room, and I brace for a fight.

"Time to get u–" He halts beside my bed, and I know what he's looking at. Rolling over, I groan as I stretch and sit up. "What's this shit? What the fuck is this, West?"

"A ticket to the gun show," I say in a flat voice, devoid of any emotion or nuance.

He sits on the edge of my bed and pinches the bridge of his nose. A frustrated sigh blows heavily from between his lips. "I'll tell you what. You better start talking right now before I lose my shit."

I clear my throat before speaking. "Take it all away. The guns, the knives, take everything and hide it from me."

Brandt hangs his head, and I have to wonder what he's thinking as he sits silently and contemplates his next move. Kindness and contact are the last things I'm expecting. He kicks off his boots and climbs over my leg to settle next to me in bed.

"What are we doing?" I ask as he wraps me in his strong arms. He chuckles and throws his leg over mine.

"Telling you it's okay. If this is where you want to spend your day today, it's okay with me. But I'm gonna spend it here with you."

Asshole. I can't be depressed and broody if he's going to cling to me like a leech and love me. "I can't forget today. And the more I try to, the more they fill my head. I wish I could wipe away the memories like rubbing sand from my eyes, but that shit is burned into my brain."

"I can remember with you. Tell me what you see."

He buries his scruffy face in my neck, and his fingers trace my collarbone. There's no way I'm going to tell him what I see. Not today. Because what I'm seeing is how I imagine they looked after the blast, with parts of their bodies missing, burned skin and bloodied. Half of their faces gone, and yet their eyeballs are intact and staring at me, blinking at me, silently begging me to help them, *to save them*, even though they're good and dead.

Instead of confiding in him, I turn my head to the door that leads out onto the deck. I feel his lips press against my skin, and he leaves a kiss on my neck. A soft lingering kiss I can't interpret. I don't know what's been going on with us lately. I just know that whenever he touches me, I feel better, or at least, if not better, I feel less alone. The bullshit in the showers, and whatever that was in the hot tub last week—it's getting out of hand. And it's not like it was before, when it was all just a game between us. This feels different, this feels like it means something, but fuck if I know what.

And it's not just that he makes me feel good because he's touching my dick. It's more than that. He makes me feel safe. And I can tell he enjoys it. Brandt *wants* to touch me, for whatever fucking reason. I don't know why anyone would want to fucking touch me. But he does, and it makes me feel… wanted, desired, desirable.

He makes me feel like I matter.

His touch doesn't feel like pity or consolation, or even comfort. His touch feels like fire—all-consuming. He makes me feel like *me* again, when I used to feel like myself, my old self. His touch brings me back to that man I used to be.

It's thrilling and reassuring, and it's addicting, and I just want to feel more of it.

The memories run through my head as he continues to trace over my skin, over the outlines of my tattoos, and like always, he makes me feel something. He makes me feel *everything*. All the hurt and the pain and the anger and the guilt and sadness rush to the surface and leak from my eyes.

My voice is barely a whisper. "Don't let me go."

"Never. I promise."

And then I keep silent for long minutes, so I can continue to feel his touch on my skin, his lips on my neck, without having to actually ask for it, until the pressure in my chest is too heavy, and I have to let it out with words.

"I'm fucking useless. I can't even protect you and keep you safe anymore. I'm your Team Leader, your Sergeant, and your best fucking friend. How am I supposed to look after you?"

"Why don't you let me look after you for a while instead?"

"Because that's not the way it's supposed to be."

"Look, you're too upset to hear me right now. I'm afraid if you hear what I have to say, you'll just push me away." Brandt raises up on his elbow and grasps my chin, turning my head to meet his eyes. "Listen with your heart, not your head. We're not going back there ever again. We're making a new life here now. I don't need you to keep me safe. I'm more than capable of looking after myself. What I need is your help with the rest of it. All the shit in here and in here." He taps his head and his chest and then laces his fingers with mine, and brings them to rest over his heart. "I need you to help me keep all of this straight. Make sure I don't get lost. Protect my sanity. Make sure I don't become bitter and hateful. Can you do that for me? Will you look after my heart?"

This motherfucker always knows what to say to pull me from my shit-spiral. "You trust me with your heart?"

"There's no one I trust more." Bringing our joined hands to his lips, Brandt presses a kiss to my knuckles. "Can I make you lunch? Or popcorn and a movie? We can stay right here in your bed all day."

Through my sheen of tears, I nod and manage a watery smile. "Will you stay with me tonight?"

"In here? Fuck yeah. Your bed is bigger and softer than mine." He laughs when I roll my eyes, and then adds, "I promised you that I'd never leave you alone in the darkness again, even if that means sleeping with you every night. But you have to promise me something in return."

I swallow past the emotions forming a lump in my throat. "Anything," I croak.

"You have to promise me you'll try to live. Giving up your weapons is a huge start, and I'm not asking you to be happy every day or to pretend to forget. I just want you to commit to your life. If you can't get out of bed, just ask me to fucking join you, but don't hide away from me. I can't watch you slip away like this, little by little, each day. I can't watch you self-destruct. I can't watch you take your life, not when it means so fucking much to me, West. *You* mean so much to me." His voice chokes up. "I don't want to be left alone in the darkness, either."

Fresh tears run down my face, and he wipes them away. "I can't promise you the rest of my life, but I can promise you today. And I can promise you that tomorrow I will try my hardest. That's all I've got, Reaper."

He lays his head on my chest and traces my belly button. "I guess that's enough for me," he says softly. "I'll be checking in. I need proof of life, every day, maybe twice a day. Maybe every other day if it's a good day, but I'll be checking in."

"Proof of life?"

"Yeah, I need to know you're in there, and that you're still holding on, still fighting. I need to know you're still with me."

All I can do is nod. *Proof of life.* I can give him that.

Sometime later, after we consume an entire batch of brownies, a bowl of popcorn, ham and cheese sandwiches, and a box of crackers, Brandt turns to me in bed, laying his hand on my chest, and asks, "Can I admit something to you?"

Jesus Christ, it could be anything. A small thrill shoots through me, wondering what I'm about to discover about him when I was sure I knew everything. "Of course."

"I'm excited about checking out that organization with you."

"BALLS? You're excited about BALLS? That's definitely something I didn't know about you."

He tucks his face into my chest and buries a chuckle. "It really is the stupidest fucking name. But I'm excited. The improved chair and the blade leg means we're not limited to the indoors any longer. We can get out of here and go hike your land like we used to. We can do more stuff."

His words carry the weight of expectation, and it's a weight I don't want to shoulder. I've had to work my ass off in order to walk on my basic prosthetic, just learning to take the smallest, easiest steps. What is Riggs going to require of me in order to use the blade? To run? To be athletic and physical? I don't even know how to relate myself to that kind of man any longer.

"We'll see. Don't get your hopes up."

"Does that mean you're not even going to try?" He sounds disappointed in me already.

"That's not what I said. I'm just saying that I don't do well under pressure lately, and the picture you're painting feels like a lot of pressure."

"I'm sorry, you're right. I just thought maybe you could feel some of my excitement and it could motivate you. I'll back off."

Great, now we both feel like shit. "I don't want you to back off. I mean, I do, but you shouldn't," I explain with a half-grin. "I just can't handle disappointing you. Clearly, I'm holding you back from living your life. I don't want to hold you back. You deserve...*everything*. I can't give you *anything*."

Brandt sits up and throws the covers back, and I feel mildly suspicious of the twinkle in his eyes, full of mischief. He takes my stump in his hands and lifts it, pushing my sweatpants up my thigh, and faintly brushes his fingertips over the bundle of scar tissue at the tip. Slowly, his head descends as he maintains eye contact with me, and he presses a soft kiss to my ruined skin. And then, with a wicked grin, his tongue snakes out, and he licks it.

With my left foot, I shove him back, and I grab my thigh from his grasp. My face twists with revulsion, and I'm absolutely disgusted by his actions.

Brandt plants his hands into the mattress on either side of my waist and raises up over me as he stares into my eyes.

"Don't give me that face. There's nothing gross about it. That's the leg that supported me when you carried me back to base after I fractured mine. It's the leg you kicked me with when I stole your last cigarette back in basic. You left a nasty bruise on my hip for almost a week, and it hurt like a bitch." With the way he's laying over my body, I can feel his thighs press against mine, and I can feel the warm hard length of him slide against my soft groin. Even through the thin cotton of our sweats, it's unmistakable. "This is the same leg I shaved when you lost that bet over Donna McPherson."

His eyes drop to my throat, watching it slide as I swallow hard, and after a tense moment, he backs off and sits up, touching my thigh again. In fact, he's touching both my thighs, like he's comparing them. "At least, I think it was this leg. I don't know, it might've been the other one. Fuck it, it doesn't matter because it's all a part of you. It's all the same." He finds my eyes again and holds my gaze, smiling like a fool. "Your body is beautiful. You're a soldier. A warrior. You use your body as a weapon and a shield to defend your country and your brothers and sisters."

Brandt tugs my pants down my hips and bends down over my thigh, bringing his face and his mouth just inches from my crotch, and I don't know if he's going to suck my dick or press a kiss to my skin, but I can't look away. My heart jumps in my chest and I can't stop swallowing. I'm not even ashamed that my dick is growing hard because of my excitement, and I realize I would let him do either one to me. It's a revelation, but not sobering enough to pull me from the moment.

His tongue slips from between his lips to drag along my exposed skin as he blazes a wet trail from the tip of my shortened limb, to the crease of my groin. This time, when he looks up at me, there's fire in his eyes instead of mischief.

"There's no part of you I wouldn't lick."

Oh shit! As that settles in, he misses the range of emotions dancing across my face as he presses a kiss to my stomach and dips his tongue into my belly button, causing my muscles to spasm. I clutch his head, but don't make a move to push him away. Instead, I grasp onto him, pushing my fingers into his dark silken hair, and hold myself still, like an invitation, waiting to see what he'll do next.

His deep blue eyes lock with mine as he moves up my chest, daring me to make him stop, and I watch with wide eyes as his tongue flicks my nipple. He's no longer playing with me; this isn't our usual game of dare. This is the real thing, or at least, it's about to be. He wraps his lips around my nipple and sucks hard, and I feel it tug in my balls and gasp. He's watching me now, watching my reaction, and it's spurring him on.

"I want to make you feel good. Will you let me?"

The sexy, manipulative way he asks, like he's begging, but at the same time dominant, has me willing to say yes to anything and everything.

"You are," I reassure him, afraid to ask for more.

"Just trust me," he promises as his lips map the colorful skin down my stomach, over the linked W and B tattoo I got branded with right after Boot Camp. He stops to nip it with his teeth before pressing a kiss to it.

As if afraid to move too fast, he makes his way slowly down the dark trail of hair that leads to my hard cock, and buries his nose in the nest of short curls that surround the base. Every neuron in my body is firing at once, and I feel juiced up and invincible, a lot like I used to feel before a mission. It's a head rush to feel that level of adrenaline again, knowing it's not from the heat of battle or the danger of risk, but from my best friend's touch.

From imagining what he's about to do to me.

Again, he checks with me to see if I'm going to resist, but my mind is stuck on stupid, and all I can do is watch. He's taking his cues from me, and I'm not going to stop him. Brandt grasps the base of my cock and brings it to his lips. The sight alone is enough to push me over the edge. It's his face, the same face I've known for a decade, but with my cock touching his lips. It's fucking blowing my mind.

"Relax, Professor," he says with a wink just before his tongue delves into my slit to catch a taste of my seed, and my balls draw up tight with need.

He's going to do it. Brandt Aguilar is going to suck my cock, and I know without a doubt it's going to be the hottest experience of my life. *It already is.*

His warm lips close around the spongy head of my engorged cock and his mouth pulls on it, drawing out more precum before enveloping the entire crown. The wet heat of his mouth is pure nirvana. As he slides down my shaft, I have to will myself not to come. There's no fucking way I'm going to end this prematurely.

He sucks and slurps like a noisy whore, like he's done this a dozen times, or more, and I'm convinced the beating of my heart is louder than the filthy sounds he's making. All of my senses exist in the space between my legs, in the parts that are covered by his mouth. I can't think of anything else—of this being awkward, of this being wrong—only how good it feels and how right.

He slides his fist up and down in sync with his lips, and I'm positive I can't take much more. "Fuck...*fuck*, your mouth. Ungh. Yeah." He grins and releases his hold on my gaze to continue with his task—sucking my soul out through my cockhead. He's going to do it too, any second. My abs burn with the effort it takes to hold my release back. Is he going to swallow me? I have a burning need to see him do it. To know my cum is pooling inside his stomach. I don't know why that seems so important to me right now, but I know it has to happen.

Grabbing his head, I slide my fingers into his hair and hold him steady as I push into his mouth. My eyes roll back in my head when I feel the head of my cock hit the back of his throat, and the sound of his gagging pulls my load from me in a hot rush.

"I'm coming. Fuck, I'm–" I don't even give him a chance to pull off, and he swallows every drop without a fight.

Even after my head drops on the pillow, he takes his time with me with slow, soft, teasing licks and gentle suction that feels as if he's pulling my balls out through my shaft. Every sensation is amplified by a thousand, and it's the best head I've ever received, by far. It's been sixteen years since my first bj, and I can't recall a single one. I can't even spare a moment to grieve the loss of those memories because Brandt eviscerated them with his wicked mouth.

He pulls my sweats back up, drops a kiss to my belly, and lays his head on my stomach. The breath of his words whispers over the fine hairs of my trail.

"Thank you for trusting me," he murmurs, then he squeezes my hip and climbs off the bed, making his way to the shower.

As I listen to the sounds of the rushing water, I realize this is the second time he's taken care of me that I haven't offered to do the same in return. I just don't know if I can. I'm not ready for that.

"Brandt," I call out.

"Yo?"

"How did it taste? How did my cum taste?" I have to know what he thought of it. Whether he liked it enough to do it again.

I don't get anything back until he shuts the water off and appears in the doorway with a towel wrapped around his waist. Drops of water roll down his chest, and for the first time, I look at his body in a different way, in a way that—I fucking want him.

At the very least, I want to taste his nipples.

"It tasted slightly bitter and salty. Kind of like my own."

"Did you like it?"

"No, I didn't like it, Wes. I fucking *loved* it." He moves towards the bed and plants a knee on the mattress, crawling over my leg to settle between my thighs. "And I can't wait to get another taste of you."

I swallow hard, and keep silent because I have absolutely no fucking clue how to respond to that.

"Do you need me to–"

"Are you offering?" I panic a bit because really, I'm not offering, I'm just trying not to be a dick. He chuckles, putting me at ease. "Relax, I'm fine. I took care of it in the shower."

Thank fucking Christ. If we were playing a game of gay chicken, Brandt would win, hands down.

BRANDT

Chapter 22

BALLS
Black Mountain, NC

"DAMN, THOSE ARE SOME HUGE BALLS!"

Shaking my head at his seemingly endless supply of ball jokes, I watch West stare out the window of the Jeep at the enormous white stucco building that houses the NC mountain region branch of BALLS.

"Yeah, well, let's go fondle them. Get your ass moving." I can make ball jokes too.

Reluctantly, he trails after me. In the lobby, an older woman standing behind the desk greets us with a warm smile.

"Welcome to Beyond the Army Legion of Love Soldiers! I'm Margaret Anne, a volunteer here. How can I help you, gentleman?"

"Afternoon, Ma'am. We're meeting with Navarro Riggs."

"Oh, Riggs! Such a lovely man." The doubtful look on West's face indicates he disagrees about the loveliness of Navarro Riggs. "I haven't seen him yet today, but you're welcome to wait right over there." Margaret Anne points to the reception area with grouped seating and a wet bar that holds a mini fridge stocked with bottled waters and a coffee maker. "If you'd rather not wait, I can give you a tour myself," she offers.

Her chipper personality isn't in line with West's brand of miserable sarcasm, and before he can chew her up and spit her out, I step in. "Thank you, Margaret Anne, but we don't mind waiting."

"No problem. Take this and look it over while you wait."

She hands West a black nylon drawstring bag that I assume is filled with promotional swag and brochures. He accepts it without thanks and walks away, and I follow after assuring Margaret Anne we're grateful.

"You could've been nicer," I admonish him when we're seated side-by-side in the plastic chairs.

"Here," he says, shoving the backpack in my lap. "Take your ball sack."

"Jesus Christ," I mumble and rifle through the bag. A heart-shaped stress-squeezy, a pen with the BALLS logo, glossy brochures, and a fridge magnet with their phone number.

His knee bounces wildly, and I can almost feel his anxiety. I know he doesn't want to be here, but I'll be damned if we're leaving. I just hope Riggs shows up before I have to physically restrain him.

"Come on, let's just g–"

"Wardell, Aguilar! Glad to see you made it," Riggs booms in a voice that carries across the reception area. He hands a to-go cup of coffee to Margaret Anne and motions for us to follow him.

He's wearing black track pants and a black T-shirt that says, 'I love BALLS', and I can already hear West's snarky joke in my head.

"Let me show you around," he offers. He makes a right turn down a long, narrow hall and points to the left. "That's the gym. You can find pickup games of basketball at all hours of the day, played by teams with two legs, and teams with two wheels." Further down, he motions to the right. "Weights and cardio. You'll usually find me in there, working with people just like you, wanting to push their recovery further."

We duck our heads in and stop short. The equipment is sick. Completely state-of-the-art. I would love to see West benefit from some of this equipment. A huge man stands under a machine with a weighted bar that he's pulling down to work his shoulders. Riggs points to the man's left leg, or rather, his prosthetic leg.

"See that? Hydraulics. We'll get you hooked up with something like that, Wardell."

I feel like a kid on Christmas morning, thinking of all the possibilities a leg like that could provide West. Uneven terrain, unstable, moving surfaces, like a boat or a floating dock—it would open up new worlds for him.

West keeps a silent, noncommittal look pasted on his face, not giving anything away. On the surface, he appears to be taking it all in, but I know the gears in his brain are working overtime.

Riggs continues down the hall, pointing left and right as he calls out room after room. "Cafeteria in there. You can eat a free hot meal anytime of day, but the vending machines are paid. Across the way are locker rooms and showers, and they lead to the indoor pool. There's also a sauna in the locker room you might want to take advantage of. It's nice," he adds with a wink.

"This place is unreal," I say out loud, knowing West is thinking the same thing. "Where do they get their funding from?"

"Private donations, military families, retired vets with pensions or successful private businesses, even some military contractors donate to us. Sadly, many families that have lost a soldier have given us a portion of their settlements as well, which we're grateful for. We also receive federal grants and state funding."

We pass what looks like a suite of offices, followed by exam rooms. "Our occupational therapists work here." We turn right again to find another long hallway. I spot what looks like a classroom with children's drawings taped to the walls.

"What's this?"

"A lot of our vets have become daily caregivers while their spouses are the primary breadwinners who have to go out to a day job, which leaves our vets with the brunt of childcare. This way, they never have to miss a session. We also offer a summer camp for our clients' families, and for children of fallen soldiers."

I was blown away by the scope of their reach and services.

"Follow me. There's something I want to show you." We follow Riggs through double doors that lead into a short hall lined with three classrooms. The first is filled with computers. A woman sits at the desk. "That's our workplace skills room. Anna will help you update your résumé and become certified in any computer program you need to find a new job. She can also get you enrolled anywhere you want to take classes and find you help to pay for them."

"What are the other two for?" I ask.

"Support groups. They meet throughout the day. Every kind of group you could imagine. Support for family members that have lost a loved one, support for vets going through divorce, or struggling with being single and alone. There's a group for PTS survivors and another for substance abuse."

We follow him into the classroom and stand by while he takes a seat. The chairs are arranged in a circle, but they're all empty. But soon, they begin to fill up as vet after vet strolls through the door. These guys are huge. With missing limbs, scars, and tattoos, full, thick beards, and even thicker arms. Most are dressed in black leather jackets and ripped jeans, and you can tell they've seen some action.

"This must be the support group for men who love leather," West snarks, and I can't help but grin. He's such a smartass, but it's one of the reasons I love him.

It's not lost on Riggs. He's struggling not to laugh as he explains, "Most of them belong to the local chapter of the American Legion of Riders."

I drop the BALLS sack by my feet, and West reaches in to

grab the heart squeezy. "And what do the ALR need support for?"

"Just listen in and see for yourself," Riggs suggests.

Six men fill the empty seats in the circle. They look comfortable, and I assume they all know each other, and have been here many times before. But when they reach into their bags, each marked with the same logo, and pull out needles and yarn, I'm floored and confused.

"Hey, new guys, get you some yarn over there, and some needles," one-man orders, pointing to a basket on the table behind us. Under his ALR jacket, his black T-shirt says, '*get stitched*', with a hot pink ball of yarn stabbed by two knitting needles.

"What the fuck is this?" West sounds pissed as he pushes to his feet.

"Sit down," I hiss, tugging on his arm.

Riggs looks entirely too pleased with himself, and I realize we've been had.

"Oh, did I forget to mention…we knit? Wardell, Aguilar, these are the Bitches with Stitches, a support group for disabled vets."

West shrugs off my grip. "I don't knit, and I don't bitch."

I practically choke on my snort. "All you do is bitch," I say with a roll of my eyes. Some of the guys snicker, including Riggs, who's heard West's bitching firsthand.

He beats me to the door, and I charge after him, grabbing his shoulder. "You can't leave."

"Fucking watch me. I didn't sign up for this shit."

"West–"

"Fucking knitting Brandt? Really?"

"Look, keep your voice down. I can hold my own in a fight, but some of these guys look like they can kick my ass with their hands tied behind their backs. Plus, you promised me."

That seems to take some of the wind from his sails and he sags with defeat. "You owe me so fucking bad."

And I chuckle because I can't help it. "I know I do."

West allows me to lead him back to the circle, and thankfully no one makes a big deal of it. They keep on stitching and bitching, as if we aren't even here.

"Stiles, how's the new job coming along," Riggs asks, kicking off the group discussion.

Stiles is a big bear of a man, with shaggy black hair and a matching goatee. He's using lime green yarn to knit what appears to be socks.

"They canned me."

"You just started there," someone points out.

"Yeah, I might've had one too many to drink and showed up late one too many times."

He doesn't sound bitter about it, and he hasn't dropped one stitch while spewing brutal honesty about his shortcomings. Either this was a very safe space, or the guy had huge balls.

Riggs sighs. "We've talked about this, Stiles. No drinking past nine o'clock when you have to work the next day. I guess you'll have to start looking for something new again."

"Yeah, I know," he admits with a heavy sigh. "I have to do better. What about you, McCormick?"

McCormick is the man who put his two cents in. He's got to weigh at least two-fifty, and he's got a nasty-looking scar across his cheek. His hair and full beard are a dark burnt orange.

"Went on a date last night. Crashed and burned."

"Again?" another man asks.

"She never even showed. I mean, she probably did, saw me sitting there and took one look at me and my bum leg, and turned tail and ran."

His *bum leg* was missing at the knee, like West's, but unlike West, he didn't hide it under pants. McCormick showed off his prosthetic with pride in a pair of cargo shorts.

"Can I ask where you're finding these girls?" Riggs inquires.

"Tinder?" McCormick scratches his beard and lays his knitting down.

"Well, that's your problem," Stiles points out.

Riggs bites back a smile. "Are you mentioning in your profile about your leg?"

"No, my profile picture is a shot of my stellar abs," he says, running his hand down his self-proclaimed washboard stomach.

The guys chuckle and shake their heads, but Riggs explains, "Nobody likes to be surprised. They deserve to know what they're getting into. Perhaps be honest about it upfront, and if they still reply, you have a better chance of them showing up for the date."

I glance sideways at West to see his reaction. I hate that he's hearing this and probably thinking he's going to have the same luck. He's already mentioned his fears about dying fifty years from now with the same load in his nuts because he doesn't think anyone wants it. Well, besides me. He probably thinks I want it out of pity. If only he knew how little I pity him.

West is seriously abusing his heart squeezy, and I make my way over to the table and choose two blue balls of yarn and some needles for us. He accepts it reluctantly, shooting me a withering glare. At least he's not making a joke about blue balls.

"What about you two?" a man asks. He has a brown mohawk, and his lip is pierced.

"Jax, they're new. Everyone gets a pass on their first meeting," Riggs says, bailing us out.

But if I pass, so will West, and I really want this to work. I need him to agree to give the Bitches a chance.

"No, I don't mind. I'm Aguilar and this is Wardell. I don't know what to say. It's been… It's been hard since we've been back stateside. Sometimes it feels like we have more bad days than good. It's a struggle, but I'm grateful I don't have to struggle alone. Also, I have no idea how to knit, but if you can point out some resources, I'll give it a try."

Jax stands up and crosses the circle, reaches into his pocket, and pulls out a folded up piece of paper that he hands to me. "That's our phone tree. If you're having a bad day, start at the top of the list and work your way down. One of us will always answer. And if you message me, I'll shoot you some website links for getting started with the needles."

"If I can convince a date to come home with me, I ain't gonna answer," McCormick insists.

Stiles looks shocked. "You wouldn't answer if you had a girl in your bed?"

"Hell no! Not like I need to give them another reason to leave."

"Well, skip his name and call me first," Stiles offers.

I glance at Riggs and see the humor dancing around the edges of his mouth. He's probably used to this back-and-forth nonsense banter, but for me and West, it's new, and it feels good, lighthearted, even. Like the way we used to joke with our team. A familiar stab of pain spikes through my heart at the memory of them, of their laughter and their smiling faces, of the countless arguments over artillery and weapons and tanks and food.

Will it ever hurt less? Would I want it to?

They ramble for forty-five more minutes until Riggs says, "That's about it for today, gentlemen. I'll see you next week. Stiles, if you need help with a job search this week, call me."

We linger as the other guys wrap it up and move past us, and each one stops to high-five us on their way past. It's a small taste of the old brotherhood and camaraderie we used to have until recently, when our world was torn apart and reduced down to just the two of us.

When Riggs moves to the door, we follow him out. "I'm glad you guys stayed. It's a good group. I hope we see you again next week."

"Hey Riggs," a guy says as he squeezes past us.

"Marx, what's up, man?" Riggs claps him on the back.

"Not much, doing good. How about you?"

"Can't complain."

"Well, that's all any of us can ask for. See ya."

We step aside so we're not blocking traffic through the door as the classroom begins to fill up for another group. "That's my buddy Brewer Marx," Riggs explains. "He runs the addiction support group."

When Riggs and I turn to leave, West lingers, spying on the group. Eventually, he catches up with us down the hall. I wave goodbye to Margaret Anne on our way out the door, and when we climb into the Jeep, West hesitates with his seatbelt.

"Reaper? Don't ever let me end up in that group."

"Dude, those guys seemed cool. Your dick isn't going to fall off because you're knitting."

"No, the other one. For addicts. Swear to me, you'll never let me end up there."

A knot of emotion gathers in my throat, and it's hard to swallow as I look into his earnest face. He means it. He's desperate not to end up like that, not that I would ever let him.

"I swear to you. I'd rather suck-start a pistol than let you go down that road." I'm relieved he had a glimpse into that dark brief ending and decided he didn't want it. "Come on, we've got a stop to make before we head to lunch."

"Can't we just drive through somewhere and head home?"

"No, I'm sick of that. We're gonna go sit in a restaurant like normal people and have a meal and a conversation."

"Easy for you to say, your life hasn't changed," he sulks.

"Why, because you have half a leg? There's nothing you can't do with that leg, except cut the toenails on it. You can still shower, work out, do laundry, shoot a gun, and fuck. Having half a leg doesn't stop you from doing anything."

"Says the man who still has both."

"So the fuck what. What are you afraid of? Some loser in a bar who says hey, did you know you only have one leg?" He gives me a *well, duh* look and I have to physically restrain myself from rolling my eyes. "Well, do the fucking math, man, you do. You've got one and a half legs, big fucking deal."

I've realized with West, being blunt and insensitive is the only way to get through to him when he acts like a toddler. His 'poor me' routine is wearing thin on my patience.

"Can you just give me a fucking minute to grieve," he sputters.

"I did. It's time you get off your ungrateful ass and return to the land of the living."

He doesn't say another word until I pull up in front of the store and park the Jeep.

"Are you kidding me? Fucking *Hobby Lobby*? Absolutely not!"

Through my laughter, I spit out, "I thought we could pick out some pretty blue yarn to match my eyes." West gives me his signature what-the-fuck expression that I love so much. "Get your ass out of the Jeep. The sooner we finish, the sooner we can go eat."

Minutes later, we're standing in the aisle, surrounded by colorful skeins of yarn, and I'm convinced West is figuring out how to stab me with the needles. I'm going to have to confiscate them in between group sessions for my own safety.

"I think this is a lovely shade of pink. You could do something great with this," I suggest, knowing he hates me even more.

"You're a dick. You can take that lovely shade of pink and shove it up your—" he swallows the rest of his threat when a soccer mom type enters our aisle with a bright smile. His face and neck flush red, and I'm dying to whip out my phone and take a picture. Instead, I give him a cocky smirk, and for the first time today, I see a hint of a smile cross his face.

He's so fucking beautiful when he smiles.

I'm going to spend the rest of the day making sure I get at least two more from him.

WEST

Chapter 23

I ROLL to my right side and reach out blindly in the dark.

When my hand connects with his shoulder, I shake him until he quiets down. Brandt is caught in the throes of a nightmare, no doubt reliving *that* day. I've relived it a hundred times in a hundred different scenarios, but they always end the same —bloody. They end in death.

I don't want to wake him because then he won't go back to sleep. There's no use in both of us being insomniacs. Some nights I can close my eyes easily and manage a couple hours of sleep until they find me in my dreams. Micah, Tommy, and Rosie, they always find me.

Other nights, like tonight, I'm afraid to close my eyes, even for a second. Others I've lost in the past have now worked their way into my worst nightmares, joining the death squad—The Street Sweepers. It's completely illogical, but try telling that to my subconscious mind.

Something outside sets off the motion-sensor floodlight, probably a squirrel or a rabbit, and sends white light shining through the sliding glass door of my bedroom. It spills across Brandt's prone body, illuminating the harsh angles of his face. Casting shadows. The light plays off his nipple, and it calls to me. I don't think I've ever paid attention to them before, but ever since we've begun exploring each other lately, I find myself paying closer attention. I study his face for long minutes, realizing that he's actually quite beautiful. That mole above his lip has become almost lickable.

I've noticed he has a fine ass. If I were looking at it objectively, not belonging to a man or a woman, I could say it was also lickable. Knowing that it belongs to Brandt? Well, it might still be lickable. Smooth and firm, rounded like a bubble, and surprisingly hairless. And now his nipples. They're small, like the size of a dime, and dark brown. I have the strangest urge to run my tongue across it and watch it harden.

But if he wakes up, I'd have to explain myself, and I'm not ready for that—not yet. The wires in my head are crossed, the signals are completely mixed up, and I know that I want him, but I can't admit it because I'm not ready to follow through, and I don't want to be a tease. Brandt deserves better than that, even from me.

Especially from me.

So softly, I drag the pad of my thumb across the tight peak, feeling it pebble beneath my touch. I'm dying to taste it. I want to know if it tastes or feels different from a woman. Would *I* feel different with my lips wrapped around it?

From his nipple, I trace down the valley of his pecs, through the faint dusting of dark hair, over numerous shrapnel scars, some still healing, until my fingertip dips into his warm navel. Brandt stirs, and I'm tempted to continue further south, but with a sigh, I roll away and sit up, maneuvering my leg over the edge of the bed. It only takes minutes to slide the protective sleeve over my stump and attach my prosthesis. As silently as I can, I move to the kitchen in search of a snack.

I'm halfway through a ham sandwich when he sneaks up behind me, making me choke on a mouthful of bread and cold cuts.

"The fuck? Shit, Reaper!"

He just laughs and jumps up on the counter, his legs dangling. "Some team leader you are. I got the jump on you in your own kitchen."

Between the tinnitus and the sound of my chewing amplified inside my head, it's a wonder I could hear at all. I wash down the ham and cheese with a bottle of water, noting and taking pleasure in the fact that Brandt's gaze is on my throat as I swallow.

Does he think that's sexy or some shit?

But before I can run my mouth, he raises his arms above his head and stretches as he yawns, and then his face pulls tight in pain.

"Are you okay?"

"I'm fine. Just the parts where my skin and tissue are missing, the skin pulls too tight when I move the wrong way or bend over too far. It's no big deal." My face isn't convincing him, so he adds, "I guess I'm like a New Jersey highway, full of potholes."

Setting down my water bottle, I move between his parted legs, and his face registers surprise. My fingers follow the same trail they mapped out in bed earlier as I touch a scar above his left pec. "Here?" Brandt nods, his eyes on my every movement. "Here?" I ask as I touch a spot over his ribs. Again, he nods. "What about here?" My fingers brush over a scar on his hip, just above the waistband of his briefs. He's fresh from bed, and it's the only thing he's wearing.

"Yeah," he breathes, sounding like he's lost his voice.

In a move that surprises both of us, I drop my lips to the first scar above his heart and press a soft kiss. His sharp intake of breath spurs me on to the next scar. This time, I let my lips linger over his ribs, like a wet caress. Brandt palms the back of my head, holding me to him, and I swallow, wondering if I have the courage to kiss the next one.

It's not about seducing him. It's about healing him from the outside in, like he's done for me. I want to show him his scars are beautiful, his battle is honorable, and that I don't care what he looks like; he'll always be perfect in my eyes.

Daring myself to continue, my lips sweep over his stomach in an arc as I seek out the scar on his hip. A soft kiss followed by a light sucking kiss, and then I nip it lightly with my teeth and Brandt hisses like I burned him. How far am I going to take this? We both know he has more scars below the waist. Am I going to kiss every one of them? A part of me wants to, but a larger part of me is scared shitless.

This would be a lot easier if it looked like an accident or a favor instead of something I desperately want.

Was Brandt this nervous when he touched me for the first time?

"I've gotta grab something. Meet me back in bed."

He stares for a moment, trying to get a read on me before hopping off the counter and disappearing down the hall. From the linen closet, I grab a bottle of scented lotion some chick left here almost two years ago and join him. He's down on his knees before me before I even have time to process it, unhooking my prosthetic and sliding the sleeve from my thigh. With my legs split wide, his face is right there, just inches from my crotch, and the more I think of it, the harder and thicker it grows. He presses a kiss to the inside of my thigh, and then another, and another, until his lips are right there, teasing the crease between my leg and my groin.

When Brandt stares up at me with those dark blue eyes, my lips part and my breath comes short and fast. It would be so easy to allow him to continue, but I want to make this about him. I want a chance to reciprocate to whatever extent I'm capable of before I chicken out.

"Lay down for me," I rasp.

Slowly, he rises and crawls over me to his pillow. My heart races faster when I straddle his hips and fill my palm with scented lotion.

"Candy cane?" he asks with a smirk. "Can't imagine where that came from."

He knows damn well it's not mine. I rub it between my palms to warm it before placing them on his chest. As I work the lotion into his skin, he shifts subtly, pressing his cock against my ass. It's not overtly obvious, but I can tell he's doing it and I can feel that he's hard. Pretending like I don't notice, I swallow and push back, just barely, but with his eyes burning holes through me, I know he's looking for any sign that I want to take this further.

The muscles in his abs ripple beneath my hands, and with the wet sheen from the lotion, they look... Fuck they look good. He presses harder against me, rolling his hips, and with his gaze still locked on my face, I just can't do it. Despite the darkness, I feel like there's a spotlight shining on me, highlighting all the dubious thoughts running through my head. It's too much pressure.

"Turn over."

I can see he's reluctant, but he obeys and rolls onto his stomach. How did I think this was easier? Now I'm being tempted by the perfect bubble of his tight ass. The swell of it rises from the top of his waistband, the dark valley between his cheeks peeking above the fabric, taunting me. As I knead his shoulders, he continues to rock his hips, probably searching for some friction from the mattress, and all I can think of is sliding my dick through his cheeks.

I did that once with a girl when I was giving her a massage that turned into more. Now I can't get it out of my head. How good it would feel to slide through his crease, feeling his cheeks squeeze my cock. Watching the head of my cock rub over his tight hole. The sight of it would probably make me cum all over his back. The tiny moans of satisfaction he makes are not helping control my dick. It seems to have a mind of its own as it demands my hips push forward, pressing into his cotton-covered crease.

The fucking slut arches his back, making his ass rise up in front of me, like an oasis, like an offering. Is he offering? This is uncharted territory I have no plan of action for. I have no training for this. What the fuck am I supposed to do? My head spins with the what-ifs and I lose focus.

Brandt rolls beneath me, lightning quick, and grabs my shoulders. "Hey, look at me. It's okay," he says, moving his hands to my face. "Come here." And because I can't bear the tension any longer, I bury my face in his chest, and his arms come around my back and squeeze.

"What's going on between us?" My words are muffled against his skin, and I'm locked in his embrace, where I feel safe.

He breathes out and the warm rush of air teases my hair.

"I don't know anymore."

"But something. You feel it, right?"

"Yeah, I feel it. I just don't know what to do about it." He squeezes me tighter.

"Oh God, why is this happening? Why now?" As if my life isn't enough of a shit salad.

"I don't know. I've been doing some thinking, and I guess we have two choices. We can either squash it, or see where it goes."

Why is it easier to discuss difficult things in the darkness when you have your head buried and you don't have to feel the weight of the other person's stare?

Brandt strokes his hand down my back. His words are a soft caress in my ear. A whispered secret. "Even if we squash it, there'll be distance between us, and things might be awkward for a little while, but I think we'll get over it."

He's giving me an out, but I'm not convinced I want it. But like a coward, I'm going to play along. "I think we can go back to being friends afterwards, like nothing happened."

"Nothing *has* happened," he stresses, "but what if we can't? What if it stays awkward because it's still there, still happening between us?"

"You've thought about this, haven't you?" I have to wonder how long he's been keeping it from me, letting these questions run through his head. "Are you saying you want to try?" Just asking the question feels like a thrill, and my stomach rises in a wave of queasiness.

His hand now rests at the base of my skull, his fingers rubbing back-and-forth through the short hairs of my neck. His touch is warm and soft and I want it to go on and on.

"I don't know. I know it feels good. Don't we deserve a little happiness after all the shit we've suffered through? Is that not fair?"

More than fair. But are we just making excuses for our impulsive behavior?

"I don't even know what that means. Does that mean we're gay?"

Brandt chuckles and presses a kiss to the top of my head. "I don't know what it means. Whatever you want it to mean, I guess. Whatever you feel comfortable saying about yourself." Then he sighs. "I don't really fucking care one way or the other. Labels are bullshit. The only thing I care about is you."

"But if we kiss and do butt stuff–"

He laughs louder this time, like a bark. "Butt stuff sounds pretty gay to me, but you can call it what you want."

"Fuck off," I say without heat, finally raising my head to look at him.

"Don't you mean fuck you, or fuck me?"

I'm so nervous, I can barely swallow, and my expression loses all traces of humor. "Are you sure this is what you want?"

I watch his throat slide, and I can tell he's just as nervous. "I'm sure. I just want you to be sure."

I'm not fucking sure of anything, besides my impressive hard-on and the relentless need to cum that's been clawing at me for hours. But I can finally admit to myself that it's not just a-hand-is-a-hand that's making my dick rock-hard. It's Brandt. I'm hard *for him*. In fact, I'm ready to throw twelve years of friendship right out the window just to feel his hand on my cock again. Or his mouth. What I wouldn't give to feel his mouth right now.

"So we're doing this?"

He just chuffs, laughing softly on an exhale of breath. "Why do you make it sound like you're executing a strategy?"

I feel like a fucking ass, and I hope my face isn't red. "Because I have no idea what I'm fucking doing." Maybe we should just go for it, balls to the wall, and push past the awkward part so we can get to the feel-good stuff faster. When I'm thinking with the head of my dick and not my actual head, I don't care about things like consequences and nerves, I'm just focused on the pleasure.

"Do you trust me?"

With my fucking life. "Should I? How much do you know about gay sex?"

He laughs again. At least we're having fun. "Just follow my lead."

Brandt scoots up so that he's half-reclined, and he urges me to sit up. I scoot back so that our cocks are aligned, and he tugs my sweats down far enough to expose my cock. It bounces up and slaps my stomach, and there's no way my face isn't bright red this time. He takes it as a compliment and smiles, looking ridiculously hot with his glistening abs and bed head.

His grin turns wicked as he works his briefs down his hips and frees his cock. It's as hard as mine, and the tip is wet. Brandt grabs the lotion and squirts a fat dollop in his palm. The sweet smell of peppermint candy taints the air and his hands are cold as he grips our shafts together in his slippery fist. It feels like the sweetest torture as he begins a slow glide down to the base and back up again.

"*Ungh,*" I breathe, feeling heat gather in my gut. "I didn't know this was a thing." My breath becomes shallow as I watch him stroke us. "Should I ask how you know?"

His chuckle morphs into a hiss. "Watch us together."

His voice sounds as raw as my nerves, but I watch, and the sight of our smushed-together cockheads, both glossy and dark red, disappearing into his fist is blowing my mind. The pressure feels incredible.

My gaze strays to his dark tight nipples, to the rapid rise and fall of his chest, his half-healed scars and his tats. I've seen his body a thousand times, and yet it feels as if I'm seeing it for the first time. Seeing him through the eyes of a lover instead of a friend, and I don't know how or why, but it's fucking working for me on every level.

"I'm close," I breathe in a husky voice. The wet squelching sounds coming from the suction of his fist sound like the filthiest porno and I can feel my balls draw up tight, ready to spill.

"Me...too," he pants.

I rock my hips, fucking into his tight grip, and when his fist closes over our heads again on the next upstroke, I lose it and shoot thick white ropes over his knuckles.

"God, yeah." I'm sweating and breathing like I ran a damn marathon. "Come with me, Reaper."

Brandt looks into my eyes and holds my gaze as he comes, a satisfied sigh crawling from his throat. He continues to stare at me as he licks his knuckles clean, and he smirks like a kitten with a bowl of cream. Fuck, I wasn't expecting that, but damn, it's hot.

He's hot.

And he's fucking mine.

BRANET — Chapter 24

WHEN I COME out of the shower, the bed is empty.

I peek through the curtains, but he's not out on the deck, either, nor is he in the kitchen, and the TV is turned off in the living room.

What the fuck?

I don't know where else to look, and fear makes my heartbeat spike. Out of desperation, I wrench open the front door, and there he is, in the driveway, sprawled out across the hood of his Jeep. A curl of white smoke escapes from his nostrils. He's smoking my last blunt.

"Jesus Christ, you just took ten years off my life."

He blows out the smoke in a lazy stream, and his eyes water. "Payback's a bitch for the kitchen earlier."

He's right. Now we're even. "How did you even get up here?"

"Upper body strength," he says with a half smirk. "I wanted to watch the sunrise. I figured since we were already awake…" West finishes with a shrug.

I jump up on the hood and prop my back against the windshield, crossing my legs at the ankles. "Pass." West passes it to me and I suck a long hit of the smooth, stinky sweetness into my lungs. Immediately, my anxiety melts away like chocolate left out in the heat.

As we watch the sun rise above the horizon, neither of us speaks. I don't know where West is, but I'm lost in my head, back in the bed we shared less than an hour ago. The first time I ever slept with a girl, my mind was blown. It was incomparable to the gratification my right hand provided. Sinking into her tight heat, getting lost in her warm body, I didn't think anything could beat that.

But West… fuck, I'm ruined for anyone else. I felt almost high from the excitement. My pleasure and lust were magnified by a hundred. Comparing what I felt with him to being with women was like comparing fighter jets to Christmas trees. They had absolutely nothing in common.

"How's your skin feel?"

"Better. Thanks for the lotion. I need to do better at keeping my skin soft while I'm healing."

I pass it back to him and he sucks it between his lips. "We're a pair, aren't we?"

"Don't start your pity party bullshit. I don't want to be

invited. We're a lot better off than everyone else we knew. We have a lot to be thankful for."

"Just sitting out here thinking." He blows up the smoke, trying and failing at perfectly shaped rings. "I don't know what to do with myself anymore. The Army doesn't want me. The rest of society probably doesn't either."

"That's not true at all, and you know it. You have a clean slate from here on out. Anything you can dream up, you can do."

"Christ, you sound like a recruiting officer. I think I read that on a poster somewhere."

He takes the last hit and crushes the roach on the sole of his boot before flicking it into the grass.

"So what is it you want to do? What does Weston Wardell want to be when he grows up?"

West chuckles. "I don't know. I haven't given it much thought." He turns on his side, facing me. "What does Brandt Aguilar want to be when he grows up?"

My lips stretch into a grin. "I should've become a fucking mailman like my mother wanted."

"Talk about trauma and PTSD. They have the highest suicide rate of any job."

"Figures. They have to deal with people's mothers all day, complaining about the inflation of stamps and lost packages." I turn on my side to mirror his pose. "My mother once mailed me a box of cookies in a care package. I never got it. A friend of mine I grew up with emailed me and told me that my mother caused a huge scene at the post office."

West's shoulders shake with silent laughter. "I've met your

mother. It doesn't surprise me at all." I had wandered outside without a shirt in my rush to find him, and now the early morning chill raises goosebumps on my skin. West traces a tat on my biceps, and between his touch and the chilly air, I shiver.

"I used to believe in something. Something greater than me."

Didn't we all? "What's that old saying? If you don't stand for something you'll fall for anything."

"Yeah, well, that's just it. The same things I used to stand for are the things I fell for. Honor, God, country—I've seen evidence there is no God. The only thing I believe in is us. You and me. Things I can touch, see, and feel."

It feels good hearing I made his shortlist, but I'm concerned he's headed for a dark place. "So you're saying you regret it? You regret your years of service?"

West blows out a frustrated sigh. "I'm not saying I regret it. The villages we saved, the people we freed. I'll never regret saving a life, no matter what country they're citizens of. What I regret is losing our team. I'm not saying the lives we saved are more important than the lives we lost. What I'm saying is, they matter more to *me*."

He scoots closer and lays his head on my chest, and my fingers automatically bury in his hair. "We're all just faceless, nameless, disposable, and replaceable casualties to the higher-ups who plan these missions. It isn't until we die that they learn our name and our rank, and see a picture of our faces for the first time. Maybe they experience a twinge of regret for their actions and their choices; maybe they don't. I'll bet anything they would do it all over again if they had to choose, as long as the mission was classified as a success. They wouldn't change a goddamn thing."

I press a kiss to his head. "But we knew that going into it, when we enlisted."

"I know, but sometimes it hits home a little harder." He turns his head to stare up at me, and a small, sad smile tugs at the corners of his mouth. "Feel better now? Now that I've proven that I still have a conscience and a shred of patriotism?"

A snort chuffs from my nose. "I don't give a fuck about your patriotism or your conscience. I just needed to know you were still in there somewhere. My West."

"Yours, huh?" But he's smiling wider now when he says it, and I know he loves the way it sounds.

"You were always mine. My best friend, my wingman, my partner in everything. Now you're just *more* mine." He lays his head back down, and an easy laugh falls from his lips. "What?"

"Nothing, I just think it's funny. I signed up for the Army before I even graduated high school. I was eighteen—so cocky and full of confidence. I thought I could take on the world. I couldn't wait to get started with the rest of my life, to go out there and blow shit up and get the bad guys. I trained hard, decided I was going to avoid the marriage trap like other soldiers I saw in the barracks, and I had my sights set on becoming a Ranger. Remember when we got called up for our first tour? Man, I was so excited. It was all I could talk about for weeks. We got over to the sandbox, and I thought, this isn't so bad, and after a year they sent us home. I hit the bar on the weekends, never took the same girl home twice, and I had a rule about not sleeping over."

I remember his list of rules for remaining a bachelor, a top-tier soldier on the fast track to promotion. He was adamant I follow the same rules.

"Then we got called up for our second tour, and I was so gung ho. I finally got promoted to team leader, and damn, we had the best fucking team out there. And then this shit happens. Now, here I am, my leg is gone, my career is over, and I couldn't pay a girl to sleep with a one-legged soldier. The funniest part is, I'm contemplating having a sexual relationship with my best friend." He shakes his head and laughs. "I just didn't see myself here."

Well, now I feel like a sack of fucking pity. Does he regret what we did? Am I his consolation prize because he thinks no one else will have him? "Is that so bad?"

He traces my nipple and then rolls it between his fingers. "Not the part about sleeping with my best friend, no. The rest of it, yeah, it sucks. It sucks hard."

"You're a real glass half-empty kind of guy, aren't you? You know what's around the corner? Any fucking thing you want. You want to join the police force and become a detective and work the narcotics squad? Do it. You want to apply to the FBI or customs? Do it. Maybe you want to go into private security. Hell, I don't know, why don't you go be a greeter at Walmart? They're always hiring."

"And I can do all of that with one leg, huh?"

"I don't see why not. Stop your bitching and start thinking about your future. Why do I gotta do all the thinking for you?"

"I don't need you to do a fucking thing for me," he laughs and flicks my nipple.

It stings from the cold and I flinch and rub my chest. "Sure you do. You need me to wipe your ass for you, too."

He's laughing now, so hard he can barely spit the words out. "Stay away from my ass. It's not up for grabs."

"Oh, so you're telling me you're a top then?"

"I don't know what the fuck I am. I'm just horny. I have no idea how it all works."

Despite his thin T-shirt, he shivers, and I wrap my arms around him and rub up and down his back, hoping to warm him up. "I realize neither of us knows much about gay sex, but how hard can it be? It's pretty much the same thing, right?" This conversation is almost surreal, and just as absurd as most of our conversations.

"I mean, yeah, except for the fact that we both have a dick. So who takes it first?"

I can't tell if he's fucking with me or if he's serious. "Doesn't really matter to me. I'm open to try anything with you."

West raises up on his elbow and searches my face. "Yeah, but what if you don't like it? Does that mean we're not gonna— we won't be–"

"Is that what you're worried about? That I won't like it and I won't want to be with you? And I'll call the whole thing off?" Is he fucking serious? My expression softens, and I grip his chin. "To be honest, because I'll always be honest with you, it doesn't matter if I like it or not. There're other ways we can be together that are satisfying. The point is, as long as we're together, the logistics don't matter." He doesn't look like he believes me and rolls his eyes. I want to convince him that I'm all in. "But to put it more romantically, there's no way being inside of you isn't going to feel good, and vice versa."

His eyes widen slightly as he considers that, possibly based on how good what we did earlier felt. He must believe me because he leans in, and I swear he's about to kiss me, and I close my eyes, lick my lips, but after a moment, I feel nothing but the kiss of the cool air. When I open my eyes, I'm not disappointed. Well, only slightly. He's grinning at me like a fucking tease, and I can't figure out if he faked me out on purpose or chickened out at the last moment, but either way, I don't fucking care, because he's smiling, and he's hot as fuck, and apparently, he's willing to try butt stuff with me.

West walks his fingers down my chest, down my stomach, and draws circles around my navel. My gut churns with anticipation.

"I've wondered about myself a few times," I admit. "I've looked at guys we served with and thought, damn, what a magnificent body. But I've never gotten hard from looking at them. My thoughts sometimes bordered on sexual, wondering what their dicks looked like, but I guess I never crossed the line." When he remains silent, I prod him. "What about you?"

"Nope. Never." *Fucking Dick, hanging me out to dry.* "Just you. The thing is, I have no fucking clue what to do with you." He laughs at himself. "I mean, if you were a woman..."

He dips his finger into my belly button, and it's an odd oversensitive feeling that makes me want to squirm. I grab his hands and place them over my pecs. "Pretend I am. Touch me, Professor."

"Fuck," he whispers, rubbing his hands over my chest, teasing my nipples into hard points.

"Yeah," I groan with pleasure, "feels so good." His hands are warm on my cold skin. His touch is solid.

"You like that?" He purrs, and I can hear the rumble underlying his voice. He's getting turned on while turning me on. I watch his hands travel over my body with hooded eyes. "All this strength makes me wonder what you could do to me," he admits, squeezing my biceps.

"What do you want me to do to you?" My voice is low and full of gravel. He's fucking killing me with his touch and his words and the promise of more.

West looks up into my eyes, and I watch his throat slide before he licks his lips. "I want you to wreck me. I want you to make me forget everything but you."

WEST

Chapter 25

"ARE you gonna blow that cucumber, or eat it?"

Brandt glances up and laughs. "Maybe I'm going to use it on you." He places it in the shopping cart and moves on to the cantaloupe.

I was a decorated Sergeant First Class in the United States Army. I've led teams of men and women on dangerous missions. I lost my fucking leg and recovered. But even I don't have balls big enough to stand here and flirt and trade gay sex jokes in the middle of the produce aisle.

I'm not there *yet*.

"What's with you today?" he asks, nudging me. "You're not in blackout mode, but something's definitely off."

Blackout mode is what he calls my black moods. "It feels so

surreal to be shopping for peanut butter and jelly after what we've been through. Everything here is so calm and clean and quiet. There are no terrorists with guns, no soldiers, no refugees, or hostages screaming in a foreign language. The difference in realities is jarring. Sometimes it hits me out of nowhere."

He places the cantaloupe in the cart and moves on to the frozen foods. "It can be hard on your psyche to switch from crisis mode to peacefulness. Most soldiers who come home have the same problem adjusting to life again. We aren't the only ones. Not by a long shot. In fact, it would be weird if it wasn't a struggle."

That's Brandt, always cosigning my shit. Always making it safe for me to feel whatever fucked up thing I'm feeling. I could tell him I want to dye my skin purple and he would tell me how it's a valid expression of my inner self or some crap. I grab a box of frozen pizza and throw it in the cart.

"This life feels so mundane. I'm used to having a purpose and a mission. Save the people, secure the village. I don't know what to do with myself anymore. I have no purpose, no mission, no *value*. Every day is the same—laundry, cooking, cleaning, and errands. What is the point of it all? What's the endgame?"

His words from last week come back to me, when we were laid out over the hood of my Jeep, and he asked me what I wanted to be when I grew up. He told me I could be anything if I could only dream it. It's a bunch of fucking bullshit, if you ask me, but there has to be *something* I can do.

"Maybe our purpose is to just be happy. Have you thought about that?"

He's asking the guy who doesn't believe he deserves happiness? Yeah, I've fucking thought about it. "Maybe, but is that enough?"

"It is for me."

Maybe it is, at least for him, but I have to serve in some way. I have to give back, to atone for the many lives affected because I failed as a leader. I have a penance to pay, and it might be a very long time before *just being happy* is enough for me.

"Maybe I could volunteer at BALLS, like Riggs does."

Brandt points at me with a loaf of French bread. "I think that's an excellent idea."

I could help out in the weight room, or even the pool. I've become pretty good at—there's a loud crash two aisles over, and the explosion of sound makes my heart stop. My lungs seize up, and the blood in my veins thickens like sludge, too thick to flow. My vision turns white and orange, like a fiery blast and the words '*frag out*' scream through my ears and ricochet around my head.

"Hey, it's okay, I've got you."

Brandt wraps his arm around my shoulders, and I panic and push him. Hard. He stumbles into a display of stacked boxes of donuts, and they crash to the floor along with the thin hold I have on my sanity. I run. Down the aisle, past the registers, through the automatic doors, and out into the parking lot, where a car lays on its horn, narrowly missing me.

It speeds by as the driver curses out the window, and then Brandt is there. He approaches me like I'm a wounded animal. Feral. Scared. Out of my ever-loving-fucking-mind. The sun is too bright, people are staring at me like there's something wrong with me, and there is. I don't belong in this world. I don't belong anywhere anymore. My heartbeat starts up again, too fast and hard, pounding away at my chest like a jackhammer. I'm covered with a cold sweat. The tinnitus is ringing loud in my ear, too loud. And then the vertigo gets hold of me, and I fall flat on my ass.

Brandt crouches down beside me, not touching me, but close. He speaks in a low, soft tone. "Wes, it's me, Brandt. Look at me."

I do. I look at him. He becomes the center of my focus. His deep blue eyes, the mole above his upper lip. My heartbeat slows. The ringing lessens. The dizziness subsides. And I take a deep breath. He counts it out.

"Breathe in. One…two…three. Hold it. Four…five…six. Breathe out. Seven…eight…nine…ten." Cautiously, he slips his hand in mine and squeezes. Anchoring me to the present, anchoring me to him.

I swipe the sweat rolling into my eyes with the back of my hand and blurt out the first thing that comes to mind. "What about the food?"

Brandt chuckles. "Doesn't matter. We'll order a pizza. Come on, let me take you home."

Still dazed and shell-shocked, I let him haul me up and lead me to the Jeep, but I'm pissed. And I'm becoming angrier with each passing second. Brandt is watching me more than he's watching the road, and his worry for me is also pissing me off. How long is he going to sit there and observe me in silence, trying to figure out how to broach the subject?

"What?" I snap.

"Why are you so angry?"

"Fuck you."

"Not today, thanks. Tell me why you're angry."

It takes me a minute to realize he made a sex joke. At the worst goddamn possible moment, he's talking about sex. I don't know whether to hit him or laugh. Maybe that's the point.

"I asked you a ques–"

"I don't know!" My voice is loud in the silent interior. No radio, just road noise, and my damn temper. We drive six more miles in silence before I crack. "I'm disappointed in myself. I'm embarrassed as fuck. And I'm tired of dealing with the fallout of what happened. The fucking side effects from the TBI, the leg and all its learning curves, endless therapies. I'm just fucking tired."

Brandt nods his head and it's not until we make the turn off for the cabin, that he finally speaks. "Why are you disappointed in yourself?"

"I thought I could handle it better. Instead, I have a fucking panic attack because someone dropped a tin of cookies in the grocery store."

The Jeep bounces along the pitted dirt road that leads up to the house, and Brandt turns off the ignition, but doesn't move to get out. "So what? So the fuck what? You had a flashback, a panic attack. Big fucking deal. I've seen housewives have panic attacks over their dog pissing on the carpet. You've got one leg, a TBI, and PTSD. You've probably got some other shit going on, and not all of it is from the blast. I've known you for twelve years; some of your issues run real deep, trust me."

Snarky fucking asshole.

Brandt gives me side-eye, checking to see if his joke landed appropriately. "I have PTSD. I've got unresolved anger issues. I have depression. I have scarring all over my body. I've lost hearing in one ear. I'm completely fucking disillusioned, and I've got no future lined up. Those people at the grocery store? They're at the bottom of my fucking list of problems, West. I don't give a damn what they think of me. I almost died for them, so the least they can do is turn a blind eye when I'm having a bad moment. Otherwise, they can fuck right off." He grabs my hand and laces our fingers together, squeezing my knuckles with his. "You with me?"

I have to fight back the rush of hot tears to my eyes. I absolutely refuse to fall apart right now. "Yeah, Reaper, I'm with you." I can barely spit the words out through my broken, gravelly voice, a dead giveaway that I'm about to cry. Like the best friend he is, he pretends not to notice.

"You owe me a pizza."

When I've got my eyes under control, I glance at him and he's wearing that smirk, the one that lately makes me want to kiss his lips. "It's a date."

"Hey, one other thing."

I can't take anymore of his pep-squad talk, it's all I can do not to fall apart. "What?"

"You ran."

"Yeah, I was having a fucking moment. I was panicked. I ran and–"

"No, you *ran*."

I don't get it. What's he trying to tell me? And then, like a ton of bricks, it hits me. I fucking *ran* on my prosthetic leg. I ran for the first time in months. He sees when it dawns on me, and he grins like a motherfucker.

"I ran!"

"Riggs is going to be so proud. That, and one more support group ought to get you a brand new leg."

My black mood gives a whole new meaning to the word disassociation. I feel completely detached—from my surroundings, from my thoughts, from life. After Brandt dragged me to support group, where I endured the Bitches who Stitch for sixty fucking long-ass minutes, listening to Stiles gripe and moan about job hunting, hearing Jax drone on and on about his ex, and the cherry on the shit sundae? Thirty minutes of McCormick whining that he can't find a date, not even if he fucking paid them.

Is that what I have to look forward to? Paid escorts? Will I have to tip them extra to stomach my stump?

I'm buried beneath the covers in my bed, and it seems like a metaphor for my life. That's where it all started to spiral: when I was buried under the rubble. Now I'm buried under the weight of the repercussions of that day. I haven't eaten, I haven't gotten up to take a piss, and I haven't showered. And to be honest, I can smell myself. The heat my body is producing under the covers is like a Dutch oven, making my BO smell worse than it is. Or maybe it really is that bad, I don't know, and I don't fucking care. My stomach growls and a pang of hunger tightens my gut. I ignore it, like I've been ignoring it for the last four hours.

The mattress shifts, and Brandt cuddles right up to me like a koala hugging a tree.

"Are you hungry? I can make you something to eat." ... "Can I get you some Tylenol?" ... "How about a shower?" ...

I can't answer. It would only lead to a conversation that I have no energy for.

"Wes, I know you're in there, somewhere. I just need…I need proof of life."

Proof of life. I promised him. I promised him I would check in with him every day, and by God, he's held me to it. "I'm here." My voice is muffled by the covers.

"Just for today, Wes. We've just got to get through today. Tomorrow doesn't matter. Not yet. Can you hang on for today?"

"Yeah," I croak. And then he's rustling the covers, making the mattress bounce under his weight, and next thing I know, his solid body is nestled up against mine under the blanket, and he's tangling his cold feet with mine, shocking me out of my stupor for the first time in hours. "Fuck, get some socks on!"

"I'm waiting for you to knit me some."

Then he's going to be waiting until his feet freeze and fall off. I'm officially the world's worst knitter. "What are you doing?"

"If you won't come out, then I'm coming to you. You want to stay buried under these covers all day? Fine with me. I just want to hold you."

He rubs his cold, bare feet over the hair on my leg, and I'm dying to fucking kick him, for touching me with his icy soles, and for smothering me with concern. Why can't he just go away and let me be miserable? Why does he have to care?

"So," he runs the tip of his finger down the nape of my neck, making the fine hairs stand at attention. "I was watching this documentary on the History channel, and they said the Leopard is a better tank than the Abrams because it runs off diesel instead of jet fuel. Can you believe that?"

"That's fucking bullshit!" I kick the covers off and roll to face him, propping up on my elbow. The absurdity of what he's saying has me fired up in a hot second. "The Leopard is shit. The Abrams has superior mobility, technology, and firepower! What kind of shitty show were you watching?"

Brandt grins, looking completely satisfied with himself. "Gotcha."

I straddle my leg over his waist and pin his shoulders to the mattress. "Say it! Say the Abrams M1A2 is the superior tank."

He's laughing too hard to say it. His full peach lips with that damn beauty mark above them are stretched wide on his square jaw. His deep blue eyes are twinkling with mirth, framed by thick dark lashes so long they look almost absurdly feminine on him.

My chest expands with warmth and my stomach churns with heat, not sexual heat, but with feeling. The fugue fog I was in has dissipated, and all of my senses are coming back online at once, and I can't focus on anything but how beautiful he is when he laughs, and that he lied about a goddamn tank to get me to wake up out of my stupor because he fucking cares so much.

I'm having a spiritual awakening at the oddest time, but not about God. About Brandt. Brandt is my religion. He's the only idol I want to kneel for and worship. The only one deserving of my reverence and respect. He's earned my trust and my undying loyalty, and slowly but surely, he's beginning to earn my love.

"Say it," I insist, keeping him pinned down.

"I don't know, the Russian T14 might give it a run for its money," he sputters through his gut-wrenching hilarity.

Tears have gathered in his eyes from laughing so hard, and I can't hold back another moment. I dip down and kiss his mouth. Just a quick peck on his lips, but it's enough to make him sober immediately. His eyes, wet now, become wide with shock, and he stares up at me like I've grown two heads. I swallow, feeling apprehensive and awkward, and second-guessing my impulse. I pushed him too far.

Or not.

Brandt's fingers grasp my head, tangling with my hair, and he pulls me back down to him. This time, when our lips meet, it's not quick, and it's definitely not a chaste peck. His mouth opens for me and my tongue tangles with his in a slow, explorative glide that sends shivers through my gut and makes my balls tighten. His mouth feels warm and velvety, and I can taste the sweetness of the soda he was drinking.

He laps at my tongue, stroking it, suckling at it, like he would the head of my cock, which, of course, makes it hard as a fucking rock. And he feels that, too, because it's pressing against his—which is equally as hard—and he rocks his hips against mine, pushing them together. The delicious pressure makes my body light up with need and I push back, seeking more friction.

The cotton covering my shaft rubs roughly over my sensitive skin, adding to the jumble of sensations igniting my libido.

The kiss goes on and on, and I never want it to end. Parting my mouth from his would be a loss I can't bear. Delving deeper, I stroke the walls of his cheeks, gloss over his teeth, even map the roof of his palate. His stubble rubs my face raw, but I welcome the burn. He laughs into my mouth, probably thinking I'm the world's worst kisser.

It's okay, let him. I plan to do this more than just once. Anything that feels this good, I plan to do every day for the rest of my life—or as long as he'll let me. His kiss is like a drug, like a shot of morphine or an antidepressant that makes all the endorphins in my body light up like fireworks on the Fourth of July. I feel alive. I feel good. No, *great*.

Brandt's kiss is giving me life.

It doesn't feel awkward to be kissing a man. At least, not *this* man. It just feels right. As good and safe and nurturing as his hugs. As thrilling and all-consuming as his touch. My head is spinning like I'm high. My stomach is riding a wave of lust, and I want to come, but that would mean I'd have to let go of his lips, which I'm not willing to do.

Ever.

He's gasping for breath, panting like he's just run a marathon. I've partnered with him on 5K PT runs in training, and he never even sounded winded, but my kiss has stolen his breath. He's tearing my hair apart, tugging at it, making a rat's nest of it, and then his hands are on my back, scratching up my skin, tracing the vertebrae in my spine, digging into my ribs as he hangs on for dear life.

Nothing has ever felt this good. No orgasm, no drug, no kill, or victory or promotion or medal. *Nothing.*

Shit, I might even come, just from the friction of his shaft rubbing against mine as we kiss. How fucking prepubescent.

Apparently, he's just as close because he reaches between us to grasp my cock and pull it free from my pants, and then he does the same to his, fisting them together in his rough grip. Brandt strokes our shafts furiously without ever breaking the kiss. All too soon I'm coming over his knuckles, soaking his stomach and mine, and he joins me with a shout that I capture and swallow with my mouth.

I come down from my high slowly, my head still spinning, my heart thundering, and even my tinnitus is kicking up, or is that just the sound of my blood rushing through my veins? Even after all that, I'm scared to look into his eyes. It's all still so new, this sexual exploration between us, and I'm always afraid I'm going to see regret when I look at his face afterward.

But when I do look, there's not a trace of regret. Brandt looks blissed out. His hair is a wreck, the short ends sticking out in every direction. His lips are red and swollen and glossy. He's smiling like a doofus and my heart soars, along with my ego. I did that. I put that goofy smile on his face. My kiss did that. *And my dick.*

"Fuck, where did you learn to kiss like that?"

"Donna McPherson," he teases, recalling the girl we competed over years ago, when we were first stationed at Bragg.

I crack up with laughter, knowing he's fucking with me. "I hope someday I get to thank her."

His expression becomes serious. "That was some kiss." His

gaze traces my lips, probably as kiss-swollen as his. "Possibly the best kiss of my life."

"Possibly?"

"Maybe if you'd brushed your teeth today, it would have ranked above Donna."

Silent laughter shakes my chest and shoulders, and I grin. He is such a sarcastic fucker. And so damn manipulative. He got me out of bed with an argument about a tank, and now he's getting me to participate in life, brushing and showering, by taunting me with past hookups.

God only knows what he's going to do to make me eat.

HE USED to complain that I hovered like a CH 47 Chinook, fussing over him, trailing after him through every room in the house, offering to wipe his ass, prepare his food, and help him dress.

Oh, how the tables have turned.

I wander into the bathroom to brush my teeth, and he nudges me aside to grab his toothbrush. Earlier, I walked down to the mailbox, and when I returned to the house, he was sitting on the front porch, waiting for me. He's hovering or trailing, or fussing. But you'll never hear me complain. I want him close. As close as he can get.

"My mother wants us to come for a visit."

"Us?" He spits and rinses, then dries his hands on the towel. "What's this *us*? She wants *you* to come visit."

"No, she said *us*."

"What the fuck for?"

"Because we've been gone for seven months? And we've been home for weeks and she hasn't seen us."

"Well, you should definitely go."

Time to play the sympathy card. "You would make me go alone?"

"Ain't no fucking way I'm going to visit your mother."

"West, don't be like that."

"Be like what? It's gonna be awkward as fuck, and I don't wanna sit through it. Is she gonna cry over my fucking leg?"

If he could only see what his face looks like, like a toddler throwing a tantrum. It's fucking hilarious. "Yeah," I laugh, "she's gonna cry over your leg, and my scars and my lost hearing. And then she's going to nag us about not having jobs and your physical therapy. Then she'll make us lunch, pat us on the back, and send us on our way for another six months."

"Six months?! If I have to put up with her fucking tears, that should at least buy me a whole year."

I lean against the door jamb, grinning, because I find him absolutely hilarious and absurd, and adorable. "So you're going then?"

"You know what? You still owe me for making me join the Bitches with Stitches. You're skating on thin ice. You better watch it." He pushes past me, purposely throwing his weight into my shoulder, and yanks open his dresser drawer. "You're asking a whole lot. Too much!"

Taking a seat on the bed behind him, I've got a spectacular view of his ass as he's bent over the drawer. So firm and round. I'd like to–

"Are you checking out my ass?"

He's standing there, holding a pair of jeans with a disbelieving expression on his face. "Maybe."

"Well, quit. It's fucking weird." But he's smiling, so I know he doesn't mean it.

"Speaking of social engagements–"

"No," he insists as he leans his back against the dresser to support his weight as he struggles to put the jeans on. "I'm not seeing anyone else. I'm not playing nicey-nice. No more. Your mother is the limit." When I don't elaborate, he gets antsy. "What?"

"Some of the guys from Bragg want to get together, catch up, like old times. They've been texting me."

"Fuck no." I admire his skills as he sits on the edge of the bed to put his boots on. Occupational therapy has taught him a lot, but also he's getting the hang of it, figuring out how to achieve what he needs and solve his own problems. Like the team leader he is.

"West, it's just a barbecue."

"It's not just a barbecue. It used to be a barbecue. The guys would come over, we'd hang out on the deck, grill, soak in the hot tub, go fishing. It's not a barbecue anymore."

I bend down to grab his other boot so he doesn't have to. "Then what is it?"

"It's a fucking interrogation. Rubbernecking on the freeway in rush hour traffic. They all want to come over and take a look at my leg, ask me a bunch of nosy-ass questions. No thanks."

"We haven't seen these guys in almost a year. They were our friends, West. Don't you think they're concerned about you?"

"They used to be my friends. I mean, it's common not to keep in contact during deployment. But now that we're home? Fuck, we're retired. What do I have in common with these guys anymore? I live in a different world. They just don't get it."

He bends over to tie his boot, and then props his prosthetic in my lap, so I'll tie it for him. I know it's difficult for him to reach because that leg doesn't bend. When he gets his new leg next week, he'll be capable of doing so much more for himself.

"So the notion of brotherhood and dying for your brother, serving for your brother, that's all well and good as long as you're enlisted, but once you become a civilian, it's out the window?"

"That's a cheap shot."

"But that's what you're saying."

He blows out a frustrated breath. "What I'm saying is, because they used to be my friends, I don't want their pity, and I don't want to feel like a bug under a microscope. Nobody wants to feel that way, Reaper. Especially not from people who used to respect them."

Placing my hand on what's left of his knee, I look into his doubtful eyes. "Why don't you just trust in me and leave everything to me? I know how you feel. Have I ever let you down?"

His throat slides, and he covers my hand with his. "Never once in all our years together." The poignancy of the moment makes me pause, and I can feel my chest warming. I'm dying to kiss him again, like he kissed me last night. He blew my fucking mind with that kiss. I lean in, hoping he'll meet me halfway, but instead, he removes my hand from his knee.

"It's gonna take a lot more than a knitted pair of socks to make up for all this, just so you know. I'm keeping score." And then he does meet me halfway, but it's not the cock-hardening kiss I'm hoping for. Just a sweet touch of his lips on mine.

It's not enough. Not nearly enough. It's never going to be enough.

The heat and smoke coming off the grill smells like charred meat and it's making my mouth water. I grab two beers out of the cooler and pop the tops off, handing one to West.

"Let's have a toast while we wait for the guys to show." He accepts it and taps it against my bottle. "Here's to hoping this barbecue goes a lot smoother than the visit with my mother did."

West scoffs, a sarcastic little fragment of a laugh. He's remembering the disastrous luncheon, where my mother definitely broke down in tears over his leg and his future, and then worked herself into a near panic attack over the state of *my* body and future. I can't even tally how much I owe him for that, for sticking by my side, and treating my mother with kindness.

An hour later, the deck is packed with old friends and some new ones. Anytime guys from base get together, they're always going to drag along stragglers, anyone who was left behind without plans, and they're always welcome. And then you have the Base Bunnies, or Tag Chasers, the guys' temporary girlfriends. West sits in the corner with his head down, trying to avoid making conversation. I've overheard him dodge a few questions already, and the more alcohol these guys consume, the looser their tongues become.

Adrian Milieu, a guy from my old barracks, sits down next to West. I've got my eyes on them, listening in on the conversation as I flip burgers.

"What's that?" Adrian asks.

West is flipping a coin. He catches it and traces the eagle with his fingertips. "Challenge coin."

They're a dime a dozen. We earn challenge coins for all kinds of things—advancement in rank, completing challenges, and meeting goals. I squint, trying to make out which one he's holding. Fuck, he must have pulled that from his wallet. It belonged to Micah.

"What's it stand for, freedom?" I don't know if Adrian is trying to be clever, or if he's just drunk, but he's pissing me off because he's pissing West off.

"Freedom," West scoffs, like the notion is absurd. "Fuck freedom. We're only free to an extent. It could be taken from us at any time. It stands for brotherhood." West stares Adrian down with a look so cold it could ice his beer. "Brotherhood means more to me than freedom. Brotherhood could make me cross an ocean, crawl through a desert, or fight in a war I don't believe in." His icy gaze tracks me and locks on. "Brotherhood is what makes me choose life every day when I would rather not.

It's a powerful motivator." He returns his gaze to Adrian. "And it's something that can never be taken from me."

Another tweedle-dumb must have overheard because he chooses an excellent conversation starter. "Yo, the eighty-second is getting deployed. It's just a matter of days before we get our orders."

Enough is enough. I tap the metal spatula against the side of the grill to get everyone's attention. "Hey, everybody listen up. We've got two rules here if you want to stay. First rule, we don't talk about deployment. What happens in the desert, stays in the desert." I let my eyes roam over each man and woman in attendance, so they know I'm speaking to them directly.

"What's the second rule," tweedle-dumb asks.

"The second rule is that nobody is allowed to tell West how good he still looks. It goes to his head," I say with a laugh, trying to lighten the mood.

As predicted, everyone starts to rip on West good-naturedly, telling him how ugly he is, what terrible aim he has with a gun, and that he couldn't blow up the broadside of a barn with a live grenade.

He smiles at me gratefully, and I breathe a sigh of relief that I made the right call. West needs this. He needs some time with these guys, to connect socially, to feel a part of again, to feel connected to the life he used to live, to the man he used to be. I know that man is still in there, somewhere, buried beneath the debris, lost in the dark. But I'm gonna find him, and I'm gonna carry him out on my shoulders if I have to because giving up on West isn't an option. In fact, I'm sure it's the only reason I'm still alive.

Aaron Schumer's loud voice cuts through my thoughts. "Remember the parties we used to have here? Man, this place brings back some memories."

When Adrian vacates his seat, I steal it. "You good?"

"When these people clear out, promise me we can spend some time out here alone, just me and you."

Does he mean alone, as friends, talking? Or does he mean alone in the hot tub, doing... other stuff? Either way, I'm dying to find out, and suddenly I want to kick everyone to the curb so we can get on with our night.

"I promise. Just me and you. Let me get you a burger."

Throughout the party, I can feel his eyes on me, following me from the grill to the kitchen, as I take out the trash, refill the cooler, and when a couple of girls surround me wanting to catch up, I can feel his gaze burning a hole through me, like a bug under a magnifying glass in the sun.

Is he feeling left out? Or is he jealous? I'm hoping it's the latter.

When the last person pulls out of the driveway hours later, I breathe a sigh of relief and grab a trash bag, making my rounds as I chuck empty beer bottles and dirty paper plates.

"Let me help you," West offers, coming to his feet.

"You just relax. I'll take care of this." It's not that he can't help, it's that I'm doing all I can to ensure he's in a good mood now that he's asked to spend time alone with me.

In the kitchen, I'm putting away condiments when West shuffles in. Of course, he didn't listen. I close the fridge and straighten, and when I turn around, he's right there, grasping my hips and pushing me back against the counter. He's so close to me, and his body is so warm and solid, his scent so familiar, that my heart jumps up into my throat.

Caught off guard by his unexpected boldness, all I can do is swallow and stare into his eyes, waiting for him to make the first move.

"I want to try something. Stay still." His hands move from my hips to cup my face, and he zeroes in on the corner of my mouth. Slowly, his lips descend, but instead of the kiss I'm expecting, they brush over the spot above my upper lip, over the small dark mole. His warm breath fans over my lips and then he gently sucks the corner of my lip between his. It's hotter than any kiss. My heart beats so hard and fast that I'm convinced I'm going to have a heart attack.

"Why am I so obsessed with this spot?" The sound of his rough voice, so deep with need, makes my cock harden. "And this spot?" he adds, trailing his mouth over my jaw, down the column of my neck, nipping with his teeth, sucking hard on my skin. His lips close over my Adam's apple, and he suckles like it's the head of my cock.

I grip his shoulders, pulling him closer, and his dick pushes against mine, hard and thick. My heart is pumping with adrenaline, and I feel lightheaded. His kisses are addicting. So is this feeling like I've become closer to him than I was, which I didn't know was possible. West doesn't continue lower, just rocks his hips into mine, and I guess he's reached the extent of his courage to explore my body, so I take over, twisting him around so that it's his ass against the counter.

My nose rubs against his temple, over his warm skin, and I can smell his citrusy shampoo. He lifts his lips from my skin with a chuckle at my maneuver, and I take advantage of the opportunity to take the lead, working my way down his neck with slow, sucking kisses. He gasps when I suck his nipple between my lips and clutches my head, tangling his fingers in my hair.

"Fuck, that's–"

He's so lost in the good feeling he forgets what he's saying. I love that. I love that I can make him feel this good, that I can have this kind of effect on him. It's empowering and thrilling and makes me want to give him everything, do anything for him, for his pleasure.

With the tip of my tongue I tease a wet trail down his flat stomach, dipping into his navel to tickle him, and he hisses like I burned him. He's not stopping me, and it's pretty obvious where I'm headed. With eager fingers, I work the button and zipper of his jeans open and tug them down his hips. Tilting my head back, I look up into his hungry eyes as my mouth follows the trail of dark hair down to the nest above the base of his shaft, gripping it with my thumb and forefinger. His lips part on a sigh and he drops his hands to my shoulders. His grip is tight as his fingers dig into the meat of my flesh, and I'll bet anything the anticipation of my mouth on him is making his toes curl.

It's all the encouragement I need to continue.

"Brandt, I'm supposed to—it's supposed to be me doing this to–"

"It's okay. You'll get there when you're ready. And if you're never ready, that's okay, too."

His expression looks almost apologetic that he's not ready yet, that he started this and then allowed me to turn the tables on him and take the upper hand. I don't mind. I've had more time to come to terms with my attraction than he has.

Through the thin cotton of his briefs, the outline of his erection is unmistakable. Starting with the plump bulge of his sack, I rub my nose into it, inhaling his musk. Fuck, the masculine scent turns me on more than the sweetest perfume ever has. With my lips, I trace the shape of his dick, mouthing the cotton until it's damp, and then warming it with my breath.

West breathes out a heavy sigh. "You're a fucking tease."

I just want to take my time and savor him. Tomorrow he could come to his senses and decide he never wants to let me near his cock again, and all I'll have are these unforgettable memories.

When I get to the swollen tip, there's a wet spot on the fabric, and I nip it with my teeth before making it wetter by sucking on it. I can taste the saltiness of his flavor on the cotton, like an appetizer before the main course.

"*Ungh*," he groans, clutching my head, as if he doesn't want me to move my mouth away. But I've had enough of this appetizer. I want the main course. I want his bare skin on my tongue. I'm dying to taste his seed again.

I have no idea if I'm good at this, no clue what I'm doing, but I want to make it the best, most memorable blow job he's ever received. I'm working off pure instinct, but from the noises he's making, and the heat in his eyes, I must be doing something right.

Starting at the elastic waistband, I peel his underwear down his hips an inch at a time, revealing glimpses of inked skin, sharp hip bones, and his veiny shaft, until it springs free, and the wet tip smacks my lips. A sticky string of his precum connects us as I pull back. It's silky, like a spiderweb, and the sight of it is turning me on as I wrap it around my tongue and lick it up.

"You like the way I taste?" The deep timber of his voice is turning me on even more.

I know exactly what he's feeling—that moment when you're on the verge of losing self control, where you want to draw out the tease, but you're ready to grab the head of the person sucking you and fuck their mouth until they choke on your load.

Yeah, he's about to lose it, and when I finally put my mouth on him, I hope he fucks it. I've never known what it feels like to be on my knees for someone, to be at their mercy, and it's fucking poetic that it's West because there's no one else I can imagine worshipping like this.

When I reach the end of the string, I dip my tongue into his slit and lick out another drop before closing my lips around his head and giving it a hard suck that makes him twitch. My lips slide down his shaft, over every vein, and his breathing becomes ragged as I hollow out my cheeks and make my way back to the tip.

"Fuck, your mouth."

Yeah, my mouth. I'm not gonna quit until it takes you to the edge.

After three slow torturous passes, I set a faster pace, working his length with plenty of suction and spit.

"Make it noisy," he requests, fingering my swollen lips as I suck. "I want to hear you slurp." I let plenty of saliva pool in my mouth without swallowing it so I can bathe his cock. Squeezing his sac, I continue to suck until my lips begin to feel numb and a string of saliva drips from the corner of my mouth. West twirls it around his finger and sucks it clean. "That's it. Make a fucking mess of me."

His words make me so hot I dig my fingers into the meat of his ass cheeks and suck him harder and faster, taking another inch of his length down my throat, until I gag and my vision blurs with tears. I have to pop his cock out for a moment to control my gag reflex, though we're still connected by ropes of thick, frothy spit.

"Can I fuck your mouth?"

Fuck, yes. I just nod, opening my mouth wide, and West slaps the head of his cock against my tongue before sliding inside. He grabs the back of my head and guides me down, slowly, watching as I swallow inch after inch. His grin is wicked and filthy, and I keep my eyes locked with his, as I do my best to deep throat his thick cock.

"You should see my dick disappear inside your mouth. It comes out shiny and wet, and your face is fucking wrecked."

He's going to fuck my throat raw, but it's worth it. So fucking worth it. The head of his cock bumps against the roof of my mouth again and again, and I can taste more of his flavor on my tongue as he leaks with each thrust.

"You gonna swallow my load?"

Every fucking drop. I can only nod, but that's enough for him. West loses himself in my mouth and buries his cock at the back of my throat with one final thrust before he bows over my head with a grunt and floods my mouth with his release. My throat convulses around his cock as I swallow, which triggers a fresh pulse of cum. He slips from my mouth and I chase his cock with soft teasing licks to the sensitive head, making him gasp a throaty laugh as he pushes my head away.

I stare up at him as I rise to my feet and go straight for his mouth. West has no problem kissing me after I just sucked him off. He doesn't mind the taste of his cum, which is fucking hot as sin. My tongue rubs against his as I get deep in his mouth, claiming it like he just claimed mine with his cock.

My throat is sore and I'm out of breath, a teary, snotty mess, and I couldn't be happier. I feel like he used me in the best way, marked me as his, a mark I bear proudly.

"I'm gonna go take a shower. I'll meet you out on the deck." I've got to finish where he left off and stroke this load out. He looks like he's about to offer... something, a helping hand, a willing mouth, but then he hesitates. He's not ready, not yet. "Go, I'll be out in a minute."

Hot water beats down on my face and chest, and with the even hotter memory of West's dick choking me, it only takes minutes to bring myself off. Dressed in a pair of gray sweats with the army logo and no shirt, I pad barefoot out to the deck where West is laid out in a lounger, nursing another beer.

I grab an empty lounger and drag it closer to his, but West stops me. "Share mine." He moves to make space for me, and I slip behind him. Settling between my legs, he reclines against my chest and sighs.

Instantly, I tense, and my mind goes on alert. His sigh isn't filled with pleasure or relaxation, it's a guilty sigh.

"I can't keep doing this to you. If I'm not willing to find out, I don't deserve to fuck around."

My mood plummets like an anchor dropping to the bottom

of the ocean. "I told you it's okay, that it doesn't matter. Maybe you'll get there, and maybe you won't, but I have no regrets." I bury my lips in his hair, feeling the soft buzz brush against my lips.

"What are we doing? What is this?"

A heavy weight settles on my chest, and it's becoming difficult to breathe because each word out of his mouth feels like another nail in my coffin. The dissolution of the dream I was beginning to have about our future. A future with him. Funny how a couple of blowjobs can start making you dream about happily ever afters and shit.

"I don't know, Professor. What is it to you?"

"Just finding a few minutes to enjoy life before all the bullshit comes rushing back."

If I don't downplay my expectations, he'll run faster than I can chase him. Then again, West is constantly surprising me, exceeding my expectations at every turn. What if I miss my chance by not being honest with him?

Closing my eyes, I gather my courage and blurt, "A few minutes? That's it? What if I want more?"

"More? From me?" His harsh laugh tells me everything I need to know. "I'm a mess. A fucking disaster. No, I'm a one-legged disaster. I can't even convince myself I deserve another day of life, and you want me to give you more? More of what?"

My fingers brush through his fuzzy hair, gently scraping his scalp. "More of you."

West scoffs and takes another swig of his beer. He takes his sweet-ass time swallowing before he answers. "What, a boyfriend? You wanna fucking date me?"

Wrapping my arms around his chest, I squeeze him to me as I lay my cheek over his hair and rub the softness against my face. "What if I do?"

"That's bullshit. It's not gonna happen. I don't have that kind of future to give you. Anyway, you can do a lot better than me."

Grinding my teeth, my jaw clenches tight, and I can feel my anger bubble up inside me and burst. "I'm so fucking tired of your bullshit. Your martyr act."

"Martyr?" he counters, pulling away from my embrace and sitting up.

"It's just a cover for you being a coward."

He turns his body so that he's facing me, and he grabs my ear and twists painfully. I shove at his chest hard enough that he lets go.

"I'm a lot of things, but I'm not a fucking coward. And I never pretended to be a martyr. I don't go around crying about all the reasons I should be pitied."

Fuck him. Heat rises to my face and I snap. "Don't you? It's all I fucking hear from you! How you don't deserve this or that."

"I don't! Not a future, not love, and certainly not happiness. I don't deserve a fucking thing."

His voice cracks, and his eyes grow wet. He looks so lost. My heart breaks for him, but he's throwing his life away and he's taking mine with him. "You're afraid to be happy. Afraid to reach for something, to want more, because it makes you feel guilty." His shoulders sag under the weight of his conscience. I just want to gather him in my arms. Instead, I grab hold of his hands.

"It's survivor's guilt, Wes, and it's killing you, and you're taking me down with you, and you're right, I deserve better than that."

West laughs without humor. "Thanks for the assessment, Dr. Phil. You're right. You deserve a whole lot more than my sorry ass. So don't ask me for *more*."

I can't reach him like this. His walls are too high. "Let me ask you a question. Just for a minute, let's pretend things went down differently. Pretend one of the other guys was in charge instead of you, and you survived just long enough to tell them one last thing. What would you say?"

A shadow flickers in his eyes and I suppose he's remembering their last words, but then he shrugs it off. "Depends who it was. If it were Micah, I'd remind him that no matter what some chick said while she was bouncing on his dick, that he was the absolute ugliest motherfucker I've ever seen."

Idiot. He would definitely have said that. "Right, but would you tell him how much you hate him? Would you tell him it was all his fault, and that you hoped he spent every day for the rest of his life regretting your death?"

His face hardens. "You're a fucking asshole."

"I guess that's my answer, then. You wouldn't dream of saying that because it isn't true. You're not responsible for their deaths." He tries to look away, but I grasp his chin, keeping his face front and center. "I was in the building with you, and I'm not responsible either."

He pulls his face from my grip. "I was in charge!"

"You didn't receive any intel that would have made you act

differently in hindsight. What you're doing is stealing their lives."

"They're dead! What fucking lives?" Tears stream down his cheeks, and I hate myself for doing this to him, but it had to be said. "He had a little girl. And Tommy had a wife. I didn't just take her husband, I took their families and their futures away."

His words hang heavy in the air. It's the truth, and it's tragic, but it's not the end of the story. "You're right, they're dead. But we lived. We have the chance to live the life they dreamed of, to do all the things they wanted to do. A chance to fulfill their bucket lists, to honor the ones they loved, and to realize their dreams. By squandering the life you were spared, fucking *gifted* really, you're stealing their futures and burying them next to our brothers and sister in the ground. It's like you're walking on their graves. Fall in love for Rosie. Plan a future for Tommy. Be happy for Micah's sake."

He swipes his tears with the hem of his shirt. "Fuck you," he says without heat. "You don't have the right to say that to me."

"Why? Because I wasn't in charge? Because I didn't have as many stars on my chest as you? What's the fucking difference? Do you think I don't feel the same guilt you do? The same responsibility for my team, no matter what my rank was? We all felt a responsibility for each other. The stars don't make you fucking special." I'm so desperate to get my point across to him, for it to sink in this time, that I feel tears rush to my eyes and fall down my cheeks. "You're all I've got left." My voice cracks on a sob and his tears fall harder. "There's no one else for me. You're it, Wes, and you're stealing what life I have left."

"You're not stuck with me," he counters petulantly.

"I am! Don't you get it? We're absolutely fucking ruined, like you said. I don't think there's one person in the world we could have a successful relationship with. We're not healthy people."

"So it's me or it's no one? You're a real hearts and flowers kind of guy, aren't you?"

If he's cracking jokes, my point must have sunk in. I hope to God he's having a change of heart. "Is that what you want? Hearts and flowers?"

"Fuck you," he laughs and wipes his nose on the sleeve of his shirt.

"I'm not saying I can't do better than you because I'm not good enough, or that you aren't good enough. I'm saying I can't do better than you because there is no one better." Sliding my hands under his arms, I pull him against my chest and he doesn't fight me. With his head cradled between my pecs, I wrap my arms around his back and lay my cheek against his head. "It's you, only you, Wes. You're my best friend, and now, you're... something more. We were given another chance at life, and somehow, we were given the added gift of wanting each other like this; of being attracted to each other. I want you in ways I've never thought of before, and that gives us a one in a million chance to build something together. To make a life worth living."

He sniffles against my bare chest, and I don't even care about the snot at this point. I'm just so grateful he's listening. "It's not gonna be the healthiest relationship. It's not always gonna be good, I get that. But you're the only person I want to do this with." West raises his head and pins his teary gaze on me. "Please, I'm asking you for more. Build a life with me that our team would have wanted to live. It's the only way we can honor them. And it's what we deserve."

West takes my hands in his. "More, huh?" He laughs and shakes his head. "I still think you're going to regret asking for this, but yeah, I'll give you more."

It's hard to swallow past the constriction of my throat. "Don't tell me pretty lies." *Don't break my heart.*

"I can try, okay? All I can do is try." He brushes his lips across my knuckles and my heart tugs painfully. It's probably the most intimate, softest gesture I've seen from him, ever. "It's not that I don't want this, Reaper. I do. But my heart might not always be in it. Not because of you, though."

Because of the guilt. Because of the bad days—the darkness, and the sometimes debilitating side effects of his amputation and TBI. "I know, I get that. It's enough for me if you just promise to try."

WEST

Chapter 17

"NOW SLOWLY SLIDE your shaft through the hole. You're doing so good," she purrs in a soft, encouraging voice. "Careful now; we don't want to ram our sticks. Just a gentle glide. Not too tight, and not too loose. When you get it just right, doesn't it feel so good?"

With my attention on the screen, I don't see Brandt sneak into the room. He pounces on the mattress, and I scramble to shut the laptop.

"Are you watching porn?"

"What? No!"

His arched eyebrow implies he doesn't believe me. "Then what are you watching?"

"Nothing. Why are you in here?"

"I live here. This is my room. What are you hiding under there?" he asks, tugging the covers down from my lap.

"Nothing." I'm only making it seem more suspicious by fighting with him in an all out tug-of-war over the blanket.

Through the bedding, his hand falls on the bamboo stick, and his face becomes serious. "Are you hiding a weapon?"

Fuck. "Really? Would I be googling how to commit suicide?"

In one swift move, he yanks the blanket from my lap. His expression is almost comical when he sees the ball of bright pink yarn he bought me stretched around my knitting needles.

Holding up the six inch wooden stick, I tease, "I guess you could turn this into a weapon, although the only thing I'm stabbing is this worsted weight yarn."

Slowly, his grin returns, and he flips open the laptop and brings the screen back to life. The woman with flaming red hair and a pretty smile comes back online. "Now that you've mastered the ins and outs of insertion, let's work on your technique."

"Dude, you can't blame me for thinking this was porn. Who is this chick?"

"Betty Beasley's tips and tricks for sexy stitches. She's showing me how to work my wool. McCormick recommended her."

He laughs and clicks on another of her videos. "She's working the wool, alright. Betty Beasley is a naughty little knitter. It doesn't surprise me that McCormick is obsessed with her." And then it dawns on him. "When did you ask McCormick for knitting tips?"

Mild heat warms my cheeks. "I may or may not have activated the phone tree while you were in the shower."

His eyebrows rise, and his grin stretches wider. "Yeah? I'm dying to know who answered first."

No way was I giving in that easily. "I guess you'll have to implement it yourself and see."

Brandt looks at me like he's seeing me for the first time through new eyes. It's unnerving, this small thrill I feel from pleasing him. Like I'm some good boy looking to be rewarded for behaving.

"Maybe I will," he breathes, his voice turning husky. Fuck, that makes my dick harder than it should. "So, what prompted this sudden desire to knit?"

"Nothing," I say airily, brushing it off. "Just thought it would be nice not to sit and mope like a moron during group while everyone else is knitting."

"So you're ready to make nice with your new friends?"

Why does he have to say it in a way that makes me want to smack him? "I'm not fucking twelve. You know, it's nice to have something to keep my hands busy. I guess you could say I've become a fidgeter. Keeps my mind busy, too."

"Imagine that," he says with a self-satisfied smirk. "I guess there's a reason the Bitches knit, and I have a feeling it's not because they like to wear homemade sweaters."

He pulls open the top drawer of his nightstand and retrieves a ball of blue yarn. "Well, let's see what other tips and tricks the sexy Betty Beasley has up her sleeve." He hits play on the video and for the next hour, we lose ourselves in the mindless complacency of working our wool.

"You think she's hot?" I ask, transferring my stitch from one needle to the other.

"Who, Betty?"

He's acting as if I asked if he thinks the mailman is hot. "Yeah, Betty. Who else?" I don't even know why I'm asking. What do I care if he thinks she's hot? She is. With her curly red hair and cleavage for days, I'd definitely do her. So why do I care if Brandt agrees with me?

"Yeah, she's hot. She's got that whole girl next door, good girl in the streets, freak in the sheets, thing going on. Totally my jam."

An irrational spike of jealousy stabs my chest. What the fuck is my problem? I'm being ridiculous, but that doesn't stop me from asking, "Anyone else you think is hot? Anyone at BALLS or the hospital?" I cringe, adding, "Liza, maybe? Or Annalise?"

"Annalise? Your occupational therapist?" He eyes me like he's trying to solve a puzzle. "She gave me her number."

He didn't answer my question. I'm familiar with sidestepping and evasion. Brandt is excelling at it to avoid this conversation, which makes me want to have it all the more.

"You gonna ask her out?"

"Why the fuck would I do that?"

Now my heart is hammering away at my chest like a jackhammer. "Because she's hot. And she's single. She's obviously interested in you."

"I don't give a fuck. I'm not interested in her. I'm interested in you."

He's saying the words I want to hear, so why don't I believe him? I used to have all the confidence in the world, and now I'm suspicious of my best fucking friend when he gives me a simple compliment. My head is so fucked. And I'm so mixed up about my attraction to him that I'm behaving like a teenage girl with her first crush.

"In me?"

He lays his knitting aside and turns his body so that he's facing me. "Why is that so hard for you to believe?"

Feeling embarrassed of my low self-esteem, I blow out a frustrated breath. "Your injuries aren't like mine, you know? You could have anybody you want still." I swallow hard and lay my knitting aside. "So why the fuck are you wasting your time with me?"

"I didn't realize I was wasting my time." He runs his finger along the inside of the waistband of my sweats, making the simple gesture look sexy. "I've been having so much fun." He drops his lips to my neck and sucks on my collarbone. "Doesn't feel like a waste of time at all." Shivers dance along my skin, and I bare my neck to his mouth for more.

He tugs my sweats down my hips and slides them off my leg, and my heartbeat kicks up, anticipating his touch. Maybe he's going to blow me again. His hand lands on my thigh, the short one, and instantly I'm in my head, feeling self-conscious. Nothing takes me out of the moment faster than reminding me of my disability. His lips find my nipple and suck hard, and my brain is warring with my libido for top spot. But when his fingers skate over the bundle of scar tissue, I shove his hand away.

"Don't pull away from me," he warns, his lips and his voice

soft in my ear. "I'll touch you if I want to." Brandt massages my thigh, his strong fingers digging into the touch-starved tissue and muscles of my leg, relaxing my inhibitions one by one.

"Fuck, that feels good." With a sigh, I tip my head back and close my eyes, soaking up his touch.

"See, don't be such a stubborn ass."

He's stealthy, though, moving back toward the tip, away from my cock. This is more intimate than sex with him. Letting my guard down, allowing him to touch the most ruined part of my body, the one that triggers me most.

Look at him. You know he's looking at you. Look at him.

Sure enough, when I open my eyes, I find Brandt's gaze hot on my face, like he was waiting for me to open my eyes. He strips out of his sweatpants without ever looking away and grips his hard cock. Brandt gives it several strokes, and I watch because lately, I can't *not* look when he does it. Why is that suddenly so hot to me, watching him stroke himself? I've seen him do it dozens of times, but now it makes me hard.

But my hungry, curious gaze turns to horror as he brings the head of his cock in contact with the end of my thigh. I'm speechless. I have no words as I watch him grind his dick against my limb. He smears drops of his cum over my skin, over my scars, and, although I'm shocked, I can't deny that the sight of it is making my dick harder. But when he looks at me, all hot and heavy, I lose my nerve.

"You know I can't feel that, right?"

"Do you have eyes? Do they work? I can see your dick works, 'cause it's nice and hard." He reaches for it and swipes a drop of pre-cum with his thumb, trailing it down my shaft.

Brandt continues to paint my skin with his cum, humping my limb, and the sight of his rolling hips, his thrusting, has heat building low in my stomach. Why do I find this so incredibly hot? He's pushing into my thigh while tugging on my cock, and the back-and-forth feels like he's fucking into my body, fucking *me*, without actually penetrating me.

Again, I push at his hand, feeling exposed and vulnerable. "Get the fuck out of here."

"I said, I'll touch you if I want to." He leans in to tease my ear with his hot breath. "Don't pretend you don't like it."

"You're a sick fuck." My voice catches on the lump in my throat.

"You fucking love it," he returns with fire dancing in his eyes.

I've known Brandt for twelve years. How did I not know he was so sick and twisted? He is one filthy motherfucker, and I can't seem to get enough of him. I lean back with my weight braced on my arms, and Brandt practically crawls over me, taking charge. I've never been one to give up control before, but when it comes to submitting to Brandt, he can have it.

"Stop thinking about me with women and start picturing me with you."

He crawls over my thigh and pushes his dick against mine. The hot, hard length of him is a new thrill I can't get enough of. How have I never noticed how velvety soft and warm his skin feels? Why has my mouth never watered at the thick veins bulging in his shaft before? The head is plump and purple and I'm dying to suck on it, but I'm such a fucking coward. But right now, I'm more afraid that he'll stop if he sees me up in my head, and that he'll rob me of the toe curling orgasm I know he can deliver.

"Feels so good when you do that," I say in a breathy, porntastic voice.

"You like that?" I can tell from his satisfied grin that he likes it just as much, if not more.

Brandt focuses on our cocks, stroking them in his fist, and he parts his lips in ecstasy. When he looks back at me, pleasure is written all over his face. He's riding a wave of lust. He takes my lips roughly, shoving his tongue inside my mouth and rubbing it with mine, sucking on it until I'm a dizzy mess.

It takes me a moment to react when he says, "Turn over."

"W-what for?"

"'Cause I told you to. Turn over."

Shit, my dick likes it too much when he tells me what to do. I'm the team leader. I outrank him. It's supposed to be the other way around, but I could get used to this bossy side of him.

Bossy Brandt.

Badass Brandt.

Balls-to-the-wall Brandt.

Reminds me of how he got his nickname, the Grim Reaper—by being a bossy, badass, balls-to-the-wall motherfucker. Yeah, I'll turn the fuck over for him. He can do…Whatever.

He nips my shoulder blade, and his teeth work a trail down my spine, making me writhe. Then he bites my ass cheek before sucking the pain from my skin. I'm sure he's left a dark purple hickey on my ass, not that I care. I kind of like the idea of wearing his marks. But nothing prepares me for what he does next.

His tongue slithers through my crease, licking between my cheeks. Wet and warm, it slides over my hole.

"Holy motherfucking shit!"

His laugh is as wicked as his tongue. "Just wait, it gets better."

I twist my neck, trying to see him over my shoulder. "How would you know?"

"The guy in the video seemed to think so."

"You watched gay porn?"

"Beats watching Betty Beasley."

"I don't know about that. That girl is a filthy freak."

Brandt spreads my cheeks and licks a wide stripe through them, lapping at me like a kitten. He continues to do it over and over, making my hole soft and loose to the point I'm ready to beg him to slide something inside of it.

But I wasn't expecting his tongue.

He stiffens the tip and pushes it past my rim, and every nerve ending in my body stands at attention and salutes him. The veins in my cock throb and I push into the mattress, seeking friction and relief. I'm almost embarrassed that I'm bucking my hips shamelessly against his face like a slut, but I'm too turned on to care. And then he's gone, the sweet fire is gone.

"I like the way you taste," he says in a voice that's pure gravel. Another glance over my shoulder shows his glossy lips, and all I can think of is fucking his mouth.

He lowers himself over my back and presses sucking kisses on my neck, and I can feel his cock, thick and hard, slide through my wet crease. He starts a slow glide back and forth as he works my neck, sending shivers dancing down my spine. My natural instinct is to push back against him because it feels so good, but I'm afraid he's going to shove it in.

"Feels so good, like I'm fucking you."

Christ, his words. I'm gonna fucking come.

"You're not really gonna–"

"No," he breathes in my ear, making goosebumps shoot down my arm. "Not today. But soon you're gonna have to man the fuck up and let me in." He snaps his hips and his swollen cockhead catches on my rim, stretching it before he glides past. "I'm gonna slick you up real good and push inside of you."

I shake my head from side to side. "You're too thick."

"You bet I am. I'm going to split you wide-open, inch by thick fucking inch." Every nerve ending in my pucker is electrified like a live wire as he continues to rub back-and-forth over my hole. "You're gonna let me in, and you're gonna fucking love it." His lips brush the shell of my ear, igniting another erogenous zone in my body. "You're gonna fuck me back, and then you're gonna come harder than you ever have before. I want to hear my name on your lips when you scream."

That's it. That's all I can take. A spasm rolls through my gut, making all my muscles clench tight, and I surrender to the wave of pleasure. Cum bubbles over my knuckles as I pump my shaft, soaking the sheet beneath me in a warm puddle.

"Brandt," I gasp, breathless like I ran a marathon.

He's still thrusting, still pumping, his breathing harsh and ragged in my ear. "Gonna...come." A heavy breath precedes a rush of warm wetness between my cheeks, and then he slows to a lazy glide. He sucks on my neck like he's making out with it and if he keeps it up, I'm gonna get hard again. "Being with you is like...I don't know what it's like. I have nothing to compare this to."

Neither do I. But as the endorphins settle and the fire in my veins cools, fear and doubt creep back in. "Does this make me gay?" I hate how small and unsure my voice sounds. And I know I'm saying stupid things, but I'm so fucking lost and confused that nothing makes sense anymore.

"Is that what you're worried about?" The weight of his body on mine is a comfort, like a warm, weighted blanket of security. He rubs his nose along the back of my neck and his breath kisses my skin.

It's easier to talk with my face buried in the pillow instead of looking at him. When he looks into my eyes, I know he can see more than just the color of my irises. He can see everything I'm *not* saying.

"I'm not worried about what people will think if I tell them I'm attracted to you."

"Then what are you worried about?"

"With all these changes lately, I don't recognize myself anymore, and I'm afraid that I'm losing myself. When I look in the mirror, I don't recognize my body, and with all the side effects of the TBI, I don't even feel comfortable in my own skin sometimes. My body is different, my head is different, my whole fucking life has changed. Everything that defined me is gone. I'm not a soldier anymore. I'm no longer a Sergeant First Class, team leader of the Street Sweepers." The gentle way he's caressing me, brushing his nose back-and-forth in the crook of my neck, his finger tracing soft patterns over the tattoos inked into my skin, gives me the courage to continue.

"This just feels like one more thing I don't recognize about myself. Something so basic as my sexuality that has identified me my entire life, long before the Army, is suddenly changing, and I just feel so lost. I don't know who I am anymore."

"I know who you are. You're Weston Wardell. You're my best fucking friend. You love military documentaries, and you're a history nerd. You're terrible in the kitchen, but somehow a whiz on the grill. You're the most loyal person I know, but you're a manipulative little shit."

He licks the shell of my ear, making me flinch and smile. "You love Mad Libs and working out." His warm breath ghosts over my ear and my dick kicks. "You act like a big baby when you're sick or injured, but you have a high threshold for pain. When you were little, you wanted to be a soldier when you grew up, just like your grandfather, and you followed your dream. Most people can't say they had the courage to follow their dreams. You're one of the bravest and strongest people I know, and nothing you've been through changes that."

I can feel his dick beginning to harden, still nestled between my cheeks. "And you're the only man who has ever made my dick hard. I know that seems scary or foreign to you, but it excites me, and I'm so fucking grateful that it's you," Brandt finishes in a barely audible voice. His soft kisses on my neck feel like affection, not seduction, and I can identify with his feelings. It *is* thrilling. And I'm definitely fucking grateful that it's him. "That's who you are, Wes, all those things and more. And if you feel lost, just lean on me and I'll show you the way back home."

Tears threaten to spill over my cheeks, but I hold them back. "Three legs, huh? Can't fall with three legs."

"We're a fucking tripod, baby. We're never gonna fall, and we're never gonna lose our way."

I know he's right. I believe every word he's saying. He's my crutch and my compass, an old familiar comfort, and my new thrilling addiction. He's everything I need and everything I want. My past and my future. Brandt is...*everything*. He's my home.

BRANDT

Balls
Black Mountain, NC

Chapter 18

WEST KEPT his promise to get involved with the Bitches, and Riggs delivered on his, hooking West up with a new hydraulic leg and a blade.

The blade is cool as fuck, in my opinion. It makes West look like a badass. Especially when he wears it with cargo shorts. It took some convincing, after his expected grumbling and excuses, but I finally got his stubborn ass in the Jeep and drove him out to the running track that circles the park. I'm hoping the more comfortable he becomes using the leg, the more active he'll be. I really think it will have a profound effect on his mental health.

Dressed in a gray T-shirt with the BALLS logo and black

running shorts, West runs through a warm-up routine of stretching and squats, getting juiced up for our run. Like a fucking creeper, I catch myself checking his crotch for a dick imprint through the thin nylon and I mentally shake myself. It's crazy how aware of him I've become, always eyeing his nipples when he's shirtless, or checking out his ass. I barely recognize myself anymore, feeling so hypersexual, but who could blame me? West provides me with plenty of eye candy.

"Come on, Professor. This track ain't gonna run itself."

I take off at a slow jog, giving him a chance to get the hang of it and build up speed. At the half mile mark, we're running at a decent pace, just starting to feel my heart pumping, when an elderly lady in a neon pink tee passes us easily. Her shirt claims she's survived breast cancer and is living her best life. West looks at me with horror, and I'm struggling not to stop running and fall down on the pavement in a fit of laughter.

"Fuck, Reaper! Are you kidding me? She's running circles around us. I'm being lapped by a granny!"

It's winding me to laugh and talk and run at once. "She's got two good legs, so quit your bitching and pick up the fucking pace."

West burns with challenge, digging down deep into his empty reserve of motivation, burning rubber, and titanium. I sprint to keep up, and when he finally passes her, he mumbles, "Not today, Grandma."

We manage three miles before calling it quits. "Proud of you, West," I wheeze through labored breaths.

"Yeah. Me too. Let's not mention the grandma thing to anyone," he insists, eyeing me with dead severity.

"I wouldn't dream of it," I lie with a straight face.

It's a twenty-minute drive to BALLS from the park, and I fill the silence by voicing an idea I've been kicking around in my head while West chugs his second bottle of water.

"When the guys were over last week, I came up with an idea."

"Like what?"

"We've got all that land, and you've got more mobility now. What if we started up a business? Like boot camp for deployment. Some of the guys mentioned the Eighty-Second getting called up. Do you remember what we were like when we got our orders the first time?"

"Fucking noobs," he laughs.

"We didn't know shit, but we were gung ho. All fired up without a clue. We could lead a training camp. Put our experience to use." He raises his brows, like he wants to hear more. "We could do some target practice, rappel that cliff on the back half of your property, do some other physical training, and then pepper them with tips and tricks the whole time."

"Like prepare them for the heat and the smell and the fucking dust."

"Exactly, and the stuff they should buy there at the Hajji Shop versus getting it sent in a care package."

"You think people would pay for that?"

"Hell yeah. You heard them, they said how much they missed hanging at your place, doing all that shit. They're a bunch of fucking POGs, they haven't seen a day of combat yet, and they're amped up for action. They'd definitely pay."

"It'd probably turn into a fucking bachelor party destination," he cracks.

"Don't care, as long as it's income, money is money. We have plenty saved from our retirement payouts. We could get some new equipment, invest in some advertising, some ammo, and bam, we're in business."

I watch as the expressions on his face range from curious to excited to determined. West has a terrible poker face, and he broadcasts everything he's thinking and feeling loud and clear.

"We're in fucking business, Reaper."

Fuck, yeah!

Today is a good day. I feel alive. I feel like I'm living my life instead of merely surviving it. Old-school alternative is playing on the radio, songs that take me way back, music that feels good. With the windows rolled down, the fresh mountain air is blowing through my sweaty hair and I can feel the sun warming my face. I've got my best friend beside me, blood pumping through my veins from the run, and West is smiling. We're dreaming together and making plans for our future, and we're getting excited about our lives again.

Today is a *great* fucking day.

"I feel the need. The need…" When I glance at West, he's rolling his eyes, already knowing what I'm going to say. "For speed," we say in unison as my foot hits the gas harder. We're tearing down the remote highway at nearly a hundred miles an hour, and I turn the radio all the way up, but it barely drowns out my howl. West grins and joins in, screaming at the top of his lungs out the window as the tires eat up the road.

For the first time in what feels like forever, we don't have a care in the world.

"Are you fucking kidding me?" Stiles shrieks. "Your bike couldn't keep up with mine if you added nitrous to it. In fact, next time I'm at the toy store, I'll pick up some training wheels for your bike."

"You're full of shit," McCormick seethes, "the only reason you beat me is because you took off from the line before the light turned green!"

"Keep telling yourself that, Carrot Stick. In the meantime, I've got a bumper sticker I was going to give my nephew, but you can have it. It says, *'Born To Be Mild'*. Get it?" he asks, smacking McCormick on the back.

McCormick glares at Stiles as I smother my laughter, but West isn't even trying to hide his.

"Looks like the boys are feeling rowdy today. This should be a great meeting," West teases as we take our seats. He reaches into his backpack and pulls out his pink yarn and needles, and the ribbing from the peanut gallery starts up again with catcalls and whistles.

"Look at those sticks! Sleek, baby, sleek."

"Real men wear pink, Wardell. Don't let anyone tell you otherwise."

"Yeah, yeah," West says with a grin, brushing it off. "Laugh it up. But don't be jealous if my stitches are better than yours. I've got skills, apparently."

"Thanks to Betty Beasley," McCormick says slyly. "No one's got tighter stitches than Betty."

"You're fucking sick," Jax mumbles. "Nobody wants to hear about Betty's tight stitches."

Stiles reaches into his black leather backpack and pulls out a canvas tote bag. He crosses the circle and hands it to me. "This is for the both of you, from the Bitches. You took the first step by activating the phone tree and reaching out, and now you're officially one of us. Welcome to the club."

Everyone's clapping as I investigate what's inside the bag— five different kinds of needles, four skeins of yarn in different colors, and some handwritten instructions that I assume are stitch techniques. On the outside of the bag is a logo someone created that says '*Bitches With Stitches, healing hearts one stitch at a time.*'

Gratitude and a sense of belonging make my chest feel tight. "Thanks guys." That's about all I can manage. I don't want to risk speaking while my voice might crack with emotion.

A man I haven't seen before breezes in and takes the empty seat between West and McCormick, and I'm immediately on guard. This guy isn't dressed like the other Bitches, in black leather ALR motorcycle gear. In fact, there's nothing about him similar to any of us. He's got to be at least 6'4", jacked with muscle, shoulder length dark hair, and eyes so intense I feel like I need to look away. Fuck, are they golden? They are! His eyes are fucking golden. Although I'm new to checking out guys, I have to say this one is definitely hot, but he's giving off a disinterested don't-fuck-with-me vibe.

Riggs walks in right behind him and takes his usual seat. "Pharo! Long time no see, my man. How have you been?"

Pharo? Get the fuck out of here.

Even his name is fucking hot. The more I stare at him, the more wary I become, and I'm pissed that he's sitting next to West. I need him to move the fuck over. *Way* over. Like, to the next classroom.

"Hanging in there, Riggs. Just got back stateside and thought I'd check in."

"Pharo," McCormick says, "this is Wardell and Aguilar, our two newest Bitches." Pharo can't be bothered with pleasantries. I guess he's too cool for that. Instead, he dips his head in acknowledgment. But McCormick continues, picking up the slack in the conversation. "Pharo's been stationed in Egypt," he explains.

Egypt? West and I share a disbelieving look. What kind of military operations is the US running in Egypt?

"So, you're still active?" I ask.

"Reserves."

That's all he's going to give me, I guess. And then Jax scrapes the legs of his chair across the linoleum as he springs to his feet.

"Where are you going?" Stiles asks.

"It's too fucking crowded in here," Jax mumbles with a pointed look at Pharo.

Of course, I can always count on West to ask what everyone else is thinking. The guy has no filter whatsoever.

"You two have a history?"

"Do you have a death wish?" McCormick hisses.

"Nah, it's fine," Pharo says. "Just some people shouldn't go making heroes out of head cases." His yellow eyes follow Jax out of the room.

That's cryptic as fuck, and I don't know what it means, but apparently they do have a history, and he clearly doesn't want to talk about it.

"Alright, gentlemen, let's get started," Riggs says, bringing the group to order. "Speaking of the Reserves, don't forget that I won't be here next week, or the week after. But Brewer Marx from the addiction support group will be taking over for me."

The Bitches bitch for forty-five minutes, and just when we're about to run out of time, West surprises me by speaking out.

"This week I realized that it's okay to have bad days. I've had some good ones, too. And the bad ones aren't all bad. Sometimes there are moments where I can smile or laugh, or feel some kind of emotion besides self-hatred. I'm learning some things about myself I never knew before." His dark eyes land on me, and I can feel the weight of his thoughts. "Confusing things. Good things. Things that give me hope. I guess I'm not the man I used to be, and I need to stop searching for him, stop looking over my shoulder in the past, and start looking forward." West clears his throat and refocuses on the group. "I'm trying. Sometimes it feels like it'll kill me, but I keep trying. Just for today, I'm grateful for the people in my life that won't let me give up."

His voice cracks on his last words, and I can see him struggle not to tear up in front of the group. I want to reach for his hand, or touch his leg, to reassure him, and lend him my strength, but

I'm afraid the simple gesture will make him fall apart completely.

When the meeting wraps, some of the guys linger, and for once West isn't beating feet out the door like his ass is on fire. He takes his time packing away his yarn and needles, long enough for McCormick to mosey over.

He scratches his thick orange beard. "So, you two want to come over to my place? Hang out for a couple hours? We can boil a package of hot dogs and fire up my laptop. Betty Beasley just dropped a new video."

It blows me away how someone who looks so confident and tough as nails can be so awkward and just... fucking bizarre. McCormick looks like an intimidating guy until he opens his mouth, and then you want to run for other reasons.

West snorts and stares at him like he's grown two heads. "Who invites people over to eat boiled hot dogs?" He looks to me for confirmation, but I'm not getting involved. "Something's not right in your head."

McCormick's face falls. "Hey, we don't make fun of people's injuries around here."

"Dude, whatever is wrong with your head was there long before your TBI," West swears. "No wonder you can't get a woman, and it's got nothing to do with your fucking leg. Did you offer boiled hot dogs to the last chick who came over?"

"No," he defends, but from the way his voice hitches, I'm not sure I believe him.

"Are you sure you're not into dudes? Inviting a couple of guys over to eat phallic shaped meat while you sit around in a circle jerk watching knitting porn? I don't know, McCormick, sounds pretty gay to me."

Of course Stiles can't resist the chance to get a dig in. "Might have better luck with the guys than you do with the ladies," he adds with a smirk.

"You're just sore because I didn't invite you," McCormick huffs.

"Last time I came over, you fed me boiled hot dogs and I shit for three days straight. No fucking thanks. You can shove your boiled meat up your ass."

I can't hold it in any longer. I'm laughing so hard my sternum hurts, and West falls into my shoulder to bury his face as he falls apart.

"Fuck all y'all." McCormick says as he heads for the door, but then he turns. "I'm going to get a beer. Are you coming?"

"This is a hell of a lot better than boiled hot dogs, wouldn't you say?" West asks as he shoves a fully loaded potato skin in his mouth.

"That's not setting a very high bar," I tease. "I'd rather eat MREs than boiled hot dogs."

McCormick doesn't find it funny. "Fine, Chef Wardell. What are you going to serve me when I come over?"

"I don't recall inviting you over."

With a smirk, I throw him a lifeline. "I'll invite you over, McCormick."

"You're a gentleman, Aguilar," he quips with a smile and a wink. "So, you two live together?"

"Brandt moved in after my... you know. I needed the extra help." His eyes land on me and they soften, and heat licks through my gut. "I guess it worked out so good he's just gonna stay."

"That's great. I wish I had someone around to help me after my accident. I had to go to a long-term rehab center until I was able to do more for myself. How long have you two been friends?"

"Since Boot Camp," I say.

"Twelve long years," West adds.

"Wow, that's a long time." He shoves a potato skin in his mouth as he glances back-and-forth between the two of us. "I like what you shared today," he says to West. "I can imagine after what you two went through, you were in a pretty dark place for a long time. I'm glad to see you're starting to crawl out."

"How do you know what we went through?" West asks, his brows drawing down tight.

"Everybody knows. It was all over the news for weeks. Every major network across the country picked up the story." He studies us, maybe taking note of our surprised expressions, and his eyebrows rise. "You didn't know? Hell," he laughs, "you two are national heroes."

Fuck, I know how much West hates that word.

"We were stuck in a hospital in Germany for weeks. I guess it was old news by the time we got back stateside."

West nods. "I didn't even know what had happened until I woke up. I was in for quite a shock when I pulled the covers back on my leg."

"Fuck, that's a terrible way to find out."

"What about you? How'd you lose yours?" West asks.

"Humvee drove over an IED. Kaboom! Next thing I know, the damn thing rolled on top of me. There were five of us. Two died, Manny lost his arm, and Margie–" McCormick swallows and bites his lip. I can see he's struggling. "–she...her face–" Swallowing again, he looks back and forth between us. "Half of it's gone now."

A sick feeling drops like lead to the pit of my stomach, souring the beer and potato skins. West covers McCormick's hand with his. "How are they doing now?"

A sheen covers his eyes, and I can see and feel what it's costing him not to fall apart in this restaurant.

"I don't know. I don't keep in touch with them. We used to be close, but... I just can't. You know?" His voice cracks, and he's barely holding it together. "I tried, but it's just it's too much, and I can't "

"Hey, you don't have to. Brandt says we're victims of the tragedy we went through, and we're victims to the aftermath and the feelings we're left with. Those corrosive thoughts eat away at us like acid. And it's not our fault. Nobody gets to tell us how to manage those feelings. They don't fucking know what we've been through, so they can't imagine what it feels like. If you did the best you can, then you did more than enough. You don't owe anybody a fucking explanation, least of all us."

McCormick laughs weakly as he sniffles into his napkin and then washes down the rest of his beer in one long gulp. "I'm glad you get it." He breathes in a deep breath and releases it harshly. "So, how's the new blade working out? It looks good on you."

"It's not bad. We tested it out on the track today, didn't we, Brandt?"

I could bring up the grandma situation because we all need a good laugh right about now, but I'll spare his ego. So instead, I just nod.

"I can't wear it for long, though. I'm already starting to feel it."

"In your hips and lower back, right?" McCormick asks. "It's because the blade is longer than your leg, and it throws everything out of alignment."

"Yes! It's nice to talk to someone who understands."

He glances at me to see if I understand, but he doesn't realize how his words cut me. It stings. I feel like I'm on the outside looking in for the first time, and that someone else understands him better than I do. The feeling doesn't sit right with me at all, but I cover my anger with a false smile. West needs this. Needs to feel like one of the guys. Needs to bond with people who literally walk in his shoes. Truth is, I don't. I'm a bystander to his struggles.

Frustrated with my jealousy, I push to my feet. "I gotta take a piss. I'll be back."

In the bathroom, I'm not alone. When I finish relieving myself, I hit the sink to wash my hands as a man empties out of the other stall, joining me at the sink. He's the same height as me, pretty much the same build, with dark hair and eyes, like West. But he's nowhere near as attractive as West, at least not to me. I feel his eyes on me in the mirror, taking his time as he lathers his hands with soap, like he's trying to seduce me with hygiene or something. Just as I meet his eyes in the mirror, West pushes into the bathroom, and he stands behind me, eyeing the guy without saying a word. The tension reaches an uncomfortable peak. He places his phone on the counter between our sinks.

"You can put your number in there if you want."

West shoulders his way between us with all the grace of a bull in a china shop and swipes the guy's phone to the side, practically dropping it in the sink. "Excuse me," he says rudely. "Are you done with that sink?"

"Y-Yeah," the guy stutters, finally looking at West. He pockets his phone and gives me one last long look before he walks out.

I play it off with a laugh and shake my head, and West's gaze is burning a hole through my head in the reflection of the mirror. He's not amused.

He rips a paper towel from the wall holder and dries his hands before chucking the wadded up ball into the trash. "It's time to go."

He's silent on the ride home, staring out the window, fidgeting with the radio, but I can feel his anger and anxiety mounting with each passing mile until he finally blurts, "Maybe you should turn around and go back, get that guy's number." I hold my breath, and he adds, "He was obviously into you."

"You think?" If I know West, and I do, he's about to have an episode the size of Texas, and I just need to remain calm while he works it out.

"So that's it? You're gay now? Checking out *all* the guys?"

I didn't check anyone out. He's being ridiculous, and it's hard not to laugh or smile because it's almost cute. In fact, I don't even have to answer because he keeps right on going.

"I mean, it's fine with me. We're just friends, right? Just having a good time? I guess you were just waiting for something better to come along."

Christ, he has the thickest skull of anyone I know. Absolutely fucking clueless. "Was I?"

"I guess so."

He's glaring, irises pools of dark fire, and if I don't put a stop to it soon, he's going to say something stupid he'll regret. "Would you cut the bullshit? I'm not interested in any man—or *anyone*—but you. Not because I'm figuring things out, and not because it's convenient, but because I've wanted you for longer than I care to admit, and more so every day." An amused chuff pushes through my nose as I watch his face morph from pissed off to disbelieving. "You're the last person I want to fall in love with for the rest of my life."

With my eyes back on the road, I miss his expression, but I almost don't want to see it either, for fear of how he'll take it.

Fuck, I have to look. He's not saying anything. And when I do, I laugh because he's grinning from ear to ear.

"Who was the first?"

"Also you," I admit with a sideways glance. "I didn't wanna push you, I just didn't want you to spin out. I thought you should know where I'm at."

"No, I'm glad you said something. You shouldn't ever keep anything from me. We promised each other." He reaches over and turns the radio down. "You're the first and last person I ever wanna fall in love with, too." Gratification like I've never known before unfurls in my chest, filling up all the empty space. Joy, contentment, fulfillment—his words make me feel all of it. "I don't know what the fuck I'm doing. I'm just starting to figure out who I am, or who I'm becoming, but I know that no matter what the future holds for me, I want you right there by my side." I glance at him and he meets my eyes. "I just thought you should know where I'm at."

WEST

Chapter 29

AS SOON AS we get home, I head straight for our room, beyond ready to change out this blade for my other leg, but Brandt follows, and it seems he has other plans for me.

He stops me as I go to sit down on the bed, grabbing my hips and spinning me into the wall so that I have to brace my hands against it to stop from crashing face first.

"Fuck."

"Exactly," he rumbles in my ear, lacing his fingers through mine. "Keep them right there."

Shivers skate down my spine from the rough possession in his voice. It's easy for me to obey. I want whatever he's going to give me.

His fingers tease my waist as he slides the hem of my shirt

up my torso. "I had the best fucking day today. Do you know why?" He pauses to finger my nipples before sliding the shirt up over my head and arms.

Fuck if I know, or care right now, about anything other than what he's doing to me. "The potato skins?"

His wicked laugh in my ear makes my dick twitch.

"No, not the potato skins." He sucks on my neck and licks his way down to my shoulder, where he lightly nips me with his teeth. "And not the beer." His hands return to my hips, and he slides my shorts down one hip, and then the other, exposing my briefs. "Not even the satisfaction of watching a grandma smoke your ass."

Fucker. I knew he wouldn't let me live it down.

He peels my underwear and my shorts down my legs in one move, and I step out of them, bracing my legs wide to keep my balance.

"It was watching you try, and then succeed today." His soft lips suck on the lobe of my ear, and the sensation travels straight to my cock, making it hard and thick. "It was seeing you smile and even laugh." He's drawing on my lobe, mimicking the sensation of sucking on the tip of my cock, and now that's all I can think of. "We made plans for our future. You made friends." I gasp when his teeth close around my ear. "You fucking *lived* today."

"Oh, that. I thought it was because I told you I love you."

He chuckles, drawing out the sound like he's having fun. "Do you?"

"Do you need me to prove it?"

"That sounds like a really good idea."

At the bar, I saw that guy checking him out and then follow him into the bathroom, and I flipped. Ugly green jealousy took hold of me like a cancer, and I was up and out of my chair before I even knew what I was doing. And then he had the balls to so boldly ask for Brandt's phone number! Yeah, fuck no. I realized then and there that if I didn't get my shit together, I would lose him. Eventually. He's only going to play this *Ring Around The Rosie* game with me for so long before someone better than me, with less bullshit and two good legs, offers him something easier, something real. Where he doesn't have to hide or lie. I had exactly three seconds to evaluate my choices, and I know I made the right call when I told him to fuck off.

Because Brandt is *mine*. He belongs to *me*. He always has, really, and I'll make damn sure he always will.

Who would I even be without him? I can barely remember the man I was before him. But without him? I'm nothing.

He dips his finger into the crease between my cheeks. "You have a sweet ass, you know that? Been wanting to touch it all day."

I pop it out so it's rounded and firm. Brandt drops to his knees and spreads me open, and I feel the wet tip of his soft tongue tickle my hole. Electric sparks run under my skin like a live current, igniting my lust.

"I love your taste. Love to watch you shudder."

And then he tongue-fucks my ass like he's chasing his own orgasm. With his hands gripping my hips, he shoves his face deep and bounces my ass against his mouth like I'm riding his tongue. I wish I could see it from another angle because I bet it's fucking hot. I'm dying to touch my cock, but he told me to leave my hands on the wall.

He might stop if I don't obey, and if he stops... I'll die.

My breaths come hard and fast as heat builds inside me like a pressure cooker. The obscene slurping and groaning noises coming from his mouth are working me into a primal frenzy, desperate for more, more of anything and everything. I'm ready for all of it.

He straightens to his full height and disappears, and I glance over my shoulder to see where he's gone. His nightstand. He rummages through the top drawer and grabs a bottle of clear liquid, shucking his pants and underwear on his way back to me. The heat of his body warms my back as he leans over my shoulder, peppering my collarbone and neck with sucking kisses. I can feel his fist bumping against my ass and know he's stroking himself. My heart kicks into a faster rhythm, wondering what he's about to do to me.

The dizzy swirl in my head, my body burning with heat, libido in overdrive, it's all too much, and I lose my balance, my good leg beginning to buckle. *Fucking vertigo.*

Brandt catches me, reaching around my waist, and his big, calloused hands stroke over my abs and across my chest. "Steady," he whispers in my ear. His slick cock rubs through my crease, catching on my rim with each pass. It's a tease, a mindfuck, because I know he wants to slip inside of me, but he's holding himself back. I push back against him, begging for a little more. The fear is gone this time, replaced by longing and jealousy from earlier at the bar. I *want* him inside me. I'm so fucking ready. I'm too horny to let my inhibitions cloud my judgment.

Brandt taps my hole with his finger, and I push back again.

"You want it, don't you?" It's not a question. More of an observation. He knows what I want. He also knows I'm too much of a coward to voice the words.

I answer with a moan.

He slides the tip of his finger past my rim, and immediately I feel full, but no pain. His finger isn't thick enough to hurt. The sensation sets my body on fire as he slowly slides in and out, and when he curls his finger and brushes over my prostate, I bang my head into the wall as my body tenses.

"Holy fuck!" I scream. He chuckles in my ear, his breath hot on my neck, making the fine hairs rise. "More," I beg, hoping he'll give me another finger.

"I've got plenty more. I'll give you as much as you can take."

Jesus, yeah. I want to take it all.

I feel a mild burn as he stretches me wider, and I can't imagine what his cock will feel like, but I'm horny enough not to care. "Right there," I breathe as he rubs over the spot again.

"You love it, don't you?"

"Fuck yes. More."

He thrusts his fingers harder, deeper, fucking me with them as I push back, meeting him halfway. His knuckles dig into my cheeks and my chest tightens as I hold my breath, trying to stave off the wave of heat gathering within me. He continues to light me up from the inside and I realize I'm fucking him. I'm the one doing all the work, begging for it like a desperate, needy bottom.

"Fuck, Wes. You should see how hot you look."

He loves this, wants me as much as I want him, and feeling awkward and out of my comfort zone is the last thing on my mind. I don't even tense when he slips his fingers out and pushes his swollen cockhead against my hole. His hands come around my chest again, like a hug as he grinds his shaft through my cheeks like he's fucking into me.

I want it. Want *him*. Want him *inside* of me.

The pressure increases as he presses harder. "Do it," I hiss, daring him to enter me. My chest hurts from how fast and hard my heart is beating.

"Relax, breathe out." His lips suck a dark spot on my neck and when he breaches my rim, he bites my skin to deflect where the pain is centered. The burn forces the breath from my lungs in an agonized gasp, and I freeze up. "Let me in," he purrs, licking at my bruised neck, and with a deep breath, I let go and open for him as I release it. "That's it." His voice is a soft caress in my ear, urging me to trust him, to relax into him.

He moves in and out, slowly, as my breath comes in fits and starts, sharp little gasps and breathy moans as his rhythm changes. In just minutes, the intense burn is replaced by an electric fire that licks through my lower half and makes my dick harder than it's ever been. The feeling of fullness is foreign and so intense, like nothing I've ever felt, and I'm already addicted to it.

"Goddamn, you're so fucking tight." He sucks in a sharp breath as he withdraws and plunges back in. "Knew it would feel this good." He drops his forehead on my shoulder and digs his fingers deeper, tightening his grip on my hips as he slams into me, setting a faster, harder pace. "Look how good you take my cock."

Damn, his words are lighting me up. I love it, being talked to like this, being on the receiving end of sex for the first time in my life. Being with Brandt is a first, and it's a memory I'll take with me to my grave.

I slap my palm against the wall as he thrusts into me, and I can feel my balls draw up tight against my body, heavy with my unspent release. He buries himself to the hilt, and I feel his cock pulse.

"Fuck, I'm trying to last," he grates with a hiss. His body stills within me as he wills himself not to come yet, and the feeling of being in control, of holding a certain power over him, fills me with the confidence I've been lacking for so long.

There is strength in submission; it certainly isn't for the weak.

Fast and frantically, I jack my cock, trying to catch up to him, chasing my release, and when he twists my nipples, I scream out and buck backward, fucking myself on his cock as he continues to hold himself still, watching as I take my pleasure.

"Take it, babe. Fuck me." His labored breath comes quick and shallow as he struggles to maintain control. "Goddamn Wes, can't fuckin' take anymore. I c–" He slams into my body with a grunt and the warmth of his release fills me.

"Fuck." I fuck him through it, my own release rushing forth like a freight train. "Fuck! Brandt." My spine arches like a cat as a deep, full-body shudder rolls through me. "*Ungh.*" He rotates his hips, rolling over that spot inside me that makes my toes curl, and ropes of thick white cum shoot over my hand, painting the wall. I'm sweating, panting for breath, my hip aches, but all I can feel is incredible bliss and satisfaction. The past weeks of wanting, teasing, and daring have become reality, and it's better than anything I could have imagined.

"Don't want to pull out," he breathes into my neck between kisses.

I chuckle, grinning like a fool. "Then don't." I cover his hands with mine over my chest, hugging him back, reveling in the warmth and comfort of his body, and to fuck with him, I squeeze my ass, clenching his softening yet still sensitive cock.

"Fuck," he barks, slipping from my heat. "I'll go run the shower for us, and then I want you in bed with me."

A night of cuddling, teasing touches, snacks, and movies sounds fucking perfect. In the shower, his hands are everywhere, washing my body, touching me, sliding his fingers into my well-used hole to wash me out. His kisses cover every inch of my skin. I can feel him clinging to me, and I can practically hear the unspoken words he's holding back; something sentimental and cheesy, no doubt. But I wish he wouldn't. I want to hear them. I think I *need* to hear them.

It's not until after he's carefully dried my body with a towel and we slip into clean underwear and climb into bed that he finally voices them.

"I never thought this would be us."

I agree with a wry laugh. "Me either. I mean, you've always been my closest friend, and we've always been tight, but I sought you out because you were familiar to me. It was comforting, and maybe a tiny bit thrilling, but not because I wanted more from you."

Brandt is quiet for a moment, rubbing his hand back and forth over his damp buzz cut, and I'm dying to know what he's thinking of. "Would you go back if you could?"

"To what? Being just friends?"

"Yeah, to how it used to be."

I blow out a deep breath and roll onto my side, facing him. He smells clean and citrusy and I want to bury my face in his armpit and breathe him in. "I don't know. It was easier then, that's for sure." His hand is resting on his chest and I cover it with mine. "I don't know if I want easy anymore. Whatever *this* is, I want *this*. What about you? Would you go back?"

"Nah, you've got a tight ass," he smirks.

"Fucking dick." Burrowing my hands under the covers, I flick his dick, and he yelps.

"Why would I go back? I want to see where this goes. Feelings change, relationships evolve. If you'd have told me twelve months ago that a year from now we'd be sleeping together, I'd have kicked you in the nuts and laughed until I stroked out, but here we are. Sometimes life is stranger than fiction," he teases, reaching behind me to pinch my ass. And then we're rolling and laughing and wrestling. He stills and catches my gaze. "I guess it's just meant to be." The words are a prelude to the sweetest, softest kiss.

"I never knew it could be like this, either, that two guys could be this close." I breathe out a soft, dreamy sigh and Brandt snickers. With a narrow-eyed glare, I clarify, "You know what I mean. I didn't know we could share this much, more than just best buds." His broad shoulders shake with laughter, and I shove him hard. "That's not what I meant, asshole. Just forget it," I dismiss with a huff.

He makes it sound like I've never heard of gay sex, which is just ridiculous. I just never considered what it would mean to be so intimate with another man. In my defense, why would I ever need to consider it? Until now.

Brandt flips us, rolling me underneath him, and straddles my hips. His smile is tender and teasing, and his blue eyes sparkle with laughter. "What did you mean?"

I lay my hand over his heart. "I meant close here, not *here*," I emphasize, pushing my soft cock into his groin. "You've always been my best friend, my brother, my teammate, but now, you're my..." I'm searching for the right word, racking my brain for something that feels right, that fits. How can I describe what Brandt means to me? My vocabulary isn't that sophisticated. "...soulmate."

He laughs again, leaning down to nip my bottom lip and suck it into his mouth until it's swollen and puffy and red. "That's cheesy as fuck," he whispers with a wicked smile.

Now I feel like a fool, and I shove him again, trying to dislodge him from my lap. *Soulmates? Really, West?*

"Nope, you can't get rid of me that easily," he laughs. "You're stuck with me."

Thank God. "God help me."

"Can we not call it 'soulmates', though? Can't we just say friends with benefits who really like each other a lot?"

He's still fucking laughing at me. *Fucker.* "The more you talk, the less I like you. Get off me, you're squashing my balls."

WEST
Chapter 20

Balls
Black Mountain, NC

THE MUTED SOUND *of bootsteps echoed above my head. It was the only sound to fill the tense silence, other than the low buzz of static through my comms.*

"All clear, Sarge."

"Roger that," I replied. The fine hairs on my neck stood at attention. Something wasn't right. It was too qu–

The clicking was all too familiar, a death toll in my ear, chilling me to the bone, freezing me in my tracks. The boom that followed was deafening, followed by two more in rapid succession, and then the heat. The heat was unbearable, burning my skin, my eyes, even through my goggles. The force, or maybe Brandt, shoved me hard, and then...

Fuck! My body shakes, and I tumble and roll, hitting the

ground with a painful thump. Sweating and shaking, I reach out blindly, in a dizzying state of confusion, for something familiar.

"You okay?"

I feel the cool wooden leg of the table beneath my fingers and grab on for dear life. "Get the fuck off me!"

"Let me help you." Brandt is right there, his worried face so close I can barely bring it into focus. "Can't believe you fell off the couch," he says with a smirk.

Embarrassed, and a bit pissed at myself for such a piss-poor recovery of a humiliating situation, I snap, "I didn't. I attacked the floor."

"Backwards? You landed on your ass."

Thanks for noticing, asswipe. "What can I say? I'm talented like that."

My hip throbs and I roll onto my good side while massaging the bruise. Brandt stands and extends a helping hand to me. I don't want to grab it. Hasn't my pride suffered enough for one day?

"What was it?"

"The blast."

"I hate that you had to see it again."

Snorting, I say, "I see it every time I close my eyes."

"You gonna let me help you up?"

"I can do it." Like a stubborn ass, I grab the edge of the coffee table and struggle to sit up, but that's as far as I can get on my own.

"Fine." He grabs a pillow and settles on the floor.

"What are you doing?"

"You want to stay here, so I'm getting comfortable."

Why does he insist on loving me in the moments I hate myself most? "Fuck, you're annoying."

"You think? I think I'm pretty easygoing and likable." He licks my cheek, all sloppy and wet, and grins. "Are we gonna be down here a while? 'Cause if so, I'll grab a snack."

"Help me the fuck up. If for no other reason, just so I can get away from you," I say with a good dose of annoyance. Brandt hops up and grabs me under the armpits, hoisting my useless ass onto the couch. "Will you grab my crutch so I can hobble to the bedroom and dress myself?"

I know I sound like a whiny toddler, brimming with self-deprecating sarcasm, but my pride took a hit, and my ego might still be on the floor, stuck underneath the coffee table. Maybe we'll find it someday when we sweep up.

"You want me to dress you, too?" he asks, handing me the crutch I use to move around when I'm not wearing the prosthesis.

"Cute, smartass. If you follow me into the bathroom, you can wipe my ass, too."

"No thanks. I can think of sexier sounding things to do with your ass."

And just like that, I'm not mad anymore. My anger is replaced with embarrassment for my attitude.

"I'm sorry."

"Yeah, you are," he teases, shadowing me down the hall. "But I love you anyway." Brandt veers toward the bathroom while I grab my clothes and I sit on the edge of the bed to attach my leg.

I have a routine now, starting with skin care. A pump of

lotion is enough to soften the scarred skin, which reduces irritation throughout the day. A sprinkle of Gold Bond powder in my nylon sleeve for odor and sweat absorption to help keep my skin dry. Then I roll it over my stump, grab my leg to attach it, and slide my pants on, standing to get them over my ass. But when I reach for my boot to slide it over the foot, I stop...

"You fucking fucker!"

Brandt's laughter carries through the bathroom door. When he opens it, he's grinning like it's his birthday. "Gotcha."

"Why would you paint the toenails of my prosthetic foot? Bubble gum pink, no less!"

"Actually, it's Marry Me Pink." He's doubled over, clutching his stomach in a fit of laughter. "The guys said it was a hazing ritual, a rite of passage to officially being a Bitch."

"Fuck, Brandt, how could you?" We had a bro code of honor. Didn't we?

"Stiles paid me twenty bucks."

"You threw me under the bus for twenty fucking bucks?" He's laughing harder now, snorting and wheezing. "You better sleep with one eye open, Reaper."

He straightens and rubs a hand over his perfectly sculpted and scarred abs, and the move draws my eyes. It's crazy to me how I can find that so sexy now, whereas I never noticed before. So many changes in me lately. Good changes. Speaking of...

"I have an appointment with a therapist today at BALLS."

"Yeah, we're working out with Riggs after group."

"No, a different therapist." I pull my boot on to avoid his gaze, busying myself with tying the laces.

"What kind of therapist?"

I can hear the concern in his voice, all traces of humor gone. It wraps around my heart like a hug, fortifying me, giving me strength. "A head shrink that specializes in trauma."

His weight drops down next to me, making the mattress dip. "Wes, that's..." He swallows, and he clears his throat. "That's great. I'm so fucking proud of you."

And this is why I didn't want to say anything. What if I can't cut it? What if it's too much and I want to quit? I'd disappoint him. It's also why I decided to tell him, because he won't let me quit.

"Yeah, we'll see."

"Okay, finish getting dressed. There's this website I found that I want to show you before we go. It's a bulk supplier of tactical gear. We can check it out, maybe place an order so we can get started with our business."

He's in full go-mode, brimming with purpose and energy. Apparently, my starting therapy is a good thing. *Really* good.

We'll see.

Standing outside of the gym, I'm ready to part ways when Brandt catches my arm, and I turn back around.

"Are you sure you're ready for this? Because we can go back to the car," he offers, thumbing over his shoulder.

"I don't know if I'm ready, but I need this. I think we both do."

"Don't do this for me, Wes, do it for you. For your own peace of mind. You don't owe me anything."

That's the biggest fucking lie ever. I owe him *everything*.

"I'll be fine. I'm a big boy."

"Look, if you feel like…If you can't do it, it's okay to just get up and leave. Try again another day. If you need me, you know where to find me. I'll be right here working out with Riggs." I offer him a weak smile that I hope is reassuring, and he squeezes my fingers. "Don't forget, just because I'm not with you doesn't mean you don't have my legs."

"And I can't fall with three legs. I won't forget, Reaper." *Goddamn, I will never deserve this man, not as my friend, and not as my lover. In no capacity, in no lifetime, will I ever be worthy of him.* "Sit tight. I'll be back in an hour."

I can feel his eyes burning holes in my back as I shuffle down the hall toward the office where I'm meeting my therapist. Riggs set the whole thing up, and I trust his recommendation, but I have no idea who I'm meeting with. When I approach the second to last door on the left, I knock twice, and I hear a muffled "*Come in*" through the door.

The office is decorated in a plain but warm aesthetic, with white walls and brown suede chairs. The color comes from the many potted plants, and a maroon oriental knock-off rug on the floor. It's comfortable and simple and helps to put me at ease.

Unlike the man who greets me with his hand out. "I'm Brewer Marx. Please, take a seat, get comfortable. Can I get you some water? Coffee?"

He's tall, at least the same height as me, with dark wavy hair that's longer on top and shorter on the sides. The careless style blends together smoothly, just barely kissing his collar. His tone sounds easy, casual, but his dark eyes are shrewd. This man is smart, and he doesn't miss a thing.

"I know you. Don't you run the addiction group?" My senses buzz on high alert, and I feel like something's off, like I'm walking into a trap.

"I do, but I'm also a trauma therapist. I'm more than just a one-trick pony." He sits and gestures for me to take the seat across from him. "What about you?"

"What about me? I'm pretty much a one-trick pony," I repeat sarcastically. "I spent my whole life chasing one dream. I was good at it, and it's all I knew, all I wanted. And now it's gone," I say with heavy finality.

So maybe he's not setting me up, but I'm still tense, sitting forward with my hands fidgeting between my knees. These pleasantries will only last another minute or two before he wants to dig up the nitty-gritty of my past.

"Look, I get it, I do, but I also get that I can't just throw that out there without backing it up. Why should you trust me? You don't know me. I'm a big believer in trust, and it goes both ways. Your recovery is only going to be effective if you feel like you can open up and lay yourself bare, and you can't do that with me if you don't trust me. So I'll go first. I'll tell you who I am and where I came from. Then, after you've heard me out, you can decide if you think I'm someone you can trust. Deal?"

Fuck me, I was not expecting that.

He sits forward with his arms braced on his knees, mirroring my pose. "My name is Brewer Marx, and I'm a recovering addict who suffers from PTS. I spent eight years in the Army. I had one deployment to the desert. One *long* deployment," he breathes out on a sigh. "Spent almost eighteen months there. Do you know what I learned?" I just shake my head, having no idea what he's about to say. "I learned that no amount of training or education can prepare you for battle. Nothing on this earth can prepare you for the desert."

That's the fucking truth.

"I was infantry. Stationed in Iraq. We were en route from a village back to the FOB. We, ah–" he pauses to clear his throat. "–took on heavy fire. From everywhere, on all sides. In a matter of minutes we were surrounded." His throat works furiously and I know exactly how he's feeling. Trying to swallow down that lump of emotion so you don't lose your shit.

"I think there were tunnels or something underground and they just, they were popping up like fucking groundhogs. Anyway, my buddy and I returned fire. He was yelling something to me, but I couldn't hear him over the gunfire. He was telling me to retreat. That one second that he took his eyes off the fight to focus on me cost him his life. One minute I was staring at him, listening to him shout at me, and the next, he took a bullet through his head. Right through the side of his face."

His voice fades as his words trail off. I know what he's seeing in his head right now. He's somewhere else, no longer sitting across from me in this office. He's reliving the day his buddy died. Like he probably has a thousand times.

When he focuses on me again, his eyes are wet, rimmed with red, and he looks visibly distraught. "I froze. I was wearing his fucking face. My buddy, the guy I trained with, the guy I bunked with. His brains were on my fucking face. In my goddamn mouth."

Jesus Christ. I can't even imagine. I was spared from having to see the carnage of my team's death. Hearing it was bad enough, but seeing it, feeling it on your skin, that's a whole other nightmare.

Brewer excuses himself and grabs a bottle of water from the mini fridge in the corner by his coffee maker. He swishes and spits into the trash can, like he's rinsing his mouth of the taste of his friend's blood.

When he reclaims his seat, he continues. "It only takes a second to make a fatal mistake. In that moment, I gave up several precious seconds, and it cost me. It almost cost me my life. Another guy was yelling at me to get my head in the game, and just as my head came back online, I was taken out of the game with a bullet. Right here." He taps the junction of his arm, where his shoulder meets his body. "The bullet hit my artery, and I began to bleed out. Thank God, the guy who was yelling at me was a medic. I could feel myself slipping away, getting weaker, my vision becoming darker, and he reached into the wound and pinched my artery close with his fingers. Can you imagine? The pain brought me back. I threw up all over myself," he recalls with a humorless laugh.

"He held my life in his hands for eighteen long minutes until air support came and cleared out the scene. On the chopper, my heart stopped beating from the loss of blood, and they gave me an emergency transfusion and brought me back. But at the hospital, they lost me again."

My emotions are getting the best of me, and I can feel them

leaking through my eyes and nose, my throat thick with it. I can only imagine the effort it takes him to hold his shit together while he tells me the story.

"As you can see, they brought me back again. But I was done after that. I kept getting lost inside my head, losing time. My short-term memory was shit. I would freeze up and have panic attacks, and I was no good to anyone like that. I was broken. Damaged goods. I finished out my contract stateside. In the meantime, I put my G.I. Bill to good use and went back to school to receive my certification as a licensed therapist and addiction counselor. As you can imagine, it cost me a lot to get up and function every day like nothing was wrong. I relied heavily on pills to get me through school, to help with my focus and my memory and the panic attacks. The anxiety was crippling most days. It's a wonder I even made it through. After I was discharged, I continued with school and received my bachelor's degree in social work and mental health."

He stops to take a long swig from his bottle and swallows so hard I can hear it. "Can you imagine?" He laughs harshly, dragging a hand through his carefully mussed hair. "There I was, high as a fucking kite during my residency, counseling others on the dangers of addiction. Most days I could barely fucking stand myself, could barely stand to look in the mirror."

I don't want to hear anymore. I thought it was bad enough, but his story just keeps getting worse. I don't want to feel for him because it reminds me of my own pain. I have no idea how to cope with that pain.

"What happened? When was your turning point?" I ask.

"You know what they say, you have to hit rock bottom

before you can begin to climb back out of the hell hole you're living in. It was the anniversary of my buddy's death, and I took his wife and two little girls to visit his grave. I was sort of uncle Brewer, guardian of his family. That was the hardest part for me, seeing this beautiful family grieve for him, an honorable, responsible, wonderful man, and yet here I was, still alive, a worthless piece of shit. The unfairness of it all just made me so fucking angry and bitter. Angry at God, angry at fate, angry at myself."

I know what that anger feels like. That self-hatred that burns deep in your gut like acid.

"But the moment that got me was when they walked back to the car and left me standing there alone, with just me and Eric. His wife thought I was some sort of hero or some bullshit, but Eric knew better. He could see me for what I really was. He was watching me from heaven, or wherever the fuck he ended up, and he could see every fucked up deed and sin I committed. He saw me for the fraud I was. I was in the middle of a long tirade of apologies and self-recrimination, making empty promises of how I would do better when I spotted a man slumped against a headstone. Maybe he was a homeless vet or something, because he sure looked like it, and I caught myself getting angry at him, like a self-righteous prick. How dare he desecrate someone's grave, their honor, and their sacrifice, by sleeping there, making a home there, with his dirty, unwashed body. He held a paper bag in his hand, and I know there was alcohol in it. I fumed with anger, so fucking full of shit. I had no right to judge him. Maybe he knew the person buried there beneath him. Maybe he felt responsible for putting them there."

Brewer paused to finish off his water and then swiped his eyes over the sleeve of his shirt to dry them. "I realized I was him. I was certainly no better than him, except my clothes were cleaner and I had a decent haircut. There I was, escorting the family of the man who died for me, high out of my fucking mind. If I could have taken my life right there in that moment, I would have. I dropped to my ass in the dirt and swore to Eric and God and myself that I would do better. That I would get clean. And that I would use my degree and my experience to help others. I owed it to Eric and his family to make something of the life I was spared, to live the life he would have that he no longer could."

I lose the battle with my tears, swiping at them as I feel them wash over my cheeks in a warm rush.

"I found BALLS, started to attend meetings here, and when I celebrated two years clean, they offered me a job. Can you imagine? Me, an addict, a fuck-up." He laughs again, but not because it's funny. "Been clean ever since. The anxiety has gotten better. But I'll tell you what, Wardell. There's no cure for this shit. It doesn't ever go away completely. It's a disease that lives in our brain and tortures us on any given day at any moment, when we're at our weakest, most vulnerable point, and it kicks us while we're down. That's why we have to get strong and steady on the good days. So we can defend ourselves against the bad ones." He clears his throat and swipes at his eyes again. "That's it. That's all I've got to say. Now it's my turn to shut up and listen."

I swallow and shake my head, swiping at my eyes again. I don't know where to begin. I feel raw, completely exposed. I can feel his pain as if it were my own, and I know he can feel mine. I'm also envious of him. I want what he has. His confidence and strength, his peace of mind. When I open my mouth to speak, my voice comes out, a warbled shredded mess, thick with emotion and pain.

"My name is Weston Wardell, former Sergeant First Class of the United States Army, and I have PTS and a TBI. I hate myself, and I don't want to live, and I hate myself because I do want to live. I just want to feel like I deserve to. Like I deserve the life I was spared. And I don't want to disappoint Brandt. I just wanna stop hurting him." My head drops into my hands. "I just want to stop hurting."

"I can help you with that," Brewer promises, and I want to believe him. Maybe I do believe him. And for the first time in a long time, I have hope.

I make my way down the hall, back to the gym, back to Brandt. He takes one look at me and says, "Fuck no, let's get you home."

We don't say much on the drive home, but I can feel his worry, and I'm silently counting how many times he looks at me, checking in to make sure I'm okay. I'm glad to be going home, to a place that finally *feels* like home, because of him.

He strips me down and gets me into bed, fussing over me like a mother hen, and we cuddle beneath the thick covers. The solid warmth of his body at my back is a reassuring weight, like a security blanket.

"Wes, I need proof of life," he says in a rough whisper. "I haven't asked in a while, but I need to know you're in there."

"I'm here. I swear I'm here." His arms come around me,

under my arms, and around my chest. "I want this, Reaper. I want to live, I want a life, and I want you, but I want to not hate myself for it."

"Do you feel this?" he asks, squeezing me. "Do you feel my arms around you? I'm never gonna let go. When we're fucking eighty years old, I'm still gonna have my arms around you, holding you tight."

"Three legs," I rasp.

"Three fucking legs," he assures me, dropping a kiss to my head.

BRANDT
Chapter 21

THIS PAST WEEK dragged ass in an endless blur of grueling rehab, doctor appointments, wings and beer with the Bitches after group, and another long day spent hiding under the covers while West suffered with a head-splitting migraine.

Today, after his session with Brewer, he fell into my arms and croaked, "Take me home", and that's what I did.

His nerves were stripped raw, his soul bared and exposed. I could see it in his red-rimmed eyes, in the slack expression on his face. The entire drive home was spent in silence, and I was convinced we would have another day in bed until we pulled up in the gravel drive. The supplies we ordered for the Boot Camp had arrived, and not even West's shit day could stop him from getting excited, like a kid on Christmas, when he saw the stacks of cardboard boxes piled up next to our front door.

I grabbed sandwiches and beer, and West grabbed the ammo and our guns, and we set off on a hike down to the area we designated as safe to use for a gun range. It was easy to burn through the emotions stirring up in his gut with each bullet fired from his gun. Even I feel lighter with each squeeze of the trigger. Target practice is my kind of therapy. The warm sun on my bare arms and face, the higher wind velocity from standing on top of a hill, I feel alive and unencumbered by stress and burdens and anxiety. The steel grip of the pistol is warm in my hand, a familiar weight, almost like an extension of my arm. I almost feel like a soldier again.

The sun glints off West's dark hair, illuminating amber highlights. He stares down the sight of his pistol, lining up his target with one eye closed, and his jaw tenses. The echo of his shot reverberates through the valley and a slow, satisfied grin spreads across his face.

I fucking love you.

That's what I think as I stare at him. It's been a long time since I've seen him in his element, with a gun in his hand and a smile on his face. He resembles the West I used to know; a little bit dangerous, a little bit careless, but always in control. A leader.

"We've got five guys signed up for our first weekend outing. Can you believe it?"

"I can, because you promised me it would work, and you wouldn't dare break your promise," West replies.

"It's gonna be great. You and me, doing our thing again, together."

"That sounds good. Really good."

A hawk caws overhead. The silence accompanies the thoughts running through my mind.

"I want to tell my mom about us."

Where the fuck did that come from out of nowhere? West must be thinking the same thing because his face tightens.

"Don't say shit like that when I'm holding a loaded gun in my hand."

"That's not funny," I chastise, glaring as I lower my pistol.

"I wasn't joking," he smirks. He squeezes off another shot, making my ears ring, and then glances at me again. "Oh, come the fuck on, Brandt. You still owe me for the last time."

"I need you. I need you to do this for me."

I understand his reluctance to get involved, but why can't he understand my need to come clean with my parents? To tell them who I am and who I'm in love with? How can we build a future together on lies?

"How do you think she's gonna take it? Besides the obvious crying jag she's famous for. And what about your father?"

Raising my pistol, I square my shoulders and choose my target, a pinecone, high up in a tree about a hundred yards away. "My father will smile politely and walk out of the room to avoid a discussion. God only knows what will follow my mother's crying."

"At this point, you're never going to stop owing me."

I can think of a few ways I'd like to owe him. Squeezing the trigger, I absorb the kick from the gun throughout my arm and shoulder.

"I know. I just..." It's ridiculous that at almost thirty-five years old, I'm afraid of my parents. Afraid to tell them something they don't know about me. "Thank you for doing this for me."

West lowers his gun and turns to me. "I'm always going to show up for you, Reaper. Always."

"I know. That's why I love you." And I know he loves me too, which is the only reason he agreed to come with me.

We finish off two more clips each before holstering our guns. I sit down on my ass, leaning my back against a thick pine trunk, and uncap the tube on my hydration pack, taking a long swig of water.

"Does this make us geardos?"

His question catches me off guard. "What, having your own gun range?"

West laughs. "No, that's just fucking awesome. All this gear we ordered. Getting excited about it, like we're gearing up to play scout camp."

I snort a laugh, shaking my head as I wipe sweat from my brow. "By definition, a geardo is someone who is obsessed with having the best military gear, and is usually someone who doesn't need it. Does that fit us?"

"To a fucking T," he snickers. "Except we kind of need it because of our camp."

"Not gonna lie," I admit with a smirk. "I would have bought this shit even if we hadn't started the business."

"Yeah, we're fucking geardos. Let's just lock this away in the vault, along with that granny incident at the track and the fact that we can knit like one."

"Deal."

"What was that bullshit with Stiles and McCormick wanting to join our Boot Camp? They act as if they've never been in the desert."

Capping my hydration pack, I can't help but smile as I wipe my lips dry. "They wanted to support us. You know, whether you want to admit it, you're still a leader. You just have a new team."

"Who? The Bitches?" The expression on his face is caught somewhere between horror and surprise.

"I can't think of a finer team. Experienced, loyal, smart—"

"That part is questionable."

"On our worst days, through thick and thin, those guys have our backs."

West looks unconvinced. "I can't think of a more ragtag bunch of misfits."

"They are a unit, and they're our new team. And that means we're family."

"*Fuuuuuuuck.* Lord help us," he teases, looking heavenward.

"Come on, let's head back. I'll make you dinner and we can soak in the hot tub."

The trek back home is slow and steady, taking almost three times longer than it usually does, back when we had four legs between the two of us. It gives us plenty of time to talk.

"I think this will be good for me. For us, I mean. Getting back to normal. Back to what we're good at," West notes.

"So do I."

"But I need more than this. I think I'm gonna talk to Riggs about volunteering at BALLS. I need to feel like I'm helping someone."

You mean you need to feel like you're saving someone.

"Yeah, I get it. I think it will be good for you. Anything I can do to support you, I'm there."

West glances at me with a soft smile. "I know you are. But this is something I've got to do on my own." His smile grows silly. "You can help me with everything else, though." He limps along, and I can tell he's hurting. West swallows his pain and grimaces as he steps over a large rock on the path. "I had a good session today with Brewer. It was hard, and it hurt, but it was good. Therapeutic, even. You know, I wouldn't be here if not for you."

"Don't start this bullshit again."

"I mean it. I would have given up long ago if not for you. You saved me. I don't know why, and I don't know for what purpose, but you saved me. You're the reason."

Because I can't live without you. I refuse to even try.

"Yeah, well, it was completely selfish of me. Why should I have to go on all alone and suffer without you? I said fuck it, if I have to live, I'm dragging your ass with me." West scoffs, rolling his eyes. "I reached down into the darkest pit of hell and snatched your ass out of there. Now you're stuck with me."

Without warning, West turns and grabs my hips, pulling me to him roughly. His lips smash against mine in a possessive, claiming kiss that leaves me panting for more.

"I'm glad you did," he breathes over my wet lips. "I want to live. For us, for me, for our future plans, and the business. I want to see what tomorrow has in store."

West devours the pork chops I make for dinner, and we grab two beers and step out onto the deck. He sits on the edge of the tub, removing his prosthetic before sliding under the water. When I see him hesitate, I smile, realizing he's waiting for me to take my usual seat on the lounger so he can sit between my legs.

God, little things like that make me want to kiss him senseless. Drag him inside and get him underneath me. Ask him to promise me forever.

Instead, I pull him onto my lap and press a kiss behind his ear. He leans back against my chest and sighs, and I feel his entire body relax and go liquid in my arms.

I clasp my hands around his stomach, and he covers them with his. The tranquil night is beautiful. A soothing balm on a tattered soul. The sky is littered with twinkling stars. Crickets and frogs are the only soundtrack playing. It's beautiful—a moment I wish could last forever.

West sighs, rubbing his thumb back-and-forth over my hand. "Do you remember our last night in the desert? We were laid out on the hood of the Humvee, and we gazed up at the stars. We pointed out all the constellations we could find. The sky looks so different from the other side of the world than it does here."

His head must be in the same place as mine. "I remember

the sandstorm that kicked up and blew dust in my eyes, and I remember the ensuing rain."

"Oh," he says, sounding disappointed. "I guess I remember that night differently than you do."

Our last night of normalcy before our world imploded. The night I admitted to myself that I was attracted to my best friend. "No, you remember that night perfectly. I'm just being an ass." I squeeze his midsection and plant another kiss on his head. "Actually, I remember seeing you differently that night," I admit.

"Different how?"

"I don't know, just different. I was more aware of you, and I felt a little uncomfortable, which is crazy, because how could I feel uncomfortable around you? But I remember looking at your lips, and I thought the stars had nothing on your eyes."

"Get out! That's so fucking cheesy," he chuckles.

I bury my smile in his steam-dampened hair. "It might have been the beginning of the end for me."

"What do you mean, the end? We're just getting started," he insists.

"What I mean is, you're my best friend, my brother in arms, my teammate. I've bled for you. I would take a bullet for you. Hell, I took a bomb for you! I would die in order to save your life. In a fucking heartbeat, I would die for you. There's nothing I wouldn't do for you, and now that we've added *this* to our relationship, what more do I need? We're compatible in every way. There's no one I trust more than you, but now that we have sexual chemistry and love, my heart feels so full. Why would I need to look elsewhere? You're it for me. This is the end of the road. You're everything I need and want, and I'll never doubt that again."

"How did I get so lucky twice? First with the bomb, we lived. We *both* lived. And now this. I wasn't supposed to be this lucky."

"Who says?"

"I don't know, Reaper, but it feels like too much goodness. I definitely need to help someone at BALLS to balance out my abundance of blessings."

His gratitude for his life fills my heart to bursting. It's about fucking time he realizes he's blessed. My hand drops lower, brushing over the soft bulge in his briefs. "How about we go inside and you can begin to show your gratitude?"

He chuckles, cupping my hand and squeezing. I can feel him growing hard in my grip. It still amazes me that I can affect him like this.

"I guess it's a good thing I didn't eat that third pork chop," he jokes.

"Actually, I thought we could switch things up tonight." My fingers steal inside his underwear to cup him in my palm. His skin feels warm and velvety, and he purrs when I stroke him.

"What did you have in mind?"

"I want you to fuck me."

"What?" he sputters, choking on his own words.

"It's all I can think about. How you would feel filling me, stretching me. Fucking into me. I want to know what makes your thighs shake and makes you cry when it's you taking it."

"I don't cry," he insists, but his voice has gone deep and husky.

"You do. Your eyes grow wet and you blink like a maniac."

"Whatever. Quit studying my O face. It's weird."

"It's not weird. Your face is the only thing I want to see when you're coming. I couldn't stop looking if I tried."

West chuckles, all low and sexy, and bucks into my fist. "I'm gonna fuck you so good, you won't ever want to top again."

I doubt that. Never again feeling West's body from the inside? Never feeling his tight, warm ass choke my cock and milk it dry? Fuck no! Never. I could never give that up.

I jump out and grab his crutch from inside, and together we make our way to the bedroom where West sits on the edge of the mattress. After a long day in his prosthesis, and the strenuous hike, I want to baby his skin. I grab the bottle of lotion from the nightstand and squirt a healthy dollop into my palm, warming it up before rubbing my hands over his limb.

He sighs with pleasure and relief, his dark eyes heavy and half-closed as he watches me. I rub his red skin with one hand while stroking my cock with the other. Every time I do this, it turns me on. Not because I have some amputee fetish, but because of the intimacy of the act. He's hiding nothing from me, and his most vulnerable parts are literally in my hands. It's a heady feeling, that kind of trust.

"Show me what this is doing to you," he says, nodding at my crotch.

Coming to my feet, I pull my pants off and kick out of them, then my shirt. Standing naked before him, I continue to stroke my cock as he watches me, stroking his own. I could watch him do that for hours. Stroking his perfect cock with tattooed hands, seeing the smooth head become wetter with each pass his fist makes. *Fuck.* It's going to feel incredible inside me.

Climbing over him, I cover his body with mine, tasting his skin, his nipples, kissing on his neck. My tongue finds that hollow spot in his throat, the scar from his tracheotomy. West lifts his longer leg, bending it to make a place for me between his thighs. His erection digs into my belly as I continue to tease his nipples until he squirms.

West gasps and maneuvers my body until we're on our sides with him spooning me from behind. Cold, wet fingers slide between my cheeks. Slowly, carefully, he opens me up, gliding over my hole with teasing touches before pushing the tip of his finger past my tight rim.

"*Ugh,*" I breathe as he stretches me. It's not unpleasant, but I know he's just getting started. He'll add a couple more before fucking me with his thick cock.

"So hot," he murmurs. His warm breath ghosting over the back of my neck makes me shiver. "Can't wait to get inside you."

Me either.

A second finger pushes inside me, and the long slow strokes brush past my gland, making me see stars. The heat in my belly lights me up from the inside, like a torch, making me desperate for more of him. When he slides a third finger in my tight passage, I can start to feel the burn, but I'm so fucking horny I don't even care.

"Just fuck me, already."

"So eager for my cock," he whispers in my ear before nipping the shell. My nerves are shot, completely overloaded with sensation and lust.

He pushes the fat head of his cock against my pucker, applying pressure until it pops through, and then pulls out and does it again, making me whimper. *Fucking whimper.* Me, a dedicated top, is fucking whimpering for him like a whore. Next I'll be moaning and begging for him to fuck me.

He repeats the in and out process three more times, and it feels a lot like dangling a carrot in front of my nose.

Here, you want my cock? Nope, sorry, not yet.

On the fourth pass, he slides in deep. Balls deep.

"Fuck," I choke, taken by surprise.

Nothing could prepare me for this, no matter how many times he pushes inside me, nor how many fingers he stretches me with. His thick cock sliding in and out of my virgin ass, stroking my gland and making my rim burn with painful pleasure, is a sensation I never could have imagined. Not until I felt it for myself. And now that I have, I'm ready to beg if necessary to get more.

West pulls back, I assume so he can look between our bodies as his hand lands on my cheek, spreading it wide.

"Fuck. I'm gonna come just from watching my dick sink into your ass. When I push in, my cock is so hard and thick, the base stretches your hole wider. And when I pull out, your rim shrinks around my tip. So fucking hot," he hisses, sliding back in.

My stomach flips, the muscles contracting like spasms. "Shit. I'm gonna come just from listening to you describe it."

"See for yourself," he says, grabbing his phone from the nightstand. His hips still as he fumbles with the camera, and then the slow thrusts resume.

It's fucking killing me that he's recording us. I'm never deleting that shit.

Ever.

"We can watch it together later. I'll make popcorn," he teases, making me grin despite my foggy, lust-fueled fever.

He sets the phone down and hitches his longer leg over my hip, cradling me against his body even tighter. He uses my body as leverage to fuck into me faster, deeper, harder, and I push back, meeting him thrust for thrust.

"Fuck, Brandt. Fuck."

I can't keep going like this or I'll come, and I really want to be facing him, for him to see my face when he pushes me over the edge. Sliding my hips forward, I pull off his dick, and he chases me, locking me in with his leg.

"Where're you going?"

"Let me ride you."

West only considers it for an eighth of a second before grinning and rolling to his back. He grabs another pillow and props it under his head so he can see me better. Gripping his shaft, now shiny from being inside me, He holds it still and stiff for me at the base. Gingerly, I straddle his hips and lower myself onto his dick, impaling myself in one slow descent.

West hisses and lets go, gripping my hips instead. "Fucking ride my cock, Reaper. Fuck me."

Planting my hands on his chest, I piston my hips back and forth over his lap, bending low to suck his nipples.

"Go up and down, not back and forth. It'll hit that spot better."

Taking his advice, I bounce on his shaft, feeling a little self-conscious, but he's right, it feels so fucking incredible I soon forget everything but my need to come. Quicker and quicker, I chase the feeling, until he pinches my nipples and I shout as I shoot thick white ropes over his chest.

"Fuck, you didn't even touch yourself." West rises up to claim my lips, thrusting his tongue deep inside my mouth, and he comes in my ass, his hips jerking as he pumps his seed deep. "Fuck. Fuck, I'm–"

He doesn't finish his sentence, just gets lost in the kiss as I roll my hips, milking him dry.

"Wish I'd filmed that part too," he pants.

With a last peck of my lips on his, I leave him to go shower. When I come back to bed, West is practically asleep. I shut off the light and snuggle up to his side, comforted by his warm body and his clean, familiar scent.

"Rack out, soldier," I say, just like we did in the barracks every night before lights out.

Surprising me, he pops a kiss to my cheek but misses and it lands on my nose instead, making me laugh. "You always do the last thing I expect from you. But it's always just what I need," I say, trying and failing to find his lips in the dark. My lips brush over the stubble of his chin, and that's where I leave my kiss.

WEST

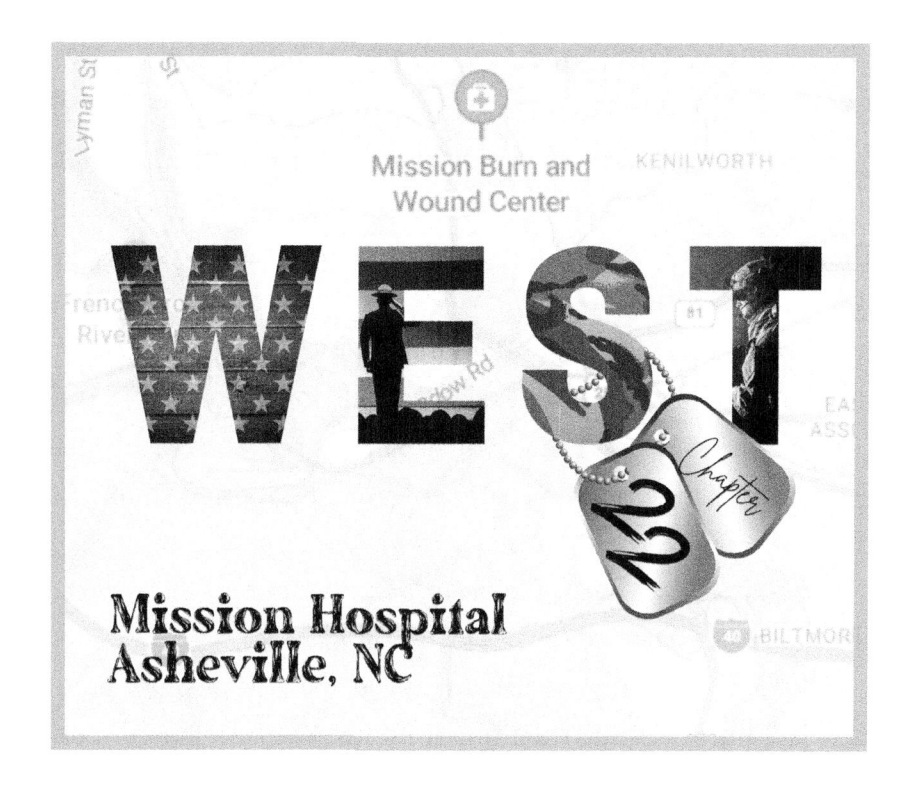

Chapter 22

Mission Burn and Wound Center
Mission Hospital
Asheville, NC

EVERY MORNING when I open my eyes to the onslaught of the morning sun streaming through the bedroom windows, my head splits with a sharp pain.

It takes me several long minutes for my eyes to adjust before the pain subsides. Pulling the covers over my head, I burrow deeper into the warm nest of soft bedding.

The sound of the TV carries in from the living room, blasting at full volume due to Brandt's hearing loss.

He's at it again.

I groan, knowing it's coming any second.

"*Son, your ego is writing checks your body can't cash.*"

Fucking Top Gun.

This has to be his four-hundred and fifty-sixth viewing.

Even buried beneath the covers, I can't tune his voice out as he recites line after line. He knows the entire movie by heart, and as much as it can be annoying, today, it's the thing that lures me out of bed. It's familiar, and routine, and it's unequivocally Brandt. And lately, anything Brandt-related makes me smile, all dopey and ridiculous.

Sitting up, I grab my crutch propped next to the nightstand and hop to the bathroom to take a piss before returning to the bed to attach my leg. I throw on a pair of gray sweats with the Army logo, a relic from my early enlistment days, and shuffle to the kitchen in search of coffee.

"Sorry, Goose, but it's time to buzz the tower," he recites, then he notices me and says, "Oh, morning, babe."

Babe. It makes me smile. I've never been someone's babe before. I like it coming from him. I fill my mug and join him on the couch. He's in full-on fanboy mode, with his mug that reads 'It's classified. I could tell you, but then I'd have to kill you.'

His favorite part is coming up. Just like he always does, he raises his mug and smiles, like he's toasting the fucking brillance of the scene or something. *Jesus Christ, I've fallen for a freaking dork.*

If there was a con for Top Gun fans, he'd be the first in line, guaranteed.

Here it comes. Three. Two. One.

"Goddammit, that's twice! I want some butts!" Brandt yells.

He cracks up, like it's the best line ever, and for the first time in the billions of times I've heard him repeat it, I laugh. Not at the genius of the script, but at him. Brandt Aguilar is fucking adorkable. And loveable. And mine. He's all mine.

Brandt glances at me and smiles. "You know, I have a whole new appreciation for that volleyball scene. Want me to rewind it and see if it does anything for you?"

Christ. "I'm good, thanks. But if you want to take off your shirt and get all sweaty for me and sing '*Playing With The Boys*', I won't stop you."

He has to do a double-take before he realizes I'm fucking with him. "Whatever. Don't ruin the ending for me."

Me? Not a chance. I'm gonna sit right here and sip my coffee and silently fall even harder for my best friend while he makes a fool of himself.

And I'm gonna enjoy every minute.

———

Riggs hooked me up with a volunteer opportunity. I didn't tell Brandt the position is called BALLS Buddies. I'm a Ball Buddy. What-the-fuck-ever. Apparently, the other nut in my sac is named Armando Cahill. I'm meeting him at the VA for a doctor's appointment he has scheduled. Riggs explained to me how some of these guys have anxiety over medical stuff, which I fully understand, even if I don't suffer from it myself. They just want a hand to hold. I'm hoping he meant figuratively and not literally.

Today, I'm holding Armando's hand.

Although I don't have medical anxiety, I can't deny a tightening in my gut as I walk into the VA. I've got nothing but bad memories of military hospitals. Shit, now I kinda wish Brandt was here to hold *my* hand while I'm holding Armando's.

I hear him give his name to the receptionist at the check-in desk and wait for him off to the side. While he's filling out papers, I check him out. Armando is tall, taller than me, maybe like six-foot-three, with dark hair cut short and dark eyes. Though he's retired now, his body still retains muscle and mass. He's built solid and thick. If his size isn't imposing enough to catch your attention, his injuries will. Armando is a burn victim. Half his face is scarred and his ear is disfigured. The burns cover his hands and one arm, and I'm guessing they continue underneath his clothes.

He turns from the counter to find a seat in the waiting area, and I step forward.

"Hey, Cahill. I'm West Wardell. I'm supp–"

"Hey, yeah. Thanks for coming. You can call me Mandy."

We take a seat and I realize we're settling in for the long haul, because everything at the VA is long. The wait time, the lines, the forms, and the recovery time. We're going to have to make small talk.

I fucking suck at small talk.

His knee bounces wildly, and I can tell he's nervous.

"So, where'd you serve?"

Mandy glances at me like he forgot I was sitting here and blows out a deep breath. "Eighty-second Airborne. I was deployed to Bagram Airfield in Kabul."

Kabul. My body flushes with heat as I remember the blast that took my leg and my team. Apparently, Kabul took something from Mandy as well.

I want to ask what happened, but he's clearly agitated as it is, and I don't want to make a bad situation worse. A story for another day, I guess.

"I know Kabul well." *Unfortunately*. He looks like he's about to jump out of his skin with anxiety, and I check my backpack, hoping my Mad Libs are still packed. Yup, they're there. "Hey, help me out here. Give me an adjective that rhymes with easy."

He looks at me like I've grown two heads until he sees the cover of my pad, and he chuckles. "Sleazy. Wheezy. Cheesy. Measly."

"Okay, okay," I laugh. "You're way better at this than Brandt."

I realize I have to explain who Brandt is, but how? Is he my best buddy? My lover? *So fucking awkward*. He's all those things and more. He's everything. But to say that is to open myself up for judgment. Then I'll have to defend myself and Brandt and our right to feel the way we do about each other. It probably doesn't make a difference to Mandy one way or another, but I feel like I'm being tested, like this is a huge decision I'm making. Whether to be honest about myself or whether to hide.

How long will I continue to hide for? When will it ever feel safe to be honest?

Now, goddammit. It starts now, and there's no looking back.

"Brandt is my best friend, my teammate, and he's my...boyfriend."

Mandy doesn't blink an eye. Just nods and continues to drum his fingers on his knee.

"Boyfriend sounds so high school. Doesn't it? He's my partner. My–"

"I get it. You're fucking. Feel better now? Now that you got that out of the way?"

His lips twist into a half smile and I realize he's not judging me; he's laughing at me. I must sound like a stumbling, bumbling gay newbie, and Mandy is amused.

"Much," I smirk, shaking my head. "The easy road is often the sleazy, measly, cheesy, wheezy road, and it is the road less traveled," I read from the page.

Mandy laughs for the first time since arriving, and I feel useful. I guess this is why I'm here, to ease his anxiety and help to take his mind off his fears, and thanks to my ridiculous Mad Libs and my baby gayness, it's working.

"I hate this shit," he admits.

"Yeah, me too. The waiting, the results that are never what we want to hear. It fucking blows."

"So, he was your teammate? Was he there when you–" his gaze falls to my leg, partially visible because my pants hiked up when I sat.

"Yeah, he was there. He threw himself on top of me and took the shrapnel hit before the second and third blasts separated us. But the building collapsed and a large chunk fell on my leg. Crushed it. I was unconscious, but I guess he dragged me out."

A dark shadow falls across his face. "I guess it could have been worse."

Well, that's one way to look at it—that I hadn't. Until now. It could have been a lot worse. I could be a vegetable, brain dead, and lost to the world. I could be paralyzed. I could be dead.

Brandt could be dead.

I'm a fucking asshole for wanting to die. For feeling sorry for myself. Brewer is going to have a field day with this shit. I can hear him now.

"You have every right to feel your feelings, and to grieve for yourself. But you are definitely an asshole. Stop wasting time feeling sorry for yourself and what could have been and go live your life."

We pass another thirty minutes trading war stories about the Middle East, and by war stories, I don't mean the blood and gore. I mean the food, the weather there, the fucking sand, and the deplorable living conditions on base.

"This is more boring than when I was debriefed after returning stateside," I joke.

"No shit."

"Mr. Cahill," the nurse announces, saving us from another round of Mad Libs.

"Thank fuck," Mandy mumbles.

The doctor checks Mandy's scarring and I was correct earlier when I assumed his body was covered in burns. His shoulder and part of his back have extensive damage. The tissue is red and angry-looking still, and I realize he has a long road to recovery ahead of him.

"You're healed enough to undergo another skin graph. I'll schedule you for surgery next month. Do you have someone to help you afterward while you recover? Or will you need to stay in rehab again?"

I remember from what McCormick told me, rehab is a PC term for nursing home. I don't even know this guy, but I can't just sit here silently and let him navigate this on his own, especially considering his fears. I've never met Armando Cahill before today, but I know him. He's just like me—alone, scared, overwhelmed, and hurting inside and out. He's a soldier, a survivor.

He's my brother.

"He has me. And Brandt. He's not alone. He can recover with us in our home. We'll make every follow-up appointment and follow all the discharge instructions to the letter."

Mandy gapes at me like I'm glowing or something. He's stunned silent.

I smile and nod my head to let him know I mean every word. Mandy shrugs and nods. "I'm with him, Doc."

And that's it. Just like that, I've got a Ball Buddy, maybe for life.

Another Bitch with stitches to join my team.

He stops me in the parking lot. "Thanks for showing up for me today. It means a–" he coughs to cover his words and starts again. "I appreciate it." Mandy looks around before his eyes settle on me again. "Did you mean what you said when you offered?"

"Every fucking word. If you don't mind staying with me and the guy I'm fucking," I tease, using his earlier description of me and Brandt. "It's a small house, and sound carries."

Mandy's face heats with color, and he laughs. "Who says I'd mind?"

Fuck, he's gay, or bi. I had no clue. It's good to know me and my nut-sac sidekick are on the same page.

"Anyway, I'll keep in touch," he adds, handing me his phone. I put my number in and he sends me a text right away so I have his, and yeah, I save his contact under the name Nutter Buddy.

Chapter 23
Balls
Black Mountain, NC

A DASH OF CURRY, *a pinch of salt, and a heaping tablespoon of cayenne.*

No wait, a dash of cayenne and a heaping tablespoon of curry? Fuck it. I can't remember what my mother told me; it's just gonna be spicy as hell.

The chicken is almost finished cooking when West wanders into the kitchen, likely tempted by the aroma. His hands come around my chest, warm and rough, and slick with lotion. With soft slow strokes, he rubs it into my scars, and the heat from his body, the scent of him so close to me, it's better than anything I'm cooking in this pan.

His breath tickles my ear. "You forgot to put this on today. Lucky for you, I don't mind touching you."

My shoulders shake with silent laughter. He's always touching me lately. Always finding any excuse to put his hands on me, or his mouth.

"I brought the mail in. There's a letter for you from BALLS."

"It can wait," he rasps, continuing to soften my skin with his hands. They slip below my sweats to cup my ass, kneading my cheeks.

"My ass isn't scarred." Like I give a fuck. He can touch me wherever.

"It will be after I tear it up."

The reminder of his cock in my ass, and the fact he's dying to do it again, makes my dick stiff.

Turning the heat off the stove, I plate the chicken while he slicks my cock with lotion. "I like where this is heading, but can it wait till after we eat? I'm starving."

"You're such a cock tease, Reaper."

Again, I laugh because it's a total lie. He can have me anytime he wants, anyway he wants me, and anywhere.

West moves to the sink to wash his hands while I add pasta to our plates.

"What's this?" he asks, rifling through the mail. He holds up a letter.

"I don't know, what's it say?"

"There's one for each of us, and it's from Bragg. Colonel Baskin."

"There's a name I thought I'd never hear again." Colonel Baskin is our ex-commanding officer. He's the last person I thought I'd ever hear from after I retired.

He tears it open and pulls out the letter, scanning it before reading aloud.

"The fuck?" he exclaims. "...cordially invite you to the Veterans Day ceremony at Fort Bragg to honor the fallen heroes lost while fighting for our freedom on October fourth, a day that will live in the hearts of brave soldiers and veterans everywhere. What the fuck is this shit, Reaper?"

I lay my fork down and take the letter from him. To my burgeoning horror, it's exactly what it sounds like. Baskin is asking us for a guest appearance to honor our team. I guess the look on my face confirms it because West curses and launches into a tirade that would make a sailor blush.

"I'd rather remove my other leg than participate in this fiasco! God himself couldn't get me to stand up on that stage and accept an award while everyone applauds me as a hero. I won't fucking do it!"

That makes two of us.

"My whole team fucking died, and I did nothing to save them! I was trapped and pinned under a wall of concrete. That doesn't make me a hero just because I was lucky enough to live. Or unfortunate enough not to die—however you wanna look at it."

Worry pools in my gut like acid. This is going to trigger him, and it's going to be bad. Like days spent beneath the covers bad. Not one ounce of my being wants to take part in this bullshit, but I've got to put a good face on it for West. Because the truth is, we really don't have a choice. The letter is dressed up and worded as a pretty invitation, but it's a direct order.

"That depends if you're a glass is half empty or glass is half full kind of guy." There it is, his signature what-the-fuck face. He's not amused with my little cliché. "Look, I completely agree with you. I have zero interest in participating in this dog and pony show either, but do we really have a choice?"

He drags his fingers through his hair, making the ends stand up like porcupine quills. "Fuck! I just feel like I've given enough to the goddamn Army. My body, my head, they'll never be the same again thanks to them. I know I signed up for this. I brought it on myself, but I'll be honest with you, I never believed in that mission. And I'm not just talking about the day we got blowed up. I'm talking about the whole fucking reason we were in the desert in the first place. We shouldn't even have been there. It was all just a political coup I wanted no part in. The only thing that mattered to me was protecting my brothers, and I failed my mission, therefore, I will accept no awards."

Tears spring to his eyes, his voice breaking on the last words, and I wrap my arms around his waist and hold him tight. I'm all out of clichés. I have no words at all. He said exactly what I'm feeling and thinking.

"I only did it for them," he cries into my shoulder, "and now they're gone. I don't have anyone to fight for anymore. Nothing matters. It's all gone."

"You have Mandy. He's got a long fight ahead of him, and he needs you, your strength. You have Jax. He's angry and closed off, and you might just be the leader he needs, or the friend. You have Stiles. I've never met anyone who needs more direction than that guy. And you have McCormick. You can't give up on him before he finally finds his true love. He's counting on you to get laid." He chuffs a snotty, teary laugh.

"Your team is still fighting. They still need you, West. Don't give up on them. There's still so much that matters."

"Fuck you," he sniffles, fighting a smile. "Those knuckleheads are a damn mess. They're tore up from the floor up. In fifty years, they'll still be fighting the same fight. If I were still enlisted, the Bitches would bomb my eval, and I'd be demoted."

He's right. McCormick is never getting laid.

"I need you to show up for me again. I can't get up there alone. I need you to hold me up. It's bullshit. We both know it. But don't make me be the only liar on that stage."

West swipes his eyes on the back of his sleeve and draws a ragged breath. "I told you, I'm always gonna show up for you, Reaper. Always."

———

"You look like a total bitch!" West cackles.

"I still can't believe I let you talk me into this," Mandy complains, hefting his borrowed Bitches With Stitches bag up his shoulder. "I don't even know how to knit."

"That's not a big deal. We'll teach you the basics. You'll catch on in no time."

Despite West's reassurance, I can tell Mandy is conflicted.

"Trust me," West swears, "you're going to fit right in."

"In case you haven't noticed, I don't fit in anywhere," Mandy gripes.

"The Bitches are just like us, imperfect. Right Brandt?"

"Imperfectly perfect," I insist, always reaching for the bright lining, the positive reinforcement to correct the negative soundtrack that plays in a constant loop in West's mind.

"Imperfectly perfect," West repeats, slapping Mandy's knee.

I bite back my smile. "Look, you're there for you, not them. You have nothing to prove to anyone. Just be yourself and you'll be fine."

It's the truth. Mandy is a likable guy, buried under layers of anxiety and trauma. He's honest and loyal and real. I liked him immediately after meeting him. He could benefit from being a Bitch. He certainly has the stitches to earn his seat in the circle jerk.

"Afterwards, if you're up for it, we can go out with the guys and grab beer and wings. It's sort of a tradition, and it will give you a chance to get to know them better, and for them to get to know you better," West adds.

As soon as we enter the classroom, I spot Riggs, back from deployment, with a scratch on his cheek.

"Riggs, glad you're back. Welcome home. I thought you were medical," West asks. "Did you see action? Were you outside the wire?"

A dark shadow passes over Riggs's face and he tenses. "Let's just say it was a close call. But I'm fine. This scratch is the worst of it."

West and I exchange concerned looks. There's no such thing as a safe job in the Army. The Bitches file in one by one, filling up the empty seats. McCormick high fives me and West on his way by. Today his shirt reads "I'm a BALLSY Bitch". The word ballsy is written in the BALLS logo.

That shirt would look great on West, I think with a snicker.

I would have to hold him down and hog tie him to get him to wear it, but it would be perfect for him. Reaching into my bag, I pull out my ball of blue yarn and get to work. The left sock is almost complete, barring a few dropped stitches, and for the right side, I'll make a sleeve to cover his stump. West pulls out his pink yarn and attempts to teach Mandy how to cast on.

Stiles takes a seat next to McCormick, wearing his ALR t-shirt and leather jacket, practically his uniform, and Pharo trails behind him, taking the seat to his right. When Jax enters the classroom, he stalls when he realizes the only empty seat is right beside Pharo.

"What-the-fuck-ever," he mumbles, glaring at McCormick and Stiles.

"Quit your bitching and take a seat," Stiles snipes.

"All right guys, settle down," Riggs says, bringing the meeting to order. "We've got fresh meat. You know what to do, gentlemen."

With a long-suffering sigh, McCormick says, "I'm McCormick, retired Army and member of the American Legion of Riders. I'm also a proud Bitch."

Stiles snickers. "I'm Stiles, former Army, American Legion Rider, and like McCormick said, I'm a proud Bitch." He looks to his right.

"Pharo, Army Reserves."

Jax snorts, rolling his eyes. "Bullshit," he coughs.

"Why don't you mind your own business and stop worrying about mine," Pharo insists. "It's your turn."

"Jax, former Army, ALR, and obviously a Bitch."

"No shit," Pharo mumbles.

Ever the peacekeeper, Riggs rolls right over them. "I'm Navarro Riggs. Former Army nurse. I'm a medic with the United States Army Reserves. When I'm not in uniform, I'm a physical therapist. I volunteer here at BALLS and I work at Womack Army Medical Center. If you have any questions, feel free to ask me. You already know these two, I assume," he states, glancing between me and West.

Mandy's eyes circle the group before he speaks. "Cahill, retired Army, and according to these two, I'd make a great Bitch."

The group laughs, and just like that, the ice is broken, and Mandy sighs with relief. The Bitches pull out their balls and begin to work their wool as they go round-robin style around the circle.

Stiles begins first. "I got a job."

"Hell yeah," McCormick cheers.

Those two have the oddest relationship, if you ask me. Constant push and pull. Like brothers.

"It's not much, just slinging grease at a mechanic shop, but it's something, and it gets me out of bed every day."

"What are your goals this time around?" Riggs asks.

Stiles huffs. "No drinking on work nights past nine. If I can't show up, I should at least give them a call."

"That would be a great start," Riggs agrees.

"You got this," McCormick insists. "Let me know if you're slow at work and I'll bring my bike by for you to change the oil."

Stiles frowns. "You can change your own goddamn oil, Cheeto Puff."

"I know I can. I just like to see you kneel before my bike. Like you're worshiping her."

Stiles's eyes bug out. "You're fucking bent in the head."

"Well, Carly doesn't seem to think so."

"Who is Carly?"

"My date," he drops casually.

"Bullshit," Stiles calls.

"No, I'm serious. I took Rigg's suggestion and changed my profile to show my leg, and I've had some interest. We're meeting up tomorrow night at the bar."

Stiles looks like he doesn't believe a word being said, but he doesn't push it.

"Pharo?" Riggs prompts. "Anything new?"

"I'm about to head out of town again. Don't know how long I'll be gone. I just really needed to be here today, to touch base and get grounded before...you know."

I did know. Civilian life is a whole other world from deployment. Like a parallel universe.

It's Jax's turn, but he remains silent, scowling at the threads in his jeans.

"What's up with you man?" Stiles asks.

"I'm here, aren't I?" he snipes.

"That doesn't mean you're okay," Riggs says.

"I am for today. Been fighting depression and anger this week."

"If you need help coping, please reach out," Riggs begs.

"Hell, I'll even break my rule and answer the damn phone if I'm on a date with Carly," McCormick offers as Stiles rolls his eyes.

I can't help but laugh when Stiles says, "Just do yourself a favor and call me first."

Riggs continues. "Well, I'm glad to be home. Like I said, I had a close call this week, some triggering moments that brought me back to a dark time, but that's what I signed up for when I reenlisted. I'm not ready to share about it. I'm not even sure if I can. It's classified. But I'm coping and I'm speaking to my therapist, Brewer Marx. I want to thank you all for being good to him while I was gone. Brandt?"

As comfortable as I feel among these guys, I hate speaking in front of the group. It's one thing to shoot the shit, but it's another to speak about things that are private, like feelings.

"I'm in a good place this week. West and I are starting a new venture and it's going well. I'm excited to see where it goes. It feels good to connect with familiar things from my past, like being outdoors, sleeping rough, shooting a gun, and having my sidekick back." I glance at West and he gives me a smile that reaches his eyes.

West huffs and pushes his fingers through his hair, making the ends stand at attention. "As usual, my week has been up and down. Both good and bad. At least I can say it's a good balance of both. We had a blast from the past," he admits, looking at me. "Our ex-CO wants us to show up for a ceremony and receive awards and...I'm struggling. I don't feel that I deserve to be recognized. And it's not coming from a place of self-pity or guilt. I honestly didn't do jack shit to deserve a hero award. I didn't save anyone. I didn't do something heroic or extraordinary. I survived by luck and the grace of God, and probably Brandt, and I don't think that's deserving of a bronze star or purple heart."

Looking around the group, I see several guys close their eyes or nod their heads. They've all been there, receiving medals they don't feel they deserve. Some of them do, and some of it was probably just a formality, but we can all relate. It's why I love this group. Who else would understand but the Bitches?

"I've also been struggling with some truths about myself, and I feel like I made a lot of progress with it this week. But more on that later."

West gives me a secret smile, and I know he's talking about us, coming out to my mother and then Mandy.

I'm so fucking proud of you.

It's Mandy's turn, and he looks to me and West before speaking. "I had a difficult week. I'm not really used to talking about my life or my feelings. I guess I don't have anyone in my life who gives a shit. The doc said I have to undergo more skin grafts, and I'm freaking out. I suffer from extreme medical anxiety and the hospitals, the surgeries, the feeling of powerlessness when you go under anesthesia, gives me the fucking heebie-jeebies. Not to mention the pain of recovery. And then the disappointment when I look in the mirror and don't see much improvement. I fucking hate looking in the mirror," he grumbles. "Somehow, I got lucky enough to meet West and then Brandt, and they offered to hold my hand through it all, literally," he laughs. "I guess I'm going to be okay, but each surgery takes a piece from me, from my soul, and I don't know what will happen if I lose too many of those pieces. Will I lose my peace of mind completely? I swear I don't have much left as it is."

"You're in the right place, brother," Stiles swears. "We'll get you a phone tree list, and you can call us anytime. I'll hold your hand."

"Yeah," McCormick seconds, "I'll hold your hand, too."

It's oddly heartwarming coming from such huge scarred guys decorated in leather and tattoos. They really are the best of the best.

The Black Mountain Tavern is pretty empty considering it's Wednesday afternoon. Stiles, McCormick, Mandy, and West join me at a round table near the bar. We order wings, potato skins, and beer, and with each glass emptied, the bullshit gets thicker.

"Man, I burned that bush with a flamethrower!" McCormick brags.

Stiles snorts. "You're so full of shit, your eyes are brown. You never fired a flamethrower, you jackass. They're practically outlawed. Mostly so geniuses like you don't hurt themselves."

The guys roll their eyes and shake their heads. He really is full of shit.

"I did," Mandy admits, breaking the silence.

"You did, what?" West asks.

"Use a flamethrower."

"Bullshit," Stiles says.

"No, really. We cleared a hole loaded with illegal weapons. We confiscated everything and destroyed it. But...first we *tested* everything," he says with a dangerous grin.

"No way!" McCormick barks.

"It was fucking awesome," Mandy laughs.

"You're a badass Bitch, Cahill," West jokes.

"No shit," he deadpans.

He's going to fit in just fine with this crowd.

The banter continues, but my attention is stuck on West, sucking grease from his fingers. If he keeps that shit up, he's going to out us right here in front of everyone.

"I'm gonna hit the bathroom and wash up," he announces, and I'm quick to follow.

The door shuts behind me, and I lock it. West turns on the sink and I corner him against the counter, pressing into him from behind, and shut the water off.

He grins, amused by my surprise attack. Burying my nose in his neck, my lips suckle on his skin, nipping lightly with my teeth. He smells like West, like deodorant and body wash and fabric softener. My fingers slip under the hem of his shirt, teasing over his warm skin.

"What are you doing?"

"It's not obvious?"

He chuckles. "It's pretty obvious," he agrees, as my fingertips brush across his tight nipples. He gasps. "Here? Now?"

"I couldn't wait."

West turns his head so he can reach my mouth. He tastes like beer and hot sauce. My tongue pushes into his warm mouth, eager to stroke his. My rock-hard dick pushes against his ass as I grind into him. He tugs his sweats down his hips, exposing his bare ass, and I let go of his nipples, using one hand to pull my cock out and the other to brace his hip.

"This is going to be quick."

"Wait, fuck. We can't–"

He's right. I don't have lube, and even a quickie isn't long enough when I'm inside him. With regret, I settle for the next best thing.

"Stroke your cock," I order, spitting in my hand.

I smear the saliva over my shaft and slide between the hot, tight crease between his cheeks. The glide feels incredible, with my fist closing over the swollen head every time it peeks through. In the mirror, my eyes catch West's, and the heat and hunger sparking in his gaze fucking melts me. The head of his cock is dark purple, his thick veiny shaft sliding through his fist as he thrusts. I can picture his balls, just below the edge of the mirror, swollen and tight, ready to burst.

"Fuck, the way your dick rubs over my hole."

"You want it, don't you?" I growl in his ear. "When we get home, this hole is mine. I'm gonna stretch it around my cock."

"Fuck," he gasps, pushing his ass out further.

My gaze drops to watch as my dick slides through his cheeks. I may not be inside of him, but it doesn't diminish how amazing this feels.

"That's it, push back against me. Chase my cock."

The pace of his strokes increase. "I'm close," he breathes.

"So am I. Come for me."

West grunts, shooting thick white ropes onto the counter. My own orgasm rushes forth and I soak his crease. I continue to thrust slowly, milking my shaft dry, enjoying the warm wet glide as I suck the lobe of his ear between my lips.

He shivers and laughs. "Okay, quit. Gotta clean up."

I grab a paper towel and wipe his ass clean. "That felt–"

"Fucking incredible," he finishes for me. "We're leaving in less than twenty minutes."

My shoulders shake with silent laughter. His enthusiasm for my dick makes me feel like the luckiest SOB in the world.

When we rejoin the guys, they're knee deep in a heated discussion about recruitment.

"Well, I don't give a fuck how you feel about it," Stiles snaps. "My nephew asked me to come talk to his ROTC unit for Career Day and I'd rather deploy again than disappoint him."

Dark clouds cross West's face, and his brows tighten. "I get that. If I had any family left, they'd be my first priority. Especially kids. I bet you're his hero. It just never feels finished. Like I haven't given enough. They always ask for more. Fucking Colonel Baskin, ROTC, it's always gonna be something. I've given too damn much," he growls, slamming his hand down on the table with a thud.

"I've bled for this country, for their wars and their causes." He sticks his arm in our faces. "I refuse to walk into a school full of kids and convince them to bleed and die for somebody else's war in the name of patriotism. It's fucking bullshit and you know it!"

Stiles slaps his arm away. "I'm glad for you. I've bled for the guys that died for me too! But those kids, for some of them, a battlefield in a dessert is better than what they have now. The Army is their escape. It's a ticket to freedom and a better life."

McCormick motions to his prosthetic leg. "How is this a better life? Tell me how this is better."

It's not just his missing limb, it's the myriad of other injuries and scars we all bear and suffer from daily that compromise our quality of life. I get his point crystal clear.

"When is it enough?" West asks.

Guilt and sadness cloud Stiles's eyes, but he stands by his point. "Someone is always going to have to bleed in order to keep the stripes red on the flag. It's the price of freedom. That's just the way it is."

They're both fucking right. Like me, Mandy remains quiet. I can only guess what's going through his head.

"There used to be a time when you didn't mind bleeding for your country," Stiles reminds him.

"You're right, there was a time, years ago, when I was young and naïve and I wanted to make a difference. My body was still whole. Cuts healed quickly. Bullets were exciting. But then it became personal. I lost my fucking team! The whole fucking team. I've lost friends to suicide and depression. I've seen friends' careers end because of injuries." My gut tightens when I see a telltale sheen fill West's eyes. "You're right about another thing. I would bleed again, for you, for him," he says, pointing at McCormick, "and him," West points to Mandy. "And especially for him," he says, sliding his arm around my shoulder. "I'd bleed and die for my team, for my brothers, but war? I'm fucking done with that shit."

"Amen," McCormick seconds.

Stiles chugs the last of his beer and slams the empty mug down before coming to his feet. He offers West his hand. "You're abso-fucking-lutely correct, Wardell, one-hundred percent, but I can't bail on my family. They're my team too. And you're right, I'm his fucking hero, as messed up as that is."

After he leaves, the group remains silent until the waitress drops off our bill.

"Did I push too far?" West asks.

"No," I reassure him, patting his back. "You spoke your truth, and you were right. Just try to see where he's coming from, too."

"I do. If I had a nephew–" He takes a deep breath and I can see him struggling to rein his emotions in. "Their needs would come before my personal beliefs."

I wish so hard he had a family. That his grandma still lived. Or that my own family were better, more loving people who claimed him as their own. It wasn't something I ever missed deeply, but West is the kind of guy who needs that kind of acceptance and love. All I can do is be that family for him, always.

"You have me, Professor."

West lays his head on my shoulder. "I know. I'll never doubt that. Just don't ever ask me to play hero."

I swallow down my laugh, because it's so ironic. I'll never ask him to play the hero, not for me or anyone else, but there's one truth I'll die by.

Weston Wardell is a fucking hero. He's *my* hero.

There's no one stronger, more driven, more loyal, more loving, or braver. He's my Team Leader. He's my best friend, my brother to the soul.

He's the love of my miserable fucking life.

WEST

Ft. Bragg
Fayetteville, NC

"CHRIST! Would you sit the fuck down? You're driving me crazy."

"Sorry," I huff, plopping down on the couch beside him.

I have enough anxiety roiling in my gut to age me at least ten years by the end of the day.

Brandt takes a deep breath and blows it out before asking, "What is it? What's wrong?"

"Everything! I'm worked up over this award ceremony tomorrow. The more I think about it, the more reasons I come up with for why I shouldn't go."

He pinches the bridge of his nose and then rubs his eyes. "I figured that's what it was. Look, there's not much I can say to make it better for you. We just need to go, get through it, and put it behind us."

"It's not just that. I can't stop thinking about Stiles showing up for that ROTC jag. I should have supported him. It's eating at him, at his conscience. He doesn't want to do it, but he refuses to let his nephew down. And I gave him shit for it. He's the real hero, not me."

Brandt's head snaps up, and he looks full of disbelief. "Stiles?"

"Yeah. And if you tell him I said he's my hero, I'll shove my prosthetic foot right up your ass."

"Kinky," Brandt teases with a smirk.

"You know what we should do? We should show up at the school to support him the day after tomorrow."

Brandt's smirk spreads into a genuine smile. "I guess you should activate the phone tree. Get the Bitches on the line, gather them together and give them marching orders."

"Yes! Great idea. Except...I think McCormick is on that date tonight with that chick Carly. So you know he won't answer."

The smirk is back in place. "You look like you need a drink. Maybe it'll help with that anxiety."

"A drink? Why do I need a drink?"

"Think about it," he says, as a wicked light shines in his blue eyes. "The Black Mountain Tavern serves two-for-one beer this time of night."

The Black Mountain Tavern... McCormick. Carly.

"I think you're right. I definitely need a drink. I'd give

anything to see McCormick macking on the ladies, in full action. I'm dying to prove he has no game."

We grab our jackets and head out, laughing the entire way. In the Jeep, speculation runs wild.

Brandt chuckles. "Do you think he makes her pay for half the bill?"

"Hard to tell. He believes in equality; it's a sign of strength to him, but he's desperate to get laid, so...It's anybody's guess."

"I bet five bucks he's wearing an ALR or Bitches shirt with a pair of jeans that has a hole in them."

"And I bet he's mentioned Stiles and the boys at least four times already," I add with a chuff.

"Maybe he's regaling her with his glory days from the Army."

"Christ, he's probably sitting alone at the bar by now because she split already."

"Do you think he would tell her about his crush on Betty Beasley?"

"Crush?" I snort, "Try obsession."

I spot his Harley as soon as we pull into the parking lot of the Black Mountain Tavern. "He either made her drive herself, or he's giving her a ride on his bike."

Only one helmet rests on the handlebars, which means he actually made her drive herself. And he wonders why he can't find a date? McCormick is absolutely the worst catch imaginable.

We walk into the bar, but it's not McCormick we see sitting alone at the counter, it's Stiles.

"What the hell are you doing here?" Brandt asks. "Spying?"

"I'm not spying!"

"Sure looks a lot like spying," I add.

"What the hell are you two doing here?" he asks instead of answering.

"Two-for-one beer."

"That's why I'm here," he lies.

We take seats on either side of him, flanking Stiles, and flag the bartender. Country music plays in the background, but nobody's on the dance floor.

"So, how's he making out over there?" I ask, glancing over my shoulder.

McCormick sits at a table with a woman with long brown hair. She's cute, and I know better than to judge a book by its cover, but it doesn't look like she has a damn thing in common with him. From her floral sundress and strappy sandals, to the cute headband in her hair. Carly looks like a nice girl, a sweet girl. Way too naïve for McCormick.

"She hasn't laughed at one of his jokes yet," Stiles defends with a frown. "He's actually a pretty funny guy, when he isn't being an ass and he isn't making fun of *me*."

I'm chuckling as I answer, "Is that right? I never noticed. McCormick is a funny guy? News to me. What about you, Brandt?"

"I'm not sure about funny, but I always thought he was real deep. Soulful," he teases.

Stiles has the grace to laugh at himself. "Okay, I'll admit, I'm not spying, it's just...buddy support."

"And does your buddy know you're here supporting him?" Brandt asks. We both know the answer is no.

"I don't want to distract him and take his focus from his date. Better he not know I'm here."

"What are you gonna do," I ask, "beat her up in the parking lot if she ditches him?"

"She better not!" He catches himself and blushes beet red. It's the first time I've ever seen Stiles blush. It's almost cute how loyal he is.

The bartender drops our mugs in front of us, and I raise it up. "A toast, to McCormick."

"To McCormick," they parrot, raising their glasses.

Brandt slips me a five-dollar bill and I assume it's because McCormick is wearing a nice jacket, and by nice, I mean not leather. But twenty minutes later, he stands to go to the bathroom, and I notice he's wearing an ALR shirt beneath the jacket that says, 'Save a Cycle, Ride a Vet.'

Classy guy that McCormick.

I slide the five bucks across the bartop with a laugh. Of course, we then have to explain to Stiles why we're laughing and exchanging money.

He snorts and then chokes on his mouthful of beer. "I could have won that bet, hands-down."

After an hour, I'm honestly floored she's still sitting opposite him. I struggle to get through an hour with him in group sometimes.

Brandt finishes off his second beer and huffs, "I was prepared to break out, *'You've lost that loving feeling'*. What good is a wingman if your buddy isn't crashing and burning?"

Christ. Thank God we're spared from that shitshow.

"I already checked. They've got it on the jukebox," Brandt adds.

I almost feel bad for him that he's never been able to reenact his favorite scene from his favorite movie. It's probably on his bucket list.

"Hey, you remember that one time–"

"Yeah, the time I pulled the plug on the jukebox right after you cued up that song, all hell-bent on singing to Thomason's date."

"I should be pissed about that," he frowns. "You owe me."

"I owe you for a lot of things. *Everything*. But I don't owe you for that. And I will never make that up to you."

The buttons on the collar of my crisp white dress shirt are choking me. It's been almost a year since I've had to get dressed up. Longer, actually. Not much call for Dress Blues in the desert.

I feel like a fucking fraud.

Not for wearing the uniform—I fucking earned that right ten times over—but for the reason I'm donning it today. Brandt slides my navy blue jacket over my shoulders and brushes imaginary lint from them, making sure I look spiffy.

"Check out that chest candy, Sergeant," he murmurs, running his fingertips over the many colorful bars decorating my breast.

I swat his hand away with a laugh.

"Almost as impressive as what you're packing down here."

He unbuttons my high-waisted blue pants and slides his hand inside my briefs to cup my soft cock.

The warmth from his hand, the friction as he strokes and tugs on it, makes me grow thick in his palm.

"You look perfect, except you're missing something."

Looking at my reflection in the mirror above the bathroom sink, I take note of my uniform. It's all there—bars, pins, stripes, cap. I can't find anything missing. He pulls a metal ring from his pocket and slides it over my cock and balls. Gasping, I pull my hips back from his grasp, which only serves to make my ass collide with his cock. His *hard* cock.

"I can't wear a cock ring under my uniform! I'll be rock-hard all night."

"So? At least you won't be thinking about all the bullshit going on around you."

He has a valid point, but... "I can't, Brandt. Save it for later tonight. I'll wear it for you when we get home."

"Fine," he concedes, pocketing the ring. "Then how about this one instead?"

He stuns me a second time as he pulls another ring from his pocket, this one a solid black band. His military ring. I've seen it a dozen times on his finger, usually when we have to get dressed up like today, but Brandt doesn't slide it on his finger, he slides it on mine. Not on my right hand, where military rings are typically worn, but on my left, in place of a wedding band. The Army crest flashes in the fluorescent lights overhead.

"Does this mean we're going steady now?" I ask with a silly grin. It's so high school, but my stomach is fluttering with butterflies. I never pegged myself as a shmoop for this romantic shit, but I can't deny how much I love it.

"Maybe. Maybe it just means that you're mine. That you belong to me forever." His warm breath tickles my ear, making my cock even harder.

He straightens my cap and then slides his thick arms around my chest, hugging me to him. In the mirror, our faces are side by side with his chin resting on my shoulder.

"There's never gonna be a day that I don't love you, or that I don't want you, Wes. This ring means I'm never going to let you fall."

Now I'm fighting back tears as I stare at the black titanium band branding my finger. I glance at my ring sitting on my right hand and slide it off, and I turn in his arms and take his hand in mine, sliding my matching black ring onto the fourth finger of his left hand.

"It means I'm always gonna show up for you. For the rest of my life, I will show up for you. Because you're mine," I vow.

I smash my lips against his in a claiming kiss that leaves me breathless and hard—no cock ring needed. He slides his fingers around the nape of my neck, teasing the short hairs and gripping them between his knuckles with a light tug, just hard enough to let me know how much he needs me.

Not nearly as much as I need him.

"Does this mean...You're not asking me to–" I can't even say it. I wouldn't put it past him, though. Brandt is a sly, manipulative genius. He has a way of getting what he wants before you even realize you're giving it to him.

"No. That's not what it means. I'm not asking you to marry

me. I'm telling you how it's gonna be for the rest of our lives. It's gonna be me and you, forever. From here on out, on the good days and bad days and all the days in between."

I don't really have an answer for him, not that he's asking me a question. He's telling me. Stating facts. And I'm totally on board one hundred percent. So, I answer with a kiss, slower, deeper than the last one. The heat he stirs up in my gut has me rethinking the rest of my evening. I'd rather ditch this charade and get back in bed. With him. And the other ring in his pocket.

The alarm on his wristwatch beeps, and he pulls away with a sigh. "You ready to knock this out?"

"Not really. Just promise me this is the last time you ask me to play the hero."

"I promise," he swears with a quick kiss to my lips.

My heart is about to spike right out of my chest. I'm certain of it. The rush of adrenaline is making me feel nauseous, and I'm sweating through the armpits of my jacket.

"I can't fucking do this," I say in a panic. "I'm not who they think I am. I'm not a fucking hero. They're dead because of me. I should have been court martialed, not decorated."

Brandt clutches my sleeve. "Listen to me," he hisses. "It doesn't matter how you feel about it. They don't give a fuck about your guilt. They don't really even care that we're still alive. They care about the ones that died, the ones they lost. The ones they're here to honor today. They are fallen heroes, and they deserve our respect. I don't care what it costs you.

You're gonna sit there and you're gonna keep your fucking shit together and smile. It's the least we can do for them. That's all these people want to see. We're just poster boys for fallen heroes. They don't care that we're dead inside, they just want to pin medals on our chests and talk about our glory, and our sacrifice, because it brings them closer to the ones they lost. They've got rose-colored glasses on because it softens the harsh glare of their grief."

He lets go of my sleeve and brushes the fabric smooth. I swallow hard, past the lump forming in my throat I will myself not to cry.

"This is fucking bullshit. The whole goddamn fiasco is fucking bullshit. they should be here, accepting these medals themselves. They fucking earned it, not us."

"You bet it's bullshit. And when we get home, you can fall apart in my arms and cry. You can bury yourself under the covers and I'll join you. Or we can sit outside and get higher than the fucking stars, until we forget how much it hurts, but for the next two hours, you're going to fucking grin and bear it. Got it?"

All I can do is nod. I'm just grateful he's strong for the both of us, strong enough to afford me the luxury of being a victim to my feelings and my conscience.

"Hey, this is just as hard for me. I need you to help me get through this," he whispers fiercely, clutching my shoulder. "I'm not okay. Can you help me?"

I'm such a fucking jackass. A piece of fucking shit beneath my shoe. Of course he's not okay. And I promised I would always show up for him.

"I've got you, Reaper. Three legs. You can't fall with three legs."

"No, you fucking can't," he agrees, bringing me in tight for a hug. "Come on, let's go smile and wave so we can get the fuck out of here."

The ballroom is packed with elegantly dressed men and women. Camera crews from local TV stations set their equipment up around the perimeter of the room. Brandt and I are lined up like we're awaiting a firing squad to take us out as a line of generals, colonels, and admirals stand at the podium, breathing meaningless words into the microphone about valor and honor and bravery and sacrifice, things they know nothing about sitting behind their desks.

"Deep breath," Brandt reminds me, and I imagine I can feel his hand squeezing mine, although he dare not touch me right now with so many eyes on us. We have to toe the line, pomp and circumstance, and all that bullshit.

Baskin holds a black box in his hand. The purple-and-gold heart lays nestled on a bed of velvet. He pins it to my chest, and I feel the weight of it, the weight of sacrifice and responsibility. The weight of the lives lost that earned me this medal. My heart pounds beneath his fingertips as he pins it to my breast.

This one I earned. As a soldier, it's my duty to risk my life to protect my country and my team. And I did. I risked it, and I was injured while doing my job honorably. Same as Brandt, who's also receiving his. Imagine that, two Southern boys who had nothing but stars in their eyes when they met, and some half-cocked notion about making the world a better place, both earning Purple Hearts.

Go fucking figure.

"...a solemn distinction, for those who have sacrificed themselves honorably, or paid the ultimate price with their life," Baskin recites.

He goes on to list the names of each service member we lost that day as he awards each of them a Purple Heart medal, accepted by their family members. The impact of their names being read aloud feels like a nail being pounded through my chest, straight through my heart. It's been a year since we lost them and it doesn't hurt any less.

The next medal hurts almost as bad as their loss. Being recognized and awarded for something I don't feel I earned. The Bronze Star. My grandfather earned a Silver Star back in World War II. I used to stare at it behind the glass of my grandma's china cabinet for hours, imagining the day he earned it, the heat of battle, the danger, and the risk.

My grandfather rescued his buddy, who was shot in the leg. He tied a tourniquet around his thigh and dragged him six miles to safety. They were behind enemy lines, and it took three days. Alone and hungry and dehydrated, separated from their unit, they finally made it to safety.

My grandfather was a true hero. I've always dreamed of following in his footsteps someday; I just wish my grandmother was here to see me today. All I ever wanted was to make her proud of me. As proud as I was of her.

Brandt's mother crouches before the stage to take a picture of her son as Baskin pins the star to his chest.

"...fourth highest military decoration for valor. For heroic or meritorious achievement in battle."

The only thing I achieved that day was doing my job and not dying, but whatever. I just want to get off the stage and get to the eating part, and then the leaving.

"Just smile and wave," Brandt reminds me.

I feel like a freak, like an oddity on display for everyone's amusement. We're sitting at a banquet table at the front of the room with the big brass from Fort Bragg. Across the room, a sea of round tables decorated with white linen cloths, host smiling faces and clicking cameras.

This is the seventh circle of hell. Achievement unlocked.

I have to bite my tongue, literally bite it, to keep from snapping at Baskin as he ducks between with his arms around our shoulders. As soon as the woman takes the picture, he walks away without a word to either of us, like we don't even exist. Like we're nothing more than cardboard cutouts designed specifically for photo ops.

"Fuck this," I mumble.

"Don't give them the satisfaction of seeing what they've done to you because they don't give a shit."

"Can we get out of here?"

"I wish," he says, placing his hand on my knee under the table. "But not yet. Come on, let's dance." My face is doing that thing again, the what-the-fuck expression, and Brandt laughs. "Dance with me," he insists.

"You've got to be kidding me."

"I'm not," he laughs.

"Dance? On my one good leg?" Hell, I couldn't even dance when I had two good legs.

"You can hop around," he teases with a twist to his lips.

"You're an ass." With Brandt standing there holding his hand out to me, people are beginning to stare, including the big brass.

"Fuck it. Dancing beats sitting here, like a fucking puppet."

The song playing is sweet and emotional, *The Wind Beneath My Wings by Bette Midler*. Many couples are dancing, but none of them are two men. With one hand on my hip, he slides the other around my shoulder, keeping his body at a respectable four inch distance.

"Everybody is staring at us."

"Of course they are." A wicked smirk tugs at his lips. "The colonel is looking."

His smirk is contagious. "Does he look pissed?"

"Oh, yeah."

"Perfect. His guests of honor look super gay right now, and it's not a good look for him."

I slide my hand around Brandt's waist, pulling him closer, close enough to smell his musky cologne. It's a powerful scent that makes me want to lick his skin. Colonel Baskin shoots me a nasty glare, with narrowed eyes and his lips stretched thin, and I lay my head on Brandt's shoulder. Baskin starts toward us, and I can feel Brandt's body tense.

"Fuck, here we go. Can we get out of here now?"

"Yeah, perfect timing," he agrees, guiding me off the dance floor with his hand on the small of my back.

We're waylaid by Brandt's parents, who want to gather us

together for more pictures. We can't tell them we're leaving because I'm pretty sure his mother will block the door with her body, so instead we just lie and say we're going to the bathroom to wash up.

I recognize Tommy's wife, and there's no way I can walk by her without stopping to say something. What I don't recognize is the infant in her arms. Tommy never mentioned his wife was pregnant. In fact, the last thing he said was that they were hoping to start a family when he came home.

I don't have it in me to hug her because if that's Tommy's baby, I can't get near her without losing my shit and crying, and if it's not Tommy's baby, I'll definitely lose my shit. Either way, I'm not okay. So I stand at attention and salute her.

"Cut that out," she admonishes, reaching in to hug me. "Don't you dare salute me."

"Congratulations," Brandt offers, looking at the tiny boy.

Angela rubs the baby's head. "I told him the day before he died, but he didn't want to say anything because he thought it would jinx the first trimester." She can barely spit the word trimester out before she's in tears.

Thank God for Brandt, who hugs her as she sobs quietly into his shoulder. I just... I can't. It's just further proof how fucked up fate is. This man had a family. He had something worth living for, just like Micah did. It's not fair these families are broken and these people have to carry on without them. It's not fair this baby will never know who his father was or what an amazing guy he was.

Brandt takes down her number, promising to keep in touch. No doubt he'll send a baby gift from the both of us. Knowing him like I do, I have no doubt that he's going to try to convince me to set up a college fund for Micah and Tommy's kids. He won't have to twist my arm very hard. I can't think of anything better to do with my money than to give it to them.

Angela is sidetracked by another well-wisher and Brandt tugs me away to make our great escape, except we're thwarted by another nail in my coffin. A tall, dark-haired man, dressed in a charcoal gray suit. He stops us like he knows who we are.

"Hi, I just had to introduce myself. I'm Jonathan Wilby."

He says it like we're supposed to know what that name means, but I glance at Brandt and he looks as clueless as I am.

"Brandt Aguilar," he says, shaking the man's hand.

"Weston Wardell," I say, introducing myself with a handshake.

"I know exactly who you guys are. Annie told me so much about you. Her team leader, the Professor. And I think she called you the Grim Reaper?" he asks Brandt.

Annie? Who the fuck is– "You're the guy Rosie was dating!"

Recognition dawns on Brandt's face, and he smiles before reaching in to hug Jonathan.

"She told us a little about you."

"Very little," I add with a grin.

"We were keeping things under wraps until she got back home. I've actually known her for years. We went to high school together, and then community college. That's when she decided to major in communications and linguistics, and she joined the Army."

I'm at a loss as to what to say to him. I feel Rosie's death as completely as I do the rest of my team, and despite the fact that she had no children, she had a family and people who love her. She had a life that was interrupted and unfinished. Ever the ambassador, Brandt mumbles something to smooth things over while I'm just standing here, completely disassociating and on the verge of falling apart. The constant ringing in my ears is louder than ever, and there's an uncomfortable pressure crushing my heart, followed by a wave of nausea that makes me feel sick.

I think I'm having a panic attack. The second one today.

He hustles me into the Jeep, but doesn't say a word until we're halfway home. "I need proof of life. I haven't asked you in a while, but I need to hear it today."

"I hated every second of that, but I'm okay. At least I will be." Swallowing, I touch the gold-and-purple heart decorating my chest. "I'm proud of you. Proud of both of us. I feel like I've waited my whole life to get this, because it says that I'm a hero. But the truth of it is, we're not heroes because we got injured. We are heroes because we served. We volunteered to serve and protect Americans. We volunteered to risk our lives, and we did, every day. Every single soldier in the armed forces risks their lives every day to keep others safe, and for that, we're all heroes, and we all deserve this."

"So you're good?" he asks, raising his brows. "I mean, yeah, you're right, we're all heroes who deserve a medal, but this isn't elementary school and we don't get participation awards. Unfortunately, only the ones who are injured or dead get recognized, and I need to know you're good."

"I promised you my life just hours ago. I promised it to you forever, and forever isn't going to end today. I'm good, Reaper. I don't hate myself anymore. I don't like feeling like I've stolen valor by accepting a bronze star, but I accept that I deserve to be recognized for my service."

"Fuck, I owe Brewer Marx more than I can ever repay him. We should send him on a cruise," he jokes, referring to the progress I've made because of him.

Brewer definitely has saved my ass, and a cruise isn't enough to thank him for all he's done for me. All that I can do is keep showing up, continue to commit to working on myself and improving, and to continue volunteering to help others. It's the only thing I have to give back and the only way I can say thank you.

Chapter 25

Balls
Black Mountain, NC

"I CAN'T BELIEVE this shit. I've come full circle. I'm right back in my worst nightmare, fucking high school," Jax bitches.

"It wasn't so bad," McCormick insists. "ROTC was my favorite subject."

"That's because you're a kiss ass. You were then, and you still are now."

"You're just grumpy because nobody's kissing your ass," McCormick snaps.

Jax snorts. "You go on one date, and suddenly you're a love guru."

I follow the guys down the hall to the classroom on the left and peek through the little window in the door. Sure enough,

Stiles is standing at the front of the class, dressed in a worn gray Army t-shirt and camouflage cargo pants. We file in and he does a double take before cursing.

"Oh fuck. What are you doing here?"

"We came to support you," McCormick says, slapping his back. "Which one is your nephew?"

Stiles stumbles, swallowing before pointing to a kid in the back of the classroom. "That's Andrew or Drew, my sister's boy." He recovers and clears his throat. "These are my brothers, my team. Or I guess you would say squad."

"What happened to your leg?" one kid shouts. He's asking McCormick, but then he looks at West and realizes they're in the same boat.

"Well, shit, now they're never gonna enlist," Stiles grumbles.

"I lost it in the war. Got myself blowed up," McCormick explains.

"What about you?" the kid asks West.

"Same story. Got myself blowed up."

Nobody asks Mandy what happened to his face, because it's pretty self-explanatory. He got himself blowed up, too.

"Look, I've talked to you about unity and brotherhood and honor and bravery. I've told you about the grueling schedule and the hell of basic training. But what I didn't tell you was that when all that is behind you, and you're staring down four years of enlistment on your contract, shit starts to get real pretty quick. I've seen guys deployed with less than a year of experience and training. It may sound exciting to you now, but I promise you, there's nothing exciting about living in the desert. There's nothing exciting about coming home broken with your body in pieces. And even the ones that come home with all of their limbs intact are still broken, up here," he explains, tapping his head. "And in here," he says, rubbing a hand over his heart. "Nobody goes over there and comes home without scars, even if you can't see them. I'm not saying don't enlist because some of you would make great soldiers. But if you have another option, take it. War isn't for everyone."

There are no questions, just silence as the weight of his words settles over the class. Then, Drew, Stiles's nephew asks, "Can you tell us what it's like over there? What it's really like?"

We spend the next hour going over the good and not-so-good aspects of living in a war zone. The not-so-good list is a lot longer than the good one. The bell rings, and we file out after the kids. Stiles high-fives his nephew.

"I can't believe you all showed up," he says, sounding choked up.

"Like you said, we're your brothers. Of course we showed up," McCormick explains. "Come on, you owe me a cold beer and a basket of wings."

As we make our way down the crowded hall, I've got a warm, glowing feeling in my gut. It feels good to be part of a team again, to show up for your friends, your brothers. To do a good deed and be supportive.

"Betty?!" McCormick stops short, bringing the rest of us to a halt.

"Do I know you?" The woman looks familiar. Flaming red hair, cat eye glasses, red pouty lips.

It's Betty fucking Beasley.

"I go by Woodward at school. Betty Woodward."

Oh fuck, I said that out loud.

McCormick blushes redder than his hair color. "We watch you online."

"Yeah, McCormick is your biggest fan," Stiles snipes.

Her pretty green eyes grow big and round. "McCormick the Bitch?"

The guys snicker behind their hands. All except for West. "Please tell me that's not your online username."

"What else would I call myself?" McCormick asks.

"It's great to finally meet you in person," Betty says pleasantly.

"What are you doing here?" McCormick asks.

"I teach home economics. What are you doing here?"

I glance at West, gauging his reaction. Is he attracted to her? Now that we know she lives nearby, is he going to engage with her? Transfer his interest from me to her? It's a stupid fucking thought to have, but there's no denying she's hot, and we're both bisexual men. It's going to take a while for me to stop second-guessing him when it comes to women. Fuck, when it comes to anyone. I never took myself for a jealous guy until West.

I also never had anything worth losing. *Until West.*

Thank God, he looks more amused than interested.

"We're retired vets. We were giving a speech to my nephew's ROTC class. In fact, we're all members of a support group for veterans with disabilities, and as part of our therapy, we knit. That's how we know you. We all watch your videos."

"Some of us more than others," Stiles teases, disguising his words with a cough.

Betty smiles like that's the best news she's ever heard. "Get out! You all knit?" We all nod collectively, and she continues, "I just have to have you do a video with me!"

"Co-host? With Betty Beasley?" McCormick sounds like he's about to have a stroke.

"Definitely. Give me your number and I will contact you with the details."

McCormick almost drops his phone as he fumbles with nerves. She hands it back to him and he stares at the screen as if it's the second coming of Christ.

"Do you mind if I give you a call?"

Betty has the grace to blush. "As long as it's related to knitting or the show. I'm afraid you're not exactly my type."

Before I can get angry on his behalf, Stiles beats me to it. "Look, if you're not into guys with disabilities, there are nicer ways of saying it. You don't have to–"

"It's because he's a man," she blurts, cutting him off.

Stiles chokes. McCormick chokes. Thankfully I recover. I grab both of them by the shoulders and drag them down the hall, glancing over my shoulder to say, "Thanks, Betty. We'll be in touch."

"Wait," McCormick hisses, "I was going to get her to sign something."

"She doesn't want to sign your fucking smelly underwear," Stiles gripes.

"Don't take it too hard," Jax assures him, "you've still got half a chance with Carly."

As we pile into the Jeep, I exchange looks with West, and we shake with silent laughter. *Betty fucking Beasley. What are the odds?*

"Good afternoon, Sgt. Aguilar," Margaret Anne greets cheerfully. "I made your coffee just the way you like it, with lots of cream and no sugar," she beams.

Returning the smile, I gratefully accept the steaming paper cup, inhaling the rich aroma as I take a tentative sip. "Have I told you yet today that you're a doll?"

She blushes like a teenage girl in high school and shoos me away.

West follows me down the hall as we make our way to support group. I can hear him snickering behind me, and I roll my eyes.

"What?"

"Did I say anything?"

"Kind of, yeah."

"She likes you."

"Who? Margaret Anne?! She's like...my grandma." He's fucking smoking crack.

"It's not uncommon for older women to be attracted to younger men."

My boots freeze on the polished concrete floor. "The fuck is wrong with you?" Raising the cup to my lips, I'm about to take a sip when I pause, suspicion making my stomach roll in waves. "I can't fucking drink this now." I shove the cup at West. "Here, are you happy now?"

Laughing, he takes a sip and makes a face before he chucks it in the nearest garbage can. "I think it's sweet."

"And I think you're jealous because I'm her favorite and not you." He laughs even louder and I feel ridiculous for letting him get to me. "You owe me a coffee," I grumble bitterly.

He strides ahead of me, and I can't help but notice his gait. I would never admit this to him, for fear that he would punch my teeth in, but the way he walks with his prosthetic on makes his ass sway deliciously. I rush him from behind, taking him by surprise, and push him through the bathroom door off to the left of the hall. He loses his balance and clutches me for support.

"What the fuck? If you have to pee that bad, just say so."

He thinks I have to pee? That's definitely not the function my cock needs right now.

Shoving him roughly against the counter, I cover his back with my body, grinding my quickly hardening erection into his ass. West braces his hands on the counter and widens his stance for balance.

"Where is the most obscure place you've ever had sex?" My whispered words are a sinful suggestion in his ear.

"Fuck no, not in the BALLS bathroom," he laughs.

"I can lock the door. Tell me," I insist, thrusting into him.

Even through layers of clothing, I can tell he wants me as he pushes back against me. "You should know. You were there."

I rack my brain trying to think of where we fucked that was so obscure. The hot tub? Our bedroom? Was he counting the bathroom at that bar? "Black Mountain Tavern?" I reach my hand around his hip to cup his cock, finding it rock-hard.

"No," he chuckles, "in a bounce house."

His words register through the fog of lust clouding my head, and I pause mid-kiss on his neck. "You had sex in a bounce house? When? Where the fuck was I?"

"The fuck if I know. You were there somewhere. Probably trying to score, same as I was." He meets my eyes in the mirror and registers my confusion. "Sanderson and his wife had that birthday party for their kid."

The name rings a bell. Sanderson was on our squad back at Bragg. "Who did you hook up with?"

"I don't know," he murmurs, cupping the side of my face as he turns his lips into my neck. "Some chick."

He covers my hand with his, pressing harder against his dick for friction. I want so badly to lock the door and fuck him over this counter. Why in the hell did I start something I can't finish?

"Did she bounce on your cock?"

"Mmm, yeah."

"When we get home, maybe you can show me how good it felt. You can bounce on mine for the rest of the night."

With the frustrated sigh, he stills my hand. "Come on, let's get this over with."

We're the last to arrive, and McCormick already has his purple yarn out, his project almost complete. Although I can't figure out what it's supposed to be for the life of me. I pull out the blue yarn I'm using to make West's socks. I've almost finished the sleeve for his limb.

"The fuck is that supposed to be, a cock ring?" Of course, West, having no filter, asks the question on everyone's mind.

"Don't be ridiculous," McCormick snorts. "It's handcuffs," he explains, holding them up like we're blind.

Stiles scoffs. "What kind of kinky freak knits handcuffs?"

"The kind of kinky freak you wish you were fucking," he retorts, before blushing bright red. "I didn't mean me,"

McCormick clarifies, looking panicked. "What? Nobody has knitted handcuffs? It makes perfect sense. They don't chafe your skin."

He has a point, actually. "I mean, I guess?" West tries to hide his smile, but it shines through. *Fuck it.* "Hey, do you happen to have the pattern for that?"

"I've got you, brother. I'll email it to you tonight."

A bark of laughter escapes West's mouth, and when I glance at him, I see his body shaking as he tries to contain it inside of him.

The cock ring idea has merit as well.

"Looks like Aguilar is tired of the buddy system. He's ready to strike out on his own," Jax teases.

Fuck me, they think I want to knit handcuffs to use on a woman. West stares at me a little too long, residual heat from earlier lingering in his dark eyes. His expression is wrongly interpreted by McCormick.

"Wardell doesn't like that idea. He likes the buddy system. Don't worry man, I think Carly has a friend who's single and looking to mingle."

West just shakes his head, like there's something fundamentally wrong with McCormick. Which there is. I'm certain of it.

"All right guys, let's get started," Riggs calls.

McCormick's big mouth kicks off the meeting. "I met Betty Beasley, and she asked me for my number."

"Yeah, so she could put you on her show," Stiles corrects.

"Yeah, but after she spends time with me, one-on-one, who knows?"

"Jesus Christ," he murmurs, scrubbing his face. "I'm still employed. So I guess that's a win."

Pharo is noticeably absent, so Jax goes next. "I had a setback this week," he admits, picking at his fingernails. "The only bright spot was when I showed up for a friend," he says, barely glancing at Stiles. "It might be what saved me." He refuses to look up and meet anyone's eyes, staring instead at the holes in his jeans. "I could tell you I'm okay, but I don't know if I really am. I might need to get with someone after the meeting."

"Jax, it takes big balls to come here and be honest about the bad days. I don't have a damn thing to do after the meeting, and I'm all yours for the rest of the day," Riggs offers.

"Yeah, we're all free," West swears, eyeballing each and every Bitch, daring them to disagree.

Mandy goes next. "The closer I get to my surgery, the more I'm struggling. Not just with medical anxiety, but nightmares and PTS. It's typical for me right before surgery. So," he says, looking at Jax, "I'm with you, man. It's a good thing we're getting together after the meeting, 'cause I don't need to be alone today."

Jax nods, looking slightly relieved.

My heart feels heavy listening to their pain. I know that pain, it's a dark and lonely place. Thank God I have West, but Mandy and Jax don't have anyone to call their own, besides the group.

In the heavy silence, I realize it's my turn, and that they're waiting on me to speak. It feels like a day for sharing secrets, and although West and I haven't discussed a timeline for coming out to the group, we told my parents, and he handled that well. He also told Mandy, and he felt good about that. I don't plan to tell them outright, but it doesn't sit right with me to have them thinking that I'm ready to start dating, especially if they're going to continue to tease me about it like I know they will. That's what brothers do.

"It's been a long week. The awards ceremony took a toll on us. And that was only one of many tough days recently, but somehow it all pales in comparison to the one bright and shining spot this week." All the good feelings I associate with West, the way he makes me feel, so complete and alive, has a smile spreading across my cheeks that I can't fight. I want to tell them I'm in love with my best friend. I want to shout it to the entire world. I want to tell them I'm happier than I've ever been and that even on his worst days, I'm still so fucking grateful for him. "It's probably the brightest spot of my entire fucking life. It really puts everything in perspective."

Am I blushing? My face feels hot.

I must be because the ridiculous cat calls start up—whistles, a slow clap—I have the worst poker face.

"What's her name?"

"When can we meet her?"

"Does she have a friend for West?"

In a move that surprises everyone, but no one more than me, West pushes to his feet. He stands before me and, with a look I can only describe as let's-fucking-do-this-because-I-love-you, he straddles my lap and hooks his arms around my neck, touching his forehead to mine. Softly, he brushes his lips over mine, waiting for me to part them, and when I let him inside, he strokes his tongue along mine in a deep, passionate kiss that almost makes me forget we're not alone.

"It's about fucking time," Riggs bitches, clapping the loudest.

"Get some," McCormick yells.

"Fucking McCormick," West mumbles against my lips. "Maybe you should consider dating dudes; it might change your luck."

McCormick looks affronted. "Fuck you." But then his expression changes as he appears to consider it. "What are you doing later?" he asks Stiles.

"Oh hell, no! And don't call me later, asking me what I'm wearing."

"And no dick pics either," Jax adds. "Nobody wants to see your junk. Again."

"I was drunk dialing! I meant to send that to a chick," McCormick swears. "Y'all are a hateful bunch of Bitches," he whines when every single one of us breaks out in laughter.

I stare up into West's eyes, and I see everything I feel for him reflected back. All the love, all the trust, it's all there clear as day. I slide my arms around his waist and press my lips to his again.

Fuck the Bitches. This is our moment.

"I love you," I breathe against his lips.

"Love you more."

WEST

Black Mountain, NC

Chapter 26

> McCormick: Are you doing it right now?
>
> Stiles: If he doesn't answer, it means yes.

"BRANDT! Can't you make them stop? This is getting ridiculous."

"You're a retired SFC. You have leadership skills. Use them," he shouts from the bathroom.

I poke my head in the bedroom and call, "Come on, before we're late. We still have to pick up Mandy." I'd shut my phone off if it wasn't such an important day.

Brandt emerges and grabs his wallet and keys from the

dresser. "I'm betting you're more nervous than he is. You need to relax because you're going to make his anxiety worse."

"You're right. Fuck. I don't know how to calm down." I'm fucking blowing this. Mandy needs a rock-solid, supportive ball buddy, not a saggy limp nut like me.

We climb into the Jeep and I'm glad he's driving because my head is a mess.

"Tell me about the Sherman."

"The M4?" The question catches me off guard. It's so unexpected I forget my panic. "It wasn't a total piece of shit like the bad rap it always gets. It had super thick armor, and because it was taller than other tanks, it was a little more comfortable and roomy inside. They were easily repaired right there on the battlefield and ran on gasoline rather than diesel, which was both good and bad. But the Panzer blew it out of the water. Fucking Germans."

Brandt laughs and shakes his head. "How many times do I have to remind you we're allies now, Professor?"

"Yeah, yeah, whatever. Thank God they replaced it with the Pershing. It had a better cannon, thicker armor, and better suspension and mobility." I reach for the knob to turn the radio down. "Can you imagine if we had that thing from the get-go? Maybe the war wouldn't have lasted so long."

I check my phone for messages from Mandy, but there's nothing.

"Feel better?"

Fucker. My heart rate has slowed and I'm not on the verge of hyperventilating. He totally played me. "Yeah," I chuff.

"You know he's going to be okay, right?" I blow out a deep breath. "Tell me, what's the worst that can happen?" he asks.

"I don't know. That he doesn't fucking wake up?"

"He's going to wake up. What's the next worst thing?"

"He gets an infection?"

"No, because we're going to take great care of him, and make sure he takes great care of himself. Next?"

I'm quickly running out of arguments, and now we're down to the real truth. "That he doesn't see an improvement and his self-esteem and confidence plummets." My shoulders droop with defeat because I've convinced myself this is a huge probability.

"I love you." His words surprise me, making my head snap up. "I love that you care about people. He's going to be fine because he has you and me and the Bitches and Riggs and Brewer, and we won't let him plummet."

What would I do without this man? "I love you, too."

We pull up in front of Mandy's apartment, and he hops in the backseat. He doesn't have much to say on the drive over to the hospital, which is understandable, so we fill the silence by playing the radio. Brandt's fingers tap the steering wheel in time to the beat. When the song segues into a commercial, a beaming smile spreads across his face.

"What?" I ask, instantly wary.

"Do you feel it, West?"

Fuck. I should have seen it coming. "I'm sorry, Mandy. He can't help it. I think he suffered residual TBI in the blast."

"I feel the need...The need for speed," Brandt shouts, rolling down the windows.

He hits *'play'* on the CD player, and the track changes to *Danger Zone* by Kenny Loggins. I'm not even annoyed because the timing couldn't be more perfect. So I roll my window down and sing along with him, word for word. Eventually, Mandy joins in, and when I catch a glimpse of him in the side-view mirror, he's smiling.

Thank God.

We park our asses in the waiting room at the hospital while Mandy gets checked in and prepped for surgery. One by one, the Bitches wander in. First Stiles, then Jax, then McCormick and Riggs.

All at once it hits me, the reality of where I landed and what I have. When I was recovering in the hospital, I thought my life was over, that I'd lost everything. I'd never felt more desolate and lost in my entire life. I was even afraid to cling to Brandt for fear that he'd leave, too.

I've seen so many retired and disabled vets fall through the cracks, fall by the wayside, and get lost. Forgotten. My greatest fear was to end up like them.

Alone and lonely.

I never could have imagined I'd have an entire support group of friends who treated me and Brandt like brothers. Guys who showed up on your worst day to hold your hand. A real family. And what's more, not just a best friend, but one who loves me to the bottom of my soul. A man who wants to spend his life attached to me. Tears gather in my eyes and when I blink, they spill down my cheeks.

I'm so fucking grateful for what I have, something I swore just months ago I'd never be able to say.

"Okay," Brandt says lightly, "enough. Pull it out."

"No! Not here. Go to the bathroom," McCormick jokes.

Idiot. I know what Brandt's referring to. Reaching into my go bag, I pull out the worn Mad Libs I carry everywhere.

"Adjective that rhymes with easy."

"Sleazy. Measly. Weaselly," Brandt answers.

"Basically, McCormick," Jax teases.

I grin, shaking my head. "Give me a proper noun that starts with an N."

"Naples, Italy," Riggs supplies.

"North American Museum of Anthropology," Stiles blurts. Everyone pauses what they're doing to stop and stare at him like he's grown two heads. "What? It's a real place. I've been. It's nice."

Choking back my snort, I record his answer. "Two verbs and a noun."

"Sneezing, shooting, and a flamethrower," McCormick answers.

Looking up from my pad, I peg him with a disbelieving look. "Really? A flamethrower?"

"What? It's been on my mind ever since Mandy said he fired one," he says with a shrug.

Unbelievable. "You know what scares me? The fact that not only did the military give you a loaded gun, but they actually paid you to shoot it."

"Oh, that's nothing, I've got stories that will make you shit your pants," he says with a wicked grin.

"I don't doubt it," Brandt murmurs just loud enough for me to hear.

"Weston Wardell?" the nurse calls.

"That's me," I say, coming to my feet.

"Mr. Cahill is prepped and ready. He wants to see you before we send him in."

She leads me to the back where Mandy is laid out on a rolling bed, dressed in a gown and surgical cap. He looks like how I feel.

Scared shitless.

Crouching over his bed, I grab his hand and lock our fingers together. "Hey, brother. You look good."

He grins. "Yeah? I'll ask for an extra set to take home."

I clear my throat. "Listen to me. This is nothing. A fucking walk in the park. Okay? You've been through worse shit than this. You're tough as fucking steel. Also, there are six badass motherfuckers out there in the waiting room who are gonna kick your ass if you don't wake up. So..."

Mandy snorts. "Yes sir. I'll do my best not to disappoint."

"You just do the best you can. Fuck everyone else. But I promise you, I'm gonna see you real soon." Swallowing hard, I press my forehead to our joined fists.

"What if they fuck up and cut my leg off instead?"

"Then we'll be twins. Just make sure they take your left leg so we can hold each other up without falling over."

He grins, and I return it, fighting back tears. Why in the fuck am I crying again?! Shit! I swipe at my eyes before the tears can fall and Mandy laughs at me.

"Stop your pouting. I'll be fine, right? You fucking promised."

"Damn right."

"Okay gentleman, it's time," the nurse informs us.

With a last hard squeeze, I let go of his hand and salute him. "Oo-rah."

Mandy returns it with a smirk.

As I'm walking out of his room, I actually hear that bastard tell the nurse not to cut his legs off by accident.

Leaning against the door frame, I poke my head into the guest room where Mandy is recuperating. "How do you feel?"

With the covers pulled up to his chest, I can only see his face, swollen and covered in bandages on one side.

"Peachy," he croaks. "My face feels like it's on fire, like it's been stung by ten thousand bees."

"I'll get you a pain pill. In the meantime, are you up for company? There are some people here who want to see you."

"Sure," he says lifelessly.

Taking a step into the room, I cross my arms over my chest and hover over the foot of the bed. "What I meant to say was, I've got some bad ass Bitches crowding my living room, and they won't leave until they make sure you're okay."

A hint of a smile tugs at the corner of his lip on the side of his face not covered in bandages. "I guess you better send them in, then."

McCormick pushes past me, followed by Jax and Stiles. "How are you doing, man? West says you look even uglier than you did, but all I see is improvement."

Mandy tries to laugh, but winces in pain when his face

tightens. "Are you saying it's an improvement because half my face is covered?"

"Yeah, what did you think I meant?"

"Scoot over," Stiles grumbles, making himself comfortable on the queen-size bed.

His huge body takes up most of the mattress until McCormick stretches out on Mandy's other side, squishing him in the middle like the cream filling in an Oreo cookie.

"Are y'all stayin'?" Mandy asks.

"Ain't got a fucking thing to do today," Stiles answers.

Jax snorts. "You didn't get fired already, did you?"

"No, I put in for vacation time."

"Dude, you just fucking started," Jax points out. "How do you already have vacation time?"

Instead of answering, he asks, "Do you have any snacks, Wardell?"

All I can do is shake my head at him. When did this turn into a fucking pajama party? Sighing, I crawl across the foot of the bed. "Make room for me."

Jax makes himself comfortable in the chair in the corner, and a minute later, Brandt pokes his head into the room. "Don't you look comfortable," he teases.

"Would you grab those bags we brought?" Stiles asks.

Brandt returns holding plastic grocery store bags. "What's in these?"

"Care packages," he answers, sitting up a little to grab the bags. Stiles starts to pull contents out of the bags, dumping them on Mandy's lap. "Brand new yarn, and these needles are for knitting in the round, in case you want to make handcuffs like

McCormick did," he teases with a smirk. "I've got Twinkies, chips, and earplugs."

"What are the earplugs for?" Mandy asks.

"So you can't hear them having sex down the hall."

As a grown man who has been to war, I don't blush easily, but discussing my sex life with Brandt in front of a bunch of men has heat blooming on my cheeks. There's no disguising it, and the guys tease me for it.

McCormick grabs a bag from Stiles. "I brought porn mags, lube, and fuzzy socks."

Mandy's chest shakes with silent laughter, and he ends up coughing, and then wincing again.

"Brandt, bring the pain pills, and some better care packages. These suck."

"Like you. You know all about sucking, don't you?" McCormick jokes.

The sex jokes are never going to end. I'm pretty sure they have an endless supply to last a lifetime. When Brandt comes back, he's carrying a tray with a bottle of pain meds and bowls of food. Steam rises from them, and the scent carries to me, something familiar that makes my mouth water from nostalgia.

"Chili Mac!"

"You made chili?" McCormick asks.

"I reheated Chili Mac MREs. It's West's favorite."

Back in the army, whenever I was sick or injured and lying in bed like a big baby, Brandt would take care of me just like this, bringing me Chili Mac and a box of tissues, cuddling in bed with me while he watched Top Gun on replay over and over as I napped on and off. And that's when I spot it, and I chuckle. I should have known. He's got a slim plastic case tucked under his arm, and I'll bet ten bucks it's Top Gun.

He sets the tray on the dresser and practically climbs over my body. "Who's ready to take a trip to Pasadena?"

Jax rolls his eyes. "Dude, you missed your calling. You should have joined the Air Force or the Navy instead of the Army."

The afternoon passes with conversations murmured around the bedroom, voices kept low while Mandy dozes on and off. We finish *Top Gun* and play two more movies back to back. McCormick pulls out his yarn to work on some project, and Stiles thumbs through the latest issue of *Guns and Ammo Magazine,* while Jax scrolls through his phone. Despite the fact I'm cramped in a bed holding three too many people, I have no desire to move. Brandt's warmth cradles me, his soft breath tickling the back of my neck, and despite McCormick's foot pushing against the small of my back, I'm comfortable, like I'm wrapped in a cocoon of coziness. I feel safe. And judging by the peaceful look on Mandy's face, so does he.

The cool sheets beneath my ass are a stark contrast to his warm weight on top of me. Brandt's lips tickle my ear, planting kisses down my neck, across my jaw, as he works his way toward my mouth.

"Do you think he can hear us?"

"Nah," he breathes over my lips, "he's got earplugs." He

teases my bottom lip by sucking it between his until it's plump. "And painkillers. He's probably out like a light."

I worried about him all day. Much of my fear was soothed by seeing him rally today, in good spirits for the most part, while the guys visited. Mandy is going to be fine. He's going to heal, and then he's going to get on with his life. His struggle is far from over. There are many more skin graft surgeries in his future, but he knows he doesn't have to face them alone, and hopefully that helps.

"Hey," Brandt says, staring into my eyes as he cups my face. "Right here, right now; that's where I need your head."

His kisses bring me back to the present. The stubble on his cheek scrapes my lips, making them tingle, and I close my eyes, losing myself in him—in his scent and heat, in the feel of his rough hands tracing my body, the hard bulge of his erection pressing into mine.

Over the years, he has taken me in his arms and hugged me countless times, but it never felt this good. Like I'll die if he stops.

His lips close over my nipple, and he sucks it into a stiff peak before flicking it with his tongue. But he doesn't release it. No, Brandt milks my nipple until it's almost sore. I've never had them sucked for so long before, and my cock is twitching from the constant pull.

I wonder if I could come like this, just from having my nipples played with.

I slide my knee between his legs and grip his ass, trying to fit my body inside of his, or at least to get as close as I can. "You want me to turn over?"

"No," he says gruffly, "I want you just like this."

This feels different. He's going slow, taking his time with me, bathing my skin in kisses, touching my body in places he usually skips over. He places his hand on my shortened limb as he moves down my body, kissing a wet path down to my navel, where he licks the sensitive hollow until I squirm and push his head away. Even as he lowers his mouth, trailing his nose through my pubes, I'm aware of his hand rubbing over the bundle of scar tissue on the tip of my leg.

Why does it make me so fucking self-conscious? It's just Brandt. I know he accepts every part of me, even the broken pieces.

Especially the broken pieces.

But there's no rationalization for things that trigger you. I wish I could learn to not feel tense when he touches me there, like all my self-worth is tied up in my amputated leg. Frustratingly, he glides right over my cock with a wet lick of his tongue and continues down, sucking kisses on my inner thighs. His nose tickles the fine hairs between my legs, but he doesn't stop there. He sucks hard on the few scars that lead down to the tip of my thigh, and when he gets to the end, he focuses his dark blue gaze on me as his tongue flicks out to lick the raised scar. I can't really feel it, besides the pressure of his tongue. Most of the time, it just feels like static, like when your leg falls asleep. But the visual, the feeling of intimacy, makes me want to cry.

I've never had this with anyone before, and I don't think I could have it with anyone besides Brandt.

Because there's no one I trust more.

With my body.

With my heart.

With my life.

It begins and ends with Brandt.

I can't take it. I need him inside of me *now*. Right fucking now. I need to feel him inside of me like he's a part of me. One body. One life. Sitting up slightly, I reach under his arms and pull him up my body, bringing his mouth flush with mine, and press my lips against his, delving deep inside for a taste of him.

He moans into the kiss, sounding as hungry and needy as I feel, grinding his dick against mine as I suck on his tongue. Grabbing for the bottle of lube lying on the mattress beside us, he squeezes some into his palm and, reaching down between our bodies, he slicks his shaft. It slides through my crease easily, tickling in the most erotic way as it glides over my hole. I'm clenching now, wishing he would just fill me already and put me out of my misery.

"Gonna slide inside of you, just like this. Wrap your legs around my waist."

Brandt moves his body like he's fucking me, thrusting between my cheeks. He stares into my eyes and the connection is too much. I close my eyes to hide from him, to focus on how good he feels, but he isn't having it.

"Uh-uh. Open your eyes and look at me." He pushes against my entrance, and I can already feel the burn. "I want to see your face when I push inside you."

His swollen crown pops past my tight rim and I gasp, arching my back.

"You feel that?" Licking my lips, I nod. "So fucking tight.

God…you feel so good," he pants, burying himself deep. "I could lose myself in your body."

He hisses as he pulls back out. My hole is on fire because he didn't prep me, but I think he did that on purpose. And I love it, that initial sting, that bite of pain that stays with me long after he finishes inside of me.

He thrusts back in and stills as my body clenches around him, adjusting to his invasion. As long as I live, I will never get enough of this feeling, when he first enters me, when he's stretching me and filling me, claiming me. Every time feels like the first time, and yet, it feels as if we've been doing this for lifetimes.

Slowly, he moves in and out of my channel, with long, deep thrusts that open me up and make me shake as I cling to him and beg for more.

"Have you ever made love before?"

This is a hell of a fucking time to ask me a question like that.

"Never."

"This belongs to us." He suckles my lips, my tongue, and I chase his mouth for another kiss. "This is ours. Making love to each other."

"Kiss me," I whisper, desperate for contact. Wanting to be connected at every point of our bodies.

I glance between us with hooded eyes, and the longing in me increases tenfold. The way he moves. His body is beyond sexy. It's almost beautiful. The deep scars, the shadows that fall between the ridges of his toned muscles. His colorful tattoos. Brandt is a work of art.

He leans down to suck on my throat, in the hollow where I

have my trachea scar, making my cock throb between us. It lies on my stomach, heavy and dripping, begging for attention. I reach for it and pump into my fist slowly, in sync with his thrusts. Fire builds in my belly and spreads through my limbs, making my skin flush all over.

"I'm close," I hiss, hoping I can hold off long enough for him to come with me.

I dig my fingers into the muscle of his back and feel the divots and ragged flesh of his shrapnel wounds—wounds he sustained while saving my life. We're two souls that were always destined to be mates, beautifully broken and carefully mended. We belong to each other. I am the keeper of his body and his heart, and he is the protector of mine. To him, my imperfections are perfect. To me, he has no imperfections. He was always perfect.

"Say it. Tell me."

He thrusts deep, making me cry out, "I love you."

"Come with me."

As my orgasm rushes forth, my heart splits wide open, my body spilling tears and cum and sweat.

I have bled for him.

I would give my life for his.

And I will be vulnerable for him. *To* him.

He is everything and together we have forever.

With a roar, he finishes inside my ass, spilling his load deep within me, and collapses on my chest in a sweaty heap.

Sometime later, he finally slips free of my body, and I feel the warmth of his seed trickle down my thighs. Brandt rests his head on my shortened limb. I run my fingers through his hair and he rubs his thumb over the skin of my inner thigh, spreading the wet mess in circles. We don't need to say a word—the silence is enough. So is the expression on his face. It screams *I love you, I'm happy.*

I don't need to tell him I love him, or remind him that we're forever. The look on his face says it all. I return the look before closing my eyes, letting my head fall back against the pillow in contented bliss, and I breathe a sigh of satisfaction and relief.

My soul is finally at rest. So is my conscience.

BRANDT

Chapter 27

Epilogue

"HEY, HELP ME WITH THIS," I pant, heaving the heavy cardboard box onto the bed.

West is just getting up for the day, although it's nearly twelve in the afternoon. He's been awake for some time, but this is how he likes to start his day usually, unhurried and alone. I've seen him stare out the window for nearly an hour many times. I can only imagine what he's thinking about. Sometimes I hear him mumble to himself and I wonder if he's talking to God or some higher power he's made peace with.

"What's in the box?" he asks, sitting up with his back propped against the pillows.

"It's the box they gave us when they sent us home from Germany. Probably everything we had with us on base."

He looks at it warily, like it's full of landmines. And for him, it probably is. It's a box full of triggers. Mental and emotional landlines. I wouldn't even be able to go through it if he weren't with me. Unfolding the flaps on top, I pull out the first item, a picture album bound in black leather. I already know what it holds inside: twelve years worth of memories of me and West's friendship—our life together in the service, trips we've taken on leave, pictures of his grandmother and my parents.

A little piece of home whenever we were homesick.

I know for a fact there're pictures of the Street Sweepers in there, and so does West. He shakes his head when I offer it to him and instead I just lay it on the bed. Next, I pull out a packet of paperwork, army legalese and mumbo-jumbo. There's another packet almost as thick, our discharge papers from the hospital, X-rays, and medical records. West's file is twice as thick as mine.

Wading through spare military gear and boots, I find something of interest. "Remember this?" I ask, holding out a rock. He smiles and takes it from me, inspecting the rough edges.

"I picked this up on our first day in the desert because it reminded me vaguely of a spearhead, which is a big thing here in North Carolina. I guess it reminded me of home."

Looking at him, I can't help but smile. You wouldn't know it from his tough exterior, but West is a very sentimental guy with a heart as soft as a marshmallow. Reaching into the box, I pull out a wide-neck beer bottle filled with Afghan afghani coins. Next is a tube of hand lotion that I can only assume is… holding it to my nose, I take a whiff and recognize the scent.

"Is this what you used to use to jack off with?"

"Give me that," he curses, grabbing it from me and shoving it under his pillow, exactly where he used to keep it. Ignoring my knowing laugh, he asks, "What else is in there?"

Reaching my hand into the box, my fingers close around a plastic bag and I pull it out. It holds our dog tags. West grabs the bag from me and takes mine out, sliding them over his head. So I do the same with his, tucking them under my T-shirt. I'm smiling as I reach into the box and pull out a manila envelope. I don't recognize it, and I'm curious but kind of afraid to open it.

"What's that," he asks.

"Beats me."

"Open it," he says, eyeing the packet.

I break the seal and peek inside. It holds a bunch of smaller envelopes, all sealed and addressed. One by one, I pull them out and read the names. Susan Lagaro. Marina Estevez. Michael and Michelle Jennings.

West isn't curious anymore; he knows exactly what this is. So do I. Goodbye letters, or death letters, whichever you want to call it. Final words from beyond the grave from our team to the ones they loved most. I hold the stack in my hands, tapping it against the box lid.

"What do you want to do with these?"

His throat slides, and he takes his time meeting my gaze. "We have to send them. They deserve to know what those letters say." With a nod of agreement, I carefully place them back inside the envelope. "Where are ours?

Reaching back in, I pull out two letters, one addressed to Sergeant First Class Weston Wardell of the United States Army.

The second is addressed to First Sergeant Brandt Aguilar of the United States Army.

I've never seen his letter, but of course he addressed it to me, I'm the only family he has left. Mine however is a surprise to him.

"You made your final letter out to me?" He looks like he's about to cry any second, and I just might fall apart with him.

"Of course. Who else would I save my final words for?"

"Your parents?"

I shrug. "They know I love them."

He flips it over and then pauses. "Can I open it?"

"I don't see why not."

Despite my casual tone, my heart is in my throat as he unfolds it. He's about to read my last words, or what were supposed to be my last words. The most important things I wanted him to know. Basically, the essence of our friendship. What it all boils down to.

West,

That's what all your friends call you, isn't it?

The luckiest day of my life was the day I sat down beside you in the mess hall and stole your biscuit. Someone up above was looking out for me that day.

Thank you for giving me the best memories of my life, my happiest days, my most thrilling adventures, my most memorable, and meaningful conversations. They were all with you. When people are gone, they say, 'he lived a good life.' Well, I did live a good life—because of you. You made it good. You made it fucking incredible, actually. Because of you, I lived the kind of life other people wish they had.

I wish I could be selfless and say that I hope you move on and find another friend like me, like what we had together, but I'd be lying. I guess I'm just a selfish bastard when it comes to you. I don't want you to move on and find another friend like me. Do you hear me? Do not lay on hoods and smoke with other guys. If you get another tattoo, go by yourself. Do not get another ink buddy. I don't want you drinking and playing cards with another guy, and if I ever find out you watched Top Gun with another guy, I'll come back and haunt you for the rest of your miserable fucking life. If you do make a new friend, I guess you can play chess together or something, or join one of your nerdy trivia groups.

I guess if you're reading this, I'm gone. God had other plans for me that didn't include you for some reason, but don't worry about it, cause we'll catch up soon. I love you, West. I love you like a brother. A real one. I love you like my best friend. I love you like someone I respect and admire and even look up to. You are one of a kind, Weston Wardell, the best of the best, and I was lucky enough to call you mine for a long time, but not long enough. Carry-on, soldier. I'll see you on the other side, brother.

Love Brandt/ The Grim Reaper

Tears distort my vision, and I swipe them away and sniffle, clearing my nose. West snorts, dropping tears onto the letter, soaking the paper, and his head hung low. I can't even imagine if he was reading this letter for real after I was gone. I can't imagine the pain he would be feeling, the overwhelming isolation and desolation. It would be enough to make my heart stop beating if it were me.

"You're a real selfish prick," he says in a warbled voice. "First, you try to leave me, hypothetically, and then you tell me I can't even move on and get a new friend."

Through my tears, I laugh, a snotty, broken sound that makes him laugh as well. Taking the letter from his hand, I lay it down on the bed and climb over his lap. He looks up into my eyes, and I push my nose against his, rubbing them together. Eskimo kisses, because I'm too teary to kiss him properly and my throat isn't working, but I need to feel close to him.

His breath feels hot against my cheek. "I can't do this without you. I refuse. There's no point to it, really, because we both know I'm only alive because of you. If you go, I'm coming with you."

"West, don't." Don't what? Don't die because of me? It's like trying to stop a flood with a paper towel, completely fucking useless and pointless.

"Wherever you go, I'm going to follow. You promised you wouldn't leave me alone in the darkness, and I can't imagine how dark it would be without you. You wouldn't do that to me, would you?"

"No," I say, sounding completely broken. I am. Fucking heartbroken to the core. Because if something happens to me, I'm taking his life as well.

"I'll see you on the other side 'cause I'll be there with you. In this life and the next, together forever."

Touching my forehead to his, I wrap my arms around his shoulders, and he does the same to me, like two koalas hugging a tree trunk. There's no beginning and no end to us. We are one. And where one goes, the other follows.

"Are you going to read my letter?"

Sliding off his lap, I sit back and grab the envelope, tearing through the seal. Taking a deep breath, I brace myself for the onslaught of emotion that's about to crush me.

Brandt,

If you're reading this, I'm sorry. Whatever I did, I didn't do it on purpose. But I'm over here wherever I am, all by my fucking self waiting on your sorry ass. So grab your gun and put your boots on and hurry the fuck up, 'cause you're late.

And don't go getting any ideas about replacing me, either! You should know better than that. Nobody but me is going to suffer through your Top Gun bullshit. Frankly, it's annoying, and I only put up with it because I love you.

You're getting this letter because I don't have anyone else to write it to. You're all I've got. The only thing in my life that mattered. But I want you to know it wasn't out of convenience. I wasn't stuck with you. I didn't end up with you because there was no one else. I would have chosen you over everyone because there's no one better than you. You're not just my best friend, or my brother or my family. You're my partner, my other half. Too bad we weren't gay because we'd have made a great couple.

It's hard to read his words through my tears, but I laugh, looking up at him. He must know what point I'm at in the letter because he laughs as well.

If you miss me, just reach out and talk to me. You know everything I would say. Please don't ever stop hearing my voice. Don't ever forget what I look like. And don't ever forget how much I love you.
 I'll see you on the other side, brother.

 Love West a.k.a. The Professor

The paper is stained with dried water marks, his tears as he poured his heart out to me. I lay the letter down and slide my hand over his knee.

"It's a good thing we turned out gay because we really do make a great couple."

West laughs. "There's something else in there."

Reaching into the envelope, I pull out a shiny enameled challenge coin. I remember it well. It was our first challenge after basic. West struggled to climb a ten-foot wall in the pouring rain, and he only completed the course because I helped him. I had no idea he kept it all these years as a token of our friendship. Clutching it in my fist, the cool metal warms quickly as it bites into my skin.

"I love you, Wes."

"Love you too, Reaper."

Gripping his chin between my fingers, I brush my lips over his and, when he opens for me, I kiss him properly this time.

For long minutes, we just sit there clinging to each other without words until Mandy clears his throat to get our attention. He's standing in the doorway, holding an envelope.

"Hey, Nutter Buddy, you good? Do you need something?" The left side of his face is still swollen from the surgery, but he's up and moving about and even dressed today, which is a huge improvement.

"I'm sorry to interrupt, but I overheard. I have a favor to ask."

"You can ask anything."

"I have a letter of my own from my buddy that I never mailed to his family." He chews his bottom lip, choking up. "There's so many reasons why I've held onto it, but it's time to let it go. I heard you say that their families deserve to hear their last words, and Sam's family deserves to hear his." He holds the letter out to me. "Would you mail this for me?"

I exchange looks with West to make sure we're on the same page, and he answers for the both of us. "I can't, Mandy. You're right, you've held onto that long enough. It's time to let it go. But I can't mail that for you. That's something you're going to have to do yourself." Mandy's shoulders droop under the weight of unwanted obligation. "But what I can do is go with you to mail it. We both can. And when we finish, we can stop off and grab a beer and toast them."

Mandy nods. His throat works as he struggles to answer. "That sounds doable."

"Grab your jacket and we'll head out."

"Today?"

"No time like the present."

"Are you sure you want to be seen with me like this? I mean, the post office is one thing, but the Black Mountain Tavern?"

"Hell, like the guys said the other day, your face is a damn improvement over what it was," I tease.

Managing a small smile, Mandy says, "I'll grab my jacket."

When he walks away, West says, "There's one more place I need to stop."

"Today?"

"No, not today. Tomorrow or the next day is soon enough."

"Someone else you need to say goodbye to?"

"No, not really. More like someone I need to say hello to."

When I step out of the shower, there's a note etched into the foggy mirror drawn by West's finger.

Meet me outside

Smiling to myself as I roll on deodorant and brush my teeth, I figure he's probably waiting for me in the hot tub, which means I'll have to shower again. But it will be one hundred percent worthwhile.

But when I open the sliding glass door from our bedroom, West isn't in the hot tub, he's standing by the rail, bathed in moonlight. There's a trail of wildflower petals leading directly to him.

Did he pick those for me?

God, I fucking love you.

"What's this? What are you doing?"

"When you promise the rest of your life to someone, you don't do it in the fucking bathroom."

"Do you do it outside on the deck under the stars?"

"Yes, you fucking do."

Closing the distance separating us, I slide up against his solid, warm body, and cup his dick. "You're wearing it, aren't you?"

"Yes, I fucking am." His wicked grin makes my dick equally as hard. No cock ring needed.

My fingers attack his zipper, going straight for the prize, 'cause I'm dying to see how mouthwatering he looks wearing it, slick and hard and throbbing.

"Hold up, first this ring, then we'll get to the other one."

"Well, hurry the fuck up and promise me forever, because I want to get my hands and my mouth on your swollen dick."

West chuckles, reaching for my hand. He slides my fourth

finger, the one with his ring, between his lips and sucks seductively. The feeling goes straight to my balls.

"If I slip, I know you'll catch me. If I get lost, I know you'll find me. And when I succeed, I know you'll cheer for me. Louder than anyone else. I owe my life to you, Brandt. You asked for proof of it every day until it was no longer at risk. Joke's on you," he smirks, "'cause now you've got to spend the rest of it with me. Right by my side."

And just like that, I forget about sex and all I can feel is my damn heart, swelling to bursting. "There's nowhere else I'd rather be." Taking his hand in mine, I kiss his knuckle right above my ring. "My whole world revolves around you, Wes. Like it spins on your axis. I pretend like I'm independent, like I have my own life, my own interests, but it's all a lie. All I have is you. You're all I want, all that matters. The rest of it is just background noise. If I get to spend the rest of my life with you, I count myself pretty fucking lucky."

Lacing our fingers together, his kiss falls on my lips and I'm reminded about his cock ring-covered cock, waiting for my mouth.

His smile is dazzling and the next words out of his mouth cement all the reasons why he's perfect for me, why he's the love of my life.

"*You can be my wingman anytime.*"

Choking on a laugh that's part sob, I say, "*Bullshit. You can be mine.*"

WEST

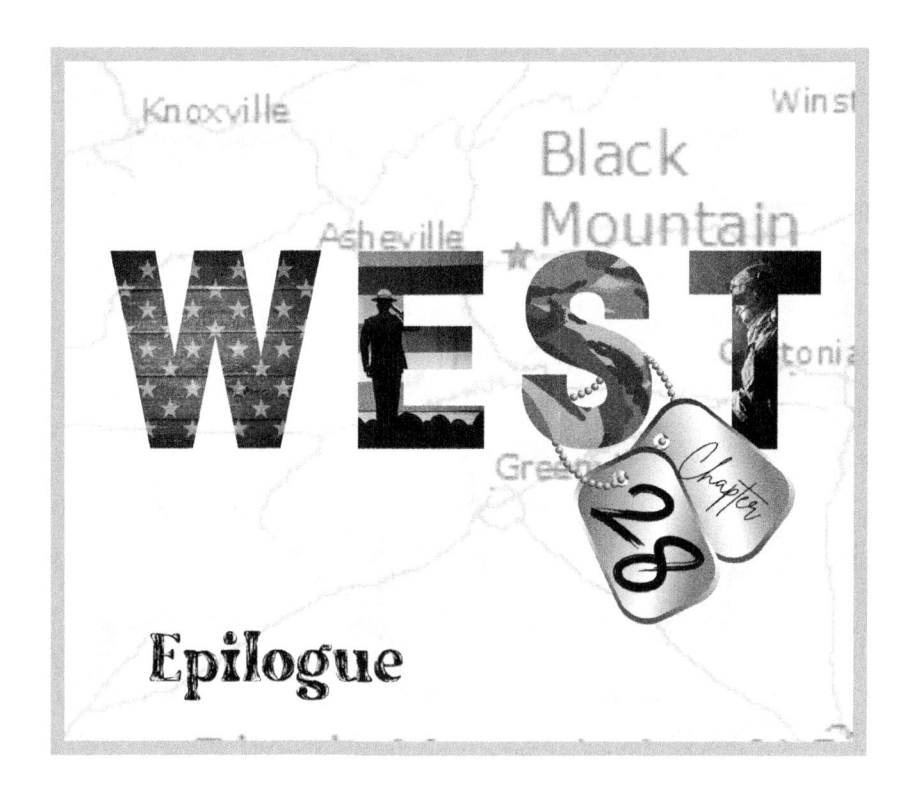

Chapter 28

Epilogue

HEAT ENVELOPS MY SHAFT, wet heat and the most intense suction, as his fingers squeeze my balls.

I'm gonna blow, and when I do, it's gonna flood his entire fucking mouth. My head slams back against the pillow and I groan and palm the back of his head, forcing another inch down his throat. He gags, and the sound makes my stomach clench. My nerves buzz as the pleasure intensifies, and I shout as I shoot my thick load.

He swallows noisily, slurping and sniffling, and drops his head on my shortened limb, pressing a sticky kiss to my scars. "You've got a thick cock, and that load was huge," he grins, sounding satisfied and a bit sleepy.

"Best way to start the day."

"Speaking of, after breakfast, what do you want to do today?"

"I want to stay buried in your mouth all day. Until my dick is so empty and spent it cries for mercy."

He's laughing before I'm even done speaking. "I'm serious."

"So am I," I tease, then sigh overdramatically. "Fine, I guess today is a good day to go do that thing I mentioned. Someone I have to visit."

"A Bitch? A Ball Buddy?"

"No, and that's all I'm gonna tell you. If you aren't gonna suck my dick again, let's get showered and dressed."

He tosses me the keys, and I slide behind the wheel and adjust the seat's position. I'm still getting the hang of driving. My prosthetic makes it difficult to gauge how much pressure I'm putting on the pedals. It's a lot of harsh jolting stops and starts. Brandt might have to file a medical claim for whiplash. He even got me a bumper sticker from the Disabled Veterans of America association that reads, *'Slightly Damaged Human: Keep Your Distance.'* The Bitches got me a handful that better not ever end up on my baby's butt, like, *'I'm just in it for the great parking'* and *'I give great rides.'* That one depicts a guy in a wheelchair with someone on his lap. McCormick used a black sharpie to draw a huge boner poking from the guy's lap.

I know the exact moment Brandt figures out where we're going. He slides his hand over mine and presses a kiss to my cheek, then he leans back against the headrest and closes his eyes for the duration of the drive.

The cemetery is well maintained, which eases my conscience because I don't visit often, so I can't complain. I approach her grave and plop down on my ass, dusting off the silk flowers that decorate her headstone.

> *Virginia Grace Wardell*
> *1934-2011*
> *Beloved Wife and Grandmother*

"Hi Gran."

Brandt plops down beside me and takes my hand. He offers me a sunny, encouraging smile.

"It's been awhile. I've been deployed. I kinda got blown up, Gran. I'm sorry. I've been recuperating, getting strong again, so I could come see you."

Already the tears threaten to spill, and I just fucking got here.

All my life, I looked up to her and my grandfather like they were invincible. I guess all children think their parents are invincible. Immortal. It's something we take for granted. But not me. I knew that wasn't the case because my own parents failed me. My Gran was the strongest woman I knew. I only ever wanted to make her proud of me, like I was of her.

But my granddad, he was larger than life. A decorated war hero and the world's best replacement dad, now buried at Arlington. I dreamed of someday following in his footsteps. I pushed myself harder than necessary, took risks I shouldn't have, just to try to be the man he was, to accomplish a tenth of what he had. He died when I was young from a heart attack, leaving me and my Gran on our own. So even though I looked up to him like he was a god, I had twenty-two extra years with my Gran. She was my whole world.

Until Brandt came along.

"Gran, you remember Brandt, my best bud."

Of course she did. He visited her many times with me in the years after basic training.

Brandt nods, like she can see him. "Hi, Ma'am, good to see you again. We miss you."

Swallowing back a fresh wave of tears, I clear my throat and continue. "Gran, Brandt isn't just my best friend anymore. He's the man I love with all my heart."

The End

Before your book hangover sets in, let me reassure you there's more West and Brandt and the Bitches in the second *Scars And Stripes* book, **The Darkness Within.**

Grab Brewer and Nash's book today!

DEAR READER

Thank you so much for reading **Proof Of Life,** the first novel in the *Scars And Stripes series*.

If you enjoyed Brandt and West's romance, **please leave a review** to tell other readers how much you loved them. Telling your friends and spreading the word on social media helps people find their new favorite book.

With love,
 Raquel Riley

NEXT IN SERIES

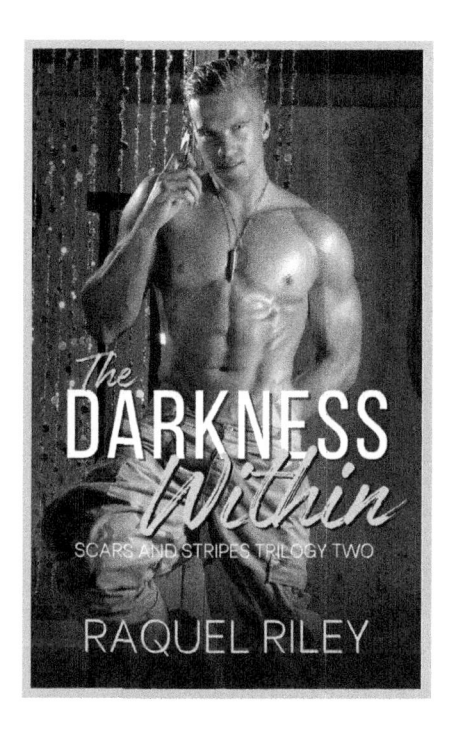

The Darkness Within is available on Amazon and Kindle Unlimited!

You can't give your heart away until you first learn to love yourself.

Nash

A mission gone sideways. My world turned upside down on a dime.

Held prisoner in the dark tunnels below ground, cut off from the world,

I was hanging onto life by a thread. Wanting to end my suffering, but afraid to let go.

And then I was rescued. Dragged into the light. My first breath of freedom in twenty-two days. But I was still trapped in my nightmare, inside my head.

A prisoner of war.

Brewer

His mind may be broken, but his soul is still intact, and it's the most beautiful thing I've ever seen. As his sponsor, I promised to help him find his way, to show him how to love himself again. I'm breaking all the rules of recovery by falling in love with him. But when you find the person you're meant to spend the rest of your life with, you don't want to waste another day apart.

The Darkness Within is the second book in the *Scars and Stripes Trilogy*. This hurt/ comfort MM romance deals with heavy topics such as addiction, mental health, PTSD, and a forbidden love that defies all the rules. A high-angst story that has a hard-earned HEA and cameos from *Proof Of Life*.

ABOUT THE AUTHOR

Raquel Riley
ROMANCE AUTHOR

Raquel Riley is a native of South Florida but now calls North Carolina home. She is an avid reader and loves to travel. Most often, she writes gay romance stories with an HEA but characters of all types can be found in her books. She weaves pieces of herself, her family, and her travels into every story she writes.

For a complete list of Raquel Riley's releases, please visit her website at **www.raquelriley.com**. You can also follow her on the social media platforms listed below. You can also find all of Raquel's important links in one convenient place at **https://linktr.ee/raquelriley**

ACKNOWLEDGMENTS

Tracy Ann, your feedback is so appreciated! You help me shape these books and characters and give them life. Thank you for your continued praise and support of my stories and for keeping me organized.

Dianna Roman, your sense of humor breathed life into this book. Thank you for the Bitches and the BALLS, and for the inside look at life in the Army.

Also, thank you to my **ARC/street team** for your insightful input and reviews and outstanding promotion.

A huge thank you to the **86'ers!** Dianna Roman, Tracy, Jenn, and Emma. You crazy bunch are guaranteed to make me laugh at least fourteen times a day.

I can't forget the **Secret Circle!** You bunch keep me accountable and sane and cheer for every one of my accomplishments, both big and small.

Marsha Adams Salmans I'm so grateful you came into my life. Your dedication to my reader group and promotion of my books is invaluable. Thank you for being irreplaceable and amazing!

Jenn Green, You are an editing wiz! Thank you for polishing my words so that they shine.

Last, but never least, thanks to my family for being so understanding while I ignore you so I can write.

Printed in Great Britain
by Amazon